Take Me Out

Martyn Clayton

Take Me Out

This edition published 2007 Lulu

In association with Garbled Noise

ISBN 978-1-84753-384-5

Copyright Martyn Clayton / Garbled Noise 2007

Martyn Clayton has asserted his rights under the Copyright, Designs and Patents Act 1988 to be identified as the author of this work

This book is sold subject to the condition that it shall not by way of trade or otherwise be lent, resold, hired out or otherwise circulated without the publisher's prior consent in any form of binding or cover other than that which it is published and without a similar condition, including this condition, being imposed on the subsequent purchaser.

Front cover design copyright Claudia Keilty 2007

Cheers & That...

Firstly special thanks go to the incredibly talented Claudia Keilty who managed to turn my vague ideas into a bang-on brilliant front cover. I'd like to thank all the Myspace friends who believed in what I was doing, Camera Obscura for providing the soundtrack to my writing, and the City of York for being my home and an inspiration. Last but never least, I want to thank Rachel without whom none of this would be possible. This book still believes in the value of public libraries, free school meals and decent social housing. The characters in Take Me Out are fictional and any resemblance to real people living or dead is probably coincidental, but you can never be totally certain can you ? Ta !

For Mum & Dad

"Each had his past shut in him like the leaves of a book known to him by heart; and his friends could only read the title." Virginia Woolf.

Life had a habit of passing her by until

The downstairs phone was ringing.
A bleary eyed Lauren picked up the digital clock on her bedside table.

3:23 AM

 Who the hell could that be ? Probably a wrong number or someone larking about. They'd had a spate of them a while back. Some gruff drunken bloke had called persistently. He had kept asking to speak to Loretta, who ever she was. Lauren would leave it. If Francis her housemate had been home he'd have chuntered his way downstairs and picked it up. The ringing stopped. She turned off the bedside lamp, lay back down and allowed sleep to reclaim her. The phone started ringing again. This time she instinctively jumped up out of bed, grabbed her dressing gown and grumpily stomped down the stairs. This had better be an emergency.
'Hello ?'
'Sorry to disturb you, but is that Lauren Seymour ?'
'Yes, yes, it is , is there a problem ? Why are you calling me now ?'
The voice on the other end of the phone was apologetic.
'I really am sorry, my name's Maggie Curran, I'm at York District Hospital.'
Mention of the 'H' word served to focus her mind a little.
'Is it Francis ? He's meant to be in Leeds. It's not my family they don't live in York. What's this about ?'
'We've got a friend of yours here. He was dragged out of the river after a passer-by saw him jump off Ouse Bridge. He's in a bad way, but he keeps asking for you. He didn't know your number, but one of your neighbours, Sally Frederick works here as a nurse, said she knew a Lauren Seymour who used to go to York University.' The voice paused but Lauren's still only half-awake brain couldn't help her fill the silence. 'I hope I've got the right Lauren Seymour ?'
'What's this person's name ?'
   She was hurriedly running a mental check through her male friends trying to work out which one of them was either depressed enough to throw themselves off a bridge or crazy enough to get so shitfaced they did it as a dare. Marcus possibly, she'd heard on the grapevine that he'd separated from Jenny. He was sure to be a bit low, but she'd not spoken to him for nearly six months. What about Ralph from work ? He was a party animal, always full of stories about the scrapes he was getting into. Lauren was sure most of them were bullshit however, and he had a wife and kids who'd be by his bedside. None of them would ask for her. She was barely more

than an acquaintance with most of them. Unless of course they weren't thinking straight, needed someone with a bit of distance. In that case it must be Marcus. They had been close once, he was always having women problems as a student and Lauren more often than not provided a female viewpoint for his latest tale of romantic woe. Once or twice he'd seemed a bit unstable.

'It's a Mr Gorman,' said the voice. Marcus had an Irish sounding surname. McIllvoy or something similar.

'Mr Gorman ?' She didn't think she knew a Mr Gorman. 'I'm sorry I think you must have the wrong person. What's his full name ? I'm sure I don't know any Gormans.'

Lauren heard the voice on the end of the phone conferring with someone else, a hand had clearly been placed over the receiver as the words became muffled and distant. Come on, come on she thought. The front room was freezing. It was November and the central heating wasn't due to kick in for another hour and a half. Then she imagined just how cold the River Ouse must be at this time of year and found an ounce more patience.

'Sorry to keep you waiting. My colleague has informed me that he says his name is Robert.'

Lauren only knew one Robert and he was an older guy from the Newcastle office of the advertising firm for which she was a copywriter. He was a perpetually cheerful fatherly type readying for retirement. And he wasn't a Gorman.

'No, I'm sorry it's still no use. I don't know a Robert Gorman.'

' Really ? Right. Ok then,' the voice sounded disbelieving. 'I do apologise for disturbing you.'

Lauren put the phone down and took herself back to bed but sleep just wouldn't come. Her mind was too alert now as she rifled through her mental filing cabinets for clues as to what the call could have been about. It seemed too much of a coincidence to just be a case of mistaken identity. How many Lauren Seymours could have passed through York University ? How many could there be in York ? Something felt wrong, and if there was a friend of hers lying in a hospital bed after being dragged barely alive out of the river then she needed to go see them. But who was Robert Gorman ?

She heard the woof of the gas boiler as the central heating flicked into life. The pipes were hissing and the house was slowly beginning to warm up. The gentle heat began cosseting her troubled mind as sleep did its best to call her back. It would be another two hours until the 7.15 alarm. Those precious hours could be made the most of and the fractured night put behind her. Then the phone rang again.

'Oh for fucks sake,' she shouted, so loud the elderly neighbours who always rose early probably heard her through the walls of the terrace. Jumping up she almost stumbled headlong down the stairs, this time in just her knickers and the oversized Franz Ferdinand t-shirt she slept in. It hung on her tall, slender frame, as she pushed her dark brown hair behind her ears and again reached for the phone.

'Is that Lauren Seymour ?' It was the same voice.

'Yes, what do you want now ?' Lauren made no effort to disguise her irritation. Sleep had become increasingly important to her of late. More of it was needed these days for her to be anywhere near functioning properly during the day. Even then it was rarely enough.

'He's asked us to tell you that he's Robert *P*. Gorman. He was very particular about that middle *P*'

The missing letter made all the difference.

It began something like this

OCTOBER 5th 1992 - Seminar Room, BA History Induction Meeting, York University.

   Next to speak was a slight boy with slicked back hair, a fading Disney t-shirt, cheap jeans and high-top trainers. Alongside all the new bohemian, black artsiness and grunge aesthetics of the rest of the group he looked out of place. Everything about him screamed awkward and even though inside Lauren was turning somersaults she was certain that she was nowhere near as nervous as this oddity.
'Robert P.Gorman,' he finally spoke, his voice suggesting an imminent stutter. The goth looking girl in a Cure T-shirt, black cardigan and black tasselled skirt across the room who until then had been affecting disinterested disaffection suddenly spluttered a girlish chuckle. She caught Lauren's eye who in turn was then finding it hard not to laugh. A moment of embarrassed connection .
'Sorry ?' Asked Dr Strickland, a drawn prematurely bald man with more than just a look of Ade Edmondson. He had been trying his hardest to be jocular and upbeat with his new youthful charges.
'My name is Robert P.Gorman,' the awkward one firmly reiterated. Now most of the room were trying to contain their collective laughter. All except a woman who had seconds earlier introduced herself as Bessie. She was a size 20, mid forty-something mother figure who looked at him as if she wanted nothing more than to take him home and feed him stew.
'Well that's great Rob, welcome aboard. And where is it you come from again ?'
'I hadn't actually told you where I'm from. And it's Robert. Nan never liked to hear me called Rob or Bob.'
'Oookaayy, Robert. Well it's…'
'No, she said that shortening a name is common. Bobs don't get on in the world, whereas Robert's get the top jobs.'
'I'm sure that's correct.' Dr Strickland had now made a point of moving his attention to the next person along, a mousey girl in a long-sleeved Wonder Stuff t-shirt who was leaning as far away from Robert as she could without falling off her chair.

'Melton Mowbray.' Robert spoke at double speed .
'I'm sorry ?' The lecturer was now looking alarmed.
'Home of the pork pie.'
'Right, could we just..'
'That's where I'm from. It's a small market town in the East Midlands.'
'Great so that's Robert from Melton Mowbray everyone.' Dr Strickland glanced around the room as the collection of young strangers ached with a painful shared hilarity. Robert sat stony faced.

After the induction meeting Lauren had sat down with the goth girl at a table in the refectory and learnt her proper name. This wasn't the stuffy sounding 'Millicent' that Dr Strickland had announced, reading her full name from his student roster. This was Millie. She was far from stuffy and Lauren thought she liked her.
'I'm Robert P.Gorman from the home of the pork pie !' Millie had mimicked to Lauren's approval. She had confidence this one. Lauren couldn't help admiring the girl's flawless make-up and willowy figure. There was no way she could ever get away with such a striking look. It was obvious to her who the lads on their course were going to be directing their attentions towards.
'What was he like ?' Lauren asked, glad to have found a topic of conversation on her first morning in this new chapter of her life.
'I know, he looks like his mum has dressed him.'
'Probably his nan actually. What was all that about shortening his name ?'
'Yeah, weirdo alert I reckon.' Millie looked as if she was pondering something .' Shame he's so odd though. He's kind of interestingly attractive don't you think ? I get bored of guys with conventional good looks.'
Lauren wasn't particularly bothered whether their good looks were conventional or merely interesting, she was just grateful for what attention she could get.
'He was alright I suppose.' It was hard not to notice his striking blue eyes.
'You'd have to give him a major sort out though. Lack of personality could present a serious problem in the fanciability stakes.' Millie drew on her cigarette. 'I'm sorry, I've not offered you one.' She held the packet towards Lauren who removed a tab and thanked her new companion.
'That old bird seemed to like him.'
'Was her name Bessie or something ?'
'Big Bessie' Lauren offered.
'Haha yeah, or Mature Bessie.'
'Mature Bessie, I like it.'
'So we've got Odd Rob so far and Mature Bessie.'
'Rob ? Wash your mouth out young lady. It's Odd Robert !'
With that they both sat giggling conspiratorially, double-checking that Robert was nowhere in sight. It was to be the start of a beautiful friendship and the first of many discussions about the oddity that was Robert P.Gorman.

Meanwhile half a world away

'Millie, Millie, is that you ?'
'Lauren hon, what's with you ?'
'Can you speak ? It's a bit of an emergency. I need your advice.'
'What time is it with you ? I'm in a restaurant with Karl at the minute. Can I call you back ?'
'No, no time. I need to chat with you now.'
Karl was impatiently arching his eyebrows at his fiancée who put her right hand over the mouthpiece of her phone.
' Aww I'm really sorry babes,' Millie raised her voice an octave and widened her big blue eyes. 'It's Lauren, it sounds urgent. Would you mind if I just…'
Karl set his face, held out his hands and sighed. Pushing his chair backwards, he put down his knife and fork and leant back in frustration.
"Just one second Lauren…." Millie got up, ran to the ladies toilet, found an empty cubicle and sat down on the lavatory. 'It must be about six with you. Karl's just finished his show and I've met him for a meal. He's going to be spitting feathers that we've been disturbed so this had better be important.'
Karl was an actor currently working in an off-Broadway production by an edgy new New York writer with the popular touch. The reviews had nearly all been positive and many were suggesting that this could be his big breakthrough.
'It's Robert P.Gorman. He's back !'
'What do you mean ? Have I just got myself into an impending row with my bloke for one of your lines about Odd Robert ? Come on Lauren, what's going on here ? Are you alright, you sound a bit weird ?'
'No, it's him. I just got a phone call from the hospital. He threw himself in the river and now he's asking to see me. It's frigging freaky.'
'You ? But why ?' She leant forward as if drawing closer to her friend across the Atlantic. Now actually, this was quite interesting. Intriguing anyway.
'God knows. I've not seen him in ten years. Last time was after our graduation.'
'Oh yeah, I remember now. His infamous nan had just died and no one came to see him graduate. We took him out for a drink the day after.'
'But only because we felt sorry for him. He was never a mate as such. Hadn't he lost his parents in a road accident when he was a toddler and she'd brought him up really oddly ?'
'Ooh that's right. Didn't she stop him playing out until he was 16 or something ?'
'That and worse from what I can remember.'
'Lauren.' Millie had just remembered an important little extra detail. 'Can you remember what else happened that night ?'
  Since receiving the phone call from the hospital, Lauren had been attempting to piece together her last few encounters with Robert. There was little sense in the clumsy narrative that found him asking for her in his hour of need.
'Didn't we decide to flirt with him for a bet. See who could be the most outrageous ?'

'That's right. You won of course when you draped yourself across him like a siren. I thought he was going to pass out with the shock. I had to buy you a multi-pack of Hula Hoops as your winnings if I remember rightly. You and your stinky crisp habit. It's diabolical.'
'But why would he want me now ?'
'I've got absolutely no idea babes. Are you going to see him ?'
'I don't see what else I can do. If he tried to top himself and he's asking to see me. I couldn't live with myself if I decided not to and he well…'
'Well, quite'. They were both momentarily silent. 'Look Lauren, I've got to go. My food's going to be getting cold. Why don't you go see Robert and then ring me back later at the apartment and we can talk about it some more. Karl doesn't get home till midnight and I was only planning on having a bath and watching TV. It'll be good to talk.'

Lauren smiled ,
'Yes, yes it will.'

Lauren put down the phone. She missed her friend. Millie was now half way across the world leading an exciting life with her wonder boy, whilst she was stuck in the house in which she'd lived for over eight years in sleepy old York city. Not having her cake and eating it did at times begin to grate. There was little that had really changed about her life in the past decade. She still worked for the same company as a copywriter which she had joined upon leaving university, she still shared the same two-up, two-up two-down in the Groves with her big gay housemate Francis. In his mid-40s, a music teacher with a penchant for bow-ties, amateur dramatics and George Clooney, he had become like a reassuring big brother . Always there with a catty line and a listening ear, they were the archetypal odd couple. With Millie's move to New York, Francis was now perhaps her only enduring true love.

There had been other contenders in her 32 years. There was snake-hipped Joe at Uni. He was an ex-public school boy and played in a band in his home town called Erstwhile. According to Joe they were always on the verge of something big and he walked around campus as if he was already a rock star. Back home he'd been a big fish in a small sea. He had a posh dope head drawl and a disarming way of looking at you that made every first year female undergraduate in their hall of residence want to get to know him better. One night at Toffs she'd comforted him as he poured his heart out about the hometown girlfriend who'd just given him the push. In his words she was ,'the only ever one,' and with all the 18 year old certainty he could muster he was sure he could, 'never love like this again.'

Before long Lauren had been stroking his hair and holding him. By the end of the evening they'd been eating each others faces and wondering how to broach the subject of where this was leading. They'd stayed together for the rest of their first year but half way through the second Joe announced that Erstwhile were up for, 'cracking London.' He was going to leave Uni and sleepy York to follow his dream in the capital safe in the knowledge that his minted stockbroker father could bale him out if things turned messy. Lauren had no such assurances and didn't fancy hanging around grotty bedsits being a wannabe rock stars girlfriend. So they'd agreed to go their separate ways. She missed his dotty daydreams, the touch of his lush soft skin and his puppy dog eyes. She missed being part of a couple - The World Famous Joe & Lauren Show, and she missed the reflected glory she received from hanging out with the coolest kid in school. The last she'd heard of Joe he was fitting solar panels in north London and living with a French girl with whom he had a baby. She wondered if he ever stopped to remember her.

   For the rest of her degree she had got her head down and tried hard to put the attractions of the opposite sex to one side for a little. Blokes since had come and gone. Nothing major , only minor diversions on the motorway of life. Stinky Pete the squaddie with the rock hard abs, gorgeous blue eyes and the charm of a rhinoceros, lecherous Creepy Tim, the thought he's it solicitor from Harrogate. Curious Chris, the artist who lived above a hairdressers on Walmgate, perpetually broke and frequently moody. Then of course there was Matt. He was not around long enough to pick up one of Millie's nicknames.

   Matt was the boy with the earth-moving smile. He was the man who always came around at the critical time, and somehow knew exactly what you were thinking. He was the one who sat up late writing reams of well-crafted poetry only to rip it all up in the morning. He was the one who could quote Dostoyevsky without sounding pretentious. He was the one who could throw on his oldest faded t-shirt and lived in jeans yet still look as sexy as hell. He was the one Lauren thought she could rely on in a crisis. He was the one with whom she was slowly falling in love. He was the one who would talk to her for hours about important things, share their histories, their ideas, treat each other not just as girlfriend and boyfriend but as partners in crime, mates above all else. He was the one who made her believe that men might be worth bothering with after all. He was also the one who struggled for years with manic depression. He was the boy who could sink into a morass of self-loathing, not answering the phone for days, not returning her calls or wanting to be disturbed. He was the one who one night took a massive overdose of sleeping pills after a night out and never again woke up. He was the one who left her in the most dramatic way possible, without an explanation or a word of warning.

  They had only been together for a couple of months but there had been something about Matt which led her to believe that perhaps he could have been the one. He was always upfront about his illness and never attempted to hide it from Lauren. She herself had seen periods on antidepressants to cope with her occasional black dog days, when the heavy grey curtains of life closed around her. There was grim stuff she'd not really dealt with from her teenage years, the bullying she'd been on the end of at school, the problems in her relationship with her mum, the brief dalliance with eating disorders. All these strands of her own history at times weighed her down a little. Made the life going a little heavy. She didn't feel as if she was in any position to make judgements and Matt, even with his illness was a lot saner than most of the guys she had dated. Together they seemed to make sense of one another. If there was true love thought Lauren, this must surely be what it's like. It's not just about lust, or attraction. It can't surely be based on prospects or earning potential. It couldn't only be about shared principles and visions for the future. It must be about helping to draw out each other's best characteristics and

being there to make sense of the worse. In these cynical times being with Matt gave her some hope that good things could still happen to decent people. Decent people like Matt. Decent people like her.
'It's like I've found the missing bit of me,' she had once told Millie in the Tap & Spile on Monkgate one evening after four vodka, lime and sodas. Millie had cautioned her against losing her head too quickly but was happy for her friend who had always seemed to be unlucky in love.

   Millie found it hard to understand why. Lauren had deep brown eyes, a quirky, questioning smile and a wicked sense of humour. She always kept you on your toes and exuded a natural sex appeal. Millie suspected that there might something about Lauren which put most men off. It wasn't her looks, or indeed her personality, but maybe it was her self-contained nature. There were very few people who could ever get close to her. She was always her own master. Millie knew that she needed men in a way that Lauren clearly didn't. Whereas she needed a boyfriend to feel as if life was complete, Lauren saw them as an optional interesting extra. If Millie had learnt anything in all her years of man-hunting it was that the male of the species seemed to like moderately needy women. As long as you stayed the right side of bunny boiler, a bit of clingy poor helpless me served to flatter their fragile egos. It helped them feel wanted, secure in themselves, as if they were still in charge of matters. It reassured them that their place in this mixed-up world was still assured. Lauren was not about to give any such assurances. Matt had been one of the few who could really get near her.

   Lauren had only learnt about Matt's death four days after the event, when she had called round his flat above a take-away on Gillygate . She wanted to know why he hadn't been returning her calls. Under normal boyfriend circumstances she wouldn't have bothered. They could do what the hell they liked. She wasn't about to start running after losers. With Matt things were different.

   In all likelihood his silence meant he had temporarily slid down into a dark mental hole. On one previous occasion when this had happened Lauren had taken him chocolate and sat with him quietly as he slowly began to emerge. She'd been on hand with cups of tea, and cooked him little manageable meals. Nothing too intense, all the time staying far enough out of his face so as not to appear as if she was making a serious emotional move on him. This time she was greeted at the door by an ashen faced guy who she knew only as Donut. He'd been sleeping on Matt's floor on and off for months and claimed to be a musician. He travelled around the country and turned up unannounced. For some reason Matt had a long held loyalty to him. Lauren had never liked the guy. He was always quick with a snide line and his presence always appeared to be accompanied by a cloud of marijuana smoke. She wasn't totally sure what kind of influence he was having on Matt, but Lauren never felt as if she was within her rights to tell him. When Donut told her what had happened she at first refused to believe him thinking it was some kind of sick joke. She contacted his workplace but the humourless receptionist refused to give out any information to 'a stranger'. Panicked she ran to the library, found the phone book for Newcastle where Matt's parents lived and set about contacting every Trethewy she could find. There was only a handful, it wasn't a common surname in that part of the world, and by the fourth query of ;

'Hi, is this the right number for Matthew Trethewy's parents ?'

A cracked female voice quietly replied in the affirmative. From its broken tone Lauren immediately began to fear the worse.

'Oh hi, I'm a friend of his and I was just wondering if you knew where he was as I've been trying to…'

Before she had chance to finish her line, Matt's mum had begun crying and the truth had painfully emerged between the heavy sobs. No, she didn't think he had never mentioned a Lauren. Yes, she was free to come to his funeral and why didn't she travel up with Donut. A few people from work were going to go as well. Did she work with him ? No. Was she a friend from university ? No, Matt had gone to St.John's, she to the University. Then how did she know him ?

   It was clear that he'd never even told his parents about her. Whatever her own feelings about their relationship she was now fairly certain that they had not been shared by Matt. The razor slash of grief that propelled her home was shoulder barged out of her consciousness by a clumsy blind rage. She took scissors to the top Matt had bought her only a week or so earlier, she torched his photos on the gas hob, screamed at the top of her voice before falling down on the bed with a bottle of cheap vodka that had been lurking with the cleaning products in the cupboard underneath the sink. When she emerged from her dark heavy sleep, she had found Francis and Millie downstairs talking earnestly about her. Through the crush of her hangover she had tried her best to explain what had happened. Her two closest friends resolved to try and take her out of herself and help her to move on. This was touch and go time. One slip and she could slide into a similarly black morass. They had both seen enough of her brooding moods to know that Lauren was herself no stranger to the darkness.

   They assured her it had been a brief ugly episode, a mistake to get involved with someone so screwed up in the first place, nothing she was responsible for. All of which may or may not have been true but it didn't prevent the incessant questions that now troubled her. Could she have been there for him ? Was it something she had done or maybe even hadn't done ? Why when everything had been so good between them and her own life had improved so much should Matt have gotten so low ? There would be no easy answers, no tidy resolution.

   Both Millie and Francis liked Matt. He seemed to be a serious, thoughtful guy. Someone with a sharp mind and a generous heart. A man who was big enough to take on their best friend. They always knew it would take more than just a few warm words, a good looking smile and a slick bit of charm to win Lauren's heart so completely. That Matt seemed to be doing just that spoke volumes about his character.

   Lauren knew she couldn't attend his funeral. She was all but a stranger to his family and friends. Only the venal Donut knew the truth about her relationship with Matt. The thought of having to stand at the back of the crowd of mourners, unknown by the majority and seen as little more than one of Matt's many casual acquaintances left her feeling sick. But just what was the truth of their relationship ? She had only been in his life for two short months. Despite the shared secrets and the exquisite intimacy of their bodies, her time in his life had been not much more than a flicker. Why should she claim any special grief as his girlfriend compared to friends who had known him most of his lifetime ? As people searched for a reason as to why he did what he did they could easily point at her. No, she couldn't go, not under the circumstances.

Francis and Millie had been their customary wonderful selves. Their decision to try and keep their best friend busy with diversionary activities seemed to be helping her maintain a modicum of stability. The grief she felt was immense and it had threatened to swallow her at any moment. She'd lost grandparents in the past , and she'd cried when Sammie her ancient childhood dog finally died a few years earlier, but this was different. This raw jagged pain gouged deep into her heart, accompanied her every action and felt as if it would never leave her. There were lakes of tears, chats into the early hours with Millie and Francis and times when she thought she'd never be able to love or trust anyone again.

Then life started to slowly change. After six months or so of sorrow, a day or two would pass when she didn't think of Matt or even feel that sorry for herself. Then three or four days, soon it was a week. Eventually Matt became a memory of sorts. She focused less on his sudden demise, more on the brief, precious, good times they had shared. Soon her memories of Matt were no longer tear-stained and pitiful but graced with enough sunlight to be bearable to recall.

A year after his death she decided to contact Mrs Trethewy again. On the phone she explained that she was a 'good friend' of Matt's from York and wondered if she could talk about him to her. They both talked and talked, two hours passed in what felt like minutes. Not once did Lauren spill the beans as to her relationship with Mrs Trethewy's son, but by the time the conversation had ended both women seemed aware of where they stood. Before she rang off, Mrs Trethewy asked if she'd like a photo of Matt. Lauren hesitated, she had destroyed her photos of him in her rage upon learning of his suicide and had not set eyes on his image for over a year. She was no longer sure if the picture in her head really corresponded to that of Matt at all.

'Yes, that would be lovely', she had finally replied.

The women exchanged addresses and promised to keep in touch. When the photo finally arrived it showed her old boyfriend standing on a beach underneath the shadow of Bamburgh Castle in Northumberland, a place where he had promised to take her when the weather had warmed up a bit. He was smiling and looked supremely content. An attached note told her that the photo had been taken during his last family visit, he had driven his mum up the coast for a walk and a chat. He had been on top form that day, full of himself and with a twinkle in his eye. His mum was sure that life was treating him good, his illness was in check and that his future looked bright. She suspected he might have started seeing someone but he was always coy about divulging too much detail out of fear of tempting fate. The date on the back was three weeks after Lauren had started going out with him. Kissing her hand she placed it on the smiling face that gazed back at her from the photo.

'My precious friend.'

Placing it in the small wooden box where she kept old keepsakes, important letters and photographs of the special people and places in her life she had finally allowed Matt to rest in peace.

After the peculiar disturbance of this dark November morning she again found herself thinking about Matt. His sudden end, their brief, abbreviated relationship. Lauren wondered how things could have been different. Where they would both be now had he not left her so suddenly, so completely . Then she thought of Robert P.Gorman.

Back to the future

'Lauren Seymour, I'm here to see Robert Gorman.'
Lauren wondered what she was doing. The nurse on duty seemed to be expecting her.
'Ah the famous Lauren. Your friend's down the corridor in the room on the second right. He's physically OK but obviously still quite shaken. To be honest he's lucky he was spotted.'
'Yes, I understand.' If only someone had found Matt in time then maybe… stop that thought right there.
'You're his first visitor.'
'Me ? His first. What about family, are they not coming ?'
'He say's he doesn't have any.'
Then some of the infamous Gorman back story returned to her.
'Oh that's right, he was brought up by his grandma and she passed away a few years ago. I think he's an only child.' Which was just about the sum total of all the knowledge she had of him.
'So he's going to need his friends around him . When he's physically better I think it might be wise for him to be psychiatrically assessed. You don't throw yourself off a bridge without good reason.' It was as Lauren feared.
'Was he not drunk ?'
'We found no traces of alcohol in his system.'
'Oh, that's…' But the nurse appeared to be in a hurry to move matters along.
'So he's just down the corridor, second room on the right. He's expecting you.'
Lauren nodded and walked down the corridor as she had been told. There was the door to the room, she opened it and popped her head inside wondering what she was going to find. There lying in bed with his eyes closed was a stranger.
'Robert ?' She whispered, not really sure she wanted to wake the sleeping figure. It seemed impertinent. It wasn't Francis or her dad lying there. It was someone who seemed to bear a passing resemblance to a person she once knew years ago. The figure opened an eye , followed by another and those eyes then began to focus.
'Lauren, is that you ?'
'Well, last time I looked it was.'

She walked into the room and sat down on the hard plastic chair next to his bed. What did you say to a guy with whom you were never really that close, who you hadn't seen in ten years and who was now lying in a hospital bed after having attempted to take his own life ?
'So Robert. How's things ?' As soon as it left her mouth she cringed at the improper inanity of her words.
'I think I've felt better.' Robert's voice was the same monotonous drone it had always been. ' It's nice to see you.'
Lauren wished she could say the same thing about setting eyes on this odd hospitalised stranger. What was she doing here ?
'Robert, look I don't know why you asked for me to be here, but I'm really sorry to see you like this.' Whatever this situation required, hesitation or uncertainty wasn't it.
'That's OK.' He went back to staring at the wall.
'Are there any friends or family I could contact for you ? People who can help you out ?'
'No one.' He still didn't look in her direction.
'At all ?'
'Not at all.'
'But, Robert there must be someone who…'
'There is one.'
At last they were getting somewhere.
'Good. Right, well tell me who they are and how I can get in touch with them for you.' She rummaged in her bag and pulled out her mobile. 'I can put their number in here and I can phone them straightaway. I've explained to work that I won't be in till later so it's not a problem. Right…'
'It's you.'
"I'm sorry ?"
'You, you're the only friend I've got.'
She looked down at her waiting mobile, switched it off and roughly shoved it back in her bag. Another escape route had just been closed.
'But Robert, I've not seen you in ten years ? There must be someone else surely.'
'No one.'
This was hard work.
'So you're telling me that a woman you've not seen in ten years who never really knew you that well in the first place is the only friend you can call on.'
He nodded.
'I really don't know what to say.'
So they both stayed silent. This was becoming beyond weird.
'And you did promise.'
Oh my god. Now she remembered. On that night out after their graduation, whilst her arms had been draped teasingly around his shoulders , she'd looked right into his eyes and whispered suggestively;
'and remember, if ever you're in trouble, you just ring your Auntie Lauren and she'll soon put you right.'

She'd drunkenly tapped his nose and then slinked off to the toilets. Millie spent weeks afterwards calling Lauren 'Auntie' , never allowing her drunken over-friendliness with Odd Robert to slip quietly away to die in a darkened embarrassed corner.

'It must be those blue eyes Laurs', she'd teased, 'they've been working their magic.'
'More like the six Southern Comfort and Cokes working their magic Mills, and if you don't mind…'
Lauren had contented herself that she was unlikely to ever see Robert P.Gorman again, not thinking for a moment that he'd ever take her up on that distant drunken promise.
'You were so good to me when nan died that I thought you'd be the obvious person to call.'

As far as Lauren could see there was nothing obvious about calling her at all.
'I'm flattered that you remembered me, I really am, but I'm not sure what I can do for you.'

Finally the head turned back towards her, his eyes were now wide open as they looked straight into her own.
'Look I know this must be strange, but I really am all on my own and I didn't know where to turn. They wanted to call a next of kin but I haven't got any, then they said friends and well…'
'You haven't got any.'

He nodded and closed his eyes again as if the act of remembering his solitude pained him. You would of had to have a heart of stone and precious little soul not to feel at least a modicum of sympathy for his predicament. What could she do now ? She couldn't leave the poor guy. She needed a minute or two to think.
'Look, can you give me five minutes. I'll be right back.'
'Promise.'
Lauren paused at the door.
'I promise. Shut your eyes for five minutes.'

She grabbed a rank black coffee from the machine in the foyer and stood just to the right of the main entrance to the hospital. Forgetting about her promise to Francis to try and cut down she drew a cigarette from the packet in her bag, lit it and took a long satisfying draw, blowing a stream of directed smoke into the damp November air. So now what ? She took out her bag and turned on her phone. Quickly texting Francis, she asked him to give her a call as soon as he received the message. He was away in Leeds for a few days visiting the mysterious Tony. From what she could gather he was a love interest, but Francis only ever referred to him as 'my gentleman friend' , which was delightfully old fashioned and very Francis. She also knew that when he was away he didn't like to be disturbed.

Within a couple of minutes, the 'Take Me Out' ringtone Millie had sent her kicked into action.
'What is it now ?' It was Francis, and he didn't sound happy.
'Oh sorry babes, don't mean to disturb you.'
'I was just cooking Tony breakfast, he's very particular about his sausage.'

Lauren didn't think that line was meant to sound as camp as it came out.
'You're cooking ? The man who makes me cook his tea every night when he's at home ?'
'Come on Lauren, it's not *every* night is it ? Anyway, you're staff. I give you subsidised bed and board and this is the thanks I get.'
'Tony giving you bed and board is he ?' Lauren couldn't resist a little tease.
'Ooh cheeky madam. Tony is a very dear friend.' He paused for second, '..and that's all I'm saying.'
Lauren laughed pleased to hear her friend had recovered his sense of humour.
'So what can I do you for ?'
'This is so weird Francis. I'm at the hospital.'
'Congratulations ! When's it due ? It must have been an immaculate conception, you never go out.'
'Haha yeah, like that's likely be happening anytime soon' she took another quick draw on her cigarette. 'No, listen it's serious. I got this phone call in the early hours.'
   Lauren then began telling her friend the peculiar details of her current situation, the curiosity that was the undergraduate Robert P.Gorman and her confusion as to what to do next. Francis was hooked. He loved a bit of intrigue, particularly if it didn't involve him.
'No friends or family at all you say ?'
'So he says.'
'Looks like you're stuck with him then.'
'Oh god, what do I do next ?'
'Think practical Lauren. He jumped in the river so he's going to need a change of clothes I'd have thought. You're going to have to go to his place and pick them up for him, then when he's discharged make sure he goes to see the shrink and that he's eating properly. It could keep you busy and you did say you needed an interest.'
'I was thinking more of yoga.'
'Well, this is probably more socially useful than standing on your head chanting to Krishna or whatever it is they do.'
'Francis, but…'
'No buts young lady. If this is for real then he really does need someone. You've been asked for a reason as far as I can see and you've got a duty to try and do some good.'
'Yes Father.' Lauren always called her housemate Father Francis when he was delivering a 'buck your ideas up' style lecture. He was forever introducing a mystical purpose into random events. He still occasionally went along to Mass at St Wilfrids and kept a small Mexican statue of the Virgin Mary on top of the television . Lauren was never sure whether it was there purely for its camp value or because of his residual Catholic beliefs.
'So get yourself back in there and you can tell me all about it when I get home tomorrow night. Oh and Lauren…'
'Yes dad ?'
'Do try and stay calm.'

'I will. Say hi to Tony for me.'

With that she stubbed out the last embers of her cigarette, chucked the cup containing the dregs of the foul coffee in the bin, gathered herself and walked back inside.

Robert had drifted back off to sleep and for the second time in less than an hour she felt guilty for waking him. If she tried to keep this arrangement on a purely practical level it made more sense. Robert had needs which needed attending to, the most pressing of which was for some clean clothes.

'Robert, where do you live ? I'm going to need your key so I can go get you something warm and dry to change into.'

Robert smiled for the first time and Lauren was struck by it's warmth, completely in contrast to his grey pallor and haunted , yet still piercing eyes.

'Oh, it's just a flat, off Holgate Road. Have you got a pen ?'

For once she was an unlikely girl guide, pulling out a black Accent Advertising biro and handing it to Robert who was now sitting up. He scribbled something down on the back of the paper coaster on his bedside table and then handed it to Lauren, pointing out his door keys which were lying next to a slowly drying leather wallet on a table near the radiator.

'Right, got that. I can go straight after work. Not going anywhere until this evening are you ?'

'I think they want to discharge me in a couple of days. I think they want me to get some bed rest.'

'Probably for the best. Do you want me to bring you anything in particular ?'

He gave her a confused look as if she had just asked the strangest question in the world.

'They're just clothes. I don't know really.'

Lauren imagined herself in the same position. She'd probably want her comfiest stuff. Her favourite old jeans with their generous biscuit allowance for fat days, and her grey washed out hoodie. They were clothes to wear when there was nowhere to go, no one to see. Ideal for lounging on the sofa, watching a DVD and drinking endless cups of tea whilst putting off the housework for another hour or so. They were grotty old things, but she'd never refer to them as *just* clothes. As a child she'd been a bit of a tomboy, never really getting the whole dressing up, hair and make-up thing. As an adult she had managed to find her own personal style. It was modest and unlikely to turn many heads but it suited her. Different clothes accompanied different moods. They were integral to who she was and she was no fashionista by any means. Maybe it was a girl thing ? No, Francis was more devoted to his appearance , despite his size, than she was. But he was very gay so he probably wasn't the best male example and she herself was hardly the best female one. Whatever, it didn't matter.

'OK, I'll see what I can find.'

To boldly go

Lauren reported into work that afternoon as promised telling her colleagues that she had had an appointment at the hospital to keep, which immediately sparked their curiosity. Diverting the conversation onto safer territory she managed to get through the afternoon without spilling the beans. Her mind had been distracted by the morning's events and her lack of sleep was taking its toll. What she craved though was a bit of normality and her desk and in-tray provided just that. The copy for a brochure extolling the virtues of a new high-rise development in Leeds was proving to be more of a challenge than she had first imagined it would. She had written countless of these dull things before but for some reason the pretentious marketing speak of the developers had thrown her head into disarray. They wanted to convince potential buyers that this was more than just another steel and glass monstrosity across the skyline and was instead 'a lifestyle opportunity,' and that a purchase of one of their overpriced boxes was 'a strong personal statement.'

Was her own lack of a mortgage perhaps a strong personal statement ? House prices had risen inexorably in York over the past few years and attempting to buy a place on her own was now an impossibility. The fabulous Prada wearing souls who popped up in frothy novels set in the capital always seemed to sustain their fabulous Chardonnay quaffing lifestyles on advertising wages but she knew that was far removed from her reality. Accent was a small provincial advertising house that maintained two offices and a modest reputation. They were known for their efficiency and reliability, not their flashy salaries. Lauren as a creative probably earned less than the nurses she was talking to earlier in the day but she wasn't complaining. Living with Francis was no problem. They were like a comfortable married couple and if she was occasionally late with her rent then he rarely pressed the issue. He liked having her around. They were more than just housemates now and each knew instinctively when the other needed time by themselves. Lauren was no longer sure that she could cope with living alone. Without Francis she'd probably sit and pine especially now that her girlie best friend had left for pastures new.

Although there had been plenty of casual friends who came and went, only Millie and Francis really knew her. They were the people to whom she could entrust the secrets of her heart. The only other sentient beings who got anywhere near understanding her. Her mum and dad were alright as far as it went, but in their eyes she was still the little girl with pig tails , her favourite blue t-shirt and Mr Pookie the imaginary friend who wore a pink fedora. Millie and Francis had only known her as an adult and the relationship was different. So maybe she was not that dissimilar to Robert after all. She hadn't suffered the misfortune of losing her parents at an early age and only had two real friends, one of whom was now on the other side of the Atlantic ocean.

It was raining as Lauren left the small office that Accent rented in a larger building just off North Street. In her rush she had come out without her umbrella, so she buttoned up her mac, turned the collar up , put her head down and headed up along Micklegate in the direction of Robert's place. She'd borrowed a York Street Guide from work and had found the name of the little street where he lived. It was in a part of town she had rarely ventured into since the Odeon Cinema had closed leaving a slowly decaying boarded-up 1930s building. There was an Italian Deli down there that Lily from work who lived near the Fox Pub on Holgate Road kept raving about. For a few weeks after it had opened she'd had a crush on one of the suitably swarthy guys who worked there and went in every day for something for her packed lunch. Only when she was greeted one morning by his stunning wife and chubby sun-kissed bambino did she go back to buying her sandwiches from M&S.

    As she turned onto Holgate Road, she saw a narrow road opening leading off to a couple of blocks of grey looking council flats. A girl with a dragged-back ponytail and acne sat outside talking to a wasted looking youth on a BMX bike which was far too small for him. They both eyed her suspiciously as she felt herself tensing. Lights were on in various windows, and in the doorway to the block an elderly man was examining the weather.

'Is it raining love ?' He asked, giving Lauren a gummy smile.

'It is, not much but you could do with a brolly.'

'P'rhaps I'll not bother then.'

'Are you going somewhere ?'

'Just up to Jacksons, I'm a bit low on the booze front.'

She took another look at him. He wasn't that old at all. Beneath the cracked skin and heavy eyes there was a younger man, perhaps a similar age to Francis, mid-40s. Then she realised, he was one of the familiar figures she saw crouched under grubby blankets in the doorways near work begging for money.

'Still,' he continued, 'a bit of rain never usually keeps me from the sauce.' He cackled at his own joke and Lauren forced a guffaw out of politeness and self-protection before heading into the block.

    There appeared to be four flats on each floor and every door had a number. Robert's was listed as 11, which meant he must be at the very top. Lauren looked at the lift , the lights on the buttons had been smashed and there was indistinguishable graffiti on either side of the doors. She'd take the stairs. The exercise would be good for her. The light on the first landing was flickering and emitted a slow metallic buzz that sounded ominous. From behind one of the doors she could hear the rumbling bass of some dub reggae. On the second floor an overloud TV broadcasted a tea time game show competing with the noise of a rowing couple behind another. Finally on the third floor, the light was completely out. One flat door was left open and looked uninhabited, and there across the landing, just opposite the top of the stair was number eleven. The door to number twelve was shut and looked well tended. It was silent. She'd put the key in her bag and like everything else she was ever looking for in a hurry gravity had taken it right to the bottom.

'Bloody hell,' she muttered under her breath, pulling out receipts and a tube of ancient lip gloss which she never wore. 'Must sort my bag out, must sort my bag out.' From behind her crouched figure the noise of a door being unlocked and a

security chain being drawn across made her start, dropping her bag to the floor in the process, the contents spilling out onto the cold damp concrete. The door to number 10 slowly crept open.
'You looking for someone ?'
A young female voice in a broad local accent asked. Lauren crouching on the floor turned her head to see a girl's face peering at her from around the door. No older than about 17, she eyed Lauren suspiciously.
'Oh sorry, I'm a friend of Robert's, I've come to collect some stuff for him. He's in hospital.' The girl continued to stare. 'Robert Gorman ?" Still no recognition. 'He lives in number 11.'
'Is 'e called Robert ?' The girl screwed her face up. 'I never knew that.'
Lauren wondered for a moment if she'd come to the right place, then it dawned on her that the girl had probably never spoken to him.
'E's alright him. Never really says much. Helped me down stairs with the pushchair when the lift was knackered the other week.'
'Right.' The light from the girl's hallways lit up the key. 'Ah, there it is.' Lauren grabbed the key and held it up.
'Nice one.' The girl smiled at her and for the first time Lauren noticed just how pretty she was. 'My bags the same, full of crap.'
'I know, I really do need to sort mine out…'
'Tell 'im I said 'ello won't you.'
'Sorry ?'
'Robert, tell him I said hi.'
'Oh yes, I will do.'
'I'm Beth by the way.'
'Lauren, I'm Lauren.'
The girl held her hand out through the opening of the door.
'Oh.' Lauren wiped her right hand on her coat and then took hold of Beth's, giving the girl a warm smile. The sound of a baby crying from inside the flat distracted the girl.
'I must go, but it's been nice meeting you…' She was searching for the name.
'Lauren.'
'Lauren. I'm crap with names.' The baby increased the volume. 'Right, see you again I'm sure.' And with that the face was gone and the door was shut. Lauren heard Beth shouting as she disappeared down the hallway. 'I'm coming, I'm coming' as the impatient cry of the baby intensified further.

 Momentarily thrown, Lauren realised she was holding Robert's front door key in her left hand. Finding the lock on the door to number 11 she inserted the key, turned the lock and then gave it a slight nudge. The door opened but the place was in darkness. Feeling the wall for the light switch she finally found it and flicked it, filling the hall with light from a bulb that hung without a shade from the ceiling. Finding her bearings she looked around. he place felt cold, largely empty. The walls were a grubby cream, the front room possessed only one easy chair in a grim 80s floral velour. The stuffing on one of the arms was coming out. The carpets were threadbare and the small TV in the corner had seen better days. The house she shared with Francis was never likely to win style awards but this was just something else. Their house might well be described as ramshackle but it was full of homely touches. When you entered it a feeling of warm, lived-in, comfort greeted you. It was a place you could relax into and be yourself. This third floor flat in a seen-better-days block was simply bleak. There appeared to be no books, no CDs, nothing on the walls to introduce even just a little colour or individuality.

   Finding the door to the bedroom she was confronted with a similarly barren sight. There was an old bed, but there didn't seem to be a mattress. It was covered with a suspiciously stained duvet . An intense, stale, male sweaty smell hit her and she had to concentrate to stop herself from retching. A white wardrobe with the door hanging off sat in the corner. Get the clothes, get out and forget all about it she told herself. Opening the wardrobe door she discovered that there was nothing hanging from the rail, instead a pile of indeterminate items sat unpromisingly on the bottom.

 'Good grief, Robert, you're not exactly making it easy for me are you ?'
Tentatively lifting stuff up she found a pair of almost completely washed out jeans, a badly misshapen T-shirt and what looked like a hand knitted jumper. It was fraying and had a wonky chevron pattern which would have embarrassed her dad. The famous Gorman nan's handiwork no doubt. None of this was very promising.
'Oh my god.' She'd just remembered. 'Bloody underwear.' If this was bad, what were his pants going to be like ? Could she get away with telling him that she'd completely forgotten about them ,that it slipped her mind ? No she couldn't , not having a change of knickers in similar circumstances would have driven her mad. Robert had just as much right to his undies as she did. What was the time ?

5.54

Too late now to nip into M&S and buy him something new. No, she'd just have to keep digging until she found them. Lifting awful t-shirt after awful t-shirt she finally set eyes on what she'd been half looking for, half dreading finding. A solitary pair of brown Y-fronts with cream piping sat at the very bottom of the pile like a dirty secret.
'This is it Lauren.'
   Turning around to face the door she picked up the offensive item between her thumb and forefinger without looking at it and quickly shoved it in the Sainsburys bag she'd been slowly filling.
'Phew…that wasn't sooo bad.' Then another thought pricked her relieved self-satisfaction. 'Oh no, socks, he's going to need socks as well.'
There on the end of the bed sat two white sports socks, both without heels and each looking as if they'd never been introduced to the joys of a washing machine. Quickly picking them up and throwing them in the bag, Lauren ran from the bedroom, out of the hall, flicking the light off as she passed and back out onto the landing. The smell. That was the worst of it. The throat-gagging stench of inadequacy and failure had been the hardest aspect to bear inside the claustrophobic walls of Robert's dingy home.

Hardly pausing for breath she jogged down the stairs, the Sainsburys bag full of awful clothes thrown over her arm as she went. Outside the boy on his bike was still there, but the girl had gone. The beggar guy was talking to him and she was sure she saw something change hands as she stepped back out into the evening. Her gaze must have lingered for slightly too long as the older man turned round and spoke.
'Alright then love, did you find what you were looking for ?' He seemed to leer at her, as the rat-like boy grinned up at him admiringly.
'Yes thank you.'
'Good , good. I got me cider so I'm sorted.' He held up a litre bottle of cheap white cider and waved it in her direction. "Ey if yer not doing 'owt, you should come join me and young scabs 'ere fer a drink.'
Scabs ? You couldn't make it up could you ? Lauren wanted to extricate herself from this uncomfortable conversation as quickly as possible.
'I've got to get off I'm afraid, I'm meeting a friend a bit later and it's...'
'Suit yerself,' he seemed slightly put out at being knocked back, as if it wasn't something that happened that often. 'But you might not get a better offer y'know.' To which he jabbed Scabs in the ribs, cackled and walked back inside the block.

The possibility that he was right bugged Lauren. Were offers of romantic evenings with alcoholic beggars and their grubby teenage mates over a £2 bottle of white cider the best she could hope for now ? Don't think like that, she was still young and being single wasn't, well, it wasn't THAT bad. You got used to it after a while. And it wasn't like she was really alone was it ? She did have Francis after all. In many ways he was the ideal male companion.

A friend in need

Robert was sitting up in bed talking to a nurse who looked Indonesian. He appeared to be smiling, relaxed almost. Lauren poked her head around his door, gave a quick attention grabbing knock and walked in.
'I'm not disturbing anything am I ?' She enquired out of politeness.
'Oh no, Mr Gorman's very well. He's ready for his visitor.' T
The nurse appeared to be in something of a hurry to get away. Lauren sat down on the bed . She had found chance to dash home, get changed and make herself a small bowl of pasta before heading off to the hospital, still wondering why she was doing any of this at all. There was a documentary about twins conjoined at the head on Channel 4 she had been intending to watch.
'So then Robert, how's you now ?'
Her tone was unintentionally businesslike to the point of being curt.
'OK I suppose.' Once again he'd drifted off into vague space-staring, neglecting to do much to acknowledge her presence.
'Well I've brought you some clothes, sorry if they're not right but it's all I could find your flat was a bit...'
'Chaotic ?' Robert helped her out.

'You could say that. No wonder you're feeling depressed.'
'Nan would be doing her nut at me if she was still around. She liked everything to be particular. I used to do all the cleaning when I lived with her and when I got my own place I just couldn't be bothered anymore.'
'That sort of makes sense, but Robert you can find a middle-way can't you ? I don't enjoy cleaning but I do a bit occasionally. It wasn't just the dirt though, the place was so bare. Where's all your stuff ? No books, no CDs, no pictures on the walls. What's going on ?'
Now Robert raised an eyebrow.
'All that's a bit superfluous don't you think ? Just makes clutter. All you really need is a bed and a few clothes for a successful life.'
She decided to bite her lip and leave the 'successful life' line to hang unchallenged. 'Speaking of clothes, yours are in a terrible state. When did you last buy a pair of jeans ?'
Robert appeared to be mildly taken aback by her directness.
'I don't see why it's any business of yours what I wear ? We can't all be fashion plates you know.'
'Robert, have you looked at me ? I'm wearing my scrags, you can hardly call me a fashion victim or whatever it was.'
'A plate.'
'Pardon ?'
'A fashion plate, I called you a fashion plate.' It was another of those anachronistic little sayings he always used to come out with.
'Just shut up for a minute and let me have my say.' Lauren never did have much in the way of patience. ' I'm doing you a favour here remember.' A bit of gratitude surely wouldn't go amiss.
   With that Robert returned to looking at the opposite wall. Lauren responded by putting the bag of clothes on the bed.
'These were the best I could find. Sorry if they're not right.'
'I'm sure they will be. I told you, I don't care.'
'Well maybe you should start caring a bit more. Perhaps that's the problem.'
'Look Lauren, I don't need a therapist, all I need is a friend.'
'Well that's just it Robert, I'm not your friend am I ? I'm someone you vaguely knew years ago. I've no idea how you got yourself into this mess and if I'm being honest I've not got much idea how to help you.'
The raised voices attracted the attentions of the Indonesian nurse who put her head around the door and gave Lauren a stern disapproving look.
'Is there a problem Mr Gorman ?'
'No, no problem. My visitor was just leaving.'
Lauren looked at him gob smacked and silently mouthed a, 'what the fuck ?' in his direction but Robert's face remained passive. At that precise moment she wanted to slap it. This had been a mistake. She should have been hard and told the nurse who phoned that she had no idea who he was or why he'd want to see her. Well, at least now it was over. This brief peculiar episode was done with. He could sort himself out. It wasn't her responsibility that he didn't have any friends. What kind of

friendship could they ever possibly have ? They had nothing in common. They were completely unalike. Standing up, she put her bag over her shoulder and walked out not looking back once and certain that this was the last time she'd ever set eyes on Robert P.Gorman.

Knowing what to do next

'You said what to him ?' Asked Millie.
'I just said that I wasn't his friend, just someone who he knew years ago.'
'Oh Lauren.'
'What ? What am I have supposed to have done ?'
'You always were a bit….'
'A bit what ?'
' A bit sharp at times. Maybe he didn't need to hear that ?' Millie was trying to make her point in as placatory terms as possible.
'Oh thanks very much, that makes me feel bloody great doesn't it.' Lauren went silent for a moment, her mind drifting back to the horrors of the Gorman flat. 'And I even touched his bloody y-fronts. Can you imagine it ?!'
Millie burst out laughing, 'oooh poor you, I'd really rather not. How do you get yourself into these situations ?'
'Don't ask me. The thing is, I feel like shit now for walking out on him.'
'I understand hon but you can't hold yourself responsible for whatever he does can you ? As you said he's not seen you in ten years and you were never really that close.'
'You're just taking my side now.'
'Of course I am, I'm your best mate.'
'Oh I miss you Mills. When you coming back ?'
'You should come out here for a while, take a break, enjoy yourself. Karl's got loads of tasty actor mates we can introduce you to.'
'Actors ? Are they gay ?'
'Actually, come to think of it…'
'No I reckon I'm destined to be an old spinster now. I think my moment in the sun has gone. You should see how skinny and gorgeous all the fresher girls look this year, it drives me up the wall.'
  Millie made an un-Millie like snort , 'come off it Lauren, self-pity's not your scene.'
'S'pose not. I'm just a bit, y'know.'
' A bit what babes ?'
'Lonely I guess.' There, she'd said it.
'Which must be how Robert's feeling as well. Why not go see him again ? I'm sure he's just a bit screwed up at the minute.'
'Judging by his flat, I think he's probably permanently screwed up. Of all the people from college to come back into my life it had to be him didn't it ?'

27

And then the thought of Robert being discharged alone tomorrow morning, making his solitary way back to his bare flat entered her head. Could she just leave him to get on with it and wash her hands of the whole bizarre situation whilst keeping a clear conscience?
'I think only you know what you have to do though babes,' Millie added right on cue, reading her mind just as she'd always done, even across the vast empty expanse of the Atlantic ocean. That was what best friends did didn't they ?

A virtual life

Lauren wondered where all the years had gone. It only seemed like five minutes since she had been one of those same stick-thin freshers , looking all young, gorgeous and lovely. It always amazed her when she looked back at old photographs just how good her eighteen year old self actually did look. She was sure that she had never felt that attractive at the time. All she could remember was standing in front of the mirror wishing away her oversized nose and wandering boss-eyes. That self-protective cloak of studied mystery she covered herself in whilst all the time her insides were like a big wobbly jelly.

If only she'd known. That though was surely the whole point, just how conceited would an 18 year old be who knew exactly how good she looked ? The thirty-two year old Lauren was certain that she wouldn't like to meet her.

Home alone, Lauren found herself passing the hours on Myspace. Three friend requests from dodgy bands, and one from a middle-aged Egyptian man offering, 'stylish riches and much romance.' No thanks love, she thought as she hit the 'Deny Selected' button. Not that she'd be entirely averse to riches or romance, just not from an overweight fifty year old with forests for eyebrows and nasal hair you could style. Where were the real people these days ? Three-quarters of her friends were bands she'd never heard of who she'd approved in the early days when she was amazed that anyone should ask her in the first place. The handful of people she kept in touch with on there were alright as far as it went but none of them really gave the impression that they'd ever be more than grinning faces on wacky pages listing their interests and taste in music.   One of her American friends had posted a survey on the bulletin board. It was made up of questions like; 'How many different types of drink have you had today ?' and 'What color would you describe your soul as ?' . Lauren began filling it in to pass the time but got stuck on the question about which celebrity she'd most like to date. Possibly John Hurt she thought. He'd be interesting. Or maybe Richard Dawkins. Failing either of those two then she'd have to go for Russell Brand for purely animalistic reasons. She put down Russell Brand. Most of her friends wouldn't have heard of the other two. Having completed the survey she then decided to delete it before posting it. This was absurd.

'Why do I waste my time on here ?' She spoke aloud as her digital alarm clock beeped on the hour.

1: 00 AM

She had intended on getting a reasonably early night. After her conversation with Millie she had taken herself in the bath, tried to concentrate on her book and then crawled into bed. But sleep hadn't come. Her mind had been too full of the weirdness of the day. Mentally and physically she was exhausted, but her thoughts wouldn't give her rest. So at five to twelve she'd accepted defeat, made herself a camomile tea and booted up the computer.

Her MSN pinged notifying her that she had a new comment on her Myspace page.
'Hey there cutie, yous up late ? Don't you need your beauty sleep ?'
Give me a break. It was from Clive, the forty-something wannabe ladies man from Croydon who she didn't have the heart to delete. The bulk of his friends list was made up of desperate looking women in low cut tops pouting at close quarters into a web cam. It troubled Lauren that she sat sandwiched between Barbara the busty divorcee from Derby and over made-up Sandra who looked as if she might possibly be transsexual in his top friends list. He was perhaps the most tedious person she had ever encountered either in real life or cyberspace. Even more boring than Robert. At least Robert didn't think he was god's gift to women. What a prospect that would be ? She was trying to ignore Clive's comments and occasional messages in the hope he'd get the message that she really wasn't interested in joining his harem. At least he had never attempted to instant message her.

PING !

'Hey there babes, can u talk ?'
Of course I can bloody talk you idiot. Go away and leave me alone.
'Oh hi, Clive, I'm just about to go to bed.'
'Mmmm…what a nice thought that is ;-)'
Fuck off and die you creep.
'It is for me as I'm really tired and it's work in the morning.'
'me too, maybe I could send you to bed with sweet dreams eh ?'
The pervy bastard wants to cyber. So that's how he gets his kicks. He must work his way around his friends list.
'Clive, I have no idea what you're talking about and if you don't mind I've got to go.'
'Don't go getting all grumpy on me babes. This is Clivey-babes here, I'd like to help you ease away some of that tension.'
Clivey-babes ? You imbecile. Tension ? I'll give you bloody tension.
'Look Clive, I'd love to stop and talk but I really do have to get to bed.'
'Ok, sweetie pie, no probs. You just know where I am when you need me right xx'
No one calls me sweetie fucking pie ! Who do you think I am ? And for crying out loud, the day I need you is the day I get sectioned under the mental health act you tosser.

The virtual online community was never all it was cracked up to be.

Sleep still wouldn't come. The clock had beeped for two, then three and just as Lauren finally began to drift into a broken sleep it beeped for the third time, waking her again. As much as she tried to remove the image of Robert in his hospital bed, the empty squalor of his flat and the vision of his semi-conscious face bobbing in the murk of the River Ouse she couldn't. When she finally did sleep it had been full of entangled thoughts and emotions. There was Robert lying dead on the floor of Matt's flat, there was Robert living with Karl in New York, there was Russell Brand being pulled from the waters of the Ouse, there was Millie in bed with Francis. Eh ?

She woke still exhausted and discovered that her period had started in the night. Looking at herself in the mirror she looked drawn and haggard. Her features were washed out, her hair a tangled mess, and to cap it all she'd found another grey strand where a brown one should be. What had happened to her 18 year old self ? There was not the slightest trace of her in the reflection this morning. Today was a day to strike off the calendar. Ignore it as if it didn't exist and try to begin anew tomorrow. There was nothing for it but to take a duvet day. She'd not had one for nearly two years so surely she must be due one now. Telephoning work before anyone arrived in she left a message on her manager's answering machine, putting on her best sickly voice as she did so. That done, she jumped back into bed, shut her eyes and let the sleep she'd been awaiting finally take her.

Knowing what to do next

'Lauren Seymour, well I ask you.'
 A shaft of light from the landing entered her room as a heavy-eyed Lauren jumped startled from her sleep. 'Half past one in the afternoon and you're still in bed.' It was Francis, he was standing at her bedroom door with his hands on his hips.
'Oh, hi Francis', the words painfully struggled out. She could feel the beginnings of a splitting headache that had arisen from oversleep. 'I'm sick, I'm off work.'
 She collapsed back down into her squishy mattress and pulled the duvet over her face. Francis was having none of it.
'Well, no one got better by just being a lazy lie-a-bed. Time to get up young lady.' She heard the curtains swoosh open, filling the room with a thin November sunlight, then the duvet was rudely wrenched from her grasp.
'Francis, I think you'll find countless people got better precisely by being lazy-lie-a-beds !'
'Well this doctor prescribes the lunch time edition of Neighbours and beans on toast made by his own fair hands.'
Lauren tried hard not to look at him.
'Now look sharpish, you've got ten minutes or I'll be back with my water pistol.' He meant it. She'd better make a move.

 Francis and Lauren sat trays on their laps on each of the battered red two two-seater sofas that sat at an angle to the small colour TV in the corner underneath the back window. Lauren knew from bitter experience that speaking to her housemate during his favourite soap opera was potentially a capital offence.

'The bitch,' he mouthed at the screen as some airbrushed stick-woman admitted she'd been cheating on her boyfriend. 'Ha !' On screen the girl's friend responded with a catty riposte which Francis clearly enjoyed, a fork full of toast, beans dropping off onto his plate, sat impatiently suspended betwixt his lap and open-mouth. Now the cheating girl was crying in a dramatically hammy way. 'Well that'll learn yer you little madam…' Cue the closing music and the resumption of normal service. Francis stood up and took Lauren's tray from her lap. 'So, now we've got that out of the way, you can tell me why you're being such a worthless malingerer today.'

Lauren hid under the hood of her faded hoodie and pouted petulantly.

'As far as I can see Lauren, as much as you'd like just to be able to forget about Robert you're not going to be able to. Your conscience won't let you just close the door on all this. You need to at least offer to help him out if you're going to get any peace of mind.'

Francis began opening the second packet of chocolate Hobnobs.

'Ohhhh Francis…' Lauren put her arms either side of her head, as she sat cross-legged on the sofa rocking distractedly. It was official. This Gorman business was now messing with her head.

'You know I just tell it like it is. You can't just leave the fella and expect to sleep easily. This is a needy person. I know you don't normally do needy but it might not do you any harm to make an exception. You like to think you're all self-contained you lot, but you're not. '

Lauren stopped her motion and looked at her friend.

'Us lot ? What do you mean ?'

'Thatcher's Children of course ! The Iron Lady's progeny. You grew up in the greed is good , looking after number one era, it's bound to have affected how you view the world.'

'I've always voted Labour ?'

'New Labour, I think you'll find. There just as bad. I'm a proper socialist. I was with Arthur Scargill all the way let me tell you. '

'Yes, alright, can we just leave the politics aside and deal with my general recurring crapness please. Isn't that what we normally do ?'

'You can't just walk away from your responsibilities to other people, that's my point. No woman is an island. You've got to go see him when he gets discharged and find out if he needs anything doing. Neighbourliness I think you'll find it's called.'

'He's not my neighbour, he lives the other side of town.'

'Don't be pedantic.'

'Why is everyone all of sudden so bothered about Robert bloody P bleeding Gorman ?'

Lauren was growing increasingly exasperated. Her escape routes back into her normal, not bothering anyone, being bothered even less routine were being closed

one by one. Damn Francis and his kind heart and common sense.
'We're not. I think you'll find it's you that we're bothered about.'

Everybody needs good neighbours

    Directory enquiries had given her Robert's telephone number. Two days had now passed since he was due to be discharged from hospital and she was now sat with her mobile in one hand, the small piece of paper torn off the back of an envelope on which she'd written his number in the other. The cold clear weather was continuing. She'd needed to get some fresh air and clear her head before attempting to make the call. The nerves were similar to those she'd felt when she was trying to contact a bloke she fancied or follow up a random snog back in her youth. It wasn't pleasant, but something was compelling her to do it. She'd walked through town, the Saturday crowds not yet beginning to build, round and past the vast awe-inspiring bulk of York Minster, dropping her book off at the library before settling down on a bench in the frosty Museum gardens. The mellow-stone remains of St Mary's Abbey caught the sunlight and frost crowned the bushes. Just beyond the gardens she caught sight of a university rowing team slicing their way through the icy waters of the Ouse, the cox hollering out instructions through a loud-hailer. If she hadn't been so preoccupied she could have enjoyed the scene. A squirrel edged closer trying to make out if the flash of white he'd seen in her hand was edible.
 'Sorry mate…can't help you today I'm afraid.'
   The squirrel cocked his head to one side and looked her suspiciously in the eye before scuttling off . 'Right, let's get this done.'
   Great Peter, the Minster bell rang out 9.30. It wasn't too early to call him was it ? No of course not, 9.30 was a respectable hour for people in their 30s or at least it probably should be. She punched in the digits. It began ringing. A weary sounding monotone finally answered.
'Yes.'
'Is that Robert ?'
"Yes."
'Hi Robert, it's Lauren.'
'Oh.' His tone remained unchanged.
'I just wanted to apologise for the other day I didn't mean to..'
'It's OK.'
'Oh, it is ?'
'Yeah, it's OK.'
'And if there's anything else I can help you with just…'
'Right. I'll think about it. Was that it ?'
'Erm, yes I suppose it was…Robert..'
His end of the line went dead.
'The cheeky bastard !'

A passing elderly couple gave her a knowing look. The woman in a tea cosy hat and grey anorak leaned towards her and touched her arm. 'Don't worry about it love, he's probably not worth it?' The man winked and they moved on. Lauren smiled when really all she wanted to do was scream after them ;

'He's not my bloody boyfriend !'

No more Robert Gorman. That really was it. She set off at an angry double-speed around town. Flinging her way through the racks of clothes at H&M, then New Look she tried to burn off some of her annoyance. It didn't work. Instead she bought a Guardian, wandered into the café at the Theatre Royal and grabbed herself a window seat. Some gaunt waifs were modelling ridiculous clothes in the magazine, and Polly Toynbee was saying something about supporting single mothers. Hear , hear and all that but it just wasn't doing the trick. It was no good. She grabbed her phone and redialled the number. The same lifeless voice answered. This time she was going to be assertive.
'Robert. It's Lauren again.'
'Hello Lauren.'
'Hello Robert, now look, I need to come round and see you and I don't care what you have to say but I'm coming round just as soon as I've finished my coffee so you'd better be in because if you're not in I swear I'll…'
'OK'
'What ?'
'I said OK. I'll see you in about half an hour then ?'
'Sure'
   With that the line again went dead. Lauren stared at her phone. One of the waitresses who had been wiping down a table top and refilling the brown sugar bowl glanced across at her. She'd clearly been eavesdropping and was now attempting to fill in the blanks in her imagination by reading the expression on Lauren's face. Her coffee drunk, Lauren decided to take a quick skirt around part of the City Art Gallery whilst building up her courage for what was in store. A striking, curly blond haired gallery assistant, possibly mid-20s, whose name badge said she was called Felicity, handed her a leaflet. There was an exhibition of portraits on loan from the National Portrait Gallery of various luminaries ancient and modern including a gaunt overbearing depiction of Mrs Thatcher. Lauren thought she'd mention it to Francis who might well want to come along with some spray-paint to do a bit of defacing. The gallery had been subject to a recent expensive re-fit and looked immaculate in its new clothes. Lauren liked the place as you could wander in for free whenever you had a spare minute or two. There was always some interesting exhibition on or other. As much as she tried to concentrate on the paintings she found it impossible to drag her mind away from the impending meeting with Robert. Within five minutes she was leaving.
'That was quick,' said the gallery assistant as she passed by.
'Yeah, I've got be somewhere, I'll come back and have a proper look.'
'You do.'

The door to Robert's flat slowly opened and the pale blank face of the man himself appeared in the opening. He looked at her silently.
'Well, aren't you going to invite me in ?'
He flung the door back dramatically and gestured with his hand for her to step inside. They walked together down the hall and Robert collapsed in his solitary chair, staring at her as she stood in the doorway between the hall and the living room. He didn't say a word. Lauren noticed he was still wearing the clothes she had taken into the hospital. The windows of the flat were thick with condensation. He wasn't about to make this easy so she may as well just grit her teeth and get on with it.
'Look Robert, I needed to see you to find out what's going on. I'm a bit confused by all of this.' Robert just shrugged. 'I don't know why you asked to see me the other day after all these years but I do know that nobody throws themselves off a bridge into a freezing cold river for no reason.' Another shrug. 'Oh for crying out loud Robert, fucking talk to me please !'
   She walked into the room and sat down on the arm of the chair provoking Robert to lean away. 'It's alright, I don't intend to snog you.' A small smile cracked his features and his shoulders began to relax. Sensing the beginnings of a breakthrough, Lauren softened her approach. 'Are you going to talk to me babes, otherwise I've had a wasted journey.' Feminine wiles. She knew she must have some hidden somewhere.
   Robert let out a sigh, then leaned forward. He perhaps needed a bit of space. 'Tell you what, you gather yourself whilst I go make us a cup of tea.' Lauren got up and walked towards the hall door, pausing in the doorway. 'You do have tea don't you ?' She couldn't take anything for granted in this stripped back place.
'Yeah, top right cupboard.' She smiled at him. 'Only powdered milk though.' Shaking her head in weary disbelief she found the door to the kitchen.
   After washing up two chipped, powdered milk encrusted mugs, and boiling the water in a saucepan as she couldn't find a kettle with a plug on it, she managed to rustle up two barely passable teas. 'There you go.' She said handing him his drink.
   After a brief, awkward conversation about the length of time he'd lived there (five years), and what he now did for a living (he'd been out of work since being made redundant from his library assistant job three years earlier), Lauren brought the conversation back round to what he'd euphemistically been calling his 'accident'.
   'I don't mean to pry Robert, but having got me involved in all this I can't really help you if you don't at least tell me some of the reasons you did what you did. If you can't tell your friends who can you tell eh ?'
   She touched his knee which produced such a spasm of pure delight on his face she thought she'd better not repeat the exercise anytime soon. This was not the normal effect she had upon men.
'I'd just gotten low that's all.'
'I get low all the time, I don't consider chucking myself under the Scarborough train though. Can you be more specific ?' God this was hard work. Perhaps a career in counselling wasn't for her after all.

'Just about everything.'
'Everything. Right.' That didn't really help much. 'Was there a girl involved or anything ?' Unlikely she knew but start with the principal reason young blokes tried to end their life.
'No, no girl.'
'Not a bloke was it ?' Cover all bases.
'God no, I'm not a…' Robert looked horrified.
'It's alright Robert, they don't lock you up for it these days.'
'My nan always used to say that God created Adam and Eve not Adam and Steve.' Which served to remind Lauren that Robert's nan had belonged to some odd god-bothering group or other. It had come out in a university tutorial about the demise of religion in post-war Europe. That was one of the reasons she'd been so strict with him.
'From what I can remember, your nan used to say a lot of things.'
'Meaning ?'
'Meaning that you were always quoting your nan at uni. Millie and I didn't think it was healthy.' She hadn't meant to be so abrupt, it had just come out. It always just came out.
'I know people used to talk about me at uni. I know they still do.'
Lauren winced partly in recognition of the cruelty of her own behaviour around him back then and partly at having just touched a raw nerve. That last line must have really hurt. There wasn't much room to back-off now.
'I'm sorry Robert, it's just you always used to come out with such antiquated stuff and then use your nan as justification for it. Don't you think it's about time you had your own opinions, like with the cleaning for instance ?'
'I do have my own opinions.'
'Ok, well that's a start. So tell me what you really think about gay men then.'
'I'm not talking about *that*'
'So I take it you don't approve then. Just like your nan.'
'I bet your parents influenced your opinions. I didn't have mine around so I got mine from my nan.'
'Robert, my dad thinks Barbara Windsor is a fox and Margaret Thatcher was the saviour of the western world, I don't happen to agree with him on either point.'

    Good job she thought to herself, particularly on the latter. Francis wouldn't allow her back in the house. Robert seemed shocked by this revelation, as if such a state of affairs was an attack on the natural order itself.
'Well perhaps you should respect him a bit more then.'
'I love him to bits, he's the first person I call on when I need directions somewhere, I'd do anything for him if he asked, but that doesn't mean I have to agree with everyone of his viewpoints.' Robert looked as if he couldn't quite comprehend what he was hearing. 'Nobody agrees with their parents about everything, it would be way too weird. We've similarities, but we're individuals. If I'm ever a mum I would want my kids to think for themselves.'
'You say that now…'
'And I mean it.' This was purely hypothetical. Lauren couldn't imagine herself ever

becoming a mother never mind what she'd want her never likely to exist children's opinions to be.

   Robert went silent as if he was attempting to comprehend the revelatory news he had just heard. It was becoming starkly obvious to Lauren that Robert had never managed to develop an adult identity separate from that of his overbearing nan. She had been such a huge figure in his life and her death had left him with a family shaped hole he had never managed to fill. People pay hundreds to psychotherapists to tell them this kind of stuff thought Lauren and she'd just worked Robert out within five minutes. Perhaps a career change was on the cards after all.

'I suppose she was a bit old fashioned.'

'Of course she was.' Lauren was just finishing the last of the peculiar tasting tea, 'that was just her generation. She was not likely to be any different.' Her own gran made the occasional embarrassing remark about Asian shopkeepers at precisely the wrong moment. She probably secretly thought that Enoch Powell was a bit of poster boy who spoke a lot of sense. Her own gran though always enjoyed the fact that her granddaughter liked to speak her wilful little-mind. The strong opinions Lauren espoused even as a little girl during heated Sunday dinner time debates had sent Granny Leonard into paroxysms of delight, particularly when Lauren was verbally jousting with her bamboozled father. From how Robert spoke of his nan, she found it hard to imagine a similar grandparents indulgence on her part.

'She just had a lot to deal with you know. With losing her daughter and son-in-law and then having responsibility for me at such a late age. She wasn't a bad person, just a bit strict.'

   There was something peculiarly engaging about Robert when he began to open up. He was clearly deeply-layered and extremely complex, all of it hidden under a thick cloak of learnt behaviour. Those rote-like lines about what his nan said on every matter were perhaps a means by which to avoid having to engage with the world for himself. His nan still answered for him from beyond the grave just as she had when he was a child. Lauren had a thought.

'Where's your nan buried Robert ?'

'She's not.'

'I thought she died over ten years ago ?'

'She did.'

'Now I'm confused….'

'She was cremated.'

The nightmarish vision of the decaying cadaver of Robert's nan falling out of the wardrobe started to recede. If she was in there, it would perhaps explain the smell that haunted the flat. No, Lauren had been in Robert's wardrobe, and it contained a lot more horrors than a dead rotting granny. Those Y-Fronts were a crime against nature.

'Ok…so where did you scatter her ashes ?'

'I didn't.'

'You didn't scatter her ashes ?'

'No they're under the bed.' He spoke the line so matter of fact it was as if he was telling her he had a packet of fish fingers in the freezer. Lauren looked at him open-mouthed.

'So let me get this straight. You've got your nan's ashes under your bed. In an urn I hope ?'

'There wasn't any money left in her pension account after I'd paid for her cremation to buy an urn so they had to go in something else.'

'Like what ?' Lauren was dreading the answer.

'An empty Quality Street tin.'

'You're joking !' She sat wide-eyed. Was this another of her surreal dreams ? Any minute Dermot O'Leary was going to come through the door, waltzing with Richard Dawkins whilst Gary Lineker accompanied them on the ukulele

'Nope.'

'You can't keep your nan in a tin of Quality Street you muppet !'

'Why not ? She's hardly likely to complain is she.'

'That's not the point is it ? Surely you should be treating her with a bit of decorum.' Admittedly she sounded like a right old hag, but even witches got better treatment than that these days. Thinking about it weren't witches a proper bona-fide, don't offend their right to their beliefs religion now ? Lauren mentally retracted that thought. She was sure most witches would have brought Robert up better than his nan did.

'Well, if she'd not given all her money to the Melton Mowbray Christian Brethren then maybe there'd have been a bit of spare for a proper urn.'

'Did they not want to take her remains ? Do the decent Christian thing with them ?' Lauren as a born-again atheist wasn't entirely sure what that might be, but it must be something.

'Just after she died the church folded. The pastor fled to Spain with a member of the congregation and took nan's money with him. I think he invested it in a strip-club.'

'Oh..erm..well..' Lauren was struggling to take all this on board. What did you say at this point ? She was damned if she knew.

'So I really couldn't afford an urn. The undertakers had just finished a tin of Quality Street they'd been given by the family of someone they'd buried and thought nan wouldn't mind. I didn't like to say that she'd always preferred Roses.'

'Urn or no urn, it doesn't explain away the fact you've got her under your bed. Did she not say where she wanted to be scattered ?'

'I don't think she ever saw herself as being dead. I think she liked the idea of being immortal.' And in Robert's troubled mind, she clearly was thought Lauren. As far as he was concerned she probably actually lived under his bed keeping a gimlet-eye on all that he did. Lauren wondered if he brought her out on special occasions - birthdays, Christmas and the like.

'You can't leave her there mate, it's just not healthy for you is it ? You've got to let go. You should scatter her somewhere pretty. I bet she'd like that.'

'Like where ?'

'I dunno,' Lauren had a think then remembered that Francis was always taking weekend drives up to the North York Moors, he'd know somewhere suitable as a final resting place for a battleaxe, sorry sweet old lady. 'Tell you what, can I call my

friend? He knows the countryside a bit better than me, he could suggest somewhere. If he's not doing anything he might even drive us up there tomorrow.'
'Tomorrow? Don't I get chance to say my goodbyes first?'
'Can't you do that tonight?' Lauren wondered just how long it would take to bid adieu to a bit of dust in an old tin of Quality Street.
'S'pose so. It'll be hard though. I could get emotional.'
'I think you're allowed.'

Lauren ventured back into the kitchen to telephone home on her mobile. Francis had been eating his morning toast and marmite whilst watching children's television when the phone rang.
'Ooh scattering ashes. I like the sound of that. We need a windswept moor, the rain lashing our crouched figures as the hot salty tears of remorse sting our faces. Very bleak. Very Bronte.'
'So you know somewhere like that do you?'
'Hole of Horcum, nice spot to park the car and there's usually an ice cream van. Even in November.'
'You don't mind driving us up there then?'
'Nothing else on, and anyway, it'll give me chance to say a few words and lead the proceedings. I do hope we're going to wear black. Shall I take a poem?'
'No, I don't think that will be necessary Francis. Oh, and by the way, Robert seems a bit weird about gay blokes, not sure he's ever met any before so if you could just be easy on him I'd appreciate it.' Francis quietly considered this news.
'Like that is it? Is he good looking your friend?'
'He's not really my friend, and he's kind of alright in a weird sense.'
'Well that gives me a marvellous mental picture to play with. You're such a descriptive girl.'
'Get back to your toast Deirdre, and I'll see you later.'
'Alright Mabel.'
'And Francis'
'Yes dearest,'
'I do love you…'
'The feelings mutual. Now get back to lover boy.'
'I'll give you fucking lover boy.' But the phone had gone dead.

Ashes to ashes

Francis sat beeping his car horn outside of the block of flats where Robert lived.
'Give him chance. He'll be on his way.' Lauren was folding and unfolding her hands nervously in the passenger seat.
'You know I'm a stickler for time-keeping. I've made an effort to be here at the stated hour, he could at least be waiting for us.' Francis checked his severely

thinning hair in the mirror, and wiped a trace of something from the corner of his mouth. He looked pensive.
'Oh, don't get stroppy babes, he's in a fragile state at the minute.'
'Fragile or not, from what you've been saying, it sounds like the boy needs a bit of order in his life.'
'I'm sure he does, but can we just keep it cool today, he's saying goodbye to his nan.'
'Oh yes, the last hard centre in the tin.' Francis had been seriously tickled by the Quality Street story.
'Francis !'
   Curtains on the second floor were now beginning to twitch and a balding man in a grubby vest was shaking his fist at the occupants of the car. Francis wound down his window and waved right back of him, blowing him a camp cheeky kiss.
'Don't do that you idiot. It's Sunday morning.' Lauren grabbed hold of his hand and pulled it back onto the steering wheel.
'Well, why don't they get up and do something useful ?' Francis tugged his hand away. 'I'm missing Mass to be here.'
'Fr Collins taking it is he ?' Lauren teased.
'Fr Collins is an exceptional young priest with a remarkable bedside manner.'
Lauren sniggered. 'I bet he has…'
   When Francis had been in hospital with pneumonia earlier in the year, St Wilfrid's had sent their good looking young curate to visit him. He'd patiently sat tending a love struck Francis who seemingly made a miraculous recovery. Father Collins put this down to the extensive rounds on the rosary that were prayed for him by some of the senior ladies of the congregation. Lauren on the other hand put it down to the energising earthly power of lust.
'I don't like you mocking the clergy.'
'Mocking ? I'm not mocking,' and as she protested her innocence, the figure of Robert in a ripped navy blue ski-jacket, the like of which Lauren hadn't seen since 1988, emerged from the doorway of the block. He was carrying a Netto bag.
'This your boyfriend is it dearest ?' Teased Francis in return.
'Stop that right now…'
'Poor old granny, if being left in a Quality Street tin wasn't bad enough she's now being carried in a scabby supermarket bag as well.'
'Please try and behave Francis.'
   He was really beginning to tire her this morning. He generally acted up more when he was feeling anxious. If he was feeling nervous then that must make three of them judging by the look on Robert's face. He caught Lauren's eye and sheepishly made his way across to the car. Lauren jumped out to greet him, opening a rear door in the process and gesturing for him to clamber inside. Settling back down into the passenger seat she introduced the two men to each other.
'Robert, this is my housemate Francis, and Francis this is….'
'Robert, I know…,' Francis twisted around, stuck his head between the gap in the two front seats and attempted to air kiss the flinching passenger. 'It's always lovely to meet one of Lauren's friends. Her and I go back a long way you know, but from

what I gather you and she have an even older history.'
'Yes, we were at university together.'
'Ah, the friends we make in our Brideshead days stay with us don't you find ?' Francis was piling on the mock cultured camp. Lauren sat glaring at him. This was difficult enough without him acting-up as well. Her beloved housemate was always one for an audience. Robert sat looking confused, then appeared to stiffen in his seat a little as if preparing to say something important.
'Mr…'
'Francis please I insist.'
'I just wanted to make it very clear to you that my feelings towards Lauren are purely those of friendship.'
   Lauren felt herself inwardly wince. She shut her eyes and stayed resolutely fixed in her seat not wanting to hear what she knew was coming next. 'I know that some men are not happy about their girlfriends having male friendships, but I want you to know that you have nothing to fear from me.'
Lauren thought it best to intervene before this went any further. She opened her eyes and caught the mischievous grin of Francis just in time to mouth a stern 'no' in his direction. He in turn carried on regardless.
'That's alright Robert. We're both men of the world. We know where we stand. My little lady here knows which side her bread is buttered.' He slapped his hand down hard on Lauren's thigh making her flinch. 'You won't be straying will you honey ?' Lauren quietly seethed. 'No we have to keep the little women in their place Robert. There's too much of this sexual equality nonsense these days. Men should be men and women, well they should know their place.'
'You're not wrong there.' Robert nodded in an approving fashion seemingly relieved at having found himself a kindred spirit and pushing Lauren past the point of no return in the process.
'Robert ! Do you mind…'
'I'm sorry, I thought…'
'Never mind what you thought.' She glared at Robert then turned her spiky gaze in the direction of Francis 'Just you get driving fat boy and keep your gob shut.'
   Francis quickly turned, rolled his eyes and mouthed a silent 'women' at Robert who by now was looking terrified, his face shrinking beneath the collar of his ski-jacket.

   The rest of the journey was accompanied by Radio 3 on the dying old car stereo, to which Francis occasionally hummed along , once or twice lifting his left hand off the steering wheel to air-conduct his imaginary orchestra. Robert said little other than a few prompted pleasantries about the weather, and just how nice the countryside was out this way. As they pulled out of Pickering, a sleepy stone town beloved of retirees, the road rose up and into the North York Moors. Clouds scurried across the sky-line as the thin light picked out skeletal looking trees which grew at odd wind battered angles on the bleak moorland. Streams coursed down inclines, weather beaten sheep huddled together for warmth as the car slipped beyond civilisation. A cloud of white smoke puffed its way through the valley as Francis pointed out the course of the steam railway that still ran services up through the isolated communities of the moors.

Previously the closest Lauren had been to any of this had been whilst watching Heartbeat. As a student, a group of them had taken the train to Scarborough for a day of wandering along the seafront, eating candy floss and building sand fortresses on the beach. Other than that she rarely ventured into the areas surrounding the city. Her world was largely contained within its boundaries.

'It's so…' Lauren was trying to find the right word.
'Harsh ?' Offered Francis.
'Yes, and…'
'Bleak' piped up Robert.
'…That as well…it's kind of breathtaking.'

She was surprised to find herself so impressed. Despite having lived just a short drive from the moors for the past fourteen years she had never felt the slightest inclination to go and visit them. Her travels were either home to Nottingham to see her parents, or into Leeds to do some shopping. She wasn't really a country girl. The trips out into the uninteresting farmland intersected by 'A' roads of the East Midlands had never really inspired her to want to linger. Childhood holidays were spent in seaside resorts in Devon and South Wales and these days when she was off work she tended to stay in York, not get dressed and read books. Wanderlust was not a condition she had ever particularly suffered from. Her world was a small one, but it was one she was quite content with. Unlike Millie who loved to travel.

'Come on, why don't you come with me…it'll be fun !' Mills would always enthuse after just waxing lyrical about her next proposed adventure to some far flung corner of the planet. Lauren usually followed the same routine in response. Leave it open as a possibility, prevaricate for a while, then say no. Her friend knew the script as well, even if she did still hang onto to the slender possibility that Lauren may one day surprise her. So far she hadn't done so. Millie instead found herself another travelling companion - Kate, who worked with her in administration at the theatre. There was much that they did share without coming down heavy about her best friend's lack of enthusiasm for seeing the world. It was a minor point of divergence in an otherwise tight understanding relationship

Lauren was not without a small pang of jealousy whenever Millie would talk of their adventures in Eastern Europe, North America and the Far East. They were always getting into scrapes, always meeting fit young blokes, always visiting amazing places, always having the time of their lives without her there. Ah well, not to worry. Millie always came back and Lauren was the first person she wanted to tell all about it. Then came the New York trip.

'Come on Lauren, it's not like we're going to be backpacking or anything. We're staying in a nice hotel, en-suite showers, breakfast in bed that kind of thing.' Lauren had been tempted. 'We're going to do loads of shopping, maybe go see a show, nothing adventurous.'

As appealing as it had sounded Lauren just couldn't bring herself to agree to go. Travels were about Millie and Kate, not Millie, Kate and Lauren. She wasn't overly fond of Kate anyway, far too theatrical and not in an over the top camp Francis kind of way, more in the tortured artist kind of sense. Lauren found her lack of humour tiring and she was sure that Kate felt she was an insubstantial little advertising hack. Millie seemed to get on with her though so she always kept her opinions to herself. Another reason for turning down the Big Apple was the fear that an extended period in Kate's presence may result in her loosening her tongue on that particular score. The last thing she wanted or needed was a row with her best friend. So no, she wouldn't be going.

   Just four days after Millie and Kate had left for New York, Lauren had received a gushing early morning phone call from her friend. She had clearly been drinking and couldn't wait to share her latest earth shattering news.
'I've met him !'
'Who ? Not Bill Clinton !' During their college years Millie had harboured unlikely lustful thoughts over the then American president. These waned after the Lewinsky incident but had recently come back strongly after she was struck by his charm and twinkly eyes during a TV interview.
'No, better than that…' Better than Bill ? Now that was going to take some doing.
'He's called Karl. He's tall, blond, an actor and absolutely bloody gorgeous.'
'You've met another bloke then ? ' This was nothing out of the ordinary for Millie on her travels. There had been any number of holiday romances down the years.
'No, not just another bloke. THE bloke, Mr Right, I've met him.'
'Millie, I can tell you've been drinking and…'
'I'm not pissed Lauren, listen to me, he's frickin lovely and we've just clicked. We met in a bar a couple of nights ago and got talking. I work in a theatre, he's an actor. He's a bit good in the bedroom department…well I say good, he took a bit of warming up but then..'
'Mills, you only met him a couple of nights ago, you said you weren't going to do that again.'
'I know, but this is different. Please try and understand Lauren. Kate's being a pain about it and I need someone to tell me I'm doing the right thing.'
'The right thing ? In what sense.'
'Oh, he's asked me to marry him. Isn't it brilliant ?'

   The car pulled into a car park just off the moorland road above a vast hollowed out bowl in the land.
'This my friends living and dead is the Hole Of Horcum.'
'Wow ,' mouthed Robert.
'Nice,' added Lauren.
Robert's nan remained characteristically silent.
Across the car park a couple in matching gore-tex anoraks with the hoods pulled up took possession of 2 fluffy ice-creams, each with a flake from an ice-cream van and proceeded to eat them as they sauntered back towards their ten year old Renault.
'You weren't lying about the ice-cream van then,' said Lauren amazed at the hardiness of these outdoor types. 'See how they cackle in the face of the cold', she

said in a mock cartoon villain fashion.

'Now if you two kiddies are good,' said Francis, looking from Lauren to Robert 'I might buy you both one after we've done the business. Wet the baby's head so to speak.'

'Baby's head ? Wrong end of the whole life business mate,' responded Lauren before wondering if her flippant tone might be upsetting Robert. He didn't really appear to be aware of much that was going on. His face looked heavy and blank, as if there was still confusion as to what he was doing on the planet. This matched Lauren's confusion at what the hell she was doing here with him and his discount supermarket bag of dusty dead relation. Francis appeared to have some idea, unbuckling his seatbelt and moving his sizeable girth out of the car door.

'Come on then kids.' He rubbed his hands together against the biting cold. 'Let's get cracking.'

As all three of them emerged from the car they were hit by the chill of the moorland air. Robert stood trembling, his ancient ski-jacket and half-mast jeans failing to keep out the tendrils of cold. Lauren in her parka, scarf and hat was slightly better off, but Francis with his oversized walkers jacket, waterproof trousers, walking boots and Nordic poles had clearly done this kind of thing before. Robert stared at him then looked down at himself.

'It's alright Robert, we're not about to climb K2,' reassured Francis. 'Is your nan all set ?'

Robert held up the bag like a bronze medal winner displaying his prize on the podium at the Paralympics.

'In that case, let's press on.'

Francis strided out across the road and onto a narrow muddy footpath that scouted the edge of the Hole. Passing a group of ramblers coming in the opposite direction, Lauren and Robert were both eyed disapprovingly by some of the senior walkers. Lauren gave them a 'whatever' look whilst Robert remained oblivious, seemingly stranded on his own personal mental island.

'Get the bloody pensioner fashion police why don't you.' Lauren shouted to the back of Francis as they walked single-file along the footpath. It was intended to be loud enough for the last of the disappearing ramblers to hear.

'The Ramblers Association do a lot of remarkable work Lauren. It's not their fault you don't how to dress for the outdoors.'

'It's not like I'm in a boob-tube and sling backs is it ?' No. That would make her Millie.

'Now that would be a sight.'

'Just watch what you're saying Mr.'

The sound of Robert's jacket crunching as he moved was the only noise that emanated from his direction. They climbed over a stile, and onto a broader path that opened out onto the scrubby moor. Rearing up behind them was the shadow of the American spy-base at Fylingdales. Their strange bulky sci-fi presence looked incongruous in somewhere so wild and primitive.

'Bloody yanks. Why don't they do their own dirty work ?' Muttered Francis pointing one of his walking poles across at the discordant looking buildings. Lauren turned to

Robert, raised her eyebrows and grinned to which he returned a sheepish smile. She noticed his face was furrowed and she wasn't sure if it was the wind or the thought of what he was about to do that had produced what looked like tears in his eyes. Lauren linked his arm, patted him on the shoulder with her other hand, gave him her best kindly smile and led them both on.

'We're talking ancient here folks.' Francis was about to begin one of his history lessons, gesturing with his walking pole in a wide encompassing arc at the view around him. 'Local folklore says that this great hole in the land was created when a giant was having a fight with a neighbour.'

'Oooh I wonder if you can get ASBOS for giants.'

'Don't be flippant Lauren.' He shot her a disapproving look. 'Anyway, this dispute eventually turned nasty and Horcum, for that was his name, began pelting his neighbour with large clumps of earth he picked up in his giant hand.'

'And the hole is the space left where he took it from.' Lauren had guessed how this story was going to end. All these little folk tales said something similar.

'Is it glacial ?' Robert finally made a contribution.

'It is sir, it is indeed,' affirmed Francis as they pushed out further , away from the road and the car park and into what passed for wilderness in these parts.

'I think this is perhaps a suitable spot to say cheerio to granny,' said Francis as they arrived at a point where the moor jutted out into the bowl below.

'Nice spot.' Lauren breathed in deeply. 'OK Robert ?'

Robert took in the vista.

'Y..y..yes..t..t.hank you v..very much' Lauren noticed his hands were shaking.

'You OK ? Do you want to do this on your own or…'

'N..n..no…p..please stay.'

'OK'

Francis walked across to the hunched stuttering figure, placed an arm around his shoulder and put a hand on the bag. 'Tell you what my friend. Why don't I take the bag here for a moment and you can gather yourself. Would you like to say a few words or should I ?' Robert looked up at him, as if for guidance.

'A few words ?'

'Y'know, cheerio, that kind of thing. We can't just empty the tin and wander off. It wouldn't be proper. I nearly considered becoming a priest you know.'

Lauren looked at him and shook her head. Not the religious vocation cut-off in it's prime story again. She'd lost track of the number of times she'd heard him tell the tale of the 'call from god' he'd decided to ignore. Robert thought about Francis's offer for a second and then stuttered his response.

'N..no, you're right. Would you mind saying…'

'Not at all, not at all.'

Francis stood facing Lauren and Robert with his back to the drop.

'Dearly beloved.'

'Dearly beloved ?' He was clearly going to milk this moment thought Lauren. Just how often would an opportunity like this present itself.

'Yes…be quiet..dearly beloved. We are gathered here today to celebrate the life of…' He looked towards Robert for a cue.
'Oh..erm..Edna, Edna Nursey.'
'Nursey ?' Trust Robert's nan to have a comedy surname. It wasn't helping Lauren contain her growing amusement. She tried to recover her slender grasp on proper decorum.
'Lauren shut up. I'm trying to conduct a service here.' Francis continued.
'Dearly beloved etc, we are here to remember our dear friend Edna Nursey.'
Lauren stifled a laugh
'Who sadly passed away over a decade ago and has been living in a sweetie tin under a bed in a council flat ever since.'
'Actually, I've only been in the flat for five years, before that I used to have a bedsit on…' Robert tried to correct.
'Yes, whatever…' Francis was growing increasingly impatient that his big emotional moment kept being interrupted, 'and is now to be given back to the world as a gift to you this fine Sunday morning in November.'
'Frickin freezing.'
'Please be quiet Ms Seymour. You are getting perilously close to being removed from my congregation by my muscular tuxedoed bouncers.'
Lauren rolled her eyes and wrapped her arms around herself trying to warm up.
'All that said, I'd now like to invite Edna's charming grandson, Robert to remove his nan from the Netto bag, open the tin and let the good lady finally fly. Robert, if you would…'
'Thank you'
   Robert stepped forward and Francis handed him back the bag containing the remains of his dead relative. Crouching down he gently took out the tin and attempted to remove the lid. Nothing happened. The lid wouldn't be eased off. He tried again, this time using a little more force. Lauren who by now was getting frozen to the point of immobility walked across to lend her assistance.
'Oh the fucking thing's stuck Robert !'
'Lauren, please, my nan hates swearing.'
'Robert, shut the fuck up about your nan and get the frigging lid off this tin please.'
'Lauren there's no need to get like that with Robert, this is a poignant moment for him. Try to show some respect. ' Francis was using his best schoolmasterly voice.
'…And don't you start. Lend a hand.' Francis in turn had a go at the lid of the tin but there was still not a millimetre of movement.
'Right, there's nothing else for it. Give it here.' Lauren roughly snatched the tin off an unprepared Francis and strode purposefully across to the edge of the moor above the vast hollow of the Hole. She pulled her arm and the tin right back and with all the force she could muster threw the rusting tin and it's contents down into the vast glacial crater. Robert and Francis stood open mouthed.
'OH MY GOD.' Francis spoke slowly, enunciating each word dramatically. 'You just chucked granny down into the Hole Of Horcum without taking her out of the tin first ! You're mental !'
   Robert just gazed, a look of speechless frozen horror across his face. The slow

creeping realisation of what she'd just done was now beginning to rise up in Lauren as she attempted to dismiss it with a wave of the hand.

'Well…the bloody lid was stuck alright.'

Robert gazed off into the distance, his eyes stuck on the curve of the arc his nan had taken on her final flight. Francis was open-mouthed and incandescent

'I really think you've gone and lost it this time.' .

'Francis, I was only trying to help the boy. I didn't want to get drawn into any of this.'

'Well you could have been a bit more sensitive couldn't you ?'

'Me sensitive ? You've been the one taking the piss all morning. I've been trying to stop him having a bloody nervous breakdown.' She pointed at Robert who by now had dropped to his knees and was cradling his head in his hands.

'Well you've not made a very good job of it have you ? Look at the state of him.'

'That's right ! You blame me, it's always Lauren's fault isn't it. It's always me who gets stuff wrong and cocks up and then needs big old Francis to ride to the rescue. Poor stupid Lauren, she just doesn't think does she..'

'No, no she never does.'

Lauren stormed across towards her housemate , put her face close up against his and grabbed him by the collar of his coat.

'Well let me tell you Francis, that I'm sick of living with Mr Bloody Perfect . When we get back I'm going to be packing my things and leaving you to it.'

'Fine, absolutely bloody fine. I'm fed up of carrying you.'

   Robert lifted his red tear stained face towards the two of them.

'Don't split up on my account.'

'Robert, he's not my bloody boyfriend. He's the campest man in York. He's gay Robert. Y'know one of those blokes your nan warned you about ?'

'Well,' Robert shrugged. 'It takes all sorts.'

'Oh give me strength.'

 Lauren began striding back to the car at double speed whilst Robert and Francis attempted not to watch. She felt like a stroppy teenager having just had a seafront row whilst on holiday with her parents. Finally reaching the car, she leant back on the bonnet with her arms folded, a face set like impending August thunder. She wasn't entirely sure how long she could keep this up for as the little voice of conscience began to bug her. Perhaps she had been slightly hasty. Perhaps she hadn't shown much respect for the dead woman. No, don't be stupid, she'd been kept in a sweet tin and was carried to be scattered in a discount supermarket bag. That was hardly the most reverential manner in which to deal with your granny's mortal remains. She furtively glanced across the car park and saw Francis handing Robert an ice-cream and taking one himself from the white-coated seller. They sauntered, chatting across to the car park. Lauren quickly turned her head again and fixed her posture. She wasn't going to be the first to talk.

'Lauren,' Francis touched her arm but she didn't answer. 'Robert has something to say to you.'

'Thanks for helping out.'

'Pardon ?'

'I just wanted to thank you for helping me get rid of the remains. I didn't know what to do with them.'
'Even though they weren't technically scattered ?'
'Yes, despite that. I don't mind. It's better that they're gone.'
'Oh'. She wasn't used to being thanked for her cock-ups.
'And as I didn't know what to get you I've bought you a choc ice.' Francis handed her a small rectangular packet. 'Plain. I know you don't like milk chocolate in relation to ice cream.' He knew all her little foibles.
'Thanks.' She unwrapped the choc ice, took a bite and shivered. 'Can we get in the car ?'

Lauren hated arguing with her housemate. They were always having petty squabbles over insignificant things, but large scale slanging matches were rare. That had been the first time she'd ever threatened to move out of the house and she'd been taken aback by how flippantly Francis had responded. He didn't seem in anyway bothered. It had always been the line she'd held in reserve in case she ever needed to really shake him up. In the event, it had been completely ineffective. Or maybe it hadn't. If he wasn't exactly being all sweetness and light now he had at least appeared to have forgotten all about their crossed words.

The journey home had been largely silent. Robert sniffed and looked out of the window wistfully, Lauren shut her eyes out of awkwardness and Francis just drove.
The car pulled up outside Robert's flat.
'So you've got my number then if you need me for any reason ?' Asked Lauren.
'Yes, I have . Thank you. Thank you Francis for driving us and the ice-cream. It's much appreciated.'
'No problem at all.' Francis appeared subdued and lost in his thoughts.
Robert climbed out of the car, closed the door behind him and waved sheepishly. Lauren caught sight of the yellow Netto bag sticking out of his pocket, looked again at his shabby coat, half-mast trousers, grubby white socks and trainers. He sauntered slowly towards the flats. Robert and Lauren both sat transfixed as the solitary figure disappeared inside.
'God, he looks so lonely.' Lauren bit her bottom lip.
'I know,' Francis sighed, 'poor fella.'
'He's alright really. A bit weird but then I suppose we all are.'
'Some of us more than others.' Francis raised an eyebrow and turned to look at his passenger.
'Yeah, I'm sorry about earlier.'
'Not to worry. When you moving out though ? I can finally start charging a proper rent for that room of yours.'
'You just try getting rid of me.' They both smiled and then fell into a meaningful ponderous silence. A light flickered into life from a top floor window. That must be Robert.
'What are we going to do about him Francis ?'
'You mean Robert ?' Francis snapped suddenly out of his contemplation.

'The very man.'
'I don't know my dear.'
'We can't just leave him to struggle along can we ? He needs sorting out.'
'True, but you have to realise what you'd be taking on. He's got any number of issues to deal with, perhaps it's professional help he needs.'
'I'm sure he probably does, but what about someone who can help him sort out his appearance and just get more confident dealing with people. Someone he can chat to when he's low.'
'Someone like you , you mean.'
'Yes, someone just like me.'
'Despite the fact you have problems looking after yourself at times I reckon you could be quite good for him.'
'You do,' she turned and gave Francis a huge natural smile. 'Nice one.'
'And he could be quite good for you.'
'The Robert P.Gorman Rescue Project. That's what I'll call it. I think I'll need a folder.'
Francis grinned and shook his head. Lauren had just found herself an interest.

What's it all about ?

Ever since Millie had quit old York for a life in it's newer and groovier offspring, life for Lauren had been beyond quiet. A routine of work, sleep, watching ever increasing amounts of dull TV and the occasional drink with colleagues from work for whom she cared little. It wasn't so desperate. Once you got into the groove of inactivity it was comfortable enough. She often had the house to herself as Francis busied himself with his many activities. Every Monday it was his meeting of the Ebor Light Operatics for whom he helped coach the singers. Thursday evenings he played bridge and then there was his general round of socialising amongst his vast array of local friends. Francis was a popular man.

   It wasn't hard for Lauren to see why. He was generally jovial, very intelligent, funny if at times a little too catty with it and always ready with a piece of choice advice. His work teaching piano to a series of spoilt kids and bored middle-aged tryers seeking a distraction from their humdrum jobs and relationships filled him with satisfaction. Once a year, every Autumn term he would run a ten-week course in music appreciation attended largely by pensioners. He never seemed to hanker after anything else, never appeared to be growing weary of his life of camp suburban respectability in a sleepy cathedral city. Francis knew who he was and where he fitted in. That was something Lauren envied.

    If she was being honest with herself, work was beginning to tire. A decade with one firm writing tedious, repetitive copy for unimaginative companies selling goods and services that didn't interest her. What was it all about ? Was this how she was destined to spend the rest of her working days ? She had watched the nurses in the hospital whilst visiting Robert. They might not be particularly well-paid or glamorous, but what they did was essential. We would always need nurses but would the world end if we ever ran out of advertising copywriters ?

At work she wondered if she was the only person who felt like this. Most of her colleagues appeared to be completely enamoured with life at an advertising agency. It had slightly more glamour attached to it than working for a packing company or doing the accounts at a building firm. Lauren though wasn't really interested in any perceived glamour in the first place. What was bugging her now was repetitive insistent questions about the meaning of all this. Was helping companies of at times dubious morals to increase their profit margins what her role on the planet was destined to be ? Unlike Francis she saw no guiding hand at work, no divine intervention that would eventually pull together all the strands of her life and make sense of her contribution. She knew that if life on the planet was essentially meaningless then it was down to her to give some meaning to her own insignificant stretch upon it. At the moment that just wasn't happening.

'Hey don't go getting a social conscience on us,' had puffed Josh Andrews one of the senior account executive's at Accent . He was only a couple of years older than Lauren and had joined the company at the same time. Whilst Lauren had managed to move up a couple of grades on the pay scale, taking on a bit more responsibility in the process, Josh had risen effortlessly year on year. Of course Lauren hated him. He had recently become a father and his spotless Home Counties wife had given up work to tend his perfect home in Heworth. When he wasn't talking about his baby , new furnishings for his "family room" or his own general brilliance, he was boring her with repetitive corporate spiel about maximising profits and the bottom line.
'Don't you ever wonder what we're doing here though Josh ?'
'I know what we're doing here Lauren. We're making money for our clients. When they make money…'
'Yes we make money I know.' Lauren sighed. 'Is making money all that matters ?'
Josh looked at her blankly, before raising an eyebrow and doing a kind of sideways wink that you'd give to a three year old.
'Well yes if you want to keep your job Laurers…' he spoke using all the condescension he could muster and tapped her on the hand. Fuck him thought Lauren. Not in the physical sense though you understand even though he was good looking in a creepy Stepford kind of way . Every feature was just a little too perfect to be true. He had a face that would perhaps benefit from going twelve rounds with Joe Calzaghe just to add a bit of interesting rearrangement.

Lauren often went further than she knew she should in her comments to him. It was hard to credit him with much authority. He was barely older than her and she found him vacuous and personally irritating. People like Josh made progress in her firm despite their clear and present intellectual limitations. This increased her feelings of being jaundiced from those around her. It was growing increasingly apparent to her that no matter how long she stayed , how good her output was she would never have the kind of face or personality for senior success. Not that she was particularly bothered. Oiling her way in the corporate world was never how she'd imagined she'd be spending her time.

   She had of late started speaking her mind much more around the senior management. She frequently spoke up at staff meetings about issues of concern or challenged points around which there had been a previous consensus. It had not gone unnoticed and Josh Andrews in particular didn't seem content to let matters lie.

'Are you having any problems at the moment Lauren ?'

  He sat on the corner of her desk uninvited. Lauren ignored him by staring at her computer screen, swapping the word 'pretty' to 'beautiful' on the copy she was currently knocking into shape. She didn't answer. 'Lauren ?'

'Sorry Josh,' she looked up, 'did you say something ?'

'I just wanted to know if you had any problems presently ?'

'Me, problems ? Oh no..' she started tapping away pointedly on her keyboard again, fixing her gaze on the on-screen text.

'It's just your change of attitude has been noted.'

  Lauren looked up and stared at him coldly. There was no way she was going to make this easy for the slimy bastard.

'Attitude ?'

'Yes, you seem a little confrontational of late.'

  Lauren snorted a derisory laugh.

'Oh you know me Josh, all I'm concerned about is maximising the bottom line for our clients.'

  Josh singularly failed to pick up on the sarcasm.

'Well, that's great Lauren. We've known each other a long time and I for one would hate to see you have to go.'

  She found these kind of clichéd smarmy lines particularly irritating when they came from the mouth of someone like Josh Andrews. They were patently insincere.

'Why would I be going anywhere ?' She snapped back. She might not be overly happy at work at present but she had as yet no plans to leave.

'It's just that given the current climate it may be that the company is looking to make a few savings in the New Year.'

'Eh ? Are you saying what I think you're saying ?'

'Look, I'm only telling you because I like you,' liar thought Lauren, 'and I thought it right to forewarn you. It may be that one or two creatives will have to be laid off to balance the books and…'

'…Wait a minute, there's only two copywriters and two graphic designers here in the first place ? You're saying you're going to get rid of two of us ?'

'It might not be two, it could just be one, or it could be three, but I just…'

'Even fucking one is too many, we're snowed under already.'

'Now I know you're busy, but from a purely financial point of view.'

'Financial ? Financial ? You see how your fucking books stack up when the work we're turning out gets a reputation for being shit and predictable.'

'Yes we realised that…'

'Bollocks do you ! You lot reckon that us in here are doing monkey work. You reckon you could give our work to an office junior and they could write what I write

don't you ?'
'Well, it's not like that…'
'Huh. I bet it isn't.' Lauren turned away from Josh and started fiddling around in a filing cabinet, she removed a folder then slammed the door shut so hard it wobbled.
'Now Lauren, you see what I mean.' Josh raised his voice and attempted to pull rank. She continued to ignore him. 'It's this kind of attitude that could put you in jeopardy.'
'Whatever.' She waved a hand as if dismissing him. Josh Andrews stood up and looked down awkwardly at the sheet of A4 paper he had been carrying.
'Just so you're aware.' Lauren raised her eyebrows and made a loud dramatic sigh as Josh sheepishly left the room. Sliding back in her chair, she threw her pen down hard on the table sending paperclips flying.
'Great, just bloody great.'

Seeking distraction

Francis had been playing the piano in the corner of the front room as Lauren arrived home. He looked at her and nodded as she crept past. His 5:30 appointment with 'cranky Christine', the bank manager's wife must have been cancelled at the last minute.

From what Lauren could gather about Christine she'd been in and out of a private psychiatric hospital whilst her husband romanced a string of attractive young juniors at the bank and did his very best to hush the whole thing up. Francis felt sorry for her. She was truly trapped in a damaging relationship and felt herself powerless to do much about it.

'I'd have chopped his bollocks off years ago', Lauren had commented after Francis had told her the whole sorry tale. Bad days followed good and Francis was always liable to receive a last minute phone-call calling off today's lesson. It left him feeling peculiar and out sorts, imagining her in a darkened bedroom sobbing her eyes out, or maybe contemplating something even worse.

Lauren threw two teabags in the pot and flicked the switch on the kettle. Before long she was pouring the tea, and adding the three sugars that Francis seemed to run on to his 'Dancing Queen' mug. As she placed his tea on the coaster on the top of the piano the melancholy piece Francis was playing came to an end.
'Do you think Christine's alright ?' He looked up at Lauren. Francis could lose himself when he was playing. It was always a tool to take him away from whatever concern was currently bugging him .Lauren cupped both hands around her mug and sat back on the sofa.
'You can't be responsible for her.'
'I wish she'd never contacted me. I'm involved now.'

'Only if you let yourself be. Try not to think about it too much.'

Francis sighed. 'Easier said than done.' He joined Lauren on the sofa and she gave him a hug, resting her head on his chest.

'Poor Francis. You can't save all us cranky old birds you know. You've got to think about yourself some times.'

He stroked her hair and kissed the top of her head.

'So tell me about your day Lauren Seymour. Just how many units of plumbing supply materials is your winning copy responsible for shifting this week ?'

'Oh don't take the piss .' She pointedly moved away from him and took a gulp of her tea.

'Is there a problem ?' Normally she'd play along. Her skills at moving building supplies were a running joke in their household. She had a way of talking about ballcocks that would have made Wordsworth jealous.

'You don't wanna know babes.'

'Try me.'

'That slimy bastard Josh told me I could be out of a job in the New Year.'

'That is bad.'

'Ahuh'

'I don't know what to say.'

'Doesn't matter.'

It was clear to Francis that his housemate wasn't keen on talking about the subject just yet. She always liked to cogitate and take on board bad news for a few days before she got anywhere near opening up about what was bothering her. Francis knew that it was best to leave time to do its usual thing.

'Anyway, how's the Robert P.Gorman Rescue Project progressing ?' Distraction, that's what they both needed.

'Ooh bloody hell, Robert.' Lauren jumped up and picked up the A4 pad that was sitting next to the phone. 'I'd nearly forgot all about him.' It had been four days since Lauren had disposed of Granny's ashes unceremoniously into the Hole of Horcum. She had made no attempt to contact him and had privately been wondering whether or not just to leave him to his own solitary devices. With the news that she may very soon be joining Robert in the cues at the Job Centre she felt she might need to earn some karmic brownie-points to cash in when and if the redundancy shit hit the metaphorical fan.

'I thought I might take him clothes shopping.' She wrote the word shopping in black biro on the pad and underlined it.

'That would be a start. Just one problem though. He's unemployed, he's got no money.'

'Oh god of course. Maybe that's why he looks so shit ?'

'I think there may be more to it than that.'

'I'm going to have to buy some new stuff for him.'

'Are you serious ? You're going to buy a new wardrobe of clothes for a relative stranger ?'

'He's not a stranger, he's an old friend. Kind of.' That was maybe stretching it a bit, but thinking of him as such made the desire to acquire him some new clothes

marginally less weird. 'And I didn't say a whole wardrobe, just a few essentials.'
   Francis looked at her as if she'd just arrived from Venus.
'Right. Are you feeling okay ?'
'Very well. I just want to give something back and rather than giving my money to charity I can help someone directly. You were lecturing me about my social responsibility or lack of it the other day.'
'That sort of makes sense', Francis scratched his receding hairline. 'I think.'

A little retail therapy

'No. Absolutely not. I can't let you.'
Robert was not about to play ball. In Lauren's mind at least, Robert would have greeted the news of their impending shopping trip with outright, overflowing gratitude. He'd see what a kind, thoughtful and generous woman she was and be forever in her debt. He'd accept this offer of charity with open-handed glee and Lauren would be able to sit back in the knowledge that she'd just won some brownie points with the big guy upstairs. Actually, scrap the brownie points. Lauren remembered she was an atheist so they didn't apply to her. Maybe karma was allowable ? That seemed vaguely scientific. Whatever. Robert had at least turned up at Lauren's place as she'd asked him to. He was dressed in a pair of bobbling brown slacks which were customarily too short, a grey misshapen t-shirt with the name of a local building firm on it underneath the by now familiar ski-jacket.
'Why not ? I only want to help.' Why didn't he just play ball and follow the script ? People were always being difficult.
'I'm not a charity case. Nan says…' Lauren raised her eyebrows stopping Robert in his tracks. 'Nan's dead.' Lauren nodded. 'It's just I like to pay my way.'
'And that's an admirable quality. But friends do this kind of thing for each other occasionally.' The magic 'F' word appeared to do the trick where Robert was concerned.
'Do they really?' His eyes lit up.
'Yeah, all the time'
   This was maybe stretching it a bit. She had in the past been known to buy Millie something cheap, glittery and fabulous from Claire's Accessories, and the occasional tie for Francis but had never once contemplated purchasing them a whole new wardrobe. If she was being honest she still wasn't entirely sure why she was offering to part with so much money to help out Robert now. Maybe it was those big eyes that prompted her generosity. They seemed to look right into your soul, full of so much depth and sadness. She couldn't help but be fascinated by them and what they may or may not say about their owner. He was an enigma was Robert.
   Francis had donated fifty pounds toward the shopping trip despite Lauren's insistence that he should keep his cash to himself. Never one to willingly take no for

an answer he'd shoved five rolled up tenners into her hand and folded her fingers closed around the money. She had decided to take his advice and withdraw a set amount of money so as not to get carried away and overspend on her credit card. Sixty pounds. That added to the money from Francis should be enough to get the basics sorted. If Robert then bought himself something every month he'd soon have a reasonable set of clothes. Anything was going to be an improvement on the current crop.

 Firstly she dragged him into the multi-coloured world of New Look his grey face going red with embarrassment as a group of teenage girls in leggings and tiny denim skirts pointedly gave him an amused once over. The stares of the elaborately, coiffured and over made-up shop girls gave him the jitters.

'Just ignore it.' Lauren single-mindedly led him to the men's section, trying to avert her gaze from a rather attractive cardigan seemingly with her name written all over it. She saw less and less in here that she liked these days, but the prices were good so she kept coming back and living in hope.

 'Right, firstly you're going to need jeans.' Quickly skimming through the rails she laid her hands on a boot cut pair she liked the look of. 'What's your size ?'

'I dunno.' Robert shrugged. He disinterestedly examining the ceiling tiles.

'You don't know ?' She pulled his chin back down so he was looking her in the eye.

'No, I've never really checked.' Not checked ? What was wrong with the boy.

'Oh for goodness sake Robert. Come here and turn around.' Lauren grabbed the startled Robert sharply by the waist and forced him around so he now had his back to her. She shoved a hand down the rear of his trousers and felt around for a label. Robert looked horrifically affronted.

'Lauren ! Do you mind.'

'Not at all,' no time for squeamishness now she thought, 'just hold still whilst I find your label.' Finally getting a couple of fingers to it she stretched it up and out of the back of his sorry slacks. Peering down at the label her face far too close to his brown clad backside for comfort she caught sight of his size. '32 inches. Nice and slim. Hey do these feel too tight or too loose or anything ?'

'No, they're fine I think.'

'You think ? Turn back round let me have a look at you.'

Robert sheepishly turned around. She grabbed a belt loop and gave it a tug. There was a bit of give but not much. 32 inches would be fine. What about length ?

 A black shirted shop assistant tapped her on the shoulder.

'Can I help you with anything madam ?' He had one of those sculpted and spiked hairdos. A solitary sparkly ear stud drew Lauren's eye. His hands were folded in front of him and his cheeks seemed too shiny to be entirely free of moisturiser.

'Ooh yes, you can. I'd like a tape measure so I can measure my friend's length.'

 The young assistant looked blankly confused, his mouth opening slightly in mild alarm as Robert's red face returned.

'Excuse me ?'

'His length. I need to measure it.'

'I don't think this is the…'

'Of his inside leg.' Why was everyone being so difficult this morning ? 'Oh no you

didn't think I…' The assistant nodded. Lauren gulped hard, feeling slightly queasy with the realisation.
'I'll be back in one minute madam.' He held up a finger and then withdrew.
'Well thank you very much ! He thinks we're perverts or something now.' Robert's face was glowing. Lauren was sure she was getting a couple of extra degrees of warmth from his embarrassed burn.
'Oh for goodness sake. Just get over yourself. You should be so lucky anyway.' Robert looked hurt.
'What do you mean ?'
'I mean that it's never likely that I'm going to be examining your length is it.' Did he think he was Russell Brand or something ? Or John Hurt . Or Richard Dawkins. Robert stayed quiet and looked down at his feet as the shop assistant returned with a tape measure.
'There you go…look I'm very sorry about..'
'It's forgotten. Could you just measure my friends inside leg for him please ? You've probably done this before.'
   The young shop assistant gave her a pronounced comedy nudge and said in his campest voice;
'Ooh who you been talking to?'. Robert suddenly looked alarmed. It was another one. A gay man that is. They seemed to be everywhere these days. 'Would you mind spreading your legs for me sir.'
   Lauren grinned as Robert looked at her to come to his assistance. She just fixed him a smile
'You heard the man Robert. Spread 'em .'
   Robert did as he was told as the shop assistant crouched down on his knees and placed the top end of the tape measure on Robert's left inner thigh.
'Brace yourself sir. This won't hurt a bit.' He cheekily tapped Robert's bottom which made him clench. Lauren was doing her best to control her impending hysterics. The assistant stretched out the tape measure as Robert gulped down hard.
'30 inches. That's a regular.' He stood up looked Robert straight in the eye and said emphatically ,'and there's NOTHING wrong with being a regular sir. Just you ignore the size queens.'
   Robert's look of panicked confusion intensified as the assistant minced off to checkout a middle aged woman who was purchasing a pair of trainers for her stranded husband.
   With this new knowledge Lauren returned to the racks and pulled out two pairs of jeans in the appropriate size.
'Right, go in that changing room and try these on for me. Come out after you've tried each one on and show me what you look like. I'm not spending my money if you look like cack.' She dropped the jeans in his arms and shooed him off. 'Go on then.' Robert lollopsed over to the changing rooms, his ungainly gait making each step look like a major effort. He didn't appear to be in any hurry. Sheepishly he entered the changing rooms and stepped out a few minutes later to display himself to Lauren in the first pair. They looked okay if you ignored the person who was wearing them.

'Hey not bad, not bad at all.' The assistant who was removing the left items which people had tried on but decided not to buy looked him up an down.
'Get you handsome. It looks kind of…ooh what's the term.'
'Geek chic ?' Lauren offered.
'That's it. A bit weird and scrawny but kind of good looking with it.'
'Like those waifish male models you get in the Sunday paper.'
'The very same.' He tapped her on the wrist, sighed admiringly and wiggled off.
'Can I go now ?' Robert stood at the entrance to the changing rooms, a picture of awkward displeasure.
'Yes, go on, try on the other pair.'

   Robert slunk off returning a couple of minutes later in the alternative pair. These were slightly baggier and looser fitting. They did the job. Lauren told him to keep them on.
'But what about my slacks ?'
'What about them ?' It was impossible that anyone could be attached to anything so horrific. 'Leave them, bin them, anything just don't wear them ever again.'

   In his new jeans the pair of them left the shop and set about a trawl of some of the city's other high street stores. The brown slacks which the shop assistant had placed in a separate carrier bag were dropped into a bin outside McDonalds. A pair of cheap passable trainers were purchased, followed by three new plain t-shirts from Next, a hoodie from H&M and a multi-pack of boxers from M&S. As they sat drinking coffee and eating teacakes in the coffee shop at BHS Lauren looked at his ski-jacket. It was taunting her with its awfulness. Any efforts she had made to help Robert look like a functioning member of the human race would be undermined in a second by his frightful top layer.
'Oh bloody hell, Robert. That coat. It's got to go.'
'What's wrong with it ?' Robert looked down at the blue and white ripped 80s monstrosity. The puffy, padded sleeves were losing some of their stuffing at the elasticated cuffs. The zip on the fold-out hood in the collar was broken and coming out of place. It had curious brown stains marked across the front, and a burn mark on one of the sleeves. How could anyone wear such a thing unless it was for a bet ? Robert was university educated for goodness sake.
'The style wouldn't look out of place in a Wham video.'
'The 80s are very fashionable these days. I saw it on Richard & Judy.'
'Yes but your coat was never fashionable the first time round it isn't miraculously going to become so 20 years on. It's got to go. It's in appalling condition.'

   Lauren examined the cash she had left over in her red purse. A ten pound note and about three quid in change. That was never going to buy the guy a decent coat. There was nothing for it, the already straining credit card was going to have to succumb to a bit more punishment in the name of public service. Not only would she be helping out Robert she'd be helping out the rest of the population of York who'd no longer have to set eyes on the thing.

   After popping in a few department stores she finally found a black reefer jacket in River Island which she decided she'd quite like if she was a bloke. Robert though wasn't convinced.

'No, it's not me.' Robert was looking over his shoulder in the mirror as he tried on the coat.

'Pardon ?' What was he talking about ? He didn't have a 'me' for it to be not.

'It's not my kind of thing.' He reiterated.

'Robert, until this morning your kind of thing was the first scrag-end you laid your hand on in the local charity shop.'

'Well, I just don't think it's me.' He moved away from the rack. 'I'm happy with everything else but I think I prefer my current coat. It's comfy.'

'You can't be serious Robert, that coat is vile. You can't wear that any longer. Anyway it's falling to pieces.' She took hold of the collar of the coat in both hands, looked him straight in the eye and did her best persuasive Millie impression, '..and anyway, this one really does suit you.' It seemed to do the trick. '

D..d..do you think so ?' Lauren nodded. He took another look in the mirror. 'Alright then. I'll have the coat but on the condition that I can keep the old one for knocking around in.'

'Knocking around in ? You're not a nine year old who's going to be shinning up trees and scrumping apples y'know.'

'Yeah I know that, it's just I might need it if the weather takes bad.'

'Eh ? I'm sorry you've lost me now.'

'Stop it. Stop bugging me. I'll take the coat that's all that matters.' Robert turned from her and started wafting his arms around his head as if trying to get rid of imaginary flies. He had been full of these peculiar little jerky mannerisms all day which seemed to manifest themselves whenever he got stressed. Lauren thought it might be best to back off a little.

'Ok, Ok. That's a deal then.' She took the jacket, paid for it and met Robert who was now standing outside, back in the ski-jacket and looking pensively around him.

'Is there a problem mate. You've kind of gone a bit weird on me.'

'It's nothing.' He batted the question aside and stood stonily quiet. Lauren looked at her watch, looked at the gathering grey clouds and tapped her foot impatiently. Still Robert said nothing. She looked up and down Coney Street at the hub of shoppers. A Chinese woman was selling stripy socks and gloves from a trolley in the middle of the street. Nearby a thick-set Aussie guy wearing oversized surf gear and a stupid expression was making annoying noises with pointless whistles he was trying to flog on the fly. Lauren wished Robert would speak.

'I think it's something. You were alright, we were having a laugh and now you've gone all odd.'

'Shut up' He mouthed coldly, as he put his hands to his ears as if to shut out the noise of the world. He was rooted to the spot but his eyes were darting all over at double speed. Lauren had taken just about enough of this.

'Wait a minute Mr, I don't know what's come over you but..' Robert turned towards her, his meek distracted expression giving way to one of annoyed rage.

'Just fucking leave me alone alright. I didn't ask for your fucking help, and all you're doing now is fucking winding me up.'

He was jabbing his fingers just inches from her face. Passers-by on Coney Street were giving them open mouthed looks as Lauren almost dropped the shopping bag containing the coat on the floor. This wasn't what she was expecting.

'Robert I don't know…'

'No you don't know and you don't fucking want to know so just get out of my fucking face and leave me alone.' He pushed her back, almost hard enough for her to lose her footing and stormed off in the direction of Micklegate.

'Robert you've forgotten your….' She shouted after him but it was too late. 'Coat.' She looked in the bag at the pristine new black reefer jacket in his size and sighed. Time to go home perhaps.

Saying the wrong thing

'Frickin' psycho alert babes !' Millie was munching on an apple as she talked transatlantic to her best friend.

'It did freak me out.' Lauren was subdued. She lay stretched out on her back on the sofa, her free hand anxiously twirling her hair.

'Don't beat yourself up about it. You didn't do anything wrong by the sound of things. The guy's clearly a nutter.'

'Oh don't say that Mills.' Lauren didn't like that term. It was too dismissive.

'Why not ? He assaulted you after you'd spent a bloody fortune on the guy. Where's the gratitude in that ?'

'It wasn't really assaulting me, it was just a push.'

'That's how it starts. If he's willing to lay a finger on you he can't be trusted. It's not like you to make excuses for violent men.'

'Come on Mills, he's not really violent.'

'How do you know ?' Millie's tone had sharpened. 'You don't really know him. You think you do but you don't.' She took a crunch on her apple but continued talking with her mouthful. 'You can't take chances with guys you haven't really gotten to the bottom of. They're a dark continent are blokes. All of them without exception. You have to find out if the secrets they're inevitably hiding are just a bit embarrassing or downright dangerous.'

'Does that not apply to Karl then ?' Lauren couldn't help but see the irony and was slightly annoyed at being on the receiving end of a telling-off.

'What are you saying ?'

'Well, you just told me not to be too trusting with men because they've all got dark secrets and you went and agreed to marry Karl within a couple of days of meeting him.' As soon as the words had left her mouth Lauren realised it might have been something of a low blow.

'Well fuck you Lauren !' She seemed to be making a habit of provoking people into expletives of late.
'Mills, I didn't mean anything…' Not again.
'I know full well what you meant. You've been having digs at me and Karl since day one. I reckon you're just bloody jealous because I've met someone who makes me happy and wants to spend their life with me, whilst your…'
'Yeah, I know, left on the shelf like an old spinster.'
'That's what you're in danger of becoming. You're getting quite bitter of late.'
'Millie, I didn't think it was a crime to miss your best mate. You know I didn't want you to leave and it was all so sudden. It left me reeling.'
Millie's tone softened a little. She could never be angry for long.
'I know that babes, but you've got to be happy for me.'
'I am happy for you,' at least she thought she was. Or was trying to be. 'Really I am.' How had this happened ? They were meant to be talking about her peculiar relationship with Robert P.Gorman, not her mixed-up feelings about Millie and her impending marriage.

Lauren thought it might be a good idea to shift the subject so she asked her friend about New York life. Millie told her about all the new people she'd been meeting, the interview she'd had for an assistant manager's job at a little independent theatre that staged lots of cutting edge productions by new writers and the shopping she'd been doing with Karl's sister Lotti who had been staying over for the past week. Apparently she had shocking blue eyes, masses of shoulder length blond curls, was stick thin and had gorgeous bedroom lips that oozed sensuality. Millie clearly enjoyed basking in a little of the reflected glory. Lauren instantly hated her.
'You'd love her. She's so funny. Comes out with some great lines. And she's just so naturally stylish y'know.'
'Really.' Lauren was trying her hardest to feign interest. Lotti was sure to be a nightmare. Lauren was already convinced of that. She never wanted to meet her. Not ever.
'Yeah, god Lauren, I can't believe this is happening to me. It was only three months ago I was dossing around York thinking I'd never meet a bloke or do anything interesting with my life.'
'And now look at you.' They'd had this conversation before.
'Yeah, it's amazing.' Unseen hands, it must be written in the stars, the miracle of it all, etc, etc.
'It is.'
'Lauren.'
'Yes, Mills.'
'I do miss you though.' That hadn't been expected. It was the first time in the three months since she had left for a new life in America that Millie had admitted to missing her supposed best friend.
'Ah, I miss you loads.' Lauren felt her heart beginning to melt. Damn that girl.
'So you're going to just have to get yourself on a plane to New York aren't you young lady.'

'Hey I like the young lady bit.'
'32 is still young.'
'You reckon ?' Lauren wasn't so sure anymore. She was twice the age of a sixteen year old. That surely made her quite venerable. Too venerable to be of much interest to anyone young and virile. Randy divorcees and menopausal men would surely soon be coming into view on her romantic radar. It wasn't a happy prospect.
'I know so. Now when are you coming out here ? Karl's dying to meet you.'

Fear of flying

   November seeped damply into December and there had been no word from Robert. Francis was off visiting Tony again. Lauren found herself going to work in the grey half-light of winter, leaving in the dark and damp, York's paltry few Christmas lights doing little to lighten the mood. Christmas wouldn't be long but the prospect of the festive season was leaving her cold. Millie had been trying to get her to agree to fly out to New York in the early part of January but Lauren had been doing her customary stalling. The idea didn't totally appal her, and if she were being honest she would jump at the opportunity to see Millie again, it was the thought of the flight which was the real sticking point.
'You should do what I do,' Francis had advised, 'Take a hip flask full of single malt whisky and a couple of sleeping pills. Dead to the world I am. Before I know it a nice young air steward is tapping me on the arm and telling me we've arrived.'
   He'd been all over the place, often on his own, taking in lots of local culture and history in the process. This was yet another reason for Lauren to be quietly impressed with her landlord. He was due to visit an old college friend in Aberdeen in the New Year. She was a mathematician called Carole who was currently working on a video for YouTube which would show clueless youngsters the correct way to draw a circle with a compass. Even the prospect of a visit to the Granite City in February seemed impossibly exotic to Lauren. She had only ever flown to the Channel Islands as a teenager on a plane which took off from Southampton and arrived in Guernsey an hour later. The plane had propellers and looked like something out of a black and white war film. That had been the holiday where she'd had her first proper snog. A good looking boy with glasses who came from somewhere like Colchester had taken her to the local Wimpy Bar for a plate of chips. They'd had a romantic walk along the harbour and ended up kissing underneath the shadow of one of the second world war defences as the sun set across the sea. When they returned home they had written to each other for a couple of months before she took up with Ian Lindsey, a seventeen year old whose parents ran a hardware shop. He rode a pimped-up scooter and took her to Skegness for the day, with her riding pillion. Unfortunately they broke down outside Sleaford and had to get the train back to Nottingham. When his dad finally agreed to go pick up the bike, they discovered it had been stolen. Ian without his scooter just lost all of his allure. Her fickle fancy faded and she promptly got off with

Freddy Nardini a boy of Italian stock who lived above a chip shop. Poor Ian was heartbroken at the loss of both his scooter and his girlfriend in the space of a week. What a teenage hussy she'd been. The emotional carnage she must of wrought across the adolescent boys of West Bridgford. Thinking about it, she'd always been the one who did the dumping. She'd generally called the shots. Not once had she ended up in a sobbing mess being consoled by a best friend back then. She'd done plenty of consoling in her time, but she'd always made the running in her own little dalliances. Girl Power. Nice one.

   The thought made her smile as she opened the Rough Guide to New York which she'd picked up from the library. All that vibrant life. All that awe-inspiring architecture. All those groovy interesting people. God, it was tempting. Booting up her computer she Googled for cheap flights. Finding herself on a holiday website she discovered that she could get there and back well within her budget.
'Bloody hell, that's cheap.' She bit her bottom lip. Bang went the monetary excuse.
'No wonder the environment's so fucked.'

   Deciding to sleep on it she turned off her computer, took her book in the bath for a long lingering soak and then went to bed. That night she dreamt of being in New York, meeting Russell Brand, who just happened to be in a bar having a drink with Bill Clinton. Millie already knew them both and introduced her. Half-way through their conversation however Russell turned into a leering Robert who suddenly, unaccountably, got irate. She woke up in a cold sweat, nipped to the loo and then settled back down.

    The next morning as she sat eating her bowl of Frosties before going to work she turned on her mobile to check for messages. A beep signalled an incoming text ;
'Hi Lauren, it's Robert. Sorry about what happened. Bought myself a mobile. Let me know if this works.'
Right. Ok, she thought. Millie would probably want to scream at her but she saw little harm in being polite and returning his very first message.
'Received OK. How r u Robert ?'
Text abbreviations were a pet hate, but she found she kept using them despite herself. She put the phone down and went back to her cereal. Nothing happened, the phone just sat there silently. She put on her coat, turned off the phone and slung it in her bag. 'Suit yourself.'

   That day at work she had been distracted by Robert's latest contact and the nagging decision she had to make about New York. If she said no then she had a feeling that Millie might begin to tire of her. There was Millie making new friends, building a busy new life for herself and all those miles away was this gloomy old friend who didn't seem that happy for her. It was natural they would drift. New friends would come along, maybe one of them would eventually replace Lauren in the best friend stakes .

   The news that potential cost saving measures were being considered had begun to emanate around work. As a consequence the mood in the office was downbeat. All but Josh Andrews who somehow managed to maintain his superciliously cheerful attitude at all times. Maybe that had something to do with the fact he probably knew that whatever else was likely to happen, his job would remain safe. Lauren had come to terms with the fact that the New Year could find her unemployed and she was slowly becoming less terrified by the prospect. If she were being honest she'd spent too long at Accent as it was but was unlikely to take the leap and leave of her own accord. The redundancy pay-off after nearly eleven years of service should be reasonable enough and she would at least get the chance to take some time for herself to try and work out where she went next. As things currently stood she was clueless.

   Her lunch time sandwich was taken at her desk . For a company that said it needed to make savings they certainly never seemed to be short of work to throw in her direction. She took her mobile from her bag, turned it on and left it on the desk next to her. Within seconds it beeped an incoming message. Robert. It had been sent at 10.30.
'Not too bad. Went to the Drs yesterday. All by myself. Wore my new clothes.'
Lauren smiled and texted back immediately.
'Hey nice one. What did the doc say ?'
This time within about four minutes a message was returned.
'I'm on anti-depressants. Can I have my coat ?'
For a moment Lauren sat wondering why the doctor would ask Robert if he could have his coat until it finally clicked. He meant that damn sexy reefer that had sat in the bag unwanted in the corner of Lauren's room for the past ten days since the fateful shopping trip.
'Well I don't want it. I was going to put it on Ebay.'
Before she knew it a message beeped back.
'What's Ebay ?'
Just where did a girl begin with Robert P.Gorman ?

Clothes maketh the man

   Lauren was sitting drinking coffee in the front room of Robert's flat. Since her last visit the single easy chair had been accompanied by a red cord bean bag. Lauren had taken the liberty of buying a jar of coffee, a packet of biscuits and some proper milk from Jacksons on her way. The bean bag was surprisingly comfy, the only problem was the proximity it gave her to the threadbare carpet allowed her to see the full horror of its filthy dried food covered nature.
'I'm going to have to get the Hoover out and give this place a good going over mate.'
Robert stretched out his legs and laid back in his chair. He looked at the fingernails on his right hand, stretched both arms out and up above his head, letting out a satisfied noise as he did so.
'Haven't got one.' He dunked a Hobnob in his mug then bit into it.

'In that case I'll bring mine from home.' Vacuuming was not her favourite pastime but this just couldn't be left.

'Nice one.' Robert grinned at her cheekily. He looked quite cute and boyish, giving a typical single bloke's response to an offer of free cleaning from a fit friendly bird. It momentarily threw Lauren who was used to obtuse vagueness and confusion coming from his direction.

'Er..OK then…and where did you get this beanbag ?' She poked it with her left index finger.

'Oh that, it's great isn't it…the girl from next door gave it to me , said she didn't want it. She's lovely, she's called Beth. She's got a baby boy called Christopher. It's her dad's name she said. He's really cute, you'd love him. The baby that is, not her dad.' He laughed to himself.

Robert was gushing forth with freely surrendered information. Had he undergone some kind of personality transplant at the doctors thought Lauren ? He seemed chatty to the point of friendliness. He'd been socialising with the neighbours. Something must surely be up.

'And how have you been finding your new clothes then ?'

'Oh Lauren, that's what I meant to say. They've made such a difference. I feel really confident and up for life when I'm wearing them. I'd never have guessed just a few clothes could make such a difference.'

'Erm…quite…yes…that's good then.' Lauren's confusion was growing.

'And you were right about that ski-jacket you know. What was I thinking ?' He flicked both hands forward as he said the word 'thinking' to emphasise the point. It was as if he was starring in an episode of Will & Grace. Either that or a body snatcher had taken the real Robert and replaced him with this good natured effusive man in the room with her. Or maybe something even more dramatic was taking place. Robert P.Gorman was changing.

There was a knock at the door. Lauren jumped to her feet. 'I'll get it shall I ?' The serenely beaming Robert just nodded at her. Opening the door Lauren was greeted by a girl she recognised from a previous visit. It was Beth, the young mum from next door. In her arms was a smiling gurgling baby boy who was shaking a teething ring.

'Oh, hello,' the girl looked surprised to see her. 'Is Rob in ?'

'Rob ?' Lauren was momentarily thrown. 'Oh you mean Robert ?'

The girl gave her a gone out look. 'Yeah, that's what I said - Rob.' A hand from behind Lauren reached round and took hold of the door.

'Oh hi Beth, come in. I think you've already met Lauren.'

The girl looked suspiciously at the older woman. The friendly face that had reassured Lauren on her previous visit when it appeared from around the neighbouring door was gone. Today Beth was clearly giving her the once over. Lauren knew immediately what was going on. The girl saw Lauren as a rival. Surely no one could really think that a woman like her would ever be interested in a man like Robert ?

'Rob babes, you wouldn't take Christopher would you ? My arms are killing me.' Beth asked.

'Sure hon, pass him here.' Lauren leant out of the way as the gurgling baby reached out towards Robert, or Rob as he clearly now wanted to be called.
'I'll get out of your way now, shall I *Rob*?'
  Robert just grinned back at her sheepishly.
'Ah don't go on my account ?' The girl gave Lauren a satisfied smile. Pointedly she put her arm around Robert's waist, widened her eyes and looked up at him adoringly. It was quite a performance. She'd clearly done this kind of thing before.
'Oh y'know, places to go, people to see,' Lauren lied, 'you know how it is.'
'I just wanted to thank you for bringing the coat round and all you've done for me. I really do appreciate it.'
  The girl from next door involuntarily screwed her face up, then lifted her baby out of Robert's arms and swayed down the hall.
'That's alright. I can see you're busy so I must go.' Three and a half was definitely a crowd thought Lauren. There was no way she was going to hang round like a spare part whilst Robert and his young love cooed over one another.
  As she made to leave, Robert touched her hand stopping her in her tracks.
'Please keep in touch.' His grasp on her hand tightened a little. 'I don't want to lose you for a second time.'
  She eased herself out of his loosening touch, as the girl and her plump baby looked on from the front room doorway, both of them smiling.

Trying not to be bothered

  The ability of Robert P.Gorman to preoccupy Lauren Seymour appeared to know no bounds. There she was the other morning going around to his flat expecting to find the usual awkward Robert - needy, insecure and as ready as ever for another educational talking to. What she found instead was this peculiar stranger, the genial, smiling Rob who appeared to have become overfriendly with an attractive young neighbour.
  Lauren wasn't entirely sure how she felt about the seeming relationship that had developed between Robert and the teenage mum next door. Was it right that a 33 year old man should be hooking up with a 17 year old? Something about it gave her the creeps. The thought of getting together with a 17 year old was just beyond weird. All that acne, all those mood swings, all that impenetrable music. God, it would be horrific. It was different for blokes though with their diabolical schoolgirl fantasy rubbish. There was no comparable female fantasy. No woman older than about 20 lusted over sixth form boys did they ? Apart from the ones who popped up alongside the strangely delectable Jeremy Kyle. They were usually pregnant by their 17 year old stepson but were undeniably freakish and therefore didn't count.
  And then there was that rage the other day. Where had that come from ? What if he gets mad with Beth or the baby ? Lauren shuddered. Maybe Millie was right. Maybe he is a bit of a dark horse. As much as Lauren attempted to extricate all

thoughts of Robert from her mind he kept returning. A Sunday spent walking by the River Foss, reading the papers, taking cat naps on the sofa and avoiding contact with Robert had done little to help matters. Despite her best intentions she had found herself regularly checking her mobile for signs of a message until finally giving in at 9pm, turning it off and putting it in her bag for work the next day. Only she went and retrieved it just before bed for one last go. Nothing. 'Get a grip Lauren, he's not your boyfriend,' she told herself, partly out of self-disgust, partly as reassurance. He might be preoccupying her thoughts but she was certain she could never fancy him. Not in a million years. Not Robert P.Gorman.

   That night she dreamt that she was the best man at the wedding of a glamorous couple called Rob and Beth. They looked a bit like Posh and Becks. He was wearing a white suit, a cream silk tie and had spiked up hair. She glided down the aisle in the most elegantly over-the-top frock Lauren had ever seen. A little boy in a velvet suit carried the ring on a cushion and Millie, Karl (who she'd never met but who in the dream bore an uncanny resemblance to Viggo Mortensen in Lord of The Rings, even down to the outfit) and Russell Brand (whose usual skin-tight jeans and flouncy shirt was complimented by a white bow-tie) sat in the congregation. She wanted to get off with Russell at the reception disco but as far as everyone else was concerned she was actually a bloke despite the fact she kept telling everyone there had been a dreadful mistake.

   'Why did he lose his job, do we know ?'
   Francis was back after his latest visit to the mysterious Tony. He'd cooked them both sausage pasta for tea which they ate on their laps whilst the regional news waffled away in the background. The weatherman, Paul Hudson was making suggestive jokes at the expense of the female anchor Krista Ackroyd. It was all a bit northern Carry On.
'Just said that there were job cuts by the council and his position went. Quite a few library staff did go a few years ago I remember.'
'I can't remember seeing him at the central library.'
'No, he wasn't there,' said Lauren in between mouthfuls of pasta. 'He was out at Acomb. That's why I've never seen him about, don't think he ever really ventured into town that much.'
'And how long has he been unemployed ?'
'He's been out of work for over three years now. I presume he's just too awkward and odd which must show at interviews.'
'Even so, that's quite a while. He's got a degree and even oddballs usually manage to get something.'
Lauren paused and looked into space. 'Hey you're right. What's going on with that ?'
'Could be his depression. Perhaps he's just not motivated to do anything.'
'I hope young Beth isn't expecting him to be a provider for her and the baby. That's not likely to happen is it.'
'Seems like our friend Robert is going to be playing happy families though…for a while at least.'

'Hmmm..'
'And how does that make you feel Lauren Seymour ?'
    Lauren put her bowl down on the coffee table.
'Me ? Oh, I couldn't care less, he's a grown man.' Her voice betrayed the certainty of her words.
'You sure ?' Francis persisted, a note of mischief in his voice.
'Totally sure. Just leave it there will you.'
    In fact she wasn't at all sure about the entire situation. If they were not having a relationship then it certainly looked as if one was in the offing. She had no idea whether or not Robert had ever had a girlfriend before. He certainly remained effortlessly single during his time at university and Lauren found it hard to imagine the shambling wreck who clattered back into her life a few weeks earlier would ever attract any self-respecting young woman, or even a lonely and doe-eyed single mum like next-door Beth. After sitting deep in thought for a while, Francis with his reading glasses tutting to himself as he read yesterday's Sunday paper, Lauren suddenly blurted out what she was thinking.
'That girl's no older than 17. He's nearly frigging 33. What the hell is he playing at ? It's not right is it, it's definitely not right.'
    Francis jumped , folded his paper and took his off his reading glasses.
'Erm, it's not a massive age difference. It's big but it's nothing that would be that remarked upon if he was say 45 and she 30.'
'Maybe not then but…' Her chain of thought was stopped in its tracks by a persistent recurring, totally unpleasant memory. 'Hang on I know what you're getting at you big snide git.'
    A couple of years previously Lauren had been embroiled in a brief relationship with a marketing director from a London PR firm who was on secondment to Accent. He was 45, she was 30. They went out to the theatre together, for the occasional meal, and she kept him company when he was in town. He was an enjoyable distraction. Quite erudite and witty, well read and cultured. He was entertaining and spirited. She enjoyed socialising with him, even if she had known from day one that it was unlikely to ever be more than a casual dalliance. An anonymous phone call to her at work had informed her that he had a couple of kids and a rosy-cheeked wife contentedly baking at a country pad in the Cotswolds. He had told everyone at Accent that he and his wife were separated. Lauren's lust filled nights at the local Travelodge immediately came to an end. Seeing her discomfort Francis raised his eyebrows.
'Just don't mention that again will you…and anyway, see that was all wrong.'
'And how old did his wife turn out to be again ?'
'29,' she muttered under her breath.
'Sorry ?'
'Twenty bloody nine, alright, just shut up about it. Bad experience, I'm not going to talk about it.'
Lauren sat silently contemplating the carpet.
'The thing is with Robert, we're presuming he's inexperienced and a bit of a loner.' Piped up Francis, not wanting to prolong her suffering.

'Not presuming anything, he is a loner.'
'So he's a bit like you then.'
'Francis, I am many things, but I am NOT inexperienced.' She gave him a mischievous grin and had a pleasant thought about the male bimbo squaddie of a few years back. If only he'd been as intelligent and charming as he was physically accomplished thought Lauren, they might perhaps still be together.
'I was thinking more about the loner aspect. You're both people who prefer not to socialise.'
'I like my own company. So what ?' She hated having her solitary nature examined. It was just who she was. It was no big deal.
'I'm not having a dig at you, you're self-contained which is a good thing, all I'm saying is that it makes you both vulnerable to falling for the wrong people. You're susceptible to a bit of attention and this Beth girl gave him some attention.'
'Exactly ! But I gave him attention ? Why didn't he prove susceptible to me. What's she got that I haven't got…apart from a screaming baby that is'
'Ooh Lauren, you sound jealous. Anyone would think you fancy him. You girls when you're squabbling over a bloke, it's never pretty.'
    Lauren stood up, grabbed hold of her bowl and began walking towards the kitchen only pausing to look at Francis, wag her finger and reiterate her earlier point in the most emphatic voice she could muster.
'I do NOT, I repeat NOT, fancy him !'
'I wouldn't blame you.' Francis took a slurp from his tea then grinned mischievously. 'He's a good looking boy is our Rob.'
'And don't call him that !'

'Your phone bill is going to be bloody huge Lauren.'
'Oh, it doesn't matter, I never go out anywhere. I only spend my money on books, cds and moisturiser these days.'
'All the more reason to get a flight to New York booked. It would probably only cost you as much as all these phone calls.'
'I'm thinking about it Mills, honestly I am.' Which wasn't a lie. When she wasn't pondering the mysteries of the Gorman, she was invariably wondering whether or not she could face that flight.
'Well don't be too long thinking will you. I'm dying to see you.'
'I thought you might be coming back to England to see the folks at Christmas or something. We could have met up then.'
'Aaah it would have been great babe but Karl and I are going to stay with his family in Massachusetts. I've not met them yet and they're dying to meet the woman who has stolen their golden boy apparently.'
'I bet they are,' Lauren sighed.
'Their house looks amazing from the photos. It's all white picket fences and candy coloured clapper-board places with tree-swings in the garden. Just like in the films. There should be snow as well. I can't wait.'
'No, I bet you can't.' It all sounded idyllic but Lauren made a point of not being

effusive.

'His mum and dad seem really nice. Well, I think they are, I've not met them obviously, but I've spoken to them on the phone and…'

'Millie..' Lauren stopped her friend mid-flow.

'Yes Lauren ?'

'Would you say that I was in anyway bloke-ish ?' The dream of the other night had been bugging her.

'Eh ? Where's this come from ? What like a tomboy ?'

'Er…yeah. Like a tomboy.'

'No, not really. You're not a girlie girl, you're less girlie than me. But not a tomboy, not like some of the butch dykes who live round here. They're more men than Karl and his mates. Why what's brought this on ?'

'Oh…nothing it's just…'

But before she had chance to explain, Millie was elaborating further.

'You're a bit kind of, androgynous possibly. You've got killer cheekbones. You could have made a brilliant surly rhythm guitarist in a cool band. Y'know, kind of hanging around on the side of the stage, all gangly good looks, cigarette hanging from your bottom lip. Boys *and* girls would have fancied you.'

Lauren thought this was a compliment.

'Androgynous you say ?' She liked the word.

'Yeah, but in a good way, in a sort of sexy like that woman who sings with Garbage kind of way. Well, if she were taller and didn't wear such gorgeous frocks. You'd never wear them.'

'Shirley whatserface ?'

'Yeah her…I wouldn't worry about it. We're all different. You're never going to be tottering around on four inch heels, giggling demurely at a blokes jokes or wearing cocktail dresses.'

'Fuck no !'

'And you're clearly never going to stop swearing like a trooper either.'

'Sorry.'

'Hey don't worry about it fella.'

Lauren was standing pulling faces in the mirror above the fireplace. The week had been crawling by, the bustle of Christmas beginning to build in town as the staff at Accent remained in the dark about the situation with their jobs. No one was willing to confirm anything either way, and rumour and counter-rumour filled the void. It was doing Lauren's head in. Francis was working all evening. A series of classes for spoilt kids who lived in big town houses on the Mount and detached mansions down Tadcaster Road. Once again, she was all on her lonesome.

She'd been looking at herself trying to make out if anything in her appearance suggested masculinity. Not really, perhaps under a certain light she had something of the ambiguous boy about her. Her build was tall, and slender, elegant rather than curvy. She should maybe be more regular in plucking her eyebrows and sticking on a bit more slap than she did. She could always wear a frock now and again. In the summer or something ? That was a possibility. Nah, fuck it. What was she on about? She collapsed on the sofa picked up her copy of Heat Magazine and flicked through the photos of rat-arsed D listers falling out of taxis.

   Next-door Beth was all woman. Or all girl. Definitely oestrogen overload with that one. Tits, smile and child-bearing hips. Even a fat contented boy-child to dandle on her knee to prove the point. Not a haggard foul-mouthed old androgyne who couldn't get a boyfriend. Lauren sighed and flicked through the TV channels. This was not good, she needed to get off her arse and start living a little. Channel 4 was showing yet another rerun of Friends. Cue the opening sequence, cue the New York skyline, cut to a group of urbane mid-90s young professionals sitting around on squishy sofas drinking latte. She reached her hand into the fruit bowl and pulled out a large Golden Delicious. She examined it and then rolled her eyes, the Mexican Virgin Mary and her chubby babe in arms gazed on dolorously.
'Yes, I get the point.' She spoke impatiently at the statue. 'Big Apple. Well done, have a bloody biscuit.'
Lauren put the apple down on the coffee table, began rolling herself a cigarette and reached for the Rough Guide. It needed to be back tomorrow.

Old acquaintance, new revelation

   Lauren was ready for the weekend. She intended on doing nothing more than cleaning the sink, ironing some of her clothes, reading, drinking endless cups of tea and starting to make a list of what to buy people for Christmas. Christmas shopping was always something she left right until the very last minute and what she ended up hurriedly wrapping up on Christmas Eve often bore little resemblance to what she'd intended buying. Friday afternoon had seen her sent out to the offices of a developers in Acomb. She had been running her eye over their literature for the past ten days and they wanted her to go in and talk them through some possible improvements. They had already spent their marketing budget on the illegible rubbish she'd been trying to decipher so she wasn't really sure what good her advice was going to do. That's what happens when you allow bean counters to write your copy she'd thought to herself. No good will come of it.
    The afternoon had been long and tedious. The grey-faced, black suited men that surrounded her and listened to her advice indulgently seemed as if they inhabited another planet entirely. One of them had rambling nasal hair and kept bringing the conversation around to golf.
'This reminds me of the time I was stuck in the bunker on the 14th at St.Andrews,' he had said after Lauren had pointed out that the glossy brochures they'd had printed contained a dozen or so typos. His colleagues appeared to find this completely fascinating and pertinent, whereas Lauren just found it ridiculous.
   The lack of any connection between her and her impatient clients meant she

managed to wrap up the proceedings early. Both parties appeared to be relieved . She had picked up on their disappointment that they'd not been sent a ditzy piece of eye-candy. Lauren Seymour sounded younger perhaps. Maybe with blond hair and big eyes, definitely an inch or two shorter and certainly more girlie than the real one was. 'This is all you're getting fellas,' she'd thought to herself. 'What you lose out on in looks you make up for with pure badass copy knocking into shape ability.' Unfortunately none of them appeared particularly interested in the latter. The nagging feeling that the whole afternoon had been a complete waste of everyone's time wouldn't leave her alone.

  Work wasn't expecting her back and she saw little reason to let them know she'd made an early escape. As she left the building she took in a lung full of the cold December air . Rummaging around in her bag for her phone which had once again sunk to the bottom, her hand grazed the spine of the Rough Guide to New York. 'Fuck it.'

  She had meant to drop the book back at the central library before heading out this way. This now meant she would have to rush back into town after all and try to make it before the library closed. Otherwise she could just pay the fine. Wait a minute, there was a little neighbourhood library out this way. Where Robert used to work.

   She nipped into Morrisons, bought a copy of The Press and a chunky Kit-Kat and asked the checkout woman where she could find the library. After a bit of confused consultation with her neighbour, both of whom had clearly never seen any reason to darken its doors they decided it was the building just round the corner with 'Acomb Library' clearly displayed above it.

   Sure enough the library was right where they'd said it would be. It was a cosy little place with dull carpets and an institutional air. Two young mums with pushchairs stood chatting freely about someone called Shannon who had badly let them both down, whilst their kids put books on their heads and turned them inside out threatening the spines with imminent rupture. At the loans desk a plump middle-aged woman in a huge hippy-dippy style frock and lots of ethnic looking hand crafted jewellery was stamping a pile of large print romantic fiction for an elderly woman with a tartan shopping trolley. The woman was complaining about the bus service and how she'd have to wait until ten to five to get one home, since the four twenty-three had been axed. The library assistant nodded at the woman and gave Lauren a brief look of acknowledgement as if to say, 'I am trying to get rid of her.'

  After another couple of minutes of discussion about back problems, the wayward son of her niece and the ever rising price of gas the old woman finally pulled her trolley off and out of the library. Lauren pondered for a moment what she was going home to? Was that the only meaningful conversation the woman would have all day ? A brief vision of herself as a duffel coat wearing old woman seeking company in casual encounters in shops skipped through her mind. Her thoughts of late had been getting gloomy. For some reason she could only imagine a future for herself in which she was old and alone. The library assistant coughed and broke her contemplation.

'Ooh sorry.' Lauren hurriedly began fumbling in her bag for the book. 'This is due back today, I took it out at the central library, but can I…'

'It's Lauren isn't it ?' The library assistant was smiling whilst peering directly at her through a pair of thick lensed glasses. Lauren was sure she knew that peery-eyed piggy look from somewhere.

'It is..I'm sorry…'

'It's me !' The woman slapped her ample cleavage with both hands. Lauren looked at her again. She was familiar but she was struggling to dig up a name.

'Bessie ! Bessie Cartwright. We were at university together.'

'Mature Bessie !' Finally the name, complete with Millie's prefix popped into Lauren's head and out of her mouth before she'd had chance to selectively edit it.

'Sorry ?'

'Bessie, yes Bessie.' Lauren quickly held out a distracting hand which Bessie took and shook enthusiastically. Odd Robert, now Mature Bessie, all she needed to chance upon now was Mike the Mysteron, the intense quiet guy who used to glare at the rest of them and eat his dinner alone and she'd be hanging out with all the former course oddballs. Maybe that's what she was becoming ? Perhaps these chance encounters were nature's way of telling her to just accept her fate.

'Gosh, how are you Lauren ? You look…' She didn't finish her sentence. Lauren knew she hadn't worn as well as she might and that of late she was taking less care of her appearance. What did it matter ? She knew who she was and had nothing to prove anymore.

'Thanks. How long have you been working here ?'

'God, I've been here for eight years now. Just part-time these days. I'm looking after my mother. She's got Alzheimers.'

'Oh, I'm sorry to hear that.'

'This just gives me a bit of a break. I've got a lovely neighbour who takes care of her whilst I'm out.'

'That's good…' Lauren never knew what to say when people shared the harsher realities of their lives. Her own little bubble was relatively untroubled and safe from the intensity of concern that must accompany the daily lives of people like Mature Bessie.

'Did you say you've been here eight years ?' Bessie nodded. 'In that case you must have worked with Robert Gorman.' For the first time in their conversation Bessie's face dropped its beaming smile.

'Robert Gorman. THE Robert P. Gorman ?' Lauren wondered what she'd said. 'Yeah, from college ?'

'Hmmph.' Bessie folded her arms across her chest and set her face. 'We don't generally talk about Robert Gorman in here.'

  Good grief thought Lauren. Why not ? She knew Robert was odd but what had he done to upset Bessie ? At college she had been one of the few people who had ever had any time for him. This was more than intriguing.

'Bessie, what time do you finish ?' Lauren looked at her watch. The time was creeping towards five.

'In about ten minutes. Why ?'

'I just wondered if you fancied a coffee at that café up the road ? I saw it on the way down. It should still be open.' Bessie's huge engulfing smile returned.
'Lauren, I'd absolutely love to.'

   The two of them sat at a wobbly mug-ringed table in a harshly lit café on the main shopping street of the little York suburb. It was far from the wannabe-chic squashy sofa strewn places that had grown up in the city centre. This was a proper old fashioned shoppers café of her youth. A huge tea urn chugged away on the counter as an impatient staff began clearing up around them. An overweight girl in a brown pinny bumped the back of Lauren's chair as she ran a mop underneath the neighbouring table. She shot Lauren a glare.
'What time are you open till ?' Asked Lauren sternly. She wasn't about to be intimidated by a kid.
'Half five' The hard faced girl drawled. Lauren looked at her watch. Ten past. They didn't have long. A grey curly haired woman came through the fly-screen separating the front of the café from the kitchen.
'Eh ! Shannon, get in here with that mop.'
  Lauren wondered if this was the same Shannon the young mums in the library had been talking about ? If so it was more than likely the girl was in the centre of some neighbourhood intrigue and was probably currently preoccupied. The girl turned towards the counter and made an elaborate sigh.
  'What have I told you about tidying up whilst we've still got customers ?' The older woman asked sharply. The girl gave Lauren another pointed glare, took her mop and disappeared into the kitchen. The older woman smiled across at their table.
'Don't you worry. You take your time, we don't close till you've done.'
 Bessie thanked the woman who started wiping the counter and re-arranging sauce bottles.
   After a few minutes of discussing old course mates, what Lauren was doing professionally and Millie's wonderful new life Lauren steered the conversation onto what was really troubling her.
'So why don't you guys at the library like discussing Robert Gorman ?'
  Bessie took a sip from her coffee, furrowed her brow and folded her fingers together.
'Let's just say, he badly let both us and himself down.'
  What did that mean ? You couldn't just come out with something like that and then clamp up.
'Why ? What did he do ?' Lauren wasn't sure what constituted a major crime in the world of libraries. Putting a romantic fiction book in with the travel perhaps ?
'Something unspeakable.'
'Unspeakable ? Blimey.' Now Lauren really was interested. She did hope Bessie wasn't going to continue in this enigmatic vein for much longer.
'Yes, unspeakable.'
'Oh. It's just that Robert is in my life again now. We've met up a few times and…'
'Well if I was you I'd leave that one well alone.' Bessie cut in sharply, her voice

emphatic and to the point. It brought Lauren up short.
'Why what's he done ? I think you should tell me now.'
   Bessie shook her head, finished her coffee and stood up returning to her default bright and breezy mode in the process.
'Well, it has been lovely meeting up with you again Lauren. I can't believe all that time has passed since we left the university. Where does it go eh ?' She slung her bag over her shoulder, pushed her chair under the table and left the café, leaving Lauren bewildered and with two coffees to pay for.
'Did your friend remember something she'd forgot love ?' Asked the woman behind the counter who had been furtively watching the whole proceedings.
'Yes,' said Lauren finding some change. 'I think she did.'

   'Unspeakable you say ?' Francis had just finished off the beef casserole that Lauren had left bubbling away in the slow cooker all day. A proper meal for once. Not something from a tin. Francis had been quietly impressed.
'Apparently so. What do you make of it ?'
'I don't know to be honest. Makes the plot thicken somewhat though.'
'You're telling me.' Lauren leaned back on the sofa and ran her fingers through her hair. 'Oh, what's going on with that boy. I need to know.'
'I think trying to get the measure of that one might be beyond even your deductive powers Miss Marple.'

Kissing on the back row

   The phone beeped an incoming message as Lauren again sat at her desk taking a ten minute lunch hour.
'L would you like to go to the cinema with me ? I've never been. R.'
   No word from him for nearly two weeks then this. She couldn't find any pressing reason why she shouldn't go with him. An evening out would do her good. That's what Francis would tell her. Maybe Robert was going to shape up to become a casual cinema and occasional drinking buddy. That could be a useful addition to her well-ordered life. A monthly get together say with another human being. If Robert kept making the kind of progress he had been making then surely he would soon almost qualify as at least semi-normal. Never been to the cinema though ? That needed rectifying straight away.
'Happy to. Why not going with Beth ?'
   Surely his darling little yummy mummy chavette would make the ideal partner for a night at the pictures ? Kissing on the back row, sharing a tub of popcorn, furtive touches during the sloppy bits. Within a couple of minutes her phone beeped again. The boy was getting better at this thought Lauren. He'd knocked at least three minutes off his normal response time.

'Can't get a babysitter. Can we go tomorrow night?'

Lauren smiled. Perhaps there were still a few advantages to being childless after all.

'Yes. What 2 C?'

Lauren had no idea what was on. It had been months since she'd ventured to the cinema and hadn't been paying much attention to what was happening in the movie world. Matt had liked his films. He was always waxing lyrical about something clever, foreign and artsy he'd just been to see.

'I think it's French.'

Fair enough thought Lauren. She had Robert down as more of an action movie kind of guy than an art house buff but whatever tickled his fancy. Actually, thinking about it, every French film she'd ever seen had been full of gratuitous Gallic love-making. Sitting next to Robert Gorman whilst a couple of French actors got all sweaty and breathless might be a little hard to swallow. So to speak.

 She decided to text him back and suggest they find a nice romantic comedy as an entrée into the world of going to the cinema. Pressing the send button her phone flashed back at her that she had insufficient credit.

'Oh fuck it,' she threw her phone down on the desk where it flickered like a dying toy-robot and then went off. 'Why don't I get a monthly subscription like normal people. Why do I have to be so bloody 2001 with my pay-as-you-go?'

 Not for the first time, Lauren felt that maybe she just wasn't measuring up in the contemporary adult stakes.

 After Lauren had switched her phone to a monthly subscription at the Orange shop, whilst batting away the derisory remarks about the primitive nature of her telecommunications equipment with strained good humour, she contacted Robert. She found making arrangements with him via text altogether easier than telephone conversations. In truth she wasn't really a fan of telephone conversations full stop. Speaking to Millie was always nice, and the almost regular phone call to her parents was never really that much of a chore, but boring everyday stuff just freaked her out. More often than not she'd let the phone ring, take down the message and then email her response. It was easier than having to deal with a real person. Real people could be difficult. Like Robert. If she called his flat there was always the possibility that Next-Door Beth could answer and say something spiteful. So the text messages flew and they decided to meet in the bar at the City Screen half an hour before the film started. Maybe they could have a drink? If Robert did drink. She wasn't sure.

 Deciding what to wear for a night out with Robert P.Gorman was not a problem that Lauren would have envisaged she'd ever have had a few months earlier. She wondered why she was in any way bothered.

'First date nerves is it hon?' Francis had teased.

'No, definitely not.' Lauren had returned, not even wanting to joke about such a thing. It was too grim a thought to even contemplate considering. She'd gone through her wardrobe a couple of times. She'd contemplated the nice brown boho

looking skirt she'd bought from River Island ages ago and never worn. It was a bit last year but what the hell, who was she trying to kid anyway ? She tried it on with her favourite brown boots which had never yet seen life outside her bedroom. No, overdoing it. It looked wrong. She'd stick to her jeans. Maybe something other than her hoodie though ? What about that pale blue top that Millie had persuaded her to buy before she'd left for New York ? Lauren thought it showed off too much and was maybe a bit on the girlie side for her. Trying it on she didn't look too bad. Maybe she would wear it. It looked OK with the jeans, not too dressy, but equally not just everyday. For the first time in ages she decided to wear a bit of slap and lippy. The overall effect was passable, particularly considering just how out of practice she was.
'Hey you look good Lauren.' Francis had complimented her as she came down the stairs. That was the thing with him. He could be a right catty old bitch when he wanted, but he was always on cue with a flattering comment at just the right moment.
'I don't look like a drag queen then ?' She looked herself up and down.
'Oh god no, they would have made much more effort.'
'You are such a cheeky bugger.' She gave her flatmate a sharp flick with her scarf.

   She purposefully arrived five minutes late at the City Screen but there was no sign of Robert. She bought a vodka, lime and soda and settled down in a window seat overlooking the floodlit River Ouse. It was quite beautiful in its winter clothes, the light dancing on the murky fast flowing water. It wasn't in flood but Lauren knew after all these years of living in the city that another couple of days of rain would push it over the edge. She had become blasé about it now. Every winter the waters rose, every year sections of the city centre lay under water for a few days and tourists took souvenir photos. Looking at the dark waters she remembered that her reacquaintance with Robert was due to its allure to troubled minds. Any number of people every year jumped in to their deaths. For some it was a drunken prank gone wrong, for others it was an escape route out of a shattered life. Remembering that Robert had sought just such an escape route freaked her out. Imagining the guy standing on top of a floodlit Ouse bridge, his feet edging towards the drop as he contemplated his last moments on the planet was too much. Just how low would you need to be to want to do that ?
   Time was passing. It had been five minutes since she arrived late and still no sign of Robert. 'Well this is nice,' she thought. Arrive early so we can have a drink and catch-up , then the guy making the suggestion decides not to bother. She knocked back the drink and looked at her watch. Ten minutes until the film started. Where was he ? She flicked on her phone and tapped out a quick text.
'*Where r u ? I'm in the city screen already. Film about to start.*'
But there was no response. There was now only a couple of minutes left before she'd either have to go in without him or go home. She moved to the foyer in case she'd misunderstood the rendezvous point, but there was no still no sign of the mystery man of the moment.

'Great,' she thought. 'I've been stood up by Robert P. Gorman. The biggest geek in class. What a vote of confidence that is.'

Her ticket was neatly folded in her purse. She had nothing else to do . She'd just have to look like a Wilhemina no-mates for an evening and watch it on her own. Matt would have been proud of her. Just as she turned to go up the stairs she felt a tap on her arm.
'Oh god Lauren, I'm so sorry I'm late. I got waylaid.' It was Robert. His face was flushed , he was out of breath and it looked as if he'd been running.
'You decided to turn up did you ? I've been sitting in here waiting for you like a prize turnip. I thought you'd stood me up.' His hair was spiked-up. He was wearing the reefer jacket she'd bought him and a dark-blue pair of straight leg jeans with a turn-up on the bottom. 'They're not the jeans I bought you ?'
'Oh these things.' Robert grabbed the material on his right leg. 'I picked these up at that retro shop on Gillygate. They're not bad are they ?' Retro shop ? Not bad ? No, they were bloody gorgeous, but she wasn't going to tell him that.
'Oh right, yeah, they're…' They looked fantastic. He was in reasonable physical shape and the cut of the jeans suited him. 'Alright.' What was wrong with the jeans she'd bought him she wondered. Too High Street ?
'Yeah I was just walking down there on the way to my interview the other day and saw them in the window. Thought I'd pop in.'
'Interview ? You never mentioned that. What doing ?'
'Oh, at St.Johns. In the library, they've got an assistant's job going. No word yet, but as nan said, no news is good news.'

For once Lauren was pleased to hear reference to Robert's nan. He was changing at a rates of knots it would appear, but at least some things still remained certain.
'Very wise woman your nan.' She looped his arm and led him to the bottom of the stairs. 'Come on groovy trousers. We've an appointment with a incomprehensible subtitled film to keep.'

The film had been a slow burner. Lots of long lingering looks from a man with expressive eyebrows and an impossibly gamine woman who discussed life and stuff in their idyllic little French town. There had been several almost quite filthy sex scenes. Lauren had cocked her head to an angle during one in an attempt to try and make out which body part was where. It all looked very strange and exotic. If that was what you did then she really was getting badly out of practice. She satisfied herself that this being French, it was in fact art rather than just soft porn. Robert had sat wide-eyed and open-mouthed at the wonder of it all. It was like going to the cinema with a Kalahari bushman.
'Phew…' He puffed out his cheeks and shook his head as they walked back down the stairs into the foyer. 'That was mind-blowing.'

Lauren threw the last bit of popcorn into her mouth.
'It wasn't bad. I wouldn't have shagged him though. He gave me the creeps.'
'Me neither.' Robert spoke in a dreamy far-away voice.
'You neither what ?'

'Shagged him. I wouldn't have.'

Lauren spluttered her half-chewed popcorn all down the coat of the middle-aged man who was walking down the stairs in front of her. Robert and Lauren gave each other horrified looks and tried to pretend nothing had happened. Nobody seemed to notice. Humour. From Robert. That was new. What else was he going to surprise her with she wondered ? No, don't answer that.

They stood outside the doors to the cinema looking at each other awkwardly. Perhaps Francis had been right, this really was like a first date.
'Well,' Lauren swayed coyly from one foot to the other. 'Thanks for that. We should do this again.'
'Yes, I'd like that' He smiled at her, his eyes lighting up momentarily sending a small tremor through Lauren. They were quite beautiful but she couldn't allow herself to start thinking such things. Instead she quickly allowed herself to be distracted by her surroundings. A stream of chin-stroking humanity came down the stairs and feathered out into the foyer and out of the cinema. Looking back at Robert, Lauren noticed that he appeared lost in his thoughts again, as if he'd taken flight somewhere and landed in a place that wasn't totally pleasant. Instinctively she hugged him.
'I'm happy for you, y'know. That things seem to be looking up for you You're a nice guy.'
'Oh. I don't know what to say.'
'Don't say anything then numptie.' She kissed his cheek causing a bright red blush to rapidly fan out across his face. Just then Lauren noticed someone standing by the entrance to the Pitcher & Piano. She was staring at them. It was a familiar face but Lauren couldn't place it.
'Right, I'd better go.' Robert sharply pulled away. 'I promised Beth I'd pop in for supper.'
'Oh, OK.' Lauren had forgotten all about her. Did they do 'supper' in northern council flats then or was it some kind of euphemism ? Maybe the film had left him feeling frisky. It had left Lauren fancying a Kit-Kat and a lie down. 'Send her my love won't you.'
'Will do. Speak soon.' And with that he departed at double-speed leaving Lauren feeling slightly stranded among the dispersing crowd.
'There goes Robert. P Gorman.'

She looked to her left but the person who had been eyeing them was gone. Then she managed to retrieve a name for the face that had been ogling their farewell. Mature Bessie. She of the unspeakable secret knowledge of Robert's past. Mad old bint, what was her problem ? She could have walked over and said hello. She must have known who they were. From the look on her face she certainly seemed aware that Lauren had been giving the unspeakable one a goodnight hug.

Lauren walked home alone through the city streets, the Christmas lights of Goodramgate looking slightly more magical than they were in reality, as voices from the doors of the pubs laughed their way through the end of their evenings. The narrow streets felt warm and friendly, the half-timbered buildings huddled above her encasing her in a homely feeling of being where she needed to be. Here she was alone. Her insignificant anonymous self just one of the countless people down the centuries who had winded their way home down these same old streets. It wasn't much at the end of the day, but it had slowly become the place in which she felt rooted and she wouldn't swap that for all the good looking actors in New York City. Passing the window of the little chocolate shop, under Monk Bar into the terraced maze of the Groves and back to the cosy house where the gas fire was blazing, candles and incense sticks were lit and Francis was playing something soft and jazzy on the piano. She took off her coat, dropped down her bag and gave a contented sigh. Maybe this life business wasn't so bad after all. There would be no appointments for her to keep with the waters of the River Ouse at anytime soon.

Surplus to requirements

'I'm really sorry Lauren but we had no choice.'
'Like fuck you did !'
   Lauren was in real danger of losing it completely. Six days before Christmas and here she was being told she'd be out of a job by the middle of next month.
'I argued your side.' Josh held out his hands as if asking for forgiveness. 'Hey, I was on Team Lauren in there I can tell you.'
   She wanted to lay a punch right on his smarmy chin there and then.
'Just leave me alone will you Mr Andrews.'
'Lauren,' he moved across towards her, attempting to touch her chin with his right hand. 'Don't be like this.'
   Lauren quickly batted it away and jumped to her feet.
'You keep your fucking slimy paws off me creep or I'll get you out of this place on a sexual harassment charge before I go.'
'Just remember who you're talking to.' He straightened himself, did the customary macho broad-shouldered thing and cast her a glare. There really was something deeply unnerving about the man. Surely she wasn't the only person at Accent to see it ? 'Just remind me again who it was having the office affair with a married man would you ?' He dropped his tone and sounded like a creepy cartoon villain as he wagged his finger at her theatrically. Lauren was open-mouthed. That was beneath low. Josh smirked , 'oh you're not the only one who can play at unpleasant Miss Seymour.'
   With that Josh Andrews was closing the door behind him leaving Lauren alone in her office attempting to pick up the pieces of what passed for her newly shattered career. She fell back into her chair and sunk her head into her hands.
'And it's fucking *Ms* you tosser.'

A friend in need

'Oh God Lauren, I dunno what to say.'
'Me neither.'
  It was the truth, she was shell-shocked. Accent had been the only workplace she'd known. She'd given nearly all her adult life to it, and a third of all the time she'd actually spent on the planet. Now they'd left her stranded. Or so it seemed.
'Hey, but your redundancy money could come in handy.' Trust Millie to see the pound signs in any given situation.
'Oh yeah, I'd not thought of that.' Lauren's mood lifted ever so slightly. The value of her pay-off hadn't yet been finalised but after over a decade at the place it should be a worthwhile amount.
'Ooh what you going to spend it on ? You really will have no excuse not to fly out here y'know.'
'Suppose not, although I will have to start job hunting .'
'Lauren ! Are you mad ? Not right away you won't. You can take some time off and travel, do a course, or even just lie in bed all day reading books if you wanted to.'
'Ooh no, I couldn't do the last one. Francis wouldn't let me. He hates people not getting up before about ten. Any later and he'd be in my room singing show tunes.'
'Awww bless Francis. He's a love. How's he doing ?'
'He's OK I think.' Lauren was aware that she hadn't been paying quite as much attention to her housemate of late as perhaps she should. 'He spends a lot of time over at his friend Tony's place in Leeds.'
'Tony ? Have I heard of him ? Is he a boyfriend do you know ?'
'Do you know, I'm really not sure. I tease him about it but he doesn't really talk much about him. It's hard to judge with Francis.'
'Yes, he's always liked his little secrets has that one. Let me know if you get any goss. It's about time that fella got himself a bit of man-love.'
'Quite.' Millie had such a lovely turn of phrase.
'And what about Lauren. Is she in need of a bit of male attention as well ?'
'Oh don't Mills.' What with everything else going on at present, she wasn't particularly sure she needed any sexual complications to add to the mix.
'Come on, this is your oldest and bestest buddy you're talking to here.'
'Alright, I don't know to be honest. It's been a while now.'
'Two years by my reckoning. Since you came over all scarlet woman.' Millie laughed.
'Don't joke about that.' Lauren cringed. 'I didn't know the guy was married. He never told me anything about it. We didn't see much of each other.'
'No, but you did get to know the inside of the Travelodge quite well from what I remember.'
'Ooh the romance of it all.' She couldn't bear the thought of the sleazy worm now, even more than she couldn't bear the thought that she'd inadvertently been 'the other woman.'
'He wasn't bad in the sack though from what I remember you telling me.'
'Hmmm…I've had better to be honest. He was OK.'

'Lauren Seymour, vamp extraordinaire. I didn't know my best mate was a sexual terrorist.'
'I feel a bit like a sexual terrapin at the minute. Oh bloody hell the film we saw the other night, it was pure filth. I didn't know where to look.'
'You need to start looking Mrs. Remind yourself what you're missing. Hey, if this were a novel, Robert would become a bit of a good looking love god, you and he would fall madly in lust with one another , get together, have a string of kids and live happily ever after in a big detached house in Heworth.'
'Well thank fuck it isn't a novel then !' What a dark and desperate scenario that was. With any man. Love god or otherwise. The thought of herself as a domestic goddess was not only absurd, it was terrifying.
'Is he really still that bad ?'
   Lauren had to consider her answer. She wasn't sure you could judge Robert on a scale of good to bad. Robert was just kind of Robert-ish, in a weird category of humanity all of his own.
'No, he's alright really. He's not a bad looking fella when he dresses right. Not good looking either, just kind of interesting.'
'Ooh sounds intriguing. From what I can remember he always had really piercing blue eyes.'
'He's still got them. Anyway, he's hooked up with his foxy teenage mum neighbour. I'm not sure I can compete with her. Not that I'd ever want to.'
'Bloody hell. Robert P.Gorman with a girlfriend.'
'You'd better believe it. He's been playing house for these past few weeks. Not sure how long it's going to last mind.'
'Well, at least if he's getting some sex he's probably not likely to want to throw himself in the river again. It's all your average man needs to keep him on the level. Teenage mum though did you say ? That's a bit…'
'Peculiar'
'I was going to say weird, but peculiar is kinder. You quite like this boy don't you ? Not in a sexy, get your pants off kind of way of course, just in general.'
'He's a bit of a mystery. I'm intrigued.'
'You've still not told me if you're in the market for Mr Right though.'
   Lauren sighed.
'To be honest Mills, I'm having a hard enough time at the moment trying to love myself never mind anyone else. I think I'm going to be single for quite a while yet.'
   As soon as she'd spoken the line Lauren realised it might have been unnecessarily melodramatic. Millie would be sure to pick up on it.
'Aww that sounds so sad babes.' Cue the heartfelt best friend emotion.
   To Mille being single was one of nature's cruellest states and she'd never spent long without a boyfriend. One had followed the other in a fairly unbroken stream of random blokedom. Some of them disasters, many of them ordinary, few of them remarkable. She just seemed to need to be a part of a couple, to have a man of some sort on her arm and as a result she often appeared to let her judgement go to pot a little. That said she was never without company.
'It's not sad.' Lauren didn't feel melancholy about her situation. 'Just realistic. I like

being me. I like my own company.' A statement that was at least partly true some of the time.

Being alone was now her reality. Being single didn't ache in the same way it once did. During her twenties everyone she knew was forming, sustaining or just recovering from a relationship of some sort. The long periods when she wasn't made her feel odd and disassociated from her peers. Now she barely gave it much thought. Sure she clocked guys she fancied all the time. Even her small world was full of more than passable blokes. Few of them gave her much notice though. Not that she cared. Perhaps that was the problem. Francis had said so on more than one occasion.

'You carry this aura of being aloof from worldly concerns,' was how he put it. 'As if you wouldn't be bothered with something as trivial as a relationship. I think a lot of men are put off by that. They like cute, attentive woman who make them feel special.'

'Well they can get lost then can't they ? What am I meant to do sit and bat my eyelids and act all coy ? I don't bloody think so.'

When she considered the kind of guy she'd like to end up with the descriptions she concocted sounded remarkably similar to herself. What she craved more than anything was someone who understood her, took account of her idiosyncrasies, treated her like an equal and respected her need for the occasional bit of space. A bloke who wouldn't bang on about doing the regular domestic stuff. A cool person. A person with wit, charm and sound personal hygiene. Someone a bit like Francis, but obviously not homosexual. Bisexual could be interesting. Maybe she should start hanging out in gay bars.

'Francis ?'
Lauren was washing up the dinner plates as Francis dried and put away.
'Yes dearest.'
"What kind of women become fag hags ?"
'Pardon !' Francis was wide-eyed and grinning.
'Are they at all like me or are they kind of in your face.'
'Darling, fag-hags are usually screaming queenie harpies who look as if they've just covered themselves in superglue and rolled around in Claire's Accessories for twenty minutes. Nothing like you.'
'Oh, I see.' Lauren seemed pensive and lost in thought.
'Why do you ask ?'
'No reason really, just always sort of wondered.'
'You never cease to amaze me with your random off-the-wall queries. Where DO they come from ?'
'Dunno,' she put the final saucepan on the soapy pile of pots and dried her hands on the tea towel. 'Stuff just swims around my head and then finally pops out unexpectedly.'
'Never mind whether or not you could cut it as a fag hag. You should be thinking about what you're planning to do from the middle of January.'

Decking the halls

  A couple of days had passed since she had received confirmation of her redundancy. Christmas was only four days away and she remained studiously ill-prepared. Francis had been decking the halls with highly-flammable sparkly tat from Poundstretcher and singing the line about 'donning gay apparel' with gusto. He'd been baking mince pies, knocking back sweet sherry and calling his extensive network of far-flung friends with Christmas greetings. Five years previously he'd made a nativity scene out of cardboard boxes, old loo rolls and pipe cleaners. He'd painted it and topped the whole thing off with a shiny silver foil star. Every year since it had been religiously dragged out of storage and placed in a prime position in the front room. Lauren couldn't help thinking that Joseph looked slightly disabled, Mary was less the comely Middle-Eastern maiden, more a misshaped Yorkshire bloke in drag and the baby Jesus himself looked more Victorian circus-dwarf than junior messiah. Wisely she'd decided to keep her counsel on the matter.

  Francis was like a big over-the-top kid at Christmas, one of those annoying junior relations who tap-dance and sing songs from Annie at family gatherings. His seasonal round robin letter had been a classic this year. Lauren had received a mention as the 'foul-mouthed lodger who continues to torment me,' which had pleased her no end. She on the other hand had forgotten to send a single card. Millie and Francis indulged her absent-minded neglect. The people at work were less understanding. It was not that she deliberately wanted to be mean, just that her mind rarely ever stopped to think about things like Christmas, birthdays even less so. She'd quite easily forget her own if Millie and Francis didn't make such a regular fuss about it all. That said, there were some people who she simply couldn't get away with not buying a present for. Mum, Dad, Millie and Francis. As Christmas shopping lists go that wasn't the longest. It was at this time of year that she was always grateful for having been born an only child. Maybe she should buy something for Robert as well. Mind you hadn't she just done that already?

  There was no easy way to try and classify the relationship she had with Robert. Never in a million years would she have called Robert Gorman her friend when the fates had conspired to throw them together as fresh faced 18 year olds. At a time when attempting to ingratiate herself with the cool crowd mattered, being seen with Robert would have been the kiss of death. Her and Millie did hang around with him at the occasional break or lunch time. This they would tell themselves and others was out of sense of irony. They were being clever and knowing in their befriending of the geek. Post-modern irony was all the rage in the early 90s. Particularly for students.

  Looking back on it now Lauren couldn't help but see the cruelty in how they'd acted around him. One minute pretending to be his friend, the next acting aloof lest someone who they felt mattered saw them being nice to the weird lad. It was

impossible to tell how Robert had felt about it at the time. His strange demeanour rarely fluctuated back then. He acted like a peculiar template on which they could project all manner of strange ideas.
'Maybe he's some kind of alien experiment,' Millie had suggested one night as they'd sat in her room in halls puffing away on something fragrant and illegal.
'Oooh yeah like the product of an abduction.'
'That's it !' Millie passed the increasingly soggy reefer to her best friend. 'That's why they can't find his parents.'

  Lauren had rolled around laughing on the floor, gotten the munchies, devoured half a packet of Hobnobs and then fallen asleep. Miss Penny Perfect , former captain of her school's netball team, officer in the Christian Union and all round good (read generally disapproving) girl from along the corridor had seen her emerging the next morning looking bleary-eyed. Millie had stood at the door in just her nightshirt, her long curly hair falling messily around her always beautiful face. Lauren couldn't resist giving her a peck on the cheek for Penny's purposes.
'Thank's for a great night babe,' she winked and then cheekily patted Millie on the bottom. Seeing Penny, Millie played along.
'Anytime sweetie.' She put her hand on her hip and bent a leg suggestively. Penny's jaw could have hit the floor and for a few weeks afterwards entertaining gossip began to circulate that Lauren and Millie were closer than just good friends.

  Lauren had at times thought it would have been easier perhaps if they had of got it on. Millie was stunning, there was no two ways about it. Even Lauren as an at least 90% straight woman could appreciate that. They had one evening in the second year after countless tequilas decided to give bi-curiosity a try and attempt a snog. In the end neither of them could get much beyond a gentle peck for laughing so much at the absurdity of it all. It did occasionally cross Lauren's mind what might have happened had they done so. Sexual tension between her and Millie ? Perhaps. Of a drunken, hilarious and not very likely kind.

  What was never in doubt was just how tight they were as a couple of friends. Few others ever entered the equation. Not properly. They would socialise in large groups occasionally but at the end of the evening they would be locked in conspiratorial conversation in some dark corner. It must have been intimidating for people at the fringes, and in time other would-be close friends fell by the wayside. No this was the Lauren and Millie show. They were friends who'd be standing alongside one another at the end of time. They were real friends, not fair-weather acquaintances. They gave the term its proper meaning. The pair who would never let something as trivial as a man come between them.

Biting the bullet

December the 23rd. This year it fell on a Saturday. The busiest shopping day of the year and here was Lauren standing in the middle of Parliament Street, being pushed one way then the other by the throng of mad-eyed shoppers. Not a single Christmas present did she have to her name and time was pressing relentlessly onwards. She had a real urge to wander up to the Three Legged Mare, find a stool in the corner, read her book and slowly drink herself into oblivion. That would be a perfect way to spend the afternoon. But she couldn't. Not today. And what was she coming to wanting to drink alone anyway. Get some self-respect girl and let's get the job done shall we ?

OK deep breaths and let's try M&S. You can never go wrong with Mr Marks or indeed Mr Spencer when contemplating a parental gift. She mouthed a silent 'sorry' at the Big Issue seller standing at the door as she braced herself for what was in store.

The place was a heaving mass of intolerant humanity. Determined middle-aged women were grimacing as they fingered scarf and hat sets. Jaded looking men sought solace in the wine aisles. Hyper children ran around as if they'd been drip-fed an E number cocktail all morning. Lauren tried her hardest to remain focused and soon found a couple of ties in a box-set. One of them had a Christmas puddings design, the other was plain red. That had dad gift written all over it. For mum she bought a pair of leather gloves and a bottle of perfume which she'd never heard of. According to the blurb on the box it had 'woody citrus topnotes.' Lauren had no idea what that meant but liked the sound of it. See. That hadn't been too hard after all.

Francis was always easy to buy for. Several bottles of red wine and a packet of jelly babies was all he ever asked for or expected from his house mate. Lauren didn't know what to buy for Millie this year. Nothing sprung readily to mind. She wasn't seeing her for some time or so it would seem so she could afford to leave her present until after Christmas. That was one gift that always needed a little more thought and effort than the others.

After having waited in the cue at the till for nearly half an hour, she got served by a cheery woman with an Australian accent and an inappropriate orange tan.
'These for your old man ?' The woman asked as she was scanning the tie set.
'Pardon ?'
'These for your fella the ties ?' The woman beamed a fixed-on filling mirrored smile.
'Oh, sorry they're for my dad,' and what business is it of yours you nosy Antipodean. Get on with your job.
'He'll like these. Very classy.' Lauren looked at them as the woman threw them in a carrier bag. Was a cheeky laughing Christmas pudding really that classy ? All gifts aimed at middle-aged men were in some way or other either wacky or studiously dull. Most appeared to be festooned with a picture of Homer Simpson. Middle-aged men it seemed quite liked the idea of being compared to a yellow, lazy, useless, beer swilling TV fiend. Or at least their wives and children saw the comparison.

Outside, she watched the dads pushing pushchairs, making failing wisecracks to which their partners laughed politely, all of them dressed identically in clothes from M&S, Next and the Gap. They appeared strange neutered creatures, devoid of much life or personality. What kind of prospect was that for your average young guy she wondered. Is this what they all must become ? It was an idea of masculinity she didn't find remotely appealing, although she understood why more conventionally minded young women might. There was a dependable safety about them which at the end of the day is precisely what you probably crave when you're on the lookout for a father of your children. Again she felt the distance beginning to grow between herself and her peers. There must be other people who felt like her surely ? Right on cue her phone beeped a message:

'Hi Lauren. Didn't get the job. Have a good Xmas. C U in the New Year. R'

She shouldn't of course, but she did for just a moment at least , find comfort in the fact that Robert was still unemployed.

Playing happy families

'So darling, tell us all about what you've been up to. We never get to hear what you're doing these days.'
   Mum was in her best blouse and skirt set, her thirtieth wedding anniversary pearls were strung around her neck and she was clearly enjoying playing happy families for the day. Lauren screwed up her face as she tried to digest the compulsory Christmas sprouts.
'Oh good, you know me. Getting by as ever.'
'Jolly good dear.' Dad appeared to be wearing a t-shirt with a contemporary design. Lauren found it disconcerting. Where were the modest muted colours he usually favoured ? She hoped this wasn't the beginning of a late onset midlife crisis. A dark vision of her dad hooking up with a 25 year old bimbo, driving a sports car and wearing a soft-leather slip on shoe flitted across her mind. It made her shiver.
'Are you warm enough dear ?' Dad asked noticing.
'Yes, sorry. I just felt like something walked across my grave.'
   Mum paused with her fork full half way to her mouth.
'Lauren. What a thing to say.'
'Eh ?'
'Talking about graves on Christmas day.' Mum was always touchy about anything to do with death.
'Mum, it didn't mean anything, it's just a saying.'
'Even so dear. At Christmas.'
   Here they were, the family all together. Not-so little Lauren, the obstinate late arrival of a daughter. Just when you thought that Keith and Hilary Seymour were going to pass their days childless, she swelled up like the Michelin man after a fortnight on a pie and cheesecake diet. Out was dragged Lauren, a month earlier than was strictly necessary , kicking and screaming at the indignity of having to be introduced to the world in a caesarean fashion.
   There had always been an air of disappointment from her parents about how

she had turned out. Mum had craved for the archetypal sweet little princess to dress up and help around the house. Instead what had arrived was an obstinate, strong-willed tomboy, happier when she was covered in filth than playing with the dolls house Granddad had made for her. When she wasn't playing out on her bike, teasing the local boys or hiding on her own up the tops of trees, she was invariably stuck with her head in a book.

'It can't be natural to want to read so much.' Mum had told her. She barely ever picked up a book, just tutted at the latest made-up indignity in her Daily Express. Dad didn't seem to be too bothered whatever his daughter got up to . He spent his time building his epic train set in the loft, complete with numerous stations, trees and people. Lauren seemed to think he had developed an elaborate social system all of his own up there. His trains always ran on time, the staff were neatly turned out, the carriages resplendent in their lovingly hand painted liveries. It was a world of order and modest efficiency. A place that Dad could control completely and into which he could retreat when the rest of the world became too much for him.

If Lauren was like either of them, then she was like her father. One of the reason she had chosen to study at York was because of a happy memory she had of visiting the Railway Museum with him as a child. He'd come alive talking about the Flying Scotsman, the Mallard and the great old days of steam. She didn't particularly share his train fascination but couldn't help but be caught up with his enthusiasm. After they'd left the museum they'd walked around the city walls, bought chips and sat on a bench in the Museum gardens. It had been one of the few moments of connection she'd shared with him whilst growing up. York had looked magical on that lazy late Spring day. The old streets, the buskers and entertainers, the sound of voices from across the globe, the sunlight on the mellow stone of the walls and the Minster. It had felt like a holiday.

'And how's work been going. ?'

Dad finally asked the inevitable question. She knew she should have volunteered the information just after she'd arrived the previous evening but somehow she couldn't bring herself to breach her parents temperamental good humour. The right moment had never presented itself. Then she had wondered if it might be easier not to mention it all and then let them know via telephone in the New Year. The meal had been uneasy for some reason. Her mum had been flustered from preparing dinner. Lauren had made repeated offers to assist but had been tetchily shooed away. Dad was being peculiarly quiet, even for him. They were a temperamental pair. Lauren was never entirely sure where she stood.

She placed her knife and fork down.

'There's something I need to tell you about work.' She hesitated and tried to find the words.

'Is something wrong love ?' Dad had been expecting a stock answer

'You're not pregnant are you dear ?' Mum stepped into the breach filled by Lauren's hesitation.

'Bloody hell no ! It's about work.'

'Oh, It's just I thought you'd put on a bit of weight that's all.' Visits to her parents were always such a confidence booster.

'Thanks.' Lauren looked down at herself. Perhaps she had been going a bit overboard of late with the biscuits. 'No, it's work. I've been told that I'm going to be made redundant next month. It's down to cost-cutting measures apparently.'

Her parents both sat staring at her silently before dad finally rediscovered the use of his jaw.

'Redundant?'

Not that it was really worth the effort.

'Yes dad, that's what I said. Redundant. Surplus to requirements. No longer needed. Unemployed.'

'There's no need for you to snap at your father Lauren.'

'Mum, I'm not snapping I'm just…'

'Out of a job, we know.' Mum could barely hide her disgust. An unemployed daughter didn't fit readily into their neatly-ordered family schema. Lauren was fuming. She could feel her face reddening as she looked down at her plate in an attempt to hold back the growing fury. What did they want from her? It wasn't as if she'd gone looking to be made redundant just before Christmas.

'Mum I'm sorry if I've ruined your Christmas day but how do you think I feel? I didn't particularly want this y'know?.'

'It's not that is it Lauren. This is just the tip of the iceberg where you're concerned.' Mum continued in the same disgusted vein. Dad remained silent, meditating on his roast potatoes and whether or not to have another chipolata. His judgement would doubtless come later after he'd had chance to brood.

'So do tell me what it is mother.' Lauren flashed her a false smarmy smile and slung her shoulders back in her chair. It was like being 14 again. Something generally happened on her visits home which led to her regressing by a couple of decades.

'Look at you. You're nearly 33, still no sign of a man, no sign of settling down and doing the normal things of life and now you're out of a job. How do you expect us to feel? This isn't what we brought you up to be.' Lauren knew that by 'the normal things of life', mum meant 'providing your father and I with grandchildren.'

'I mean,' her mother continued barely able to constrain her now freely coursing spite. 'You've always gone on about how much more intelligent and important you are than dull little housewives like me when it looks like you're going to end up alone, unemployed and bitter.'

'Hilary, that's enough.' Dad reached across and touched his wife's hand in an attempt to restrain her by now runaway tongue.

'I'm sorry Keith, but she needs to hear some home truths.'

Dad took hold of his plate, sighed dramatically and got up from the table, leaving the dining room and banging the door behind him.

'Well thanks for your support mum. Has it ever crossed your mind that I might want to make my own choices in life? That I might just want to live my life how I see fit. I don't want to conform to some plan you had worked out in your head.'

'And how do you think your father and I feel? When people ask if our daughter is married yet or if we have any grandkids. We don't know what to make of it. You never tell us what you're doing or what's happening in your life. We feel as if we don't know you anymore. You don't feel like our daughter. You've become someone different entirely.'

Lauren was thrown by the strength of her mum's remarks. This wasn't what she'd been expecting at all. There had always been an unspoken feeling that countless grievances might lie under the surface but Lauren had not expected them to surface with such vehemence. Especially not on Christmas Day as the three of them attempted to be on their very best behaviour. Maybe the news of her redundancy was the necessary spark for the brooding embers to finally catch alight.
'Mum I have no idea how I feel about kids or settling down or anything. I've never met the right bloke but it's not through want of trying.'

That was at least partially true. Since reaching her thirties she had felt less and less compulsion to make any actual effort to find a man. The thought of a boyfriend was becoming increasingly superfluous. It always had been to a degree.

Mum's face appeared to soften slightly. They never seemed to talk about much other than the surface things of life. A lack of communication that had hardened into a neatly choreographed social script in which they had both come to play their part.
'Is there no-one love ?' Mum reached across the table and placed her hands on her daughters. It was heartfelt on her part but it just made Lauren tense. She didn't need this emotional drama. There wasn't a problem. Her mum seemed set on having a mother-daughter moment that she really had no intention of sharing.
'No mum, and it's just not even that big an issue anymore. I've come to like my own company and being independent. It's kind of what I'm about.'
'But what about your biological clock. Is it not ticking ? I read an article in the Sunday paper about you career women and your biological clocks. How it comes out the blue and you have to go getting gay men to inseminate you.'
'If it is ticking, it must be digital because I've not yet heard it. And I've no intention of getting inseminated by anyone, gay or otherwise. I'm happy as I am.' Lauren had to work hard at omitting the swear words when she was talking to her parents.
'Just don't leave it too late though love will you, not if you do want a family. Not like your dad and I.'

Her parents had often talked about how they'd intended on having a handful of kids. Lauren was never meant to be an only child. Fate just conspired to make her so. Lauren tried hard to remember this basic fact about their family life. She never nearly happened at all, therefore the expectations that came to be placed on her were intensified. Her parents had been facing childlessness at a time when it was still seen as a curse, not a lifestyle choice. Now their daughter appeared to voluntarily be choosing to be childfree. It was never going to make much sense to them.
'Mum, I know you mean well and want the best for me, I just really don't know how I feel about all that.' This was the truth. 'I'm not unhappy.' Which was also true. Having had periods of her life when misery hung heavy on her every moment she knew the difference between her current state of apathetic listlessness and being truly down. Something needed to change for sure but what that change was currently escaped her.

The rest of Christmas Day and Boxing Day passed in a surface niceness that suited Lauren. The mood was definitely lighter than it had been between them for some time. She even managed to share a joke with her dad as they took a family walk along the Trent on Boxing Day. It had actually been quite pleasant not just bearable. Her mind though was beginning to be distracted by the thought of what she was going to do with herself from mid-January onwards. The realisation that she was going to be out of work was creeping up on her. As much as she'd fallen out of love with Accent, it was a comfortable place to be. Her role there was well defined. She didn't have to strive too hard to get anything done or impose herself upon the place. Given the right circumstances she could probably cruise along in her current job in perpetuity. Should she now take the opportunity to go and do something entirely different? Common sense told her that she should get her head down and start applying for similar positions with other firms. Openings for copywriters were hardly plentiful in York. Leeds might offer slightly better prospects but her real chance of securing gainful employment might lie in London.

Another unexpected phone call

'Of course I'd be sorry to see you go but the capital could be good for you.'
　The two of them sat on a sofa in the foyer café at the Theatre Royal. Francis was due to meet his friend Stephen who worked back stage. Lauren with nothing to do until she went back to work on the 2nd January thought she'd hang around until he turned up. When Millie worked here Lauren had regularly sat on the same sofa waiting for her to finish her shift.
'I'm not sure I want all the upheaval. I mean all my friends are here.'
'You mean your friend is here.'
'OK, I mean you're here.' Leaving the colleagues and contacts she'd accrued from work aside, there were few people other than Francis she'd be likely to miss. Even fewer who would miss her.
'No you can't sit around in York waiting for life to happen for you. It's a big world out there.'
'I think the bigness is exactly what I'm scared of.'

'Is that Lauren I'm speaking to?'
Back at the house the phone had been ringing determinedly all afternoon. Lauren had said hello to Stephen, bought a copy of the Christmas NME and wandered back to spend an afternoon reclining on her bed whilst listening to CDs. Just as she'd have done at home when she was 17. Her original intention had been to try and ignore the ringing phone but it's persistence shifted her from her reclining position.
'Yes, it is. Who am I speaking to?'
'Oh hello Lauren, it's Bessie here. We met the other day at Acomb library.'

'Right, Bessie. Hi. How did you get my number ?'
'I was a bit naughty and looked it up on your library record. I needed to talk to you quite urgently.'
'Urgently ? Why what's the problem ? Is a book overdue or something.' If Bessie saw the funny side of Lauren's remark she didn't laugh.
'Can we meet up ? This evening perhaps. I need to talk to you about Robert.'
'Robert ? Oh, right.' This was actually quite annoying. Why couldn't she just have told her the doubtless crappy gossip about the Gorman boy back in the café the other day? Lauren was starting to feel mildly protective towards him, just as she would Millie or Francis. Given time and a bit of patience he might even become friendship material.
'Yes, it's quite delicate. Do you know The Ackhorne pub just off Micklegate ?'
Lauren had a think. Yes she did know it, Matt used to drink in there all the time. It was a proper smoky beer lovers place full of colourful locals. Delicate though ? That was an odd word to use in conjunction with Robert.
'I do.'
'Good. Can I meet you there at about seven then ? It won't take long.'
'Sure, I've nothing on.' Which was true and it was how she'd been intending on keeping it. Going out intruded on valuable sitting and reading time. The prospect of learning more about the history of Robert however did intrigue her. It must be important if Bessie was so desperate to see her. For Bessie going out would require her to get someone in to look after her mother. Whereas for Lauren it meant getting changed and withdrawing some money from the cash machine. Perhaps she didn't have many grounds for complaint. Francis would be pleased she'd be getting out from under his feet for the evening. He was always complaining about her lack of a social life.

   The Ackhorne was just down a little cobbled alley called St.Martin's Lane. It was pretty much how she remembered it from her one previous visit with Matt. He used to pop in a couple of times a week but never seemed that bothered about taking Lauren along at the time. She never bothered asking why. It was clear that his visits there were all about taking time to chew the cud. He'd sit in the corner, read the paper, drink a couple of pints of the guest beer and then wander home. He wasn't really the hell raising type and Lauren appreciated his stillness and understood his need for time apart. It was one of the reasons she found herself falling for him in the first place. There was no forced zaniness about Matt. He didn't see the need to impress with verbal dexterity or wacky behaviour. He was just his interesting and intriguing self. A welcoming mystery which she'd hoped to explore. That was the kind of people she liked best. The upfront, in your face types were generally a bit of a disappointment after the charade was dropped. The quieter ones, the people more coy about their motivations and less sparing with their affections usually merited further attention.
   As she sat at a stool by a little round table near the fire she wondered where Matt used to sit. The one time they'd come in together had been a Saturday afternoon when they'd sat by the window and ordered food. Where did he sit when he was on

his own ? Could it have been the stool that she was now propped on nursing her half pint of lager ? Perhaps. No amount of speculation would ever give her the answer. For the second time in less than a fortnight she found herself sitting nursing a drink whilst waiting for an ex-university colleague to arrive. With better timing than Robert, the saloon door heaved open and a red-faced Bessie appeared, this time without her customary beam.

'Hello Lauren,' she blustered, flamboyantly unravelling her scarf. 'Sorry I'm late I had problems with the bus, they're running a peculiar service over Christmas. Can I get you another drink ?' It was the familiar ten words to the breath approach that Lauren remembered of Bessie from way back. The woman never shut up when she got going. This could potentially be a long evening.
'No thanks, I've just got…'
'You might need it.'
'Oh. In that case I'll have vodka lime and soda then please.' Something stronger than lager was probably called for. She watched Bessie wander to the bar. It was an interesting place this with a pleasant fuggy atmosphere. It wasn't overly busy. A man with a long straggly beard puffed a pipe at the far end of the bar, a gaunt guy with an earring and a red t-shirt sat poring over the Guardian. An artsy looking girl with a jagged fringe was reading a book in the corner. Lots of solitary types, all being cosseted by the low lighting and gentle nature of the place. She could see why Matt liked it. She could imagine herself sitting here reading, or maybe writing even. Places where loners could go to be apart together were few and far between in Lauren's experience, but this one seemed to fit the bill quite nicely.

Bessie returned to the table with the drinks, a tomato juice for herself and a vodka for Lauren. Either Bessie didn't drink or purposefully intended staying totally sober.
'So how was your Christmas ?' Breezy Bessie had returned.
'Fine.' Lauren didn't fancy playing another game of pleasantries. Keep your responses short and cut to the chase.
'Good. Mine was good too.'
'That's good.' The pair of them were silent. Bessie was not normally lost for words. As long as those words didn't really matter. Perhaps that was the problem.
'So Bessie, what's this all about ?' Bessie's brow furrowed and her whole demeanour shifted.
'I don't think you should be seeing Robert P.Gorman. There are things that you don't know about him.'
'I'm not seeing him, seeing him. He's just a friend.'
'A friend, oh I see, perhaps I don't need to tell you then.'
'Bessie you've dragged me out on a cold December evening when I could have been in drinking cocoa and reading to tell me some urgent information. I think you have a duty to tell me now.' Lauren was growing tired of Bessie's cat and mouse tactics. She just needed to know where she stood. Bessie took a sip of her drink and looked pensive.
'Alright, alright. But this kind of thing doesn't come easy to me. I'm not one of nature's gossips .' Lauren resisted the urge to raise her eyebrows or even worse,

splutter her drink all over the table. From what she remembered of Bessie that disclaimer didn't really ring true. Bessie continued; 'Robert lost his job at the library because of certain allegations.'

'Allegations ?'

'Yes. Allegations.'

'Please don't get cryptic on me again, could you just tell me what you mean.' Bessie had become no less tiresome with age it would appear.

'I mean that allegations of a sexual nature were made against him.'

'Eh ? Robert ? Are you thinking of someone else ?' Robert must be the most asexual adult Lauren had ever encountered. 'Who made these allegations ? What the hell happened ?'

'Now don't get annoyed Lauren, as I said this isn't…'

'Easy for you, yes I know. Please just tell me what he was meant to have done and to whom.'

'A thirteen year old girl said he attempted to molest her.' That really was cutting to the chase.

'You what ?' Lauren wasn't really sure what she was hearing. 'That can't be right. Can it ?'

Bessie nodded, her usually red face turning ashen.

'It was meant to have happened after a reading group he was supposed to be leading for one of the local schools. A group of them came in every Thursday afternoon to read and discuss some book or other. Robert had just started taking it. Apparently this one girl stayed behind to ask him something and he made a play for her. She told her father, who stormed into the library and threatened to kill Robert there and then. It caused a dreadful scene.'

'This is unbelievable.' It couldn't be right.

'You're telling me. I wasn't sure what to think.'

'Then what happened ? Were the police involved ?'

'Yes, the police investigated but at the end of the day it was her word against his. There wasn't enough evidence to prosecute but there were lots of grey areas.'

Lauren's head was spinning. The enormity of what she was hearing was difficult to grasp in one go.

'So he got made redundant ?'

'Well he got suspended whilst the investigation was on, then the council were making cutbacks on library staff and conveniently decided that they should get rid of Robert. It was a bit of an embarrassment all round. They managed to keep it out of the local paper for the girl's sake but it was clear that Robert couldn't be trusted.'

'And he's been unemployed ever since.' That would explain a lot.

'I can't say I'm surprised. The library won't be giving him a reference anytime soon.'

'And the girl. What happened to her ?'

'That's the saddest part. She was so shaken by the whole thing that she started playing truant. Very problematic at school apparently. The family decided it might be best to take her elsewhere to start again, so her dad got a new job and the family moved to down to Sheffield. No bad memories there.'

'What did the library staff make of it ? Didn't they think he wouldn't be the kind of

person who'd do something like that. I can't believe it's possible. Not Robert.'
'Actually, it confirmed a lot of peoples prejudices about him. He was always quite aloof and cold with some of the staff. He wasn't popular. I always tried to have time for him and involve him in things as I knew him from university, but he never seemed very interested. A bit of a loner I think.'
Lauren knew what that meant. Serial killers were always described by the neighbours as 'a bit of a loner' and as a bona-fide, card-carrying member of the loner non-club herself she resented the accusation that anyone who preferred their own company to that of others was somehow a murderer in waiting.
'Wanting to be alone is no crime is it ?'
'No, perhaps not. But Robert seemed secretive with it. I don't think I ever felt I could entirely trust him.'
Lauren remembered the incident with the coat on Coney Street, the sudden shift in mood the anxious and awkward twitches, the erratic behaviour and the words of her best friend warning against getting too involved. Now this news. Something was clearly not right here. Bessie looked at Lauren who was completely lost in thought, her mind totally distanced from her surroundings.
'Lauren, are you alright.' Bessie touched Lauren's hand snapping her out of her contemplation.
"Oh, sorry, yes. I was just…'
But she was far from alright and didn't know what she was just.

Knowing what to do next

It was clear that both of them had wanted to make their excuses and leave as soon as possible. Lauren couldn't honestly say that reacquainting herself with Bessie had been a pleasant meander back down memory lane. There had been little real connection between them, less so even than there had been during their three years together at college. Then Bessie had been indulged as an interested motherly figure by the younger students, now she just appeared to be an interfering old busybody. That said, she couldn't be blamed for the news she had to deliver. If it was all true of course. It was hard to know what to think.
Lauren had remained deliberately vague with Francis when she got in, complained of a headache, took a couple of paracetamol and then went for an early night.
Her hope had been that sleep would help her opinions form into some kind of coherence and that she'd wake in the morning sure of what to do next. In the event there was to be no such clarity of mind. Instead she woke with a pressured feeling on her forehead. She knew that she'd just been party to something dreadful. Robert the pervert ? Her mind was swinging from pulling the pieces of her encounters with Robert in one direction, then doing the same in another. One minute it was obviously not true, the next it almost certainly was and if it was then what should she do next ? If it had just been her involved then her usual route out of tricky social quandaries would have been followed. Delete his number from her phone, do her

damnedest not to think about him and ignore his calls and messages. This never normally failed, even if it sometimes took a while for the person being written out of her personal script to get the message.

This though was no dodgy geezer who had bored her half to death on a night out, or a ditzy friend of a friend from work trying to get her to join an aerobics class. This was serious, important stuff that involved other, possibly vulnerable people. The most telling piece of evidence in the mental case she made for the prosecution was the fact that Robert, a man about to turn 33 appeared to have formed a relationship with a 17 year old girl. Now that not only seemed unusual it was beginning to look sinister. If the girl he was alleged to have attempted to hit upon had been 13 when the incident took place, today she would be approaching the age of Beth. The image of a grinning Robert, holding the baby of a teenage mum whose arm is wrapped around his middle appeared in her head. She had to talk to someone about this. She needed to know where to go next.

'Hi is that the Samaritans ?' It was the first thing she could think of.
'Yes that's right, how can I help you today. Is there something troubling you ?' A soft, gently well-spoken low female voice immediately put her at ease.
'Erm, yes, well there is yes.'
'Right, OK. Would you like to tell me a little bit more about it ?' The voice sounded so soothing, so patient, like honey or something. It was helping Lauren to open up.
'It's my friend. Well, he's not really my friend. He tried to kill himself.'
'I'm sorry to hear that. Is he OK now ? How are you coping with this ?'
'Me ? Oh, I'm coping well enough. No, it's just…'
'Yes..'
'He'd not seen me in ages, then I got a call out of the blue to go to the hospital, except I didn't know who he was and then….'
'Right..'
'I'm not being very clear am I ?'
'No, not really, but do try and carry on.'
'OK. Well this guy..'
'The one who tried to kill himself.'
'Yes, him. I thought he was OK, then I got a call from an old college friend who used to work with him who told me he'd been made redundant for making advances towards a teenage girl.'
'That doesn't sound good.'
'My thoughts exactly. The thing is, I don't know who to believe.'
'You have to ask yourself how well you think you really know your friend.'
'That's just it, I'm not sure I do know him really.'
'So perhaps you need to talk to him about this. But it might be best to do it somewhere public, for safety reasons.'
'Right.' It was the obvious course of action, but that didn't make it any easier.
'There's another problem as well though.'
'Carry on.'
'He's seeing a girl who I think is only about 17. She's got a baby boy as well. I'm

worried for them.'
'And how old is your friend ?'
'Almost 33.'
'In that case I think you need to have this out with your friend immediately, and if necessary inform social services about the situation.'
'Social services ? Oh god no, I don't want to be a trouble-maker and I don't think he was convicted or anything…'
'Even so, you have a duty to pass this information on. If there's nothing to worry about then no one will get hurt. If there is and you withheld information can you imagine how bad you'd feel ?'
'Yes, I can.'

The soft reassuring voice had spoken the truth. Lauren felt an increasing sense of aggrieved injustice that her precious sense of mental equilibrium had been unbalanced in this way. Two months ago she had known who she was. Life had found a comfortable self-contained groove. She bothered no-one and was bothered even less. Now she was soon to be without a job and had to deal with the most salacious and important piece of gossip she'd ever had the misfortune to receive.

'You're well off out of it. Leave the guy alone and come see me.'
For once the fear of the transatlantic haul that stood between Lauren and her reunion with Millie didn't seem quite as immense. Getting away from the situation would perhaps be the best thing she could do. Every part of her fight or flight mechanism told her that fleeing this messy set of circumstances was the best way for her to survive. Her conscience though was nagging. What about that girl and her baby ? If there was truth behind the rumours what could this possibly mean ? At 17 Beth was over the age of consent and no longer technically a minor. What was so wrong about their relationship apart from the age gap ? Plenty of couples did survive where the gap was as large if not larger than it was between Robert and Beth. If on the other hand it was true that he tried to molest a young girl then there is clearly something very wrong with the relationship. For the first time the 'P' word entered her head. There it sat flashing like a neon warning sign above the blank blue-eyes of Robert P. Gorman.
'What if he's a y'know ?' She couldn't bring herself to verbalise it. It was a hard one to utter in connection with someone she actually knew and was feeling increasingly fond of.
'Paedo y'mean ?'
'Yeah.'
'All the more reason to leave well alone. Tell social services about what's happening like the nice lady at the Samaritans said and then leave them to sort it out. You can't realistically be expected to do anymore than that.'
'Oh Mills, I'm not sure I can do that to him.'
'Lauren, what are you talking about ? The guy's a kiddie fiddler for gods sake.'
'We don't know that for sure do we ?' Everyone seemed to be certain except Lauren. Maybe her judgement was going to pot as well.
'No, but we've got a pretty damn good idea. He's loony, he tried to assault you, he's

hooked up with a teenage girl and he's got previous with some kid in the library. Everything about him is screaming nut job. You're well out of it.'
'It just doesn't all fit though, you don't know him like I….'
'Lauren, you don't know him.'
'I'm beginning to.'
'No you don't you said yourself he's a mystery.'
'Yeah but…'
'No yeah buts or anything. Leave him alone for your own safety as much as anything else. I don't want to be getting a phonecall from Francis saying you're in hospital after an incident with the nutter, or even worse.'
'No. I s'pose not.' Millie wasn't generally known for her nuanced thinking, and understanding nature, maybe Francis would have a different take.

   'You go anywhere near him Lauren and I swear I'll never talk to you again.' Francis was waving a wooden spoon at Lauren. They stood in the kitchen, he was heating through a Covent Garden soup, she had her hand in a bag of Hula Hoops.
'Oh don't be like that.' What was it with everyone ? Why all this overreaction ?
'I mean it. Why the hell didn't you tell me he attacked you ?'
'He didn't attack me…'
'He tried to..'
'No he didn't.'
'That's not what you just said.'
'Oh I don't know.' Lauren threw her arms in the air in frustration and huffed off into the front room, collapsing on the sofa with her hands shoved down in her jeans pocket. A look of total self-pity crept across her face. None of this was fair. Francis followed shortly after, his face as black as thunder, carrying his soup and a brown roll on a polka-dot tray. Neither said anything.
'So when are you back at work.' Francis asked perfunctorily.
'January 2nd. I thought you knew ?'
'No, I didn't.'
'Any plans for New Year ?'
'I shall be at Tony's.'
'Right.'
'You ?'
'No, not yet. Probably stay in and read.'
'Oh for crying out loud, get yourself sorted out and get a bloody life other than worrying about that oddball you've gone and got embroiled with. You used to be fun.'
'I am fun !' At least she thought she was. 'You've been the one telling me that I needed to give Robert a chance and look beyond the surface.'
'Yes, you've looked beyond the surface and seen he's a lunatic. The guy attempted to fiddle with a little girl ? I really think you must have lost it to want to have anything to do with him any further. What would you be telling Millie now if she was in your position ?' Francis didn't try to hide his disappointment.

'I don't know'
'Yes you do. You know full well you'd be telling her to ditch the creep and report him to the authorities ASAP. You can't take chances with men like that.'
'Men like what ?'
'Paedophiles.'
'Don't call him that.'
'Why not ? That looks like what he is, amongst other things. Did you not think it strange he kept his granny under his bed for a decade.'
'That doesn't make him a paedophile does it ? I thought that was more to do with eccentricity than anything else.'
'There is a point where eccentric becomes downright weird and where downright weird slides into dangerous. I think he's rapidly approaching the latter.'
'I just can't see it though.' It didn't make sense.
'Perhaps you can't, but I'll tell you something, if you don't pass on his situation to social services I might be inclined to. He's got access to that young woman and her baby. God knows what he could get up to.'
'You wouldn't dare.'
'Just you try me young lady, just you try me.'

    That afternoon Lauren decided to go for a walk along by the River Ouse. Crossing over the elegant arch of the Millennium bridge and down where the towpath ran into open fields and out beyond the city. There was a low lying mist and hardly a soul about. A middle-aged man in an old parka coat sat fishing on the bank, one of the houseboats had its back door open and the light from inside looked warm and inviting. It was good to feel grass beneath her Converse. She hoped that the walk might provide her with some answers. Her two closest friends had already made their own thoughts on the subject crystal clear, particularly Francis whose vehemence had surprised her. He usually sought the bigger picture, attempting to understand people in the round, but not this time. She had needed to escape the house to get away from his brooding bad mood. Lauren wasn't sure if it was just her news about Robert which had provoked it or if something else was going on in his life that he hadn't told her about. He was due to go to Tony's in the morning, that would at least give her some breathing space for a couple of nights. Whatever the reason, the tension in the tiny two-up, two-down terrace had been impossible to escape. Out here she could at least breath a bit of fresh air and try to get some perspective. Life always had a way of kicking you like this when you thought you had it sorted. Then came the inevitable text message.

'Hi Lauren, it's R. Doing anything NYE ? Come 4 dinner with me and Beth.'

    Overhanging the river which was coursing and swirling at a maximum capacity for its banks, was a tall old tree. One of the branches was broad and low. Lauren used her arms to lever herself up onto it. It supported her quite easily. Leaning against the trunk with her legs stretched out along the branch she watched the passing peaty water. Dinner with Robert, a probable sex offender and his 17 year old girlfriend. That'd be interesting. She knew what Francis and Millie would have to say on the matter, but maybe they didn't need to know. If she could watch them together then perhaps she'd be able to come to some kind of judgement about him. Now she had this news from Bessie surely it was right to see how that related to how Robert acted ? It was still possible of course that the whole thing at Acomb library had been a misunderstanding. Or that the girl herself had been making it all up. Of course, she had known plenty of girls when she was that age who probably wouldn't have thought twice before making accusations like that. No she couldn't think like that. It was the kind of thing her mum would say. That said, Lauren had never thought that every man was a potential sex offender. Just because someone was accused of something did that automatically make them guilty ? She'd see Robert again, and Beth and reserve her judgement.

Should auld acquaintance

'Come in Lauren. It's lovely to see you.'
Lauren stood at the door in her mac, clutching a cheap bottle of Cava, a New Years card and a bunch of flowers she'd picked up at Newgate Market earlier in the day. They were going to be for home, but she decided under the circumstances that maybe Robert's place needed them more. Robert leaned forward and kissed her cheek, helping her with the wine and flowers.
'They're for us ? Oh thanks Lauren. I've never been given flowers before.'
Lauren thought about it for a second.
'Neither have I.'
   The flat appeared to have undergone something of a minor renovation. There was the smell of fresh paint everywhere, the chair and bean bag had been joined by a soft squishy sofa and a couple of lamps sat in opposite corners on the floor. You couldn't yet call it homely, but it was beginning to resemble a well-established student house where the residents had tried to make a bit of an effort. The carpet looked as if it had been vacuumed as well. A couple of prints in wooden frames were on the wall. Lauren studied them briefly. They were abstract, colourful and moderately tasteful. The whole room felt like it might actually belong to a member of the human race. There was no sign of Beth.
'You look as if you've been doing some decorating.'
   Robert re-entered the room with two glasses of Cava. The glasses looked reassuringly new and clean. They certainly appeared to at least be a pair.
'Yeah, I've been hard at it. Beth's been helping. She's been an angel she really has. I picked up the sofa, the lights and the pictures at that house clearance place down Piccadilly. Do you like them ?'
'Yeah, it's made a real difference.'
'Oh, and I've sorted out the bedroom as well. D'ya wanna see ?'
   Lauren hesitated for a second. She had no great desire to repeat her last experience of that dark hole again.

'Err..'

Robert grabbed her arm.

'Come on, you'll love it.'

Lauren was stunned into silence by the transformation. The mattress free frame had been replaced by a rustic looking pine bed, the dingy carpet pulled up and the bare boards stained and covered with an attractive old rug that looked as if it might once have been expensive. The collapsing wardrobe was no more. In its place was a basic canvas covered one like you might see in the Ikea catalogue. Nothing was out of place.

'Robert, this is incredible. You've done good here.' She turned and looked at him. His face was open and smiling, his piercing blue eyes twinkled with satisfaction as he saw Lauren's reaction. His hair was again slightly spiked.

'Thanks,' he took hold of her hand. 'I'm really glad you like it.' Lauren was transfixed by those remarkable eyes. They seemed to look right through her, as they held each others gaze for slightly longer than was strictly necessary.

'Yeah..I..'

But before she had chance to even work out what it was she wanted to say, Robert leaned forward and placed a soft kiss on her cheek. Lauren felt a small tremor at the contact and she looked at him, her expression frozen, her mind completely lost for words. Then there was a knock at the door.

'Oh shit, that'll be Beth. Could you sit down in the front room?'

Robert pulled away, leaving Lauren standing there confused. What the hell had that been all about? Without thinking, she straightened herself up and dashed towards the living room, finding a perch on the end of the sofa. She didn't fancy Robert. Really she didn't. As the sound of Beth's eager voice came down the corridor, Lauren tensed and tried to fix a grin on her face.

'Hiya Lauren.' Beth appeared around the door. She looked stunning in a little pink tunic dress and leggings, her hair was up and her make-up flawless. There was nothing of the teenage single-mum about her appearance this evening.

'Oh hi Beth. Lovely to see you. No Christopher tonight? ' Lauren felt positively dowdy in her long-sleeve t-shirt and jeans. Perhaps she should have made an effort. Even Robert was wearing a shirt, not one that Lauren had bought him either.

'Nah, he's at his nan's.'

In bustled Robert with another glass of wine.

'You look gorgeous babes.'

'Thanks hon.' Beth's face lit up and she kissed him coyly on the cheek. Lauren winced. Robert sat down in the chair as Beth took the other end of the sofa.

'This is nice,' said Robert rubbing his hands. Lauren and Beth sat in silence. 'So now what do we do ?' Asked Robert after a seconds pause which felt like a couple of extended lifetimes.

'Play some music perhaps ?' Suggested Lauren, trying to remain bright and upbeat.

'I haven't got a stereo.'

'No stereo, right.'

'Let's just eat Rob. I'm starving already.' Beth scratched her belly impatiently and glanced at her watch.

'Er yeah,' Robert touched the back of his head. 'There's just one thing. I actually forgot that we were eating and didn't buy anything in. I only remembered this evening as Lauren arrived.'

'Oh Rob you fucking dong ! This was meant be a nice night in with a meal and you've gone and fucked up you useless fucker.' Beth angrily jumped to her feet and stormed out of the front room.

'Beth babes' Robert meekly called after her. He shrugged and tried to smile at Lauren, but his face gave away the hurt he was clearly feeling. He scurried off behind his mouthy girlfriend like an eager to please lapdog.

   Well there was an insight and a half thought Lauren who now felt even more uncomfortable than she had done already. There were raised voices from the kitchen but Lauren couldn't make out what was being said. Just then she had an idea and knocked discretely on the kitchen door. Someone needed to try and take charge of all this.

'Erm, just a thought, why don't I go to the Chinese takeaway around the road and get us something ? My treat.'

Beth glared at her.

'I didn't want a fucking Chinese, I wanted chicken, Rob said he was going to get a fucking chicken.' She jabbed Robert in the chest with her forefinger.

'Beth sweetheart, I just forgot, honestly I did.'

'Ah go fuck yourself you idiot. Can't trust you to do owt.' Beth waved her hand in the air, shoulder barged past Lauren and stomped off.

'Sorry about all this. I don't know how I forgot.' Robert's face had gone white. He looked as if he was about to cry. Lauren touched his shoulder.

'Hey, don't worry about it. These things happen, we all forget stuff. Does she always talk to you like this ?'

'Not always no.'

'But sometimes.'

'Quite a lot.' Robert was trying to hold back the tears. It was becoming increasingly clear to Lauren who held the upper hand in the relationship.

'Why do you stand for it ?'

'I think I love her.'

'Oh Robert, I don't think you...' But before she had chance to finish what she was about to say she felt eyes driving their glare hard into her back. Turning she saw Beth leaning against the door frame, her arms folded across her chest, a face like thunder.

'Is it any of your business ?' It wasn't so much a question, as a warning.

'Look Beth, I'm not after trouble.' Lauren wondered why any of this was really necessary.

'I bet you're not.' Beth gave Lauren a shove to her shoulder, not hard but enough to skew her balance and force her back against the dour green kitchen unit. Robert attempted to intervene.

'Hey Beth, that's just not on.' He reached to steady Lauren, and held a hand out towards his young girlfriend as if signalling her to stop. Beth spun around and aimed a slap on his left cheek.

'And you can shut your fucking stupid mouth as well.'

Lauren couldn't stand and watch this any longer. Robert might have problems being assertive but she was a sure as hell she wasn't about to be intimidated by an angry little kid.
'Just you wait one second. What the hell do you think you're playing at ?'
'I'll tell you what.' Beth reached towards her but Lauren swerved to miss.

Lauren grabbed her arm and pushed it down forcibly despite Beth's resistance.

'Robert made a mistake that's all that happened. You need to calm down and I'll go get us something to eat.'

Letting go of her grip, Beth did at last seem temporarily pacified. She stood still, sticking out her bottom lip and folding her arms across her middle making her look every inch the temperamental teenager she was. It was useless attempting to reason with her as if she were an adult. 'Right, what do you fancy ?'
'KFC'
'KFC?'
'Kentucky. I fancy a Kentucky. Can we have a family bucket ?'
'We can have a family bucket.'
'Yay !' Beth was delighted at this news, instantly forgetting her furious rage of a second or so earlier. She walked across to the bottle of Cava, poured herself a glass, took a box of cigarettes and a lighter from her bag and left the kitchen. Lauren directed a wide-eyed gesture at Robert who mouthed a silent 'sorry'.
'Family bucket do you as well will it ?'
'I've never had one so I don't know.'
'Me neither, but I'll try to forget some of the stories I've heard about their food for the evening.'

Lauren was grateful to get away. Far from playing happy families as Lauren had believed, on the evidence of this evening Robert had been childminding an ASBO kid. The Kentucky was just around the corner from Robert's flat. She had often been subject to its cloying fatty smell when she'd ventured over this side of town to visit the now redundant Odeon cinema. It sat next to a tattoo parlour in a row of low shops in an area that always seemed to attract winos and track suited kids. An alleyway down the side of the cinema stank of stale male piss and the litter quotient here seemed to surpass the rest of the city's put together.

There was a cue at the Kentucky, a sorry line of pale-skinned people in bad caps and cheap looking jewellery. An overweight man in a tired fleece jacket with huge bags under his eyes took hold of his order and shuffled past glumly. Lauren caught sight of the huge sovereign ring and swallow tattoo on his right hand and wondered what she was doing here.

She wasn't a food snob by any means, but there was something about KFC which seemed to uniquely symbolise naff. This was not the New Years Eve she had intended on having but it was interesting if nothing else.

Beth's behaviour and Robert's reaction had been telling under the circumstances. It was hard to square the clearly henpecked, appeasing Robert she had just witnessed with the idea of him as a predatory sex pest. The kiss had been confusing as well. What did it mean ? Was it just a kiss between friends ? The moment preceding it had been electric, thinking about it now gave her the shivers. And yes, she did have to admit, there was something very compelling about those eyes. He didn't seem to lack confidence when he leaned in and kissed her like that. For a moment she thought what Francis and Millie would be saying about this evening's events. They'd no doubt think she had finally lost her marbles, allowing herself to be taken in by this peculiar character. Robert with his charm one minute, his helplessness the next, the confusing signals he gave her about his feelings, and her own increasingly mixed-up feelings about him. All this set against the backdrop of Bessie's little tale. Her words and earnest troubled face in the pub repeated themselves over and over in Lauren's mind. Was Robert really still regarded by his former colleagues and doubtless many others as a would-be sex offender ? Activity outside broke her contemplation.

A group of eight girls all dressed in red devil catsuits, horns and feather boas tottered by on high heels cracking dirty jokes. A gang of six tough looking men with Geordie accents hollered across the road at them, prompting the largest of the group to pull down her outfit and expose her cleavage to the delight of the blokes. One of whom began fiddling with the zipper on his jeans. Surely he's not about to…

'Next please.' A wan spotty youth looking thoroughly miserable behind the counter was ready to take her order.

'Family bucket and a bottle of coke please.' Did she really just ask for that ?

Outside the stream of drunken humanity milled, bellowed and bickered. After a couple of minutes the grim youth handed her a bag containing a steaming bucket of greasy fast food and a large bottle of Coca-Cola. Outside, she dodged the revellers, catching sight of the silhouette of a man urinating down a cobbled alley. He caught her glance and gave her a cheery wave. Once upon a time she would have felt uncomfortable surrounded by all this leery beery humanity, but nowadays she tended to look on in part amusement, part amazement and with a degree of anonymity. It made a change to be recognised for once, even if it was only by a carefree drunk relieving himself down a ginnel.

Back at the flat, an uneasy peace appeared to have broken out. Beth stretched out on the sofa necking back Cava, like the council estate equivalent of some ancient Middle-Eastern princess. Robert was on the beanbag, but jumped up when Lauren popped her head around the front room door.

'Grubs up folks !'

Beth looked up at her.

'Ooh, nice one. KFC rocks.' That must almost count as effusive.

'Indeed'. But Lauren's agreement probably lacked much conviction.

'Go on then divvy, get some plates.' Beth gestured at her ever eager older boyfriend to make a move.

'Ooh sorry, yes.' Robert scurried off to the kitchen. Lauren started to follow behind him.

'Does it need two of you ?' Beth stopped her in her tracks.

'I'm sorry.'
'Does it need two of you to sort out the food ?'
'No Beth, but I was just going to lend a hand.' Lauren's voice had slipped into a school ma'am tone which she seemed unable to help.
'He can manage. He's not an idiot.'
   That's not what you've been telling him all evening thought Lauren but decided against saying anything. Lauren lowered herself into the threadbare chair. Beth eyed her suspiciously.
'You've been helping Robert decorate I hear.'
'Aye.' Beth's surly glare didn't shift.
'You made a good job of it.'
'Cheers.'
'Did you have a good Christmas ?'
'It were alright.'
'Good.'
   There was silence. Lauren awkwardly examined the sole of her Converse as Beth continued to glare, take a drag on her cigarette and finally speak.
'Do you fancy him ?'
'Pardon ?' That was a bolt from the blue.
'Do you fancy Robert ? I reckon you fancy him.'
'Robert ? God no, I don't fancy him. He's just….' Lauren was searching for the words. She didn't fancy him. She was almost certain she didn't fancy him.
'Just what ?'
'Just a friend, we've known each other years.'
'My mam says blokes and lasses can't just be friends. It's impossible. She reckons you're sniffing around. Told me to watch what you're up to.' Beth pointed towards her with her lighted cigarette.
'Well you can tell your mum I've never had any problems just being friends with men.' Which was true of course. The problems generally started when the men in question wanted to take things further.
'Why ? Are you a lezzer ? D'ya fancy me then ?'
'No, I'm not a lesbian. I do fancy blokes.'
'Have you got a boyfriend ?'
'Not at the minute no.'
'So you fancy Robert then ?'
'Beth, this isn't going anywhere. I don't fancy Robert. He's a friend, just try and accept that and let's try and have a nice New Years Eve shall we ?' Why did everything have to be so difficult with her ? Why was everyone being so bloody complicated ? Couldn't they just have a bit of surface niceness for a few hours without all these interrogations and aggressive mind-games. Lauren felt herself tiring quickly.
'You can do what you like.'
'What do you mean ?'
'Do you really think I got done up like this to sit in Rob's skanky flat on New Years Eve with him and an old bird ?'

'Old bird ! Well, thanks very much.' Lauren was trying her hardest not to be offended. At 17 someone in their early thirties is middle-aged. 'Are you going out then ?'
'I am, I'm off out with Karen from downstairs. I just want my tea then I'm going to get out of your way.'
'Oh, does Robert know ?'
'Dunno. I've not told him.'
'Well, don't you think you should ?' It was no skin off Lauren's nose if the obstreperous little cow didn't want to spend time in her company, but Robert was bound to feel differently.
'Who do you think you are, me fucking grandma ?'
'How old do you think I am ?' Nearly thirty-three admittedly wasn't the first flush of youth, but neither did it mean she was about to be put out to grass.
'Dunno, older than my mam. She makes an effort.'
'And how old is your mum ?'
'36, which is fucking ancient in my book.'
'So she's older than me then.' Only by four years though. With a seventeen year old daughter and a grandparent already.
'Really. I'd never have guessed.'

   Robert came through the door with two plates stuffed with fries, deep fried chicken and coleslaw. Despite her better judgement Lauren momentarily thought it looked quite appealing.
'I fucking hate coleslaw.' Beth turned her nose up at the big dollop of it on her plate. 'Scrape it off will you.'
'Oh sorry babe I didn't realise.' Robert's forced cheery smile dropped like a bridge thrown brick.
'You didn't ask did you ?' Beth shoved the plate back towards him. Lauren jumped to her feet and grabbed it, before Robert could sheepishly take it back. This was cruelty.
'I'll do that Robert, Beth's got something to tell you.'

   In the kitchen Lauren glanced at her shadowy reflection in the glass fronted wall unit. It looked drab. Definitely ageing. She pulled at the beginnings of bags under her eyes and sighed. Old enough to be a grandma. Getting older had never previously been an issue. Hitting thirty had been a breeze. There was no anguished gnashing of teeth at the passing of her youth. Not like Millie. She'd been more than just a bit neurotic. With her ever-ready credit card she'd hit the clothes racks quite badly, going through a phase of dressing like an 18 year old nymphomaniac. It was embarrassing to be seen out with her. Lauren in her androgynous shabby chic walking through town with a would-be member of a piss-poor Girls Aloud tribute band.
'Just because you want to dress like a mum Laurers doesn't mean I have to.' Millie had retorted after being teased by her friend for her latest skimpy disaster.
'Mills, I do not dress like a mum.'
'Maybe not, but you look a bit kind of…' Millie was trying to find the right word.

'What ?'
'Blokey.'
'Oh cheers Mills, that's kind of you to say so.' Lauren shook her head, looked down at her long legs in their straight-leg jeans and smiled. Not bad pins for a bloke though.

   Thankfully, after a couple of months, Millie appeared to accept her fate. She stuck much of her new wardrobe on Ebay, repaid some of her credit card bills and rediscovered her sense of style. Lauren wasn't sure whether it was just the presence of Beth that was now making even her feel increasingly decrepit, or whether something deeper was beginning to take place. A premature mid-life crisis was not something she particularly wanted to contemplate. It had naff self-obsession written all over it.

   When Lauren returned to the front room. Beth was smoking another cigarette whilst Robert sat looking vaguely shell-shocked. She must have told him.
'So, do we all know the score now ?' Robert nodded.
'It's no big deal. People do go out on New Year's Eve. Well young people do. Old farts sit in and watch the telly.'
   Give it a rest on the age thing you sly, devious, little…Lauren stopped her thoughts before they had chance to leave her mouth and spark another futile conflagration.
'But I thought…' Robert's face was a picture of rejection.
'Well let's just eat our tea shall we before it gets cold.'
   Lauren had picked up Robert's plate from the kitchen and three sets of cutlery. She handed Beth her now coleslaw free plate which she took without acknowledgement. Robert attempted a weak smile as he took hold of his. It wasn't convincing anyone. The meal passed in relative silence. Beth made the occasional satisfied groan, and slapped her lips as she ate. Robert seemed to spend an inordinate amount of time staring down at his plate. Lauren was grateful that the little madam was going to be leaving them soon. She couldn't have been more objectionable if she tried. Robert's doting behaviour was only serving to encourage her.
   At first the food had tasted reasonable, quite nice even, but by the third piece of chicken Lauren's stomach was beginning to rebel. In truth it was foul, but that didn't appear to bother Beth who greedily stuffed her face with fries. Robert played with his food listlessly, barely putting any of it in his mouth. Finishing her last mouthful, Beth wiped her fingers on the sofa and stood up.
'Get my coat Rob.'
   Robert seemed pleased to at last be getting some attention and did as he was told. Lauren made a point of shaking her head . Beth flashed her a look of undisguised contempt. At least you knew where you stood with her. Lauren didn't flinch though. She wasn't about to be intimidated by a gobby kid.
'Bye Bye Beth. Have a good night. I'm sure Robert and I will.' Lauren couldn't resist a sarcastic riposte accompanied by a suggestive raise of the eyebrow. Two could play at being unpleasant. Even though she had no intention of attempting to jump Robert's bones, it wouldn't do Beth any harm to think she did. Beth looked at her.
   For a second they both realised who was the senior of the two, which of them was

better equipped to play manipulative games if it so suited her. The younger woman's brash, surly confidence instantly departed. As stunning as Beth looked in her outfit, her girly dinky ballet pumps and flawless make-up she knew that she couldn't compete with what Lauren had. That single phrase, that knowing lift of the eyebrow had been enough to demolish her. The last look Beth gave Lauren that evening was one of fear. It was the fear that Lauren might try and take a small part of what little she actually possessed. As the door slammed and Robert shuffled back into the front room, Lauren didn't feel quite so decrepit anymore.

For the sake of Auld Lang Syne

   Robert looked uneasy and confused, an embarrassed smile across his face.
'She's great isn't she ?'
'Are you mad ? Great ? The girl's a headcase.'
'Hey now Lauren, come on that's not…' Surely he wasn't going to defend her.
'Fucking hell Robert, did you not hear the way she spoke to you ?' Lauren was becoming increasingly animated.
'Are that's just…'
'Just nothing, she treats you like you're dirt.' She wanted to scream at him. Shake him. Tell him to snap out of it.
'Perhaps.'
'You know she does. You shouldn't let her.' Robert sat down, seemingly deep in thought. 'To be honest mate, I don't really know what you see in her.'
   That wasn't strictly true. She was attractive girl. Sure she had an air of the school of hard-knocks about her, but she was certainly not your run of the mill pram-face. Slim, yet curvy and potentially quite dirty in the bedroom. Stroppy girls often were. On that score, mens minds were pretty easy to read. They'd put up with all kinds of rubbish if the pay-off was a good regular shag.
'She's not like that all the time. Sometimes she's helpful.' He really was smitten.
'How often ?'
'Now and again.'
'Not very often then.' Lauren's tone was sharp and impatient.
'Not often no.'
'It's time for you to ditch her mate I reckon. Get someone nearer your own age.'
   The last line unintentionally reminded her of why she was here in the first place. It had slipped her mind in the comedy drama of the evening's proceedings. She was looking for clues. So far they had been thin on the ground. What would they be like anyway ? Robert was hardly likely to wear a flashing sign on his head advertising the fact he went after young girls. Now was perhaps the time to do a little probing.
'I don't ever meet women my own age.'
'You met me didn't you ?' It sounded like a come on, but that hadn't been intended.
'Yes, but that's different.'

'Why is it ?'
'Well I know you from years ago. I can talk to you. I can't talk to women my own age.'
'You talk to me ?'
'Like I said, that's different.'

   Lauren wasn't entirely sure what he could mean by that. Why was talking to her so very different to talking to any other woman in her late twenties or early thirties ? It didn't make sense, but then so many things about Robert P. Gorman didn't make sense. Not having the answers was infuriating. Usually people were so easy to read. Her confidence bolstered by a third glass of Cava, Lauren spotted an opportunity to pose the vital question.
'Robert, there was something I needed to ask you ?'
   Robert looked at her. Those eyes full of sadness and mystery, he looked so hurt and alone this evening, as if someone had just attempted to pull out his heart with their bare hands.
'Yes, ask away.' His gaze held hers and those blue eyes did that thing they did. Lauren faltered.
'Oh, it was nothing. Another time maybe.' And with that she left the room and made for the bathroom.

   Robert was turning out to be quite pleasant company. No doubt the alcohol was helping to loosen his tongue and oil the conversational cogs, but his manner had been easy and relaxed. His reclining figure, stretched out across the sofa was far from that that of the awkward stuttering inadequate he had presented just a few short weeks ago. They were going over old times, the three years they had shared together at university.
'So why did you stay in York ?' Robert asked.
'I dunno really. The job came up at Accent, I was settled here. There are worse places to live. You ?'
'I didn't really have anywhere else to call home after nan died. I had got settled over those three years at college and a chance to leave never presented itself. Or at least, I never really looked for one. You wonder about all the opportunities you've missed.' He drew a pattern with his finger on the arm of the sofa. 'Do you think you'll stay around ?'
'Ah…'
'I have asked a bad question ?'
'No, not a bad one,' she fingered her hair distractedly and looked at the carpet, 'just quite a pertinent one at present. I didn't tell you, but I'm going to be out of a job within a couple of weeks.'
'Oh god, I'm sorry to hear that. What's happened ?' He reached across from his position on the sofa and tapped the hand of Lauren who was slumped in the beanbag.
'Hey, don't worry.' She made a point of gently pulling her hand away. His touch wasn't unpleasant, she just wanted to avoid any mixed signals. There was no room for complication of any kind. 'Cost cutting and all that. Usual story I guess. The only

thing is I should now be looking for employment, and jobs in my line of work are not easy to come by.'
'Could you have to leave York ?'
'It's a distinct possibility I guess. Most of the work is in London.'
'Oh.' He didn't try and hide his disappointment.

 Despite her best attempts to remain friendly but uninvolved, Lauren couldn't help but be touched. Someone other than Francis was going to miss her.
'If I do go though, I'll keep in touch mate. It's only a couple of hours on the train and all that.'
'Seems a shame after we've only just met up again. It feels like we're getting to know each other properly and now you're going to be off again.'
'Yeah, I know. It's been cool meeting up with you.' Actually, she wasn't sure whether 'cool' was the appropriate word to use in the circumstances. Interesting maybe. It was what he needed to hear so perhaps it didn't matter too much.
'Really ?' It had clearly done the trick.
'Yeah, really.' What else could she say at this point ? She had to stretch the truth a little. 'I was a bit dubious at first if I'm being honest but you've surprised me.'
'Have I ?'
'Yeah, pleasantly so. I like your company. You're an interesting man.'
'Oh, cheers. That's…'
'Now let's change the subject before your head gets any bigger shall we ?'

 Robert asked about Millie. Lauren told her all about the New York adventure and her sudden and dramatic departure for pastures new. They discussed old course mates and Lauren filled him in on the snippets of gossip she'd heard about what everyone was up to. Her own knowledge of what everyone was doing wasn't that great, but compared to Robert, who knew nothing, she was an encyclopaedia.
'Seems like everyone has moved on.'
 Robert concluded after listening attentively. He seemed genuinely interested in all those people who had singularly ignored him when he was a student. She wondered if they still laughed about him when they got together at their neat little dinner-parties in their tidy suburban semis. In the eyes of her more conventional university peers Lauren herself was perhaps something of an oddity. Her aloofness, her unwillingness to get involved in the social round. She'd lost count of all the invitations she'd politely forgotten to decline over the years. Now they'd dried-up. No one bothered asking her to any of their get-togethers. Not that she was bothered. She had little time for the charade of professional perfection that they all liked to play out. Air-kissing and tales of promotions, talk of house prices and impending parenthood did nothing for her. She'd rather be with Robert. Hanging out with the weird kid.
'I think most of them have. I keep hearing of weddings and kids on the gossip grapevine. Bessie's still around.' That had just come out. It was unintentional. It hadn't been a cue to discuss Robert's time of employment at Acomb library. Her companion sat up from his reclining position.
'You know Bessie ?'

'Er, well I see her around.' Lauren knew she'd touched a raw nerve. Robert had made a visible flinch at the mention of Bessie's name. His twitching returned. It was like watching an electric current be applied to a dead frog. It made Lauren tense a little. It was just as he'd been prior to the coat incident on Coney Street. For the first time that evening, Lauren began to wonder if Bessie had been right to warn her off.
'D.d.d.do you see her to t.t.t.t.talk to ?' He stuttered urgently.
'I say hello, y'know…' Lauren thought it was probably wise to end the conversation as quickly as possible. She tried to remain calm and not look in any way concerned about his behaviour. The last thing she wanted to do was escalate the situation.
'H.h.h.h.ave you told h.h.h.her you've r.r.r.run into me again ?' His head was being flung violently to the side as he tried to force the jammed words out. It was painful to watch. Now Lauren was herself finding it difficult to hide her growing aggravation. She really didn't need this. She could have stayed at home.
'Well it wasn't really running into you was it.'
'You're not going to keep reminding me about all that are you ?' Robert bristled, gathering back some of his self-control.
'About what ?'
'About how we met up again. It's not good to be reminded.'
'I was only trying to be a bit light hearted. I didn't mean anything by it.' This was genuinely annoying. Why did everyone this evening want to turn the slightest little thing into some major diplomatic incident ? Why couldn't everyone just chill-out ?
'Perhaps you didn't, but even so. I'm not a nutter you know.' Twitching, freaky Robert was again superseded by poor-me Robert. He seemed to turn it on and off like a hot water tap.
'I never said you were.'
'But you've thought it haven't you ?' Lauren was becoming increasingly unsure about exactly what she thought.
'Robert, do we need this tonight ?' Avoid the question, change the subject, try and lighten the mood. 'Can't we just chill and try and enjoy ourselves.'
'OK, just don't tell Bessie you've seen me will you.' It seemed to have worked, but his little performance had been telling.
'Why not ? I don't understand.' She wanted him to tell her all about it. To explain why it was all a dreadful mix-up, how everyone got the wrong end of the stick, how he'd been cruelly persecuted just for being a bit different. He wasn't about to oblige.
'Just please respect me on this. Can we change the subject ?'
'Sure.'

    But she wasn't sure at all. Everything that had happened this evening had only served to deepen her confusion. The one thing she did know for certain was that she didn't particularly want to be cooped up alone in a flat with Robert. Just running out on him would probably make matters worse though. She needed to think 'We're nearly out of wine, so why don't we make a night of it and head to the pub. Have you ever been in The Ackhorne ?' Just like the lush voice from The Samaritans had said. Meet him in a public place. She was getting somewhere now, she was sure of it. Maybe a little more alcohol, a bit more gentle probing and he'd open up. If he did turn twitchy again at least in there she wouldn't be in any kind of

danger.
'Don't think I have. Do you want to do that with me ?'
'Er, yeah ? Why wouldn't I want to ?' Lots of reasons probably, but she wasn't about to let on. Not when she'd got this far.
'It's just I got the impression that you might not want to be seen around with me.'
'Well lose that impression right away and get your coat on mister. We're off to the pub.'

Her investigations could continue in there. If Matt was looking down on her, he'd see her right. That was his pub and she was his bird. By the end of the evening she'd have unravelled the mystery of Robert P.Gorman to her own satisfaction. There was no way he'd be leaving her this evening with his secrets intact.

Ringing in the new

The pub had been heaving with people when they arrived but they found a place to lean against a windowsill towards the back. Robert had left the house without any money and Lauren ended up standing him drinks. Outside the claustrophobic confines of the flat Robert appeared to forget some of his earlier discomfort.
'So what have you been doing with yourself for these past three years whilst you've been out of work ?'

Robert momentarily paused before answering to let a crop-headed fifty-something with a well-cultivated beer gut step past to get to the toilets.
'Nothing much really. I used to go and sit by the river. Watch life pass by. I've watched a lot of TV. Cookery programmes, chat shows. That kind of thing.'
'God man, three years of that would turn your brain to mush.'
'I think it has. My concentration's gone.'
'We need to get you fixed up with something in the New Year.' She lifted her wine glass and clinked it against Robert's. 'Here's to new beginnings.'

The conversation had been flowing as freely as the alcohol. First a couple more glasses of wine, then two pints of lager followed by three vodka lime and sodas in quick succession.
'I've not been this drunk in years Rob.'
'Rob ?'
'Oh yeah.' She pointed at him. 'I've never said that before. You don't like it do you ?'
'I don't mind anymore. Beth can't say Robert. She reckons it makes me sound like a pensioner.'
'Rob sounds like a whole different person to me. Hey, maybe you should go with Rob now. It could be like a signal to the world that you've changed and moved on. Become a new person sort-of.'
'Maybe.'

He'd knocked back just as much as Lauren over the evening but didn't appear to

be anywhere near as drunk. She was really beginning to feel the effects. Her focus was going, the room had started to spin and every inch of her body felt enveloped in a fuzz of good feelings. Then came the bright idea to round the proceedings off with a couple of single malts. Francis collected bottles of the stuff which he kept in a little pine cabinet in his room. She'd never tasted one before but liked the names - Talisker, Laphroig, Glenmorangie. They sounded warm and grown-up. She necked back a measure from the Oban distillery which she only ordered as she could easily pronounce it. Her face contorted as the sharp hot fluid hit the back of her throat.
'Brrrrrrr.' Her top half made an involuntary shake.
'Are you cold or something ?' Robert touched her shoulder, resting his hand there. He'd declined her offer and instead stood sipping on a glass of tap water.
'No, it's not that. It's the drink. Man, that's harsh.'
'Awww….didn't you like it ?' He began stroking her shoulder gently with his thumb. He was leaning in towards her but she was barely capable of noticing.
'No, I liked it. Kind of. It was weird.' She looked up and saw his head was only inches from her own. His blue-eyes were dancing around as he came in and out of focus. 'Actually, I think I need the toilet.'

Lauren splashed her face with water and tried to concentrate on her reflection. It wasn't easy.

Back in the bar Robert had been urgently awaiting her return. His twitching had started again and it wasn't going unnoticed. A group of young women were staring at him, the man on the nearby fruit machine momentarily lost his concentration to glance at Robert's jerky head. Then Lauren reappeared and the jerky movement appeared to subside. A tall, thin member of the bar staff with a spike through his bottom lip was wiping clean a glass whilst keeping an eye on what was happening. For some reason Robert and his drunken female companion were starting to set-off professional alarm bells. Something didn't seem right. No matter. He finished drying the glass and took the next order from an impatient bald man in a faded denim jacket. In no time at all it was 11.30.
'Hey I've had a thought,' a drunken Lauren pawed Robert's chest.
'What's that ?'

If you were an onlooker in the pub that night you would have seen that his body language was difficult to misinterpret. He moved as close to her as he could, his head cocked in imitation of hers, his hands regularly grazing her body. Lauren remained oblivious.
'Why don't we go outside the Minster for midnight ? That's where everyone gathers for the New Year. I've been there with Millie before.' Her face lit-up as she tried once again to bring Robert back into focus.
'And what do they do ?'
'Well, they kind of mill around and sing Auld Lang Syne, shake hands, kiss each other, that kind of thing.'
'Kiss each other.'
'Yes, they kiss each other.'
'What with tongues.'
'Sometimes. Hey you perve, I didn't kiss Millie with tongues if that's what you're

thinking.' She playfully slapped his chest and pretended to look offended.
'No, I wasn't thinking that.' He slid an arm around her back and gently stroked it.
'Shall we go then ?'
'Why not.'

  Lauren unsteadily linked his arm and together they tottered off into the night, up Bridge Street, across the bridge where only a few weeks earlier Robert had stood and contemplated calling it a day on this whole vexed life business. Groups of drunken revellers swung and sang in their own tiny worlds. For a night at least they felt heroic and legendary, creating stories they'd repeat for years, jokes that would bind them together through the trials of life, friendships sealed, friendships lost. Lauren and Robert walked together arm in arm, like any other couple. But they weren't a couple, not in that sense. They were a pair of solitaries, given permission in each others company, and aided by the alcohol to be out with the herd. This was not Lauren's natural territory by any means, and it sure as hell wasn't Robert's but together they could roam through it freely.

  Coney Street wobbled and shook with random life. A teenager was climbing the Christmas tree in St. Helen's Square. A group of girls in a long line, their arms around each other skipped up Stonegate singing ,'We're off to see the Wizard', as a gaunt homeless man carrying a tired sleeping bag in one hand, a bottle of Lambrini in the other grinned relentlessly at the madness.

  Outside the mighty towering gothic of the Minster people were gathering. Bottles of champagne were in evidence, as too were cameras, the crowds of milling young drunks supplemented by well-dressed relatively sober families, tourists and the homeless. Together they stood awaiting the turn of the year and the chime of Great Peter, the Minster bell. It signified nothing, just a random delineation of time. Lauren knew that, but tonight with Robert it felt more significant than usual. Change had a way of creeping up on you, no matter what you did to try and stave it off. Like the turning of the year and the chiming of Great Peter, its arrival was inevitable.

'Dong'

  The first of the sky-rattling chimes. Noisy, drunken cheers begin to emerge from the gathered crowd, party poppers fly, a middle-aged man with an unseasonal tan struggles with the cork on a bottle of champagne. Someone nearby launched beerily into Auld Lang Syne. Lauren linked Robert's arms and joined in.
'Should auld acquaintance be forgot and never brought to mind.' She tunelessly bellowed.

  Robert didn't sing. He just looked at her as she leant into him. He stared. Hard and fixed. His arm moving in time with the disassociated voices around them, but his face showing not a flicker of emotion. Lauren had her eyes shut, the influence of the alcohol and the cold air racheting up the discomfort Her brain had by now completely cut loose on a fuzzy stream of comforting logic. Everything would be alright, of that she was certain. The New Year would make everything better. Here she was with this special old friend of hers. What an interesting guy he was. How could they have so badly misunderstood him all those years ago ? Kids are just shallow and fickle she thought. Not like now. She was a much better judge of character these days, she could look beyond the surface and see the inner-person. In the case of Robert, that was a kind, gentle and thoughtful soul. He was naïve and honest, charming without trying to be and someone who could become a really close and special friend. Really close.

Robert's stare had now been replaced by the beginnings of a sneer, but Lauren was too drunk to notice. She took his head in her hands as much to steady herself as anything else, and placed a drunken kiss on his lips. Lauren's inebriated frame fell into his. He took it, steadied her, held her and kissed her. Hard, purposefully and with intent. The final chime of Great Peter found them wrapped in each others arms as people began to slowly move away and off into the night.

All is quiet

'Fucking hell.'

Lauren's head felt as if someone had just repeatedly hit it with a mallet. She rubbed her brow and reached out for the little battery operated alarm clock she normally kept on her bedside table. Her hand couldn't find it and the act of moving her arm intensified the agony. So she closed her eyes again in an attempt to shut the pain out. It had been a while since she'd experienced the exquisite torment of a full-blown hangover. She tried again for the alarm clock. There was nothing there. No book, no coaster, no bedside table even. Tentatively she flicked an eyelid open. There was no sign of her table. Actually, she couldn't see anything she recognised. Opening the other eye her sense of confusion grew further. This wasn't her bedroom. Where the hell was she ? She couldn't remember going home last night and why had she been sleeping completely naked. ..

…oh no…

It was then that next to her she noticed the sleeping figure of Robert. Naked. This was his bedroom. This was his bed. Neither of them had any clothes on. It wasn't that difficult to try and fill in the blanks.

Her physical symptoms, the crushing headache and the stomach which threatened to aggressively rebel against last night's excesses at any moment seemed nothing when compared to the creeping horror of her current situation. Glancing cautiously across the room, she saw a pile of clothes, some she could see were her own, others belonged to Robert. As she gently crept out of bed Robert turned and muttered something in his sleep. Lauren froze to the spot, naked and exposed, until he appeared to have settled again. Her heart rate was driving relentlessly. Its thump in her chest mimicking the angry thump in her hungover head. Moving painfully towards the pile of clothes, a floorboard made a loud creak but Robert, now lying

on his back didn't make a sound. Rifling through the clothes she found her t-shirt and jeans alright. Her socks were just to one side but there was no sign of her knickers and bra. Then she glanced at the bed and saw a bra strap peeking out from the duvet which was now hanging precariously off the bed. She tugged at it and pulled it out. Gently lifting the end of the duvet she looked to see if her knickers were in there as well. No sign of them, instead she caught sight of Robert's boxers and was momentarily grateful he hadn't been wearing any of his old y-fronts. Suddenly Robert coughed in his sleep. She couldn't take anymore chances, she needed to get out of the bedroom , the flat and the whole miserable block as quickly as she could. There was no shortage of undies back in her draw at home. She'd leave her knickers just as Cinderella left her glass slipper when she had to make her own hasty exit. Lauren wasn't sure though if Robert could ever qualify as a Prince Charming. He was lying flat on his back, his head slightly to the side. His skinny frame looked utterly sexless. Why had she…. no time for those questions now. Out in the hallway she pulled on her clothes and saw that her mac and her Converse were scattered on the floor next to Robert's reefer jacket and trainers. They'd clearly been in a hurry. Now the coughing started again, this time more prolonged.
'Fuck, fuck, fuck,' she muttered under her breath.

She struggled to find the arm holes in her t-shirt, as the coughing continued. Surely he must be awake and if he was awake.
'Beth,' a sleepy confused voice came from the bedroom. Lauren hurriedly pulled on her jeans, picked up her coat and shoes and ran out of the flat barefoot, trying not to bang the door behind her. 'Beth,' the voice repeated. All was silent again until the peace was broken by a ringing tremor of a snore.

Barefoot, clutching the clothes she hadn't managed to put on she ran down the stairs and out of the block. Leaning against the wall she attempted to steady herself and pull on a sock. Her head was pounding mercilessly, every step had been intensified by the lack of cushioning on her feet. Her flight mechanism had carried her this far, but now her physical reality was clawing for a bit of attention.
'You in a hurry love ?' Sitting just to the side of the doorway was the beggar guy she'd seen previously, he was grinning at her and tapping a bottle of wine with his ring finger. Lauren wasn't really in the mood for small talk.
'None of your business.' Her voice was cracked, hoarse and husky as she pulled on her right Converse and tried to keep her balance.
'Lover boy not live up to expectations then ?'
'Pardon ?'
'Your fella, not much cop were he ?' He took a drag on a skinny roll-up and smiled to himself. 'I'd 'ave seen ya right,' he winked at her and took a swig of his wine.
'Just piss off will you.'
'Oooh, charming. I would if I had anywhere to piss off too love. I was only trying to make conversation.'
'Well don't. I've got a fuck-off hangover and I'm in a hurry.'
'I never get hangovers. I don't stop drinking long enough for them to kick-in.' He held out his bottle to her as a consolatory gesture. 'Ere, do you want some. Hair of the dog like ?'

As she pulled on her other Converse the feeling of an imminently impending hurl overcame her. She doubled up as an empty retch coursed through her midriff.
'You not well then ?'
But she couldn't answer as a stomach full of vomit was propelled up and out of her system, splattering the wall and pavement. There was clear evidence of last night's KFC in the stinking discharge as it oozed its way down the wall of the block.
'You're not well. Do you want me to fetch owt like ? Can I get you some water from somewhere or summat ?'
'No, thank you, but no. I just need to get home.'
Wiping her face, she didn't particularly care what she looked like. All she knew was that she needed to get back to the safety of her own place, her own bed and to try and forget about this whole sordid experience. None of this was right.
'Well take care won't you love.' The beggar guy's voice was full of concern.
'Yes I will.' Looking up from her vomit she caught his gaze, its gentleness momentarily softening the pound in her head and the soreness of her insides. 'Thanks.'

She had no idea what the time was, she hoped it was early before the tourists had chance to emerge from their Bed & Breakfasts for a New Year's Day saunter around the city. If she looked anything liked she felt, then the sight of her would not be pleasant. As it happened, Blossom Street was almost empty, one middle-aged man was walking a Yorkshire Terrier, he gave her a long studied gaze, filing her in his brain in the section marked, 'New Year's Eve casualties'. A young woman in a pinny was sweeping up glass from the front of the Premier Lodge, a look of abject misery plastered across her face. She probably had to forego a night out to get into work on New Years Day morning, cleaning up the mess of other peoples revelries. If it still was morning of course. Lauren couldn't be sure of anything at present.

Micklegate stank of piss and vomit. It must still be early. She knew from experience that the smell would subside as the day passed and shopkeepers and residents began their regular clean-up exercise. A couple of shop windows were smashed and a security alarm was still screeching for attention from the wall of a hair salon. Tell-tale blood drips were dotted across the pavement at irregular intervals. A traffic cone sat on top of a BMW which had had its wing mirrors bent inwards. Two large blokes with shaven heads in expensive white and striped shirts were sitting in the doorway of a clothes shop, fast asleep on one another, half-drunk bottles of Smirnoff Ice falling out of their failing grasp.

With her head down she pushed on, across Parliament Street giving any sign of life a wide-berth, down Goodramgate, through Monk Bar, across Lord Mayors Walk and into the Groves. As she turned the corner into her street, she saw Sally their neighbour running in her direction looking toned and immaculate in lycra. Her hair in a high pony-tail swung like a perky schoolgirl's and a cheesy smile was fixed across her face.
'Oh hi Lauren.'
Devastatingly, Sally decided to stop and chat.
'Hi.'

So near yet so far. Lauren thought nurses were meant to be hard-faced and careworn. Sally looked as if she'd just stepped out of a tampon commercial.
'Were you out last night ?' Sally and her perfect boyfriend were hard to bear at the best of times.
'Yes, I was out last night.' No, she just walked around with vomit in hair as a fashion statement.
'Oooh, lucky you. Muggins here had to work didn't she.' Sally rolled her eyes.
'Oh, right.' She wasn't feeling particularly lucky at the minute.
'Yes, it was my turn. I've avoided a shift on New Years Eve until now so I suppose I can't complain. Poor old Luke sat in on his own all evening bless him.'
'Poor him.' Right now Lauren would have loved to have turned the clock back herself and spent an evening sitting in, not drinking, not falling into the bed of a dodgy old college friend.
'Ooh that reminds me. I've not had chance to speak to you since I gave them your phone number at the hospital.'
'Sorry ?'
'Y'know about that old friend of yours who they found in the river. I told them I knew a Lauren Seymour. It was me.' Of course it was. 'Do you see much of him ? How's he doing ?'
'Oh, he's OK.' Clearly she'd just seen rather more of him than was strictly necessary.
'Good. The poor guy. Fancy jumping in the river. I can't imagine how anyone could ever do something like that ?'
 At this present moment Lauren understood precisely why some one would want do something like that. To get away from a braying Sally she'd probably even consider setting herself on fire, such was the exquisite nature of the torture she inflicted.
'No, me neither,' she lied.
'Anyway,' Sally tapped her arm. 'Must dash. New fitness regime.' Sally made a running gesture with her arms. 'I'm feeling like such a porker after Christmas.' From what Lauren could see, Sally didn't appear to have a millimetre of superfluous flesh on her body. 'No more Quality Streets for me.'
'No'
'Glad you had a great night anyway. Catch ya' later !' She hollered with a mock Californian intonation as her pristine white trainers and dinky sport socks began to make off down the street.
'Ah go fuck yourself.'
 Lauren scratched her head and sauntered off towards her front door. Feeling in her coat pocket for her key it wasn't in its usual place. Cue the inevitable panic and the feeling that yes, she was in a cheesy novel, and yes she was going to have to head back to Robert's flat to find the damn thing. Alternatively, she was going to have to sit on the step and bear the curiosity of the neighbours until Francis got back from Leeds. Mind you, she didn't think he was back until tomorrow so it could be a long wait. To her relief she placed her hand on the front door key which had been zipped-up in an inside pocket for extra-safe keeping. At least some small part of her had been planning ahead last night.

There were clearly benefits to being anti-social. The house felt like a sanctuary. Making straight for the kitchen she filled up the kettle and looked for the coffee. Her usual mug hung from a hook under the wall unit. She found the aspirin in the draw , poured herself a glass of water and knocked them back. As the cold water hit her stomach it turned a somersault forcing an audible groan from her mouth. Why oh why had she done this too herself ? There was just enough milk in the fridge for one hot drink . She had forgotten to buy any yesterday as Francis had requested. Taking her mug she sat down on the sofa in the front room, her head leaning back against the soft of the cushion. There she sat and tried hard not to contemplate what she had just done. Her brain for once wanted to play ball. It had thankfully gone into hangover recovery shut-down mode. It was in no mood for probing the whys and the wherefores of her latest disaster just yet.

The wall clock said it was ten to eleven. Morning at least. She wondered if Robert had yet managed to rise from the bed they'd been sharing only an hour or so ago. Was he now starting to realise what had happened between them ? If indeed anything had happened between them. She had no way of knowing, other than the circumstantial evidence of having woken up naked in bed with a similarly unadorned man. This usually only meant one thing.

At nearly 33 it didn't seem right. That was the kind of high-risk irresponsible thing you did when you were in your late teens and early twenties. Not now. Her peers were happily settled, some with families, or at the very least were assured singletons unlikely to ever end up having a random forgotten shag.

Now was not the time to try and work this out. Now was the time for sleep. Leaving her coffee half-drunk she took herself upstairs. Peeling off her smoky clothes, she pulled on her oversized Franz Ferdinand t-shirt and fell into her own bed. The way it fitted her body and the smell of it reassured her. Everything was sure to be alright. The sanctuary of sleep came soon enough.

Regrets, she has a few

When she finally woke, her room was dark. The streetlights sent out shafts of aggressive light. Her alarm clock said it was 4.30 PM. For a moment she lay in bed blissfully unaware of the circumstances in which she'd found herself earlier in the day. Then slowly the crushing recollection of the night before crept mercilessly back into her consciousness.

'Oh fucking hell no !'

She kicked the mattress with her right leg in angry appalled frustration. She needed to have a bath and wash away the dirt of the previous evening's adventure. She needed to rid herself of the mental and physical grime as quickly as possible. Pulling herself out of bed she picked up all her clothes and hurled them violently in the wash basket. Even looking at them was troubling, and their mixed mingled smell of smoke, alcohol, vomit and Robert's flat irritated her agitated brain even further.

The bath though was soothing as her hangover slowly began to ebb away. She found a carton of orange juice in the fridge which she drank whilst lying in the hot foamy water. Physically at least she was feeling more human again. Now she needed to get to grips with all this and try and plot a way forward. In her past experience the bath was always a great place to try and work things out. This was a time for drastic action.

There was nothing for it but to completely sever her ties with Robert. It wouldn't be easy but it was for the best. This whole business had been a mistake. What had led her believe that she could help turn his life around ? What great catalogue of success stories could she point to that would qualify her for the role of informal life-coach ? Robert was not her responsibility and if she had after a very drunken night fallen into his bed then it meant absolutely nothing. It was just one of those unfortunate incidents which happen sometimes. It's pointless trying to turn the clock back or attempting to make them into something they're not. Robert wouldn't be playing any further part in her life. Of that she was absolutely certain.

'Lauren we need to talk. R xx'

The message on her phone stopped her in her tracks. She sat eating cheese on toast in her dressing gown as some forgettable romantic comedy played on the TV in the background. How did she respond ? Her first reaction was to delete it, erase his number from her phone and divert her brain every time it tried to consider Robert P. Gorman. She soon found his number in her mobile's address book. Staring at it, her finger paused about to hit the key to send it into the nothing . But for some reason she hesitated. She just wasn't able to. For now she'd do nothing. Watch the film. Have an early night. Then the phone beeped again.

'Don't blank me Lauren. Rxx'

She sat, her mouth open as she stared at the screen. Now what ? Despite needing to drop off her now empty plate in the sink and to nip to the toilet she found herself unable to move from her perch on the sofa. Time appeared to stop. Then the phone beeped again.

'If you don't answer me. I'm coming round.'

This immediately shook her out of her dumbstruck inaction. She couldn't allow that to happen. Wait a minute. What if he did come round ? Maybe she could get out before he arrived. Alternatively she could just shut all the curtains , turn off the lights, lock the door and pretend she wasn't in. Why should she let herself be intimidated into responding when she didn't want to ? It was no good. She started trying to type a message.

'Can we talk later in the week ? I'm tired.'

She paused a second before hitting send. If she could buy herself a little more time then maybe she'd be able to work out how she was going to handle all this. Under normal circumstances she would now be in conversation with Millie or Francis about where to go next. Doubtless they'd back her up, provide the necessary support she needed to do what was right. They always did. This time though, things were different. Having been told by her two closest friends that under no circumstances was she to associate with Robert again, informing them that she'd woken up in bed with him this morning would probably not go down too well. No, this time at least she was entirely on her own.

The text messages stopped. No further word was forthcoming from Robert. This could be viewed one of two ways. On the one hand it could mean that he had decided not to press the issue any further this evening, alternatively it could mean that he was already on his way round to her house. Keeping all this from Francis was going to be difficult. The last thing she needed was Robert deciding to be persistent and knocking on her door at any time soon. Partly out of fear of what the night might have in store for her she took yet another early night. These were becoming something of a habit, but in her own bed at least she couldn't do anyone any harm.

Not letting matters lie

There was a loud vigorous knock at the door. The house was otherwise dark and silent.

1:52 AM

Lauren jumped up with a start. She sat frozen in the black of her room, the dull thump of her heartbeat audible in the silence. Then there was quiet. Then another knock, this time longer, louder, more persistent. Angrier perhaps ? Lauren crept out of bed as if she was being watched and slowly stepped down the stairs. She'd seen all the movies where the heroine had decided to face the impending danger rather than just running away. In every case Lauren had been screaming at her not to open that door, not to go down that dark alleyway, not to go and find the lost little puppy. Now she found herself instinctively doing something similar. Perhaps she'd be more understanding in future.

The knock had been half expected, her sleep had been broken and filled with short aggressive dreams, a sure sign of a troubled mind. Part of her was relieved. At least if this was happening now, the nervous waiting had come to an end. Another part of her felt anger. This was in no way called for or justified. How dare they attempt to frighten her like this. She wasn't about to lie there and wish it all away like a passive victim.

It had all gone silent again. Sitting at the bottom of the stairs she could hear footsteps in the backyard. The dodgy lock on the back gate meant that it had been effectively left unlocked for months, allowing access for anyone who wanted to get inside. Francis had been talking about getting it fixed for weeks, but like everything else in their elegant hovel, it remained undone. Picking up a metal tray from the kitchen she crept towards the backdoor. Shadows flitted across it and then suddenly a face pressed itself up against the frosted glass.
'I know you're fucking in there Lauren.' It was a female voice.
  Her mind paused for a second trying to adjust its thinking to take account of this revelation. Of course she was expecting Robert.
'If you don't open the bastard door and let me in I'll kick it in.' It was a voice she recognised.
'If you don't go I'll call the police.' Lauren's voice hadn't been anywhere near as commanding as she'd intended.
'Call wonder woman if you like, I'm not going anywhere until I've spoken to you.' That sneering aggressive and sarcastic tone of voice could only belong to one person.
'Is that Beth ?'
'No, it's bloody Abi Titmuss. Now are you going to let me friggin in or what? I'm freezing me tits off out 'ere'
  Despite her better judgement, Lauren began to turn the key in the lock but before she had chance to open the door, Beth had forced her way in. She made a dive for Lauren, pushing her down onto the kitchen worktop. Holding her by her t-shirt, her nose was almost touching Lauren's as her angry contorted face spat the words.
'You fucking shagged him didn't you ?'
'What are you talking about you fucking mentalist ?'
  It was not easy to think straight in this prone position, but Lauren was determined she wasn't going to be freaked by a girl. The sharp edge of the kitchen unit was digging into her back. Stiffening, she tried to slow her racing heart beat and look her attacker straight in the eye. Beth would be sure to exploit even the slightest trace of fear. She knew she had the beating of Beth, it was just a case of trying to box a little clever.
'You fucked Robert.' Beth was not about to let up, but this time her spitting accusation sounded less angry, more desperate. It was enough of an insight for Lauren to begin to fight back. What else propelled a young woman like Beth around to another woman's house in the early hours of the morning if it wasn't jealousy ? And jealousy was a weakness. She would have a need to be reassured.
'I don't know what you're talking about.' Lauren deliberately softened her tone.
'Yes you bloody do. You slept at his flat last night.' Beth's grip loosened slightly.
'Oh, you think I…' Think quickly Lauren. Beth was in the same clothes she'd been wearing the previous evening. Her breath reeked of alcohol and cigarettes. 'I slept on the floor. I just kipped over it was no big deal.'
'That's not what Robert say's.' Bloody hell, what had he been telling her ? 'He told me he'd shagged you.'
'Well you can tell Robert that he's a fucking liar then. I didn't have sex with him

Beth. I don't fancy him. Nothing happened. You've got to believe me.'
 Whatever the truth of the situation, and Lauren didn't honestly know what that might be, there was no way she was going to tell Beth or anyone else anything. Nothing happened . That was her truth and everybody else would just have to accept it. Beth glared at her. Her eyes were red raw and bloodshot. They looked as if she'd been crying.
 'Nothing happened ?' What remained of her grip dissolved.
 Lauren gently began to pull away.
'No, nothing happened. Now can I make you a cup of tea or something seeing as you came all this way.' It was hardly a social call, but what the hell. Needs must. Beth stood in the kitchen looking foolish, alone and helpless.
'Er, 'ave you got any Diet Coke ?' She giggled girlishly and made for the front room.

 Beth sat cross-legged on the floor eating Pringles and drinking her diet coke. Her sparkling New Year's Eve dress was dishevelled, her hair was matted and greasy. She pushed her bottom lip out and kept casting Lauren self-pitying looks. Lauren in turn wondered what the hell was happening. It was 2:30 in the morning and here she was entertaining a slightly mental teenage single-mum with fizzy pop and crisps. Something was not right somewhere.
'So why did you come all this way then ?'
'Gonna kick yer 'ead in won't I.' Beth crunched down on a crisp and forced her tiny hand into the tube for another.
'Charming.' Beth had been so matter of fact about it. As if it were obvious. She looked at Lauren with her hand still forced down the crisp tube .
'Well, I thought you'd shagged Rob so I was within my rights.'
 Lauren couldn't ever remember reading anything about that particular inalienable dictum in the human rights act but decided not to say anything.
'Well I didn't shag him.'
'So you say.' She shot her a suspicious glance. Clearly she still wasn't totally convinced.
'Nothing happened.' Lauren hoped she wasn't protesting too much. ' It really didn't. What has Robert been telling you ?'
'Oh 'e were bragging about it.' Finally she secured three Pringles, eased out her hand and looked at them.
'He was ?'
'Yeah, I told him I'd got off with this lad I used to go to school with, make him jealous like. It were only a snog, nowt happened. He wanted to touch me tits but I wouldn't let him.' She put all three crisps in her mouth at once and crunched down dramatically.
'Sorry, this happened when ?' Lauren was trying not to be distracted by the sight of Beth noisily snacking.
'Last night, well, this morning it were.' She spoke with her mouth full. ' Or yesterday morning. I've not been to bed yet.' No wonder she looked so tired. She put her hand to her greasy looking hair, ran it over her ponytail, sniffed it and pulled a face.
'Carry on, you were with this lad'

'Oh aye, inside Toffs. That's where we ended up. We were having a laugh together and then it just sort of happened.'

From what Lauren remembered about her times of visiting Toffs nightclub it was almost impossible to leave without having at least one random tongue sandwich with someone dodgy.

'Of course.' She was in no position to take the moral high-ground.

'Yer not mad then. That I got off with someone when I'm going out with yer mate ?'

'No, I've been there myself.' Getting off with someone other than her boyfriend that is, not just Toffs.

'Oh, nice one,' she smiled, 'and he's a right fit lad 'an all.'

'Robert didn't take this news well then ?'

'He went piggin mental. Ranting and raving. Calling me a slut and all the names under the sun.'

'He didn't try and…'

'What ? Hit me ?' Lauren nodded. 'Nah, he just went ballistic for a bit then sat down on the sofa crying his eyes out. I told him I thought he weren't a real man, for crying like, then he told me that you'd spent the night and you'd been shagging.'

'Beth…'

'What ? Did you shag him ?'

'No, it's not that. I just wondered if you thought that the age difference between you and Robert might be a bit big.'

'Saying I'm too young for him ?'

'Not that, it's just that some people might say that he was a bit too old for you.'

'Course he's too old. He's a boring old fart. Don't know what I see in him.'

'Really ?' This was a revelation.

'Oh aye. I'm right bored of him now. He's good with Christopher and he's kind, but he's not as fit as Pikey'

'Pikey ?'

'E's the lad I got off with. They call him Pikey cos he used to look like a gypo. He's dead horny now though.'

'Does he fancy you then ?'

'I reckon he does. Problem is though, as soon as I tell blokes about me little lad then they don't wanna know me.'

'But Robert didn't ?'

'No, he were alright about it. Which is why I like him. Beggars can't be choosers and all that.'

Lauren wasn't sure whether Beth meant herself or Robert was the beggar. From what she'd seen of Beth she was even beginning to wonder if Robert might be punching above his weight.

'So do you think you'll stick with him ?'

'Probably for a bit. I don't know to be honest. See if I get any better offers.'

'And where's Robert now?'

'Fuck knows to be honest. I came off round here and he headed up Holgate Road into Acomb. Could be anywhere. He's probably got another 17 year old girl up there

he's shagging. I reckon he thinks he's a right Mr Stud Muffin.' Beth was cackling to herself, giving Lauren a full view of her semi-masticated crisps. 'Ey, can I kip on your sofa ? I don't want to go back to the flats tonight. Would you mind ?'
'Considering you came round here to kick my head in I should probably say no.' Beth made her eyes big and wide. She looked young and vulnerable. Lauren felt her resolve beginning to melt. What harm would it do ? Just for one night.
'Oh go on', Beth reached across and touched Lauren on the leg. Looking up at her like a mannered little girl lost she began flickering her eyelashes.
'Oh, alright then. But you've got to get off early in the morning. My housemate will be back and if he finds you here there'll be some explaining to do.'
'Ahh nice one. You're alright you y'know.' Beth patted Lauren's knee and smiled. Stretching out on the sofa, her heavy eyelids dropping she was soon asleep. Lauren looked at her lying there in her soiled party dress and leggings. Sleep came instantly, as if someone had just flicked an off switch. With her knees tucked up underneath her, and her soft delicate features finally at rest she looked a picture of innocence. Lauren wondered how such a childlike creature could already be a mother. Turning off the light, she took herself up to bed and thought about the passing of the years.

Decisions come back to haunt her

'Lauren, please explain to me why there is a grubby looking teenage girl stretched out on my sofa in the front room please ?' Francis, his face bright red, was standing with his hands on his hips at the door of Lauren's bedroom. Lauren jumped up suddenly from her woozy semi-conscious state.
'Eh ? What is this…fuck !'
'Fuck indeed miss .You do realise that you're meant to be back at work this morning and it's now 11:30.' He was tapping his watch impatiently.
'Oh no, I…' She tried to hide her head from the burning of her housemates angry glare. But it was no use.
'I'd get your arse out of your pit ASAP. You've got some explaining to do.' He stomped down the stairs, the force threatening to put his foot through each step as he did so. Francis was clearly not a happy bunny.
  Beth sat crossed leg on the sofa eating a bowl of dry Sugar Puffs looking on as Lauren attempted to explain away her presence to an irate Francis.
'You know how I feel about random young women Lauren.'
'Eh less of the random mate.' Beth shouted.
'Don't you know it's rude to listen in to people's conversations young lady ?' Francis retorted.
'Well don't talk about me then and I won't have to listen will I.'
  Francis glared at her and pulled the kitchen door shut. They moved to the far end

of the galley kitchen out of earshot and lowered the tone of their voice.
'Where did you find her?'
'She's Robert's girlfriend.' Replied Lauren sheepishly.
'The child molesters girlfriend? That's her? She's only a kid. What's he doing with her?'
'It's not a sordid as it seems. She's quite feisty.'
'You're telling me. She told me to piss off when I came in. Said I was perving at her. In my own house, me? Perving at a teenage girl. Who does she think I am?'
'Look, it was just for one night. She came around here in the early hours after having had a really bad row with Robert. She needed somewhere to stay so I said she could.' It wasn't that complicated. Why was he being so unreasonable?
'Hasn't she got parents? Doesn't she have family or friends her own age? Why did she come round here?' Francis was clearly not buying any of this. Attempting to conceal the truth from possibly the most perceptive man in York was never easy. Thankfully Lauren had never previously had much cause to try.
'She couldn't go there. It's complicated. Please just trust me on this one will you. She'll be gone in a while.'

Despite wanting to hide the full story of the previous couple of nights, Lauren felt as she was in the right here. What kind of person would have kicked that exhausted and confused young girl out onto the street in the early hours of the morning? Not her certainly, and she suspected that had Francis actually been there he wouldn't have done so either. He had a softer heart than she did.
'You've seen him again haven't you?'
'Seen who?'
'You know full well who.' Francis was impatient.
'No I haven't seen him, I promise.' She blustered unconvincingly.
'Don't lie to me Lauren. I can tell by your face.' Lauren didn't know what to say. Just then the kitchen door opened and Beth poked her head around the door.
"Ey Lauren, yer left yer watch at Rob's flat. Brought it with me.' She was grinning at her.
'Oh, thank you.' At least she hadn't just produced Lauren's left behind knickers. A watch might be easier to explain away. Francis had a face like thunder.

The little bitch knew full well what she was doing thought Lauren. There was nothing innocent or childlike about the scheming little gob-shite. Beth had beaten her. In her own home as well. At that moment Lauren could have walked over and slapped her smug grinning little face.
'I'm going for a walk and by the time I get back I want this young lady out of my house.' Francis barged past them both and made for the front door.

Beth was leaning back on the sofa picking dirt out from under her nails, which she rubbed between her forefinger and thumb before dropping it onto the carpet. She didn't appear to be in any hurry to leave just yet. Lauren sat opposite her cradling a cup of tea.
'You in trouble then?'
'Mind your own business.' What did she think the nasty little bitch.

'I was only asking.'
'Well don't. I've had enough of you.' The time for small talk had long since gone.
'Oooh, listen at you mardy-arse. I come round to see you and this is the thanks I get.'
'You wanted to kick my head in if I remember rightly.'
'Perhaps I should have done anyway. Is that bloke going to have a go at you ?'
'Which bloke ?' Momentarily Lauren thought she meant Robert. In this drama she'd forgotten about him. Probably for the best.
'The fat gay one.'
'Yes, Francis is more than likely going to have a go at me. There. Satisfied.'
'That's a shame.' Beth grinned. There was a knock at the door.
'Oh god, who's that now.' Lauren flung a frustrated hand up in the air.
'I'll get it shall I ?'

Before Lauren had chance to stop her Beth was up and darting towards the front door. Shortly after Lauren heard the sound of Beth speaking to someone. Her tone was becoming raised and irate. After about a minute Lauren heard the front door slam and saw Robert's head appear sheepishly around the door to the lounge.
'What the fuck are you doing here ?'
Beth barged past him and sat back down on the sofa.
'I texted him didn't I. Told him to come round and see me here if he wanted me.'
'You did what ?' Talk about making yourself at home. Now she had another headache to add to the mix of this morning's complications.
'I just told you. Were you not listening ?' Beth looked across at Robert who was anxiously hanging onto the door frame. 'Get your dozy arse in here Rob and stop standing there looking like a melon.'

Robert crept inside. He caught Lauren's eye and gave a little pathetic wave of acknowledgement. Lauren thought she must have been exceptionally hammered to ever consider jumping into bed with this nervous inadequate.
'Do you two mind ? This is my house here.'
'It's not though is it. It belongs to the fat bloke and he's mad with you.'
'Don't call him that, and he doesn't want you here either, so if you don't mind.'
'Don't mind what ? I don't mind anything.' Beth was now conducting the proceedings flawlessly. Every line, every gesture asserted her mastery of the drama she'd initiated. Despite her bubbling anger, Lauren had to admit that it was quite a performance.
'Beth shouldn't we just…' Robert tried to half-heartedly intervene.
'Just what Rob ? You tell me what we should just do.'
'I don't think we should…'
'No you shouldn't be here Robert. You shouldn't bloody be here.' Lauren had had enough and rose quickly, pointing towards the door for them both to go but directing her sight at Robert who was now under siege from both women.
'Don't you speak to him like that you old cow.' Beth jumped to her feet and stood hard against Lauren, who made herself big and refused to budge. Who did the little squirt think she was ?
'I beg your pardon.'

'You heard me first time.' Beth jabbed Lauren in the stomach. 'Don't speak to him like he's some kind of idiot. You're always doing it.'
'And you're not ?' Lauren jabbed her back.
'He's my fucking boyfriend love, I can speak to him how I like.'
'Can we just…' Robert attempted to pacify the two of them, putting a dividing arm between to the two women as they squared up to take things further.
'Go Robert. Just go and take this slag of yours with you.'
'Now Lauren, I don't think that's very fair of you.'
'Yeah, you're the one who slept with someone else's boyfriend.'
'I did not sleep with him Beth.' Robert looked at his feet. 'Tell her I didn't sleep with you Robert. Tell her.'
'Lauren I…'
'Are you going to tell her ?'
'I don't…' Lauren turned to face Robert, grabbed him by the collar of his reefer jacket and gave him a quick angry shake.
'Tell her Robert. Fucking tell her.'
'Tell her what exactly Lauren ?' It was the clear baritone voice of Francis who was now standing watching the three of them argue at the other end of the front room. How long he'd been standing there, none of them could say. This was Beth's cue to really let rip.
'Oh, your slag of a housemate slept with my boyfriend the other night.' Beth had a smug look of supreme satisfaction on her face. 'So what you gonna do now then eh ? She's a slutty, lying little bitch who shags other girl's blokes.' Beth walked across towards Francis who looked down his nose at her , surveying her gravely and wondering how she'd ever got to be in his quiet little house. Beth in turn stood on her toes , peered right into his eyes, and whispered. 'She lied to you.' Tapping him on the shoulder she sauntered out, leaving the chaos she'd initiated behind her. As the door slammed shut, Lauren fell to her knees dramatically and began to cry.

   Robert crouched down next to Lauren and began stroking her hair.
'Robert, if you wouldn't mind leaving my house please.' Francis stood over the crouched couple, pointing in the direction of the door.
'But I just want to make sure Lauren is alright. This is my fault.' He looked up at Francis and pleaded.
'Could you just go please Robert.' He reiterated firmly with little expression in his usually colourful voice. Francis walked to the far end of the room held the door to the hallway open and gestured for Robert to leave.
'Lauren ?' He stroked her back, tears now beginning to well in his eyes, his voice becoming broken and thin.
'Go Robert, please go.' She sobbed. Robert stood up, walked across to the hallway door, paused and looked back. He was about to say something, but his words were lost before they'd found a voice. He took one last tear-filled glance at the crouched figure of Lauren on the floor and then he left the house. Francis walked across to Lauren, slowly eased his bulky frame down onto his knees and held his housemate. After a few minutes of holding her and allowing her to cry, he pulled away and stood up.

'Now I'm going to put the kettle on and you're going to sit down and tell me what all this has been about.'

The truth will out

Lauren's face was red raw from crying. She sat cradling another mug of tea and staring blankly into the middle-distance. The statue of the Virgin Mary looked at her dolefully, seeming to at least partly understand. When Francis had handed over the tea she'd noticed that his hand was shaking. He looked white and drawn. He hated confrontations of any kind and it felt as if she had betrayed his good nature by bringing this one into his home.
'It's a good job I bought some milk on the way home. I knew you'd forget.' Francis took a sip from his mug . 'So, where do you want to begin ?' Lauren just shrugged. 'The last I knew you were going to be spending New Year's Eve sitting in watching TV. Then what happened ?' She shrugged again. 'Look, you either start talking to me or I start considering whether or not to continue with your tenancy.'
'Oh I'm a tenant now am I ?' It was the verbal equivalent of giving her a slap around the face.
'Well, the minute you decide that we're no longer friends as you seem to have done, then you become a lodger.'
'I never said we weren't friends ?' That hurt. That wasn't nice.
'But that's how you've been acting. You've been getting very secretive.'
'Am I not allowed some privacy then ?'
'Of course, just don't go behind my back like this. You promised me you wouldn't see him again. So I need to know what happened and what you're planning on doing about it.'
'I went round to his flat on New Year's Eve. He invited me. I wanted to visit just once more to see if I could tell anything from his behaviour.'
'Tell what ?'
'Well, whether or not he was likely to be the kind of person to do what he was meant to have done.' It all seemed so perfectly clear to her. It really wasn't a big deal.
'Stop being so bloody vague Lauren. Men like that are tricky, manipulative bastards. They don't go around advertising the fact. The guy got the sack from his job as he was alleged to have tried to make a move on a 13 year old girl.'
'Yes, alleged. Only alleged.'
'You are still making excuses for him.'
'I'm not. I'm just trying to see both sides of the story.' This was becoming exasperating.
'You really disappoint me.' Francis shook his head and turned away.
'I think you've already made that fact abundantly clear.'

'I thought you had more gumption than this.'
'I have Francis, I bloody have. I know what I'm doing.'
'So you knew what you were doing when you slept with him did you ?'
'I didn't sleep with him. I know I didn't sleep with him.' Why couldn't he just let up ?
'That's not what the gobby girl said is it ? Tell me the truth.'

   Lauren blew her nose on the slowly fragmenting piece of toilet tissue she'd been holding. The chances of keeping any of this to herself now were minimal. Francis had slipped into his Grand Inquisitor mode and was not about to be thrown off the scent.
'Ok, Ok, It can't get any worse I suppose.' Francis raised an eyebrow. He didn't seem convinced. 'Robert and I went out drinking that's all…'
'And ? Carry on.' This was painful. She didn't want to have to think about it.
'We went to the Minster for midnight and ended up kissing. The next thing I knew I was waking up in his bed.'
'Next to him ?'
'Yes.'
'Naked ?' Lauren nodded and then held her head in her hands. 'So you're telling me you were drunk and you don't know what happened ?' Lauren nodded again. 'For once Lauren, you've left me completely speechless.' Just shut up then thought Lauren, but he continued anyway. 'I know you said you wanted to help him out but isn't this taking it a bit too far ? I do hope you took precautions.'
 Good god no. Lauren hadn't considered that. She had no idea whether or not anything actually happened, never mind whether or not they'd used a condom. She couldn't say anything and instead just sat there, her face frozen in horror.
'You don't know do you ?'
Lauren shook her head. This was just getting worse.

Forced to face up

   Lauren phoned work and made apologies for her no show. Some excuse about having a stomach bug or other. Not that she cared what they thought anymore. They were hardly likely to sack her. The mood in the house had been strained. Francis spent much of the afternoon playing the piano, seemingly deep in thought. She'd sat in her room reading and listening to her Ipod, only venturing out to go to the toilet or make a cup of tea. Her brief encounters with her housemate had been tense and few words were spoken. The next morning Lauren was grateful to get back into her office, if only for a little discipline and order. A pile of assignments filled up her in-tray. There was stacks of stuff to tie-up before she left, still none the wiser about where to go next. The thought had crossed her mind to chance her arm at going freelance. The idea of sitting on her computer in her bedroom seemed deeply attractive. That way she would be able to minimise further her dealings with the rest of the world. Every time she attempted to take herself out of her comfortable little box disaster appeared to strike. Maybe it would be better to just sit inside.

Work had been relatively easy. She flew through stuff, including items that should have been dealt with before Christmas. It was better to keep her mind busy. She knew that there was a clear and present need for her to regain some control over her life. This random chaos in which she'd been living of late was doing nothing for her mental well-being. The first step in imposing some order would be to sever all her ties with Robert. It was the obvious thing to do. All this had begun with that fateful phone-call in the early hours, now she needed to end it. He had no further role to play in her life. After the incident of yesterday morning she hoped he would be in no hurry to push matters further. It was perhaps better that their peculiar relationship should have ended in the way in which it did. A sudden dramatic situation like that at least served as a neat full-stop. There would no drawn out drifting apart. This way they could both make a clean break knowing exactly where they stood. It wouldn't be easy. Despite everything she had to admit to herself that she did have feelings towards him. He had been an interesting and intriguing diversion, but where would a friendship, never mind a full-blown relationship with Robert. P.Gorman actually go ? There were far too many grey areas in his past, far too much oddness about his character for her to totally fall for the little-boy-charm and quirky good looks. No, she could at least tell herself that she'd been there for Robert when he needed her most. Now he was slowly getting back on his feet it might perhaps be time to leave him be . She was no longer sure that she could be much use to him. Not with all the complications of what happened the other evening. There was though one other possible complication that could have come out of her recent entanglement with the weird kid. One she didn't want to particularly contemplate but knew she had to.

Millie would have known what to have done. Lauren stood staring at the row of pregnancy testing kits on the shelf at Boots. A middle-aged shop assistant was hovering behind her.
'Can I help you at all?' She inquired.
'Oh erm no I was just…' The woman smiled at her, touched her on the shoulder and walked off. Finally laying her hand on the cheapest she could find Lauren picked it up and looked at it. It looked wrong in her hand. Hurriedly reading the back of the box she realised it would be of little use to her yet. She needed to find out as soon as possible, whereas most of the tests didn't seem to be able to tell her much until the first day of a missed period. That was too long for her to wait. Not knowing was the worst part. Another box had a more impressive design and the word "early" in the title. It claimed to be able to tell between seven to ten days from the date of conception. Today was the 7th January. She'd take that one, try it and if it came back as negative she do the same test in a week's time. Picking up eye-cream and a bag of low calorie cheese and chive crisps to go to the checkout with, she placed all the items down on the conveyor and tried not to catch the eye of the operator.

The passive faced assistant told her the total, she handed over a twenty pound note, picked up the change and hastily shoved the lot in her bag. Leaving via the Coney Street exit she put her head down, walked up through St.Helen's Square, down Stonegate, around the Minster and out of the walled city centre towards home.

Her progress was charted as she went. A few steps behind her, always far enough not to be noticed had been another pair of feet. They had lurked in shop door ways and hidden behind larger pedestrians heading in the same direction, all the time never allowing the quarry to leave their sight. As Lauren made her way into her street, those same feet and the eyes that directed them had hidden around the corner at the end of the terrace. They'd watched as she struggled to find her door key. They'd seen her finally find it, turn the lock and go inside. They'd watched the light go on in the front room and they'd waited whilst a bedroom light accompanied it. Then they slid back into the shadows and disappeared, taking their secrets with them.

Lauren sat on the toilet looking at the box which had contained the pregnancy testing kit. She'd followed the instructions to the letter. It hadn't seemed very dignified, in fact the whole process had left her feeling disembodied. This surely wasn't her this was happening to ? The Lauren Seymour she thought she knew was self-contained, careful, cautious, never likely to get herself into one of these kind of scrapes, but that wasn't what the tester was now saying.

Pink = Positive

Read the little leaflet. That surely couldn't be right could it ? Whichever light she looked at it under it appeared the same weak shade of girlish pink. What were the chances of that happening ? The first sexual action she'd had in a couple of years and the first time in her life she'd been caught without protection. There had been girls at college who were regularly falling into bed un-prepared with any vaguely attractive young guy they chanced upon. They never seemed to land themselves in trouble. The one time that Lauren gets drunk and has a regret-filled shag with a loser she becomes pregnant. She had imagined this moment would have left her filled with absolute terror. Prior to beginning the test she had presumed that in the unlikely circumstances that it turned out positive then she would be sitting in floods of tears wondering what the hell to do next. In reality, she felt nothing. In fact something in her brain had kicked into gear filling her with a degree of clarity that she normally lacked. There was nothing else for it. She needed to get a doctor's confirmation that she was indeed pregnant and then she needed to seek a termination. Nothing about this was right.

Although in her head she hadn't altogether ruled out the possibility of children she had no desire to become a single mother to the child of Robert P. Gorman. How Robert would take the news of his fatherhood would be anyone's guess. She had seen enough of the man to know that his responses couldn't easily be predicted and even if she attempted to keep the child from his attention, it would be near impossible in a place the size of York. Soon she'd run into him when she was pushing a pushchair through town, or news on the gossip grapevine would reach his ears. Add to that her own job insecurity and the prospect of attempting to manage with a baby, alone on benefits. It just wasn't feasible. Once in a magazine she'd read that it took a strong woman to carry an unplanned pregnancy to term. Lauren wasn't sure she had that strength.

Currently she had little feeling towards whatever it was that was beginning to grow inside her. Was this moment meant to feel life-affirming or in some way significant. ? Maybe it was the latter, but emotionally at least she couldn't make out what she felt. It was all merely an unfortunate accident that needed to be cleared up. She found the Yellow Pages and looked under Family Planning & Pregnancy Advice. There was a contact number for Marie Stopes, which she quickly keyed into the phone book on her phone. Francis would be home at any moment. As far as he had to be aware the test had come out negative. Millie need not know anything about it at all. This was something she had to do on her own. Lauren always liked to believe herself to be good in a crisis. It was the general everyday stuff that sometimes bogged her down. Now she was in the middle of a proper bona-fide life incident everything felt strangely alright. Her life appeared to have a bit of short-term purpose at last and for once she felt as if she could get back on top of it. The sound of the front door opening accompanied by the shrill tinny whistling of a song from Oklahoma signalled the return of the housemate who must never learn about any of this.

Lauren had taken five minutes in the privacy of her own office to contact the Marie Stopes Advisory Service. They had outlined the procedure for securing a termination along with the current legal status. She was ashamed at her own lack of knowledge and apathy towards the issue. Perhaps she'd never felt as if it would ever be something she'd need to consider. Did any woman really give it much thought ? Weren't most too busy living their lives to take time to wonder about what would happen if…

Her GP practice had been extremely helpful. She was booked in for a pregnancy test with the practice nurse for the day after tomorrow and if this again showed up as positive options for a termination could be discussed. It was all very matter of fact, all quite businesslike, something which Lauren appreciated.

At home her conversation with Francis had been difficult. He was being far from his usual jovial self at the moment. Their relationship had suffered after recent events. Lauren hoped that this was merely a short-term blip which they'd overcome. As they'd been eating their tea, Lauren had looked at the camp Virgin Mary statue on the TV with new insight. There she was dandling her fat baby messiah, sublimely content with her lot. Despite being pregnant at the age of thirteen, seemingly without male intervention and being engaged to an old bloke she still had time to smile benevolently at her peculiar offspring. It just wasn't real was it ? Whoever had concocted that peculiar painted plaster vision of perfect womanhood had never felt like she did right now. It seemed more like male wishful thinking than anything else.

She wondered just how much the residual Catholic beliefs that Francis maintained would influence his own feelings towards abortion. As a gay man, Francis was hardly a walking advertisement for traditional Christian doctrine, but then again you never could tell. They had never had cause to discuss such matters. Lauren looked at him as he was eating. He lived in his own tidy world for sure. He was a good man with a generous heart but there were aspects of his life that remained a total secret to her. All men are a dark continent according to Millie, a feeling that Lauren was increasingly coming to share. It must apply whatever the man in questions sexual orientation. Francis, as open, as kind-hearted and as funny as he was, was still something of a mystery to her. After all this time of sharing a kitchen, a TV, a sofa, countless chats late into the night and arguments over the bathroom, her housemate still kept part of himself firmly under lock and key. Not that she could blame him. She did exactly the same. Maybe that was one of the reasons they got along as well as they did.

Doing the deed

The practice nurse had been straightforward but with just enough compassion in her manner to take the edge off the awkwardness of the situation. Lauren had made it clear from the outset that this pregnancy was unwanted. Nothing would shift her opinion on that, nor should she be treated as if there were any other options open to her. She was as certain as she could be that there were no other options. It was impossible for her to imagine a life with a child. Maybe in a few years time if she was happily ensconced as part of a settled couple, but otherwise absolutely not. She couldn't manufacture maternal feelings that she just didn't possess.

An appointment was made for the following week. Termination would be quick, relatively painless and as matter-of-fact as the test had been. The nurse had handed her leaflets offering counselling to help her come to terms with what she was about to do but they seemed to speak in a language that she didn't understand. Was she expected to feel some sort of emotion towards the miniscule, inanimate, indistinct collection of cells that was growing inside her ? Part of her wanted to. A small piece of her would have quite liked the emotional drama of it all, but she felt nothing. Just a desire to be done with all this. The whole procedure was a nuisance to be gotten through. If that made others think she was a hard hearted bitch then so be it. In her own less than stony heart she knew the real story.

Two days prior to the termination she visited the practice nurse again and was given a pill to take. The nurse at this point had attempted to broach the subject of future contraceptive options. Lauren had told her in reply that she wasn't in a relationship and knew it all anyway. Which was true. There was just no accounting for what had happened on New Years Eve. Even if she had been carrying a whole stack of condoms it was doubtful she'd have been capable of trying to use them.

The two days quickly passed with Lauren wondering exactly what that pill she'd taken was doing. A leaflet did explain what was happening inside her womb at this point, but she'd been unable to read it. It had been put through her desktop shredder and buried at the bottom of the outside bin in the backyard. She had taken the advice of the practice nurse and had worn a skirt ,one of the few she possessed. Lying in a small room with about half a dozen beds an Asian doctor, accompanied by a sober faced looking nurse pulled the curtains around them and inserted what looked like another pill inside her. Then she lay back and waited. Time passed slowly. She couldn't relax. One by one , she'd hear the women in the other beds emerge from behind the curtains around their beds. Soon Lauren too was in a cubicle just off to the side of the room passing urine and a tiny indistinct jellyfish of a foetus into a sterilised container. She wasn't meant to see much but grim curiosity forced a glance . So this was the product of her and Robert's night of disastrous passion ? It wasn't much, but something inside her pulled a deep hidden heartstring. No, she wouldn't cry for frog-spawn. Not now, not ever.

   Handing the container over as she'd been told to beforehand by the doctor, the duty nurse gave it a quick expressionless look and nodded. That was the end of it. She'd been offered and accepted a cup of tea and a biscuit, dressed herself and left. She could have stayed longer. Took time to properly recuperate but hanging around the place made her feel queasy. All those furrowed solitary female faces of every age from teens up to their forties. The occasional guilty looking boyfriend or husband clutched his partner's hand and tried to find the right words. The men who were there were perhaps the more responsible. The rest of the phantom inseminators were conspicuous by their absence.

   As she left the hospital, if she felt anything, it was vague. She would go home, rest up for the remainder of the day and keep check on her bleeding.

   It was shortly after 2pm as she crossed the car park of the hospital and out onto Wigginton Road. The sun was shining, but the weather was sharp, patches of frost still defiant in the shadows despite the late hour. There was nothing much to be proud of in all this, but she did take comfort from the manner in which she'd handled it. By refusing to hesitate she had managed to act decisively and could now move on. Some self-control had been reasserted.

   A chattering young mum walked hand in hand with a blond toddler in dungarees who was pointing at a squirrel in the branches of a tall tree in someone's front garden. The woman's face was alive to a degree that Lauren rarely saw. Here was someone content in her world. Her wedding ring caught the sunlight as the little boy tried his hardest to pronounce the creature's proper name. Lauren had smiled at the child, the mum had noticed and beamed back at her, full of maternal pride and goodwill towards everyone. Her life must have its frustrations but for now at least they were nowhere to be seen.

   This would be the point thought Lauren where her heart would sink and she'd lapse into a deep grief for what she'd just done, the life she'd denied, the chance to fulfil her maternal destiny she'd nipped in the bud. But it didn't. She looked at the two of them and knew immediately that what they had was for them. What she had was her freedom back and the possibility of charting her own route through life in the manner in which she saw fit. For Lauren that was the greatest gift. We all had to make our choices in life and this was her's. Others could judge all they liked.

As secretive as we try to be, there is little in life that remains totally unseen. Even though Millie would be too wrapped up in her own happy good fortune to care, and the questions of Francis could be successfully negotiated, today's deed would not go unnoticed . Blank eyes pry around corners, dead lost souls linger in the shadows, and from the gutter silent folk watch everything pass them by. In a city as old as this there is nothing new under the sun, only stories weaved from the threads of all our histories.

The Pay-Off

This was perhaps the most productive period at work she'd had in months. Her focus had returned and the copy she was producing was some of the sharpest she'd produced in years. Maybe it was the knowledge that her time at Accent was now limited that was doing it. Only another 6 actual working days remained and then she along with Barry the hairy monosyllabic metal-head Graphic Designer and Cara the sweet as honey young creative support assistant who made their tea would be looking for new jobs. Josh Andrews had been giving Lauren a wide-berth. His man-made fibre covered arse had not been perched on the corner of her desk at any moment since they'd returned from the Christmas break. That was until the knock on the door announced his arrival

'Ms Seymour..erm..Lauren..can I come in ?' The ridiculously quiffed blond head of Josh appeared around the door.

Lauren looked up from her computer screen, mildly irritated at having her train of thought broken. She was determined to clear all the work in her in-tray before she left. It was a matter of professional pride.

'Yeah, come in.' Her anger towards him had dissipated somewhat. He was a toad, that was without question, but a toad she would soon never have to set eyes on again. She could afford to be a little indulgent.

Josh walked in and took a spare plastic chair that sat against the far wall, carried it over to her desk and sat down opposite. Clearly he didn't want to provoke her wrath by proprietarily sitting down on her desk like he normally did. Maybe we are at last getting somewhere thought Lauren.

'Erm right, ' he folded his hands together and crossed his legs. Lauren was sure she saw sparks fly from the chaffing of the nasty fabric in his trousers. 'I've just come out of a meeting with the other executives.'

Lauren had heard that they were having one of their regular strategy meetings this morning. Previously these would have filled her with dread. The diktats and decisions that came out of them were always an inconvenience if nothing else. It had been at the last such gathering that the decision had been taken to let go of her services. How this passed for any kind of well thought out strategy was beyond her, but she had accepted it and was trying to hold her tongue. Whilst her first instincts had been to go out in a blaze of expletive riddled, in-yer-face truth telling, her better judgement had decided it was probably best not to mess up any potential reference or endanger her redundancy payment. If she walked, it meant her money disappeared. 'It's about the redundancy settlement.'

'Oh yes.' Lauren looked up furtively. Was she about to be told that it was not going to be forthcoming due to some elaborately legal scam dreamed up by the rapacious board ? It wouldn't surprise her. The bastards.

'We've worked out a final figure for you.'

'Oh.' It was bound to be rubbish from this gang of criminal tight-wads. Josh started fiddling around in his top inside pocket and pulled out a letter which had been folded into three.

'It's all down on there.' He handed it to her. Lauren unfolded the paper and scanned down. There in bold block print was the final figure. It was considerably larger than she'd been expecting.

'Is this for real ?'

'Sure.'

'That's…'

'A thank you for all you've done over the years. You've been an asset.' Lauren resisted the temptation to ask why if she'd been such a benefit to the company were they now getting rid of her.

'Thanks Josh. This is incredible.' She meant it.

'No problem. Just sorry to see you go that's all.' Josh stood up and put the chair back by the wall. 'It wouldn't have been my decision.' He sounded sincere for once.

Lauren gave him a smile which he sheepishly returned, then sat staring at the piece of paper. That would certainly cushion the blow of losing her job.

'Hi is that Forward Arc ?' Lauren was on the phone to a London agency she'd seen advertising in the Guardian for a senior copywriter.

'Yes, how can I help you ?' A bright, breezy well spoken female voice returned.

'It's the copywriting job in today's Guardian. I wondered if you could send me an information pack and an application form.' The voice took down her details and promised to get something in the post immediately. It was time to take the bull by the horns.

A surprise gift

'Ta-Da !'

Francis walked into the front room as if making an entrance in one of his local amateur dramatic society performances.

Lauren looked up from the regional news. Harry Gration was talking to an Ossett man who used to sing in a punk band and who had now written a book about rearing pigeons. It was strangely fascinating. She had a bit of a thing for Gration. He had a cheeky school boy smile and a crinkly face. He was like a kindly history teacher. Apparently he lived in York. Francis had seen him having a pot of tea in the window at Betty's Tea Rooms , but to Lauren's continued disappointment she'd not once laid eyes on the living legend of local television in the flesh.

'I have in my hand a piece of paper.'

'Hello Chamberlain. I've some bad news for you, that nice Mr Hitler has just invaded Poland.' She could remember something from her History degree after all. She was sure she would have remembered more if Harry Gration had been teaching her.

'What ? Oh yes, I see. A joke. Very good.' He undid his coat slung it over the back of the sofa and collapsed down next to her. 'No, this is much more exciting than peace in our time I can tell you.'

'Is it ? Go on then.' She took hold of his arm and looked up at him expectantly.

'This my dear friend, is confirmation of our tickets to the Big Apple.'

'What are you on about ?'

'Do I have to bloody spell it out for you ?' Lauren looked wide-eyed, clueless and nodded. 'I've bought a couple of plane tickets to New York for the end of the month. You and I are going to be paying a visit to young Millicent and her hunky beau.' Lauren sat open-mouthed.

'You are joking ?' Francis shook his head. 'But I…' This was a bolt from the blue. Hardly any words between them for days, and now this.

'No buts, this is my treat. An early birthday present if you like.'

'But you normally just get me a CD or a book for my birthday. Don't you think a plane ticket to New York is going a bit far ?'

'Oh stop being so down about it and just say thank you.'

'Thank you,' Lauren hesitated. 'I think.'

'You think ! You think ! I've arranged the trip of a lifetime for you and all you can say is you think you're grateful.'

Francis stood up, chucked the computer print out confirming the booking on the sofa and walked off into the kitchen. Lauren picked it up and examined it. Two seats on a flight from Manchester to New York leaving on the 31st January returning on the 6th February. Lauren hoped Millie would be fine about all this.

'And before you ask, I've spoken to Millie about it and she's fine.' Francis was entering the front room with two mugs of tea. 'You really have no excuses Lauren.' He put the tea down on the coffee table, and flung her a copy of the Rough Guide to New York which he'd just removed from his briefcase.

'Thought I'd buy you a new copy. Better than the scraggy things you bring home from the library. I don't how you can go in there, all those diseases.' He shuddered.

'Why are you doing this Francis ? This must have cost a bloody fortune.'

He sat back down next to her. 'Because you need to go see your friend, you need to get your head together and because I have always wanted to see New York.'

'I really don't deserve you do I ?' She put her arms around his neck and hugged him.

'No you don't. And we'll have less of that sentimental crap thanks very much. You're my hard nosed mate and that's how I like you. Anyway, we need to get you away from the oddball for a bit. Have you heard from him since the incident ?'

'The incident ? That was very delicately put.'
'You know me.' Francis raised his eyebrows.
'No I haven't.' Lauren took a sip from her tea. 'Thank god.'
'He's bad news that one. Thank goodness he didn't leave you with something more than just a headache and feelings of self-loathing and regret.'
   Lauren inwardly winced.
'Yeah, thank god.' For once, she didn't think her voice had betrayed her. Francis had picked up nothing.
'I mean if you'd have got knocked-up I'd have had to turn that bedroom of yours into a nursery, I'd have to start thinking about paternity leave, I might even have had to have made an honest woman out of you.'
'Are you saying you'd have married me ?' He'd clearly been giving it some thought.
'Probably not married exactly, but I'd have brought the kid up as my own certainly.'
'Francis ? Are you for real ? You had all this worked out did you ?'
'Yes, I had to prepare myself for the worse.'
"But you didn't consider whether or not I'd want you to do all that ?'
'Why not ? You wouldn't have wanted to have played house with the Fred West of Holgate Road would you ? I would have said that after all this time of living with you, I'd finally succumb to your feminine charms.'
   Lauren laughed.
'Well, I'm glad you think I'm feminine enough to have awoken your latent heterosexual tendencies.'
'Erm…you'd kind of made quite a good looking boy, in a soft skinny girly kind of way. Maybe it's not beyond the bounds of belief.'
'Regardless of whether or not you think I look like a boy, surely no-one is ever going to believe that you're likely to start fancying women. You are the biggest, campest, gayest, forty something music teacher in York that I know.'
'Well thank goodness for that. I'd not want anyone to steal my highly encrusted crown now would I.'
   Francis turned to the section marked "Gay Lifestyle" in the Rough Guide to New York and showed the open page to Lauren who glanced down. 'Ooh, some of these places sound interesting.' Francis enthused.
'I thought you didn't like sceney stuff.'
'In my own backyard maybe, but take a look at the torso on that podium dancer. It's enough to make you want to swim the bloody Atlantic.'
'Mmm…not bad at all. Do you think he's got a well-groomed straight friend he could introduce me to ?'
'Who cares…' Francis's eyes were wide-open and admiring.
   Lauren finished her tea and placed her mug down on the coffee table.
'Are you sure you'd want to marry me then ?'
'On second thoughts, probably not.'
'Well that's a bloody relief. I can imagine trying to explain that one away to my folks.'
'And how are Mr and Mrs Seymour currently ?'
'Oh y'know. Still the same. Mum spends all her time knitting metaphorical baby

booties for her never likely to appear grandkids and dad is busy with his train set.'
'They are the picture of suburban contentment those two aren't they. Hey, if you carry on with this newly found slapper around town routine you've just started your mum might be able to get the wool out sooner than she thinks.'
'Don't even joke about it.' That was a bit too close to home for comfort.

   Francis flicked around with the TV remote and then went to get himself ready for a rehearsal of his amateur dramatics society. Lauren took herself for a long bath with the Rough Guide. The realisation that she'd been rushed headlong into this New York trip began to creep up on her. She wasn't entirely sure how she felt about it all. There was still the question of the seven hour flight to contend with, and there was no prospect of an escape route. It would be more than churlish to be angry with Francis. It had been a lovely thought, a touching sentiment to do something as grand as this. Even in this age of cheap flights an air ticket to New York cost slightly more than a CD or box of chocolates. She knew at the bottom of it all there lay a deep concern for her welfare. At times it could be overbearing. He did come across as a surrogate father and his interventions did at times suggest a certain lack of confidence in her own ability to manage her life. From anyone else this would be irritating. From Francis, it was largely tolerable. From what he had said, it sounded as if Millie was already in on the act. Just what had he told her exactly ?

   'Oh, he said you'd been having problems with the freak-deaky guy and needed to get away.' Millie didn't seem to know the whole story. Or if she did she wasn't letting on. 'Anyway, I'm glad he bought two tickets as there was no way you were going to get round to it on your own.'
'I would have eventually.'
'Oh yeah, right.'
   Lauren was momentarily hurt by her friend's disbelief.
'I would have.'
'The main thing is, you're coming over in a few weeks time ! Yay ! We're going to be back together again.'
'Yay !' Lauren tried to mimic her excitement.
'So, tell me more about what's been happening with the dodgy geezer. Did you tell social services about him ?'
'Erm..' In her haste to deal with the pregnancy that particular task had been far from her mind.
'You didn't did you ?'
'No, I never got the opportunity.' Please don't ask why Millie.
'What opportunity would that have been exactly ? All you have to do is phone them up. I'll do it if you like. Anonymously of course.'
'No, don't you dare.'
'Why are you so bothered about protecting him ? What if he's up to no good with that girlfriend of his ?'
'I think she can take care of herself.'

'What makes you say that ?'
'Let's just say she isn't a shrinking violet by any means.'
'I'm not sure I get your meaning but I'll take your word for it. Feisty is she ?'
'You could say that.'
'Why are you being so bloody vague Lauren ? There's something you're not telling me here.'
'There's not, honestly there isn't.' She lied.
'Oh, OK then.' Millie sounded far from convinced but didn't seem inclined to want to push the issue. 'Just make sure you give him a wide-berth and get your ass over here so I can fix you up with some tasty bloke or other.'
'Millie, I will not be requiring your matchmaking services thanks very much. I'm quite happy as I…'
'Ah, happy, shmappy , you're in need of a bit of serious loving doll.' Millie was doing an average job of mimicking a New York Jewish accent. Lauren tried hard to force a laugh.

So where next ?

She had submitted a perfunctory application for the senior copywriting job at Forward Arc. Her mind had been too distracted to give it her full attention although the job itself both intrigued and scared her in equal measure. The starting salary was considerably larger than she'd been earning at Accent. If she secured the position she'd be heading up a department of three full-time copywriters as part of a much larger creative team. They'd worked on any number of impressive magazine campaigns and their offices in Soho looked swish and exciting. It was all a real far-cry from what she was used to. At first her self-doubt looked as if it was going to conspire to keep her from applying. The application pack had sat barely looked at on the floor of her room. Francis had nagged her about it endlessly, but she'd resisted. Then one evening after work a sudden rush of blood found her filling in the form, attaching some samples of her previous work and preparing the envelope for posting. Then she hesitated again. It sat in her bag for a full day before she got round to walking into the Post Office, having it weighed and sending it off. The proof of posting sat in the pocket of her mac as evidence of her increasing willingness to tackle life head on. She hadn't told her parents yet.

'Oh and I've applied for a new job.'
'That's good dear,' replied mum. 'Is it in York ?'
'No, not this time. It's in London. A more senior position with a much bigger agency.'
'Oh, that sounds exciting.' She was clearly doing her best to be more interested in her daughter's career. Maybe the Christmas set-to would benefit their relationship in the long-term. Lauren could maybe live in hope.

'Yeah, I think I need a much bigger challenge now. I've kind of been stuck in a rut for a while.'
'Well as long as you know that whatever you do, your father and I will always be proud of you.'
Lauren was touched.
'Ah thanks mum, that means a lot to me.'
'We don't always show it but we're more than happy with what you've done with your life.'

That was a bit of a retraction of her earlier sentiment, but again, Lauren was trying to restrain her cynicism.
'That's a really lovely thing to say.'
'Well, I'm your mum, that's what I'm here for. You know if you can't tell me things then who can you tell eh ?'

It was an obvious line to insert at this point in a mother to daughter conversation even if both of them knew it wasn't really true. There was Millie she could tell. Or Francis if she had to. In most cases there was no need to tell anyone anything. Then the memory of lying on the hospital bed , all alone as she terminated her mum's potential grandchild returned to her. There was no way she could ever share that particular story with the one who bore her.

Goodbyes and new beginnings

The last day at work had been easier than she'd expected. It had glided past in a fug of goodwill, cards and occasional tears from staff Lauren barely knew. Clearly she had made more impact at Accent than she'd ever realised. Some of the management team had invited the redundant trio out for drinks as a farewell gesture but they'd stuck together and collectively declined. It was a small act of defiance but one that gave them all a feeling of satisfaction. Instead, Lauren had suggested that the three of them go to the Chinese Buffet and then into The Ackhorne, her newly re-discovered favourite watering hole.

They made an unusual party. Cara had been unable to stop talking about her new boyfriend and the renovations they had planned for the flat they'd just bought in an old Georgian townhouse along Bootham. Barry sat quietly, fiddling with roll-ups, occasionally saying something sage which Lauren was sure came straight from the mouth of Yoda. He was intending to set up a design practice of his own and Cara wanted to re-train as an aromatherapist.

'I could be off to London.' Lauren had casually mentioned as she knocked back a pint of Rooster, a real ale that Barry had recommended. It turned out he was an Ackhorne regular and a former aficionado of the local Campaign For Real Ale. Despite her better judgement, Lauren was enjoying the beer, even more so when Barry had informed her that bitter contained far less calories than lager.
'Ooh London, how exciting.' Cara had enthused, her permanent grin threatening to rupture her face.

'Highly overrated in my experience.' Barry looked nonplussed.
'I just think it might be time for a change. New challenges.'
'You could always take up kick-boxing.' Barry offered as an alternative to relocation.
'Pardon ?'
'Kick-boxing. If you need a new challenge. Here, can I roll you one ?' Barry was sealing his cigarette and gestured towards his baccy tin.
'Oh go on then.' Lauren succumbed. Cara giggled nervously. 'I just think I might be stagnating if I stay here much longer.'
'You could be, alternatively, you could just be settled, happy and content with your life. Like me.'

From what she knew of Barry he was sublimely content. He lived with his long-term girlfriend in a small terraced house in Acomb. He went to countless gigs, drinking with his mates, enjoyed long motorbike touring holidays around Europe and generally chilled out.

'There's too much emphasis put on achievement.'
Lauren couldn't really say she disagreed.
'Petey is mega-ambitious.' Cara sipped at her diet Coke. 'He wants to be one of the senior account executives and possibly then start his own financial services company.'
'He's living the dream baby.' Barry blew a smoke ring and slipped Lauren a crafty wink.
'Yeah, yeah he is.' Cara put her blond hair behind her ears and looked at the table. 'I think London would be way-cool Lauren. Good luck with the job'
'Thank you Cara. I'm sure it would be.' But in her heart of hearts she knew her sympathies were probably more with Barry the rooted Acomb behemoth. He was stretched back now in his seat, looking like a mad druid as he sank the remainder of his third pint. He was actually quite a likeable guy thought Lauren. All these years of working with him and she'd never realised.
'Of course,' he held his roll-up between his fingers and wiped a fragment of cheese and onion crisp from his beard. 'They were all cunts at Accent. Present company excepted of course.'

Cara looked horrified, Lauren doubled up in laughter. Two miserable looking middle-aged men at the next table, who had been sitting largely silently in individual meditation of their beer and cigarettes , stared across at them disapprovingly. Barry waved. 'Alright fellas. Just enjoying a quiet night with me bitches…don't you mind us.'
The men shook their heads and went back to their drinks. Lauren was finding it hard to maintain her drunken balance as her entire upper body wobbled with a belly laugh.

'Barry, make sure you don't leave here without putting your number in my phone please.' Lauren wiped the tears of out her eyes and took a large slug of her drink. Barry was funny and uncomplicated. Barry was a dude.

By the end of the evening Lauren was feeling decidedly worse for wear. She'd necked four pints of Rooster and had been persuaded by Barry to round the night off with a measure of single-malt whisky. It had been a great evening. Cara had been largely superfluous, instead Lauren enjoyed listening to Barry's wry observations and dry sense of humour. It had been a blokey few hours with Barry conducting the proceedings. If his girlfriend didn't mind Lauren wouldn't mind nicking Barry for the occasional evening of shooting the breeze in the warm friendly confines of The Ackhorne. He suited the place. Lauren wanted to as well.

Pete had turned up at five to eleven to collect his darling intended. He was a smart, well-groomed boy with a Radio Four accent who smiled nervously as he looked around the pub. This was clearly not the kind of place he would usually make a point of visiting.

'Oooh hello babes.' Cara, stone-cold sober, but fizzing on five Diet Cokes threw her arms around him. Pete looked mildly alarmed at the company she was keeping.

Lauren stood up, swayed a little and took his hand.

'It's a pleasure to meet you young man.'

'Yes and you. You must come round to the flat for dinner for sometime.'

Lauren leaned forward and touched his chest flirtatiously .

'Ooh a dinner party. That would be lovely.' She was drunk and Pete was attractive in a catalogue cut-out kind of way. What a nice young man. What a lovely offer. She had so many lovely friends didn't she ?

Cara was giving her boyfriend a look that said, 'don't go there.' Pete in turn took a step back from the lanky grinning woman wobbling precariously before him.

'Yes. Wouldn't it C ?' He stuttered.

'Yes, it would.' Cara lied.

Lauren, put a steadying hand down on the neighbouring table, forcing the two middle-aged men to drink up their dregs and leave. She blew a kiss at their backs as they left and then scratched the back of her head.

'Such nice boys.'

'Peter is it ?' Barry finally piped-up.

'Well Pete actually.'

'Pete, let me speak to you mano to mano. Draw up a stool my friend.' Cara's face was a picture but before she had chance to warn her boyfriend off, Lauren grabbed her by the arm almost pulling her over in the process.

'The menfolk need to discuss manly things dear, we should go to the toilets and powder our noses.' Lauren had no idea how you powdered your nose but had heard it mentioned in films. By now Cara looked flustered and annoyed, but Lauren was leading her off in the direction of the ladies. Barry watched them wobble off and then gestured for the young man to join him at the table. Pete perched on his stool and looked earnestly at Barry.

'Now listen here kid. You got yourself a pretty little lady there.' He was gesturing across the table as if he were a gumshoe detective talking to a new client. Pete nodded, his face breaking out into near ecstasy at the mention of his girlfriend.

'She's sweet.'

Pete nodded.

'She's pretty.'

Pete nodded.

'She's clearly besotted with you.'

Pete shrugged sheepishly with mock modesty.

'But there's just one thing you should know.' Pete's expression changed to one of slight concerned curiosity. He leaned in, Barry did likewise and their heads were almost touching. Barry carelessly blew cigarette smoke in Pete's face and then continued.

'She's had four plates of Chinese food and five diet cokes this evening.'

'Golly, yeah, she's got a big appetite.'

'And that means only one thing.'

'What's that ?'

'That dainty little creature of yours is going to be farting like squaddie tonight my friend. Make sure you have a window open and if you're even thinking about anything physical I'd forget about it. In my experience there is nothing more off-putting than a woman letting off a depth-charge as you're going down on her.'

Pete had turned white as a drunken Lauren stumbled back to the table arm in arm with an equally ashen-faced Cara.

'Ready then Pete.' Cara let go of Lauren who nearly wobbled over before landing on her stool.

'Yes, shall we head off ?' Pete jumped up relieved to see the return of his bloated princess. He looked her up and down and remembered Barry's warning.

'Sorry to be a pain, but I fancy a bit of an early-ish night.' She simpered. Barry caught Pete's eye, gave a quick knowing wink, stuck out his lips, touched his nose and shook his head.

'Don't go there son. Not tonight.'

'Did I miss something ?' Cara asked confused.

'OK C, let's get going shall we.' Pete took her arm and began to lead her off.

'Seeya Barry, seeya Lauren. Good luck in London.' She waved energetically as Pete with his head down bundled her out of the door, down St.Martin's Lane and back towards their safe little domestic world.

'Have you been being a naughty boy Barry ? That lad looked horrified.' Asked Lauren.

'Let's just say, I've been letting young Peter know that not everything that grows in the garden has the sweetest of fragrances.'

'Aah that almost sounds like poetry dude.'

'When poetry's wing-ed muse takes flight Lauren, you cannot predict its trajectory.'

'Now you're just talking bollocks.'

'Big hairy ones .'

'I can well imagine.'

'Don't you go getting ideas.' Barry leaned back in his chair and started rubbing his large belly contentedly through his XL Iron Maiden t-shirt. 'I'm spoken for love. Although I fully understand why any red-blooded woman would want a piece of Barry love-action.'

'Yeah, you're like a big walking pheromone.'

'And you Lauren, are one slinky foxy lady.' He pointed towards her with his roll-up and raised an eyebrow suggestively.
'Do you really think so ?' It had been a long time since anyone had paid her such a compliment voluntarily. Normally she had to drag it out of them with expletives and threats of violence.
'Aye, I do. You're quite fit you. Like one of them Chrissie Hynde, Patti Smith, beanpole birds.'
'Ah cheers Baz. Nice one.' She thought. Not conventionally attractive then, but then she'd never had any illusions that she was. Interestingly attractive was good. Even Millie had once said so.
'No worries. Here, have we got time for another ?'

Out of the darkness

The two of them hugged on the doorstep of the pub as midnight rolled around. They sauntered down St.Martin's Lane together before finally saying goodnight as it ran into Micklegate and their paths diverged. They'd promised to do it again some time and Barry reckoned Lauren would get along handsomely with his partner Ellie. If she was anything like Barry then Lauren was almost certain of it.

From the old church yard of St.Martin's a darkened figure emerged from behind one of the lichen-covered Georgian tombstones. It had been waiting there for them to step outside, resting its back on the stone of someone who had been dead for nearly two hundred years. From its position in this quiet hidden corner, it could see right into the belly of the pub. From behind the stone it had peered. It had watched the activity, heard the laughter when the door had opened and closed. Unable to make out much but a low burr of mingled conversations, it had been forced to provide its own commentary on the snippets of random events that caught its vision. It had seen Pete and Cara make their exit, and watched as Lauren and Barry had emerged from the door of the pub. It had seen the hug, and listened to their drunken conversation. It had stood up against the wall, watching the two figures at the end of the lane say their good byes. Then it had quickly jumped the wall and furtively darted through the shadows of the narrow cobbled lane. It stayed behind as she walked up across the river and through the city, all the time keeping enough distance not to be seen.

Too far under the influence to notice much, Lauren found her feet somehow kept moving towards home. Her mind again fuzzed with warm feelings. The past few months had been beyond peculiar but they had served to shake her out of her comfort zone a little. Now they were over it felt as if life was beginning to open up . The shadow behind her watched her wobbling footsteps as they veered across the path onto Lord Mayor's Walk and down into the snickleway that led into the terraced maze of the Groves. Then the shadow gathered pace, moving towards her. Its footsteps ceaselessly, methodically gaining one after the other until they were within a foot of the oblivious figure of the inebriated Lauren. Only then did

something deep within her sense the danger, breaking her dramatically from her benign stream of mental consciousness. She glanced quickly over her shoulder, her mind finding a fraction of sobriety as her survival mechanism kicked into life. There was a figure. It stood staring at her in the middle of the path. Lauren was transfixed with sudden fear. Now the figure with its hat pulled down over most of its face, and the collar turned up on a dark coat moved towards her. Finally, she managed to move, turning quickly she attempted to break into a run, but her legs refused to co-operate, she stumbled, almost falling to the pavement. The figure reached out and grabbed her by the collar on her mac and pushed her down the end of an alley between two of the terraces. In the light of the streetlight, her confused reasoning attempted to make out who it was.
'You killed our baby.' It was Robert's voice.
'What,' Lauren put a hand to her now thumping head.
'You went and killed our baby. I saw you.'

As her focus returned, her brain laboured to make sense of what was happening. There was Robert. She could see his eyes were red raw, presumably from tears.
'What are you talking about ? What baby ?'

He pushed her back again against the wall causing her to make an audible yelp. Every part of her felt numb and beyond her control. Her stomach turned over, her head angrily demanding more oxygen.
'You were pregnant. I saw you buy a tester. I saw you leave the hospital.' He gave her another shake. His voice was cracked and broken, as if he had been sobbing. 'I know what women like you do to babies. I've been watching you.' Again, he shook her. Lauren felt her eyelids closing and her consciousness beginning to slip. 'You can't just sleep with someone then leave them you fucking heartless bitch. ' Snot was dribbling down his face, his mouth was thick with saliva.
'Robert please let me go. This makes no sense.' Lauren could feel tears beginning to well. Please let this end.
'Why should I ? Why the fuck should I ?' He was shouting at her, shaking her as he spoke, his mouth inches from her ringing ears.
'Please can we talk about this tomorrow. I need to go home Robert. I'm drunk.'
'Yeah, you're fucking good at that aren't you, you fucking whore. I saw you with him.'
'With who ? Who are you talking about. Please let me go.'
'Your fucking fat boyfriend. Drinking with him in the same pub you drank with me you slut. Is that where you take all your men ?'
'Please just let me go Robert. I can't think straight tonight. Please let me go. Please Robert, please just let me go.'

Her whole body was shaking with fear as her wide-eyed assailant stared hard at her, globs of spittle in the corner of his mouth, his seething face hard up against hers. She felt herself losing control of her beer swollen bladder as a warm trickle of frightened urine began running down her leg, the ultimate indignity.
'You're fucking pissing yourself you dirty fucker. What kind of woman are you ?' Robert watched transfixed with disgust, momentarily loosening his grip.

He threw her to the ground, making her land in a puddle of icy rain water mixed

with her own hot piss. Now the tears overcame her, furious sobs bellowed up from deep inside her turning belly. All she wanted was to slip out of consciousness and be taken from this place. If Robert was going to kill her why didn't he just do it and give her some relief.
'Don't think I'm finished with you Lauren.' He leered above her. 'I'll be watching you every step of the way you fucking murderer.' He spat violently towards her face but the globule of thick sputum missed her by millimetres. His shadow retreated. The sound of his disappearing footsteps as he ran off into the night echoed around the alley.

Lauren's head swam as her sobs began to slowly subside. The whole world was spinning. How had she allowed herself to get like this again ? It was only meant to be a night out after leaving her job. Nothing unpleasant, just a simple evening with friends. As she lay crouched in her own urine in a cold wet alley a few streets from her home, her face stung with salt tears she couldn't find much sense in her wondering.

Rising slowly to her knees she noticed her coat was torn and her hands were grazed. The cobbles still spun and her nostrils were full of the rank stench of mingled fear, sweat and piss. She staggered the remaining way home. An elderly man walking his dog crossed over the street to avoid her. He shot her a look full of contempt and hurried on his way, shooing his dog who had paused to cock its leg up a street lamp. The night was now clear, occasional clouds scurried across the moon, as the sound of cars on Huntington Road subsided and she entered her own street. At the door, she had no idea whether or not she had her key, but her legs were giving way beneath her and her head continued to spin. Her heart was thumping mercilessly, defiantly sending tremors through her body as it did so. Life was coursing hard within her, determined that her temporary condition would not serve to snuff it out.

She slammed hard on the door with the open palm of her hand, making the black Labrador from two doors up launch into an aggrieved throaty bark. The alcohol numbed the worse of the stinging in her hand, but what pain she felt reassured her that yes, she was still alive. Most of the houses on the street were in darkness, including her own. Francis would have gone to bed. There was no response, so she banged again. Still the house remained silent, her anxiety growing out of fear that Robert may still be around, watching her latest indignity. Again she hammered, this time rat-tatting out a series of knocks, trying to place some basic rhythmic order on all this madness. That and her heartbeat were all that made sense to her now.

A light came on in a next door bedroom. A curtain began to move. Then, the hallway light behind the frosted glass of her own front door flicked on and the familiar cumbersome shape of Francis slowly came into distorted view. Lauren fell onto her knees again and started crying with relief.

'What the hell has happened to you ?' Francis stood open-mouthed at the door, frozen by the sight before him. Partly regaining his composure, he kneeled down and lifted her up. 'Come on Lauren, help me out here love.' His voice was full of tenderness and concern. She tried to raise herself a little, allowing Francis to carry her into the hall, slamming the door shut behind him.

'I wondered who the hell that was at this time of night. Not like you to forget your key.' He didn't seem angry. 'Now can you walk through to the front room?' He put his arm around her waist, she placed her weight down on his shoulder and they staggered through. He sat her down on the sofa and then awkwardly eased her out of her ripped mac. 'You got into a bit of a mess didn't you?'

Lauren sniffed and collapsed onto the sofa where her eyes slowly began to close. Francis fetched a spare old duvet and a blanket from the airing cupboard, filled a glass of water and placed it down on the floor next to her with a couple of Nurofen. He then sat down in the easy chair opposite, pulled a blanket over himself and turned out the light. There would be time for talking in the morning.

Trying to make sense

'Cup of tea for the invalid.'
Francis was rattling a cup and saucer at Lauren's head height as she slowly came around. Her eyes regained their focus as she realised she was in the presence of her housemate. Just as consciousness returned, so too did the angry hammer blows of a hangover to her protesting head.
'Oh fucking hell.' She put her hand to it.
''Ere, have these,' Francis picked up the Nurofen from the floor and handed them to her. She took the tablets and knocked them back with a swig of tea. Now the broken memories of how her night had ended began to piece themselves together in the drained wreckage of her drink heavy mind.
'Oh this is bad.'
'You're telling me.' Francis sat back down in his chair, but leaned forward towards her. 'You're in a right old mess. What have you been up to?'
'I don't know.'
'Heavy night was it?'
'No, it was a good night, then…'
'Then what?'
She looked at him, the realisation of why she was how she presently was had returned and the tears once again began to flow. Francis got up from his perch, knelt next to her, wrapping his arms around her bruised and battered frame as she started to sob.
'Eh, come on now. It's not like you to cry my darling. This is twice I've seen you do it in the past three weeks.' He stroked her hair and placed a kiss on her cheek. Holding her for a while as her tears began to subside, she sat up. Francis handed her a tissue, she blew her nose, took a sip from her water and tried to gather herself.
'God I stink.'
'I didn't want to say anything, but yes, you absolutely reek.'

'This is bad Francis.' Her voice was cracked and broken. She sounded like Keith Richards after a night on the sauce celebrating a sex change.
'Oh we've all had drunken episodes Lauren, don't beat yourself up about it, you'll be laughing about all this once the hangover has worn off.' She looked at him with her grey, washed out face and heavy red eyelids. 'Won't you ?'
   Lauren shook her head.
'I got attacked last night. Well, I say attacked…'
'Attacked ! Fucking hell. By who…no, let me guess.' Francis jumped to his feet and started pacing the room.
'No Francis, it wasn't like that.'"
'It was him wasn't it ? The Gorman character. He attacked you. Lauren I told you not to see him.' His raised voice increased the pounding in Lauren's head. This was agony.
'I didn't see him Francis, please sit down I need to tell you properly.' Francis looked at her, paused for a second and then sat down, his face bright red, a small vein above his left ear was visibly throbbing. There were beads of angry sweat beginning to form on his forehead.
'So what happened ?'
'I was just coming home from the pub, I turned down into the Groves and he appeared from out of nowhere.'
'He'd been following you.'
'I think so.' Lauren blew her nose.
'The fucking creep. Then what ?'
'He pushed me into an alley and started shouting at me, banging me against the wall. He was just so angry.'
'This is mental stuff.' Francis shook his head in disbelief.
'Then he pushed me to the floor and left me there. I don't think he's finished with me.'
'He will be finished with you when the police get hold of him. I'm calling them now.'
'No Francis, please, not yet. I've not finished.'
'Well finish, then we're calling them, and social services. The guy's a lunatic, he needs locking up.'
'I don't know.' Lauren shook her head, feeling the tears begin to well again.
'You don't know what ?'
'Well, he had his reasons.'
'You are surely not still making excuses for him are you ? What possible reason could he have for doing this to you.'
'There's something I've not told you.' There could be no more hiding. He had to know the full story.
'I'm sure there are countless things you've not told me, you're very secretive.'
'No, this concerns me and Robert.'
'Go on.'
'You know the other week when you said you were glad Robert hadn't left me with anything else, other than regret after I slept with him.'

'Yes ? He's not given you an STD has he ?'
'No Francis, I was pregnant.'
'You're pregnant ? And he did this to you.'
'No, I WAS pregnant. I had a termination.'
'You what ? This isn't possible. I'd have known.'
'I didn't want to tell anyone. I was pregnant, I made an appointment at the doctors and got referred to the hospital for a termination. It was all very quick and painless. I didn't want to make a massive issue out of it.'
'So you have an abortion just like that and don't think it worth telling me ? Clearly you told the maniac or he wouldn't have done this to you.'
'No, that's just it. I didn't tell anyone. He's been following me for ages I think. He saw me buying a pregnancy tester and then leaving the hospital and he's put two and two together.'
'And came up with four.'
Lauren nodded. Francis stood up, holding his brow and pacing the room.
'But Lauren…an abortion ?'
'I know, I know. I'm not proud of it. I didn't have any other choice. No job, no partner. No maternal feelings. What else was I supposed to have done ?'
'But I'd have helped bring it up.'
'I know you would, and I don't deserve you. You would have made a lovely father. But it just wasn't right for me. Not now anyway.'
'I understand.' Francis appeared to relax a little. His brow slowly unfurled, the gentle twinkle in his eyes showed its first sign of returning, his voice took on that familiar reassuring gentle tone.
'You do ?'
'Of course I do. I always understand you remember ? It couldn't have been easy.'
He looked her directly in the eye, stroked her hair and tried hard to contain the tears which threatened to reveal the depths of his compassion.
'I'm sorry for not telling you.' What a bitch she'd been. Shutting her old friend out of such an important event in her life like that. Sometimes she didn't always think straight.
'It would have been nice to have been told, but I can see why you wouldn't want to.' He gestured across to the statue of the Virgin that had been dutifully watching the proceedings.
'I didn't know if it would offend your beliefs.'
'Beliefs ? Lauren, I only go to Mass to ogle the good looking young priests. What else could I be doing on a Sunday morning. According to the church every time I get frisky with a fella I'm committing a mortal sin, I can hardly claim the moral high ground now can I. No, we're all fallen.'
'Some of us more than others.' Lauren stuck out her bottom lip.
'That goes without saying.' Francis flicked her lip with his finger and smiled.
'What am I going to do ?'
'Firstly, you're going to get yourself cleaned up. Secondly, you and I are going to spend some of that redundancy money of yours on a new coat, then we are going to inform the police and social services about the menace of Robert P. Bloody,

Stinking, Looney-Tune, Gorman.'
'I haven't got any choice have I ?' Francis shook his head.
'And you're not going anywhere without a chaperone until this is cleared up.'
'Now that's going a bit far.'
'I don't think so. He just roughed you up this time, took advantage of the fact you were drunk. Next time it could be a whole lot worse. Promise me you'll report him.'
'OK, I'll do it. I'll definitely do it.' But even as she spoke the words she could begin to feel her certainty going the same way as her resolve.

More retail therapy

Lauren took a long bath. Francis had cancelled his appointments for the day due to ill-health, hers not his. He never missed an appointment, even when he was almost laid out with illness. Only during his spell of pneumonia earlier in the year did his patient one to one tuition have to be cancelled. He was clearly taking all of this very seriously. When she emerged from the bathroom wrapped in her bathrobe, Francis presented her with a large white envelope with a London postmark. Lauren wiped her hands on her robe, and opened the letter. It was from Forward Arc, the advertising agency which had the job she applied for.
'Well ?' Asked Francis impatiently, jumping from one foot to the other like an excited overweight school boy. Lauren looked at the letter.
'I've got an interview.'
'Brilliant.' He clapped his hands together triumphantly. 'You clever girl. When is it ?'
'Next Tuesday. Bloody hell, that doesn't give me a lot of time.'
'Ah, you don't need it. Just wow them with your charm and good looks and the job's yours.'
'Thanks for your confidence.'
'No problem.' He was grinning from ear to ear.
'Oh but Francis.'
'What now ?'
'It's London isn't it.'
'Yes, so…' He couldn't really see a problem.
'So, I don't know anyone there. I'm not sure I want to live in London.'
'Look Lauren. The fact you don't know anyone there is a massive bonus as far as I can see. I think you've exhausted York. You need a fresh start and as much as I'll be gutted to see you leave, I think it would be good for you.'
'I can sort of see where you're coming from.' Lauren sat looking pensively at the carpet wondering where all this was going to lead.

She had little choice but to wear her grubby old parka for their shopping trip.
'That mac cost me sixty quid.'
'Last of the big spenders eh.' Francis teased.
'It's only a year old. There was loads more wear in it.' She was examining the rip at the seam. 'The bastard.'
'So the prospect of Robert stalking you for three weeks is nothing, yet he puts a rip in your coat and it's a hanging offence?'
'Well, yeah. Duh.'

In town Francis stuck to her side like glue looking around furtively all the time, sure that behind every cumbersome tourist their lurked a demon from down the road. Lauren by way of contrast was somehow relatively relaxed.
'It's like having my own security staff.'
'Pardon ?' Francis was eyeing someone suspiciously among the crowd of people crossing Parliament Street.
'Don't worry about it.' She flicked her hand dismissively. 'You're beginning to freak me out.'
'You should be freaked out. You've had a stalker.'
'I know, I know.'
'You shouldn't be so dismissive Lauren. You were in great danger last night.'
'Francis, can we just change the subject.' It was true of course, she just didn't want to think about it.
'OK, just please take this seriously. The state you were in though.' Francis shook his head.
'Francis, now please. Concentrate. I need a coat.'
A new coat was duly purchased. Lauren wasn't a lingerer when she needed to buy clothes. She went in the store, found something she liked in her size and purchased it. There was never any need to try things on, she had learnt over the years what suited her tall, skinny frame and what didn't. It was another knee-length belted mac. The look worked on her so why bother changing now ?

After they finished their shopping he had suggested they go and sit in the bar at the City Screen and have a coffee. She felt far more relaxed than perhaps she should under the circumstances. Her legs and arms still had a dull ache, and her hangover which looked as if it was going to be merciless in the beginning was still clinging on defiantly. Francis remained hyper-attentive throughout. He seemed sure that someone was behind them but Lauren didn't care. As long as Francis was next to her Robert was unlikely to approach. What was he going to do in broad daylight anyway ? This incident would perhaps curtail her going out on her own at night for a while, but it was unlikely to change her daytime behaviour. These could well be the last few weeks she had in her lovely adopted city, she wasn't about to have them limited by fear.

Unfinished business

Francis was holding the downstairs phone and looking at her.
'Now are you going to do this or am I ?'
'Yes, yes, I'll do it.'

Francis handed her the phone. On the back of an envelope he had jotted down the telephone numbers of the city social services department and the police station. Police first thought Lauren. Let's get the law out of the way. Despite everything, she couldn't help but feel a certain sense of betrayal that she was even contemplating this. It had to be done. A dull institutional female drawl in a low register answered at the other end.
'Oh hi, I'd like to report an assault.'
'And can I have your name please madam.'
'Lauren Seymour'
'And your address please ?' She gave her address.
'Just putting you through to a duty officer.' There was a click at the other end. Lauren's butterflies returned as a connection was made and a telephone rang.
'Hello this is WPC Sykes speaking.'
'Oh hello, I'd like to report an assault.'
'Is this a Lauren Seymour ?'
'It is yes, I was walking home last night.'
'Last night you say. Had you been drinking ?'
'Yes, I'd had a few drinks with my friends and I was followed home.'
'OK.' Lauren could hear papers being rustled. There was little in the policewoman's monotone voice that put her at ease.
'And then he grabbed hold of me and pushed me down into an alleyway.' Her words were quick to the point of almost being garbled.
'Do you have any idea who the attacker was ?'
'Yes, his name is Robert Gorman and he lives…'
'Is Mr Gorman a boyfriend or partner? ' There was something dismissive, almost accusing in her tone. As if Lauren was somehow wasting their time with this probable little domestic.
'Er no, he was a friend.'
'And had you had an argument ?'
'No, not really. There had been a misunderstanding of sorts but nothing major. I'd not seen him for a few weeks.'
'And you say he had been following you ?'
'Yes, he's been doing it for a number of weeks on and off I believe.'
'Do you have his address ?' Lauren gave them the address of Robert's flat. She heard a speedy tapping on a computer keyboard at the other end.
'Do I need to come in or anything ?'
'We may need you to make a statement, in the meantime could you leave it with me.'
'Yes of course.'

With that the deed was done. Francis, who had been watching on attentively picked up the paper and pointed to the number of the social services department.

Lauren sighed and keyed it in. Within seconds a gentle male voice with a southern accent answered.
'Oh hi, I wanted to report something .'
'Report something ? OK.'
'I've got a friend, well, he was a friend. He's nearly 33 and he's formed a relationship with a 17 year old girl who has a baby boy.'
'Ok,' the voice intervened to pause her story. 'The thing is there, the girl is actually over the age of consent and unless her parents complained we couldn't really do much. She is under 18 still so if they did then we may have to investigate further.'
'Right, the only thing is I believe the guy in question has been investigated in the past for a possible assault on a teenage girl at his former workplace.'
'That changes matters somewhat. Was he charged ?'
'I don't think there was enough evidence to press charges but there were lots of grey areas apparently.'
'Again, as he wasn't charged it would be difficult for us to do much. That is of course unless the girl's parents sought our help.'
'Oh, I see.' Lauren wasn't sure whether she was annoyed or relieved at this news.
'But I'll take your details and get back to you should we require any further information.'

'There's only one thing for it then.' Francis was incensed by the inaction of social services.
'Can we just leave it now ?' Lauren had been explaining the contents of her two awkward telephone conversations.
'No we can't, we need to inform the young girl's parents about Robert's past.'
'Francis, we can't do that. That is going too far.'
'Not at all. We'd just be providing them with some information and they'd be free to make of it what they like.'
'I really couldn't do that to him.'
"You might still have some misplaced loyalty to the nutter but I certainly don't. '
'Please don't get involved.'
'I think it's a bit too late for that don't you ?'
'No, I can't tell her parents. It wouldn't be right. I've only ever heard her talk about her mum. God knows where her dad is. Robert did mention something about prison.'
Lauren needed to think and quickly. If she didn't do something Francis might be liable to take matters into his own hands. It wasn't Robert now she wanted to protect, it was her housemate. She couldn't abide the thought of him becoming anymore embroiled in this sorry mess than he already was. Just then, the beginnings of a plan began to form.

Spilling the beans

Lauren sat cradling a cup of stewed tea at a table by the window of a greasy spoon café on Bridge Street. Not many of these places were left in the centre of York these days. They'd been replaced by countless identikit coffee shops and trendy café bars. It was a real blast from the past. Elderly shoppers were eating full English breakfasts, a man in blue overalls and a yellow reflective jacket scoured his Daily Star and chewed on a bacon sandwich. Two teenage girls in tracksuits, puffed on cigarettes and necked back the contents of Coke cans. The café door opened and a young woman pushing a jammy-faced baby in a pushchair edged inside. She saw Lauren and gave her a begrudging nod of recognition.
'Thanks for coming Beth.' Lauren stood up to greet her and helped her with the pushchair. The little boy looked at her keenly, his face smiling beneath his blond mop of hair.
'S'alright.' She eyed Lauren suspiciously.
'Can I get you anything.'
'Full English please. Oh, and a diet coke.'
   Lauren had thought perhaps she might like a small Danish, but if that was what the girl wanted then that was what the girl would get. What she was about to tell her was hardly likely to make her day. As Lauren returned from the counter she saw Beth feeding Christopher from a small jar of baby food. She attentively wiped the corner of his mouth and spoke lovingly to him as he contentedly chuckled and cackled. At 17 Lauren had spent most her time hanging around in town, listening to her Wonder Stuff records , under-age drinking with her mates and obsessing over lads. It was a world away from Beth's reality. Her daily life was one of self-sacrifice and care for another small helpless little being. At her age Lauren's only concern had been with herself. Even at nearly 33, Lauren still didn't feel as if she would have been able to take on the upbringing of a child, particularly not on her own. Add to that the fact that Beth managed on a barely subsistent income of state benefits her daily struggles looked almost heroic. She presented a tough exterior to the world, she had to. She coped with what was thrown at her and had a curious mixture of streetwise intelligence combined with youthful naivety, but the care she administered for her child couldn't be doubted. She was not alone. There were hundreds of mothers like her around York. Pushing pushchairs in discount store clothes, chain smoking cigarettes, flaunting their cheap jewellery, receiving the contempt of the better favoured. They were hard people to feel much sympathy for and hadn't they brought it on themselves with their irresponsible behaviour ?
   Lauren now knew that whilst girls who got pregnant from better-off families were made appointments at abortion clinics, girls like Beth carried the pregnancy to term. Whilst the middle-class girls could dream of careers, future wealthy husbands and partners, girls like Beth thought they had little to look forward to. A baby became a route to gaining some respect and credibility. A way to shortcut the road to adulthood. The young men in all this were anarchic creatures, devoid of much responsibility, rarely made to face the consequences of their actions. The young women on the other hand carried the whole thing. Head towards the earthier parts of the city and see who it was who kept the place from falling into chaos. It was a

tough matriarchal world that had been crafted in the space left as jobs and self-respect retreated.

The gap between the increasing wealth of the city, with its upmarket apartments, stylish boutiques and spiralling house prices and the world in which Beth lived was increasing daily. Beth was a born and bred Yorkie in a city increasingly made up of wealthy incomers, drawn to the place by the beauty of the medieval streets and its access to some of the most breathtaking countryside in England. Lauren doubted if Beth had ever seen that countryside or whether she really appreciated the narrow lanes and snickleways that so appealed to tourists the world over. Her reality was very different and although they both inhabited the same small northern city their experience of it was disparate. Lauren was by no means wealthy, or even snobbish, but she had rarely encountered anyone like Beth in all her time of living here. Sure she'd seen them about, cued behind them in the Post Office, avoided groups of hard looking teenagers in hoodies on street corners, but she'd never really spoken to any of them. Not properly.

Despite Lauren's determination not to be intimidated by the younger woman, she had to admit that she did carry a small degree of fear towards her. It was Beth's hardness, her unpredictability, her determination to use every trick she possessed to try and gain the upper hand. She also knew that whatever Beth did she felt to be in the best interests of Christopher. Robert for all his social oddity was probably still a better prospect than the average chaotic young male contemporary of hers. They couldn't be trusted around her precious son, her one constant possession in an unpredictable and denuded world. Robert had shown himself to be tender and caring. With him she could perhaps fall for the myth of the happy family. Lauren's presence had seemed to endanger that. Now Lauren knew the news she had to share with her was likely to send her already confused world spinning a little faster. For all that had happened to Lauren, she knew that when this whole messy business was concluded that she herself could walk away. Beth though would have less options available, less places to run. In her heart, Lauren was struggling towards compassion.

'Did you tell Robert you were coming ?'

'Nah, kept quiet like you said. He's at home watching the telly. I called on him before I left. What did you want anyway ?'

Lauren had decided to write a note to Beth and post it to her. It asked her to text her mobile to arrange to meet up and not to tell Robert. Lauren guessed that the note of intrigue about the arrangement would keep Beth's lips sealed. It was a risk of course and if Robert found out she dreaded to think what might happen. But in Lauren's mind there was little now to lose. He had overstepped the mark badly. Violent threats in dark alleys after weeks of stalking her were not playing ball. If he still laboured behind delusions of friendship then he was more than just badly mistaken. Lauren took a hand-rolled cigarette she'd prepared earlier from the baccy tin in her bag. She needed it to steady her nerves.

'Do you want one ?' She gestured towards Beth.

'Trying to give up. For Christopher's sake.'

'Oh, right of course.' Lauren opened her baccy tin and put the roll-up back inside.

'Thanks for coming.'
'You've said that once.' A middle-age waitress in a blue pinny brought across a plate of bacon, egg, sausage, mushrooms, fried bread and beans. Beth's eye's lit up. 'Ah nice one. I've not had full English in ages.' She smeared her plate in brown sauce and began tucking in.
'You must be wondering why I wanted to meet you.'
Beth looked up from her plate, chewing on a piece of bacon.
'Aye, I am.'
'Well, it's not easy.'
'Eh, I'm all ears me. Like whatsisface.' The food had clearly served to lighten her mood. Job done thought Lauren.
'Who ?'
'Y'know, big eared bloke. He were married to Princess Di.'
'Oh, Prince Charles.'
'Aye, him. Dozy bastard. D'you reckon he had her killed ?'
'Sorry ? Oh right.' Lauren was thrown off her chain of thought before realising that Beth was referring to the conspiracy theories. 'Probably not. Seems a bit unlikely.'
'Me mam reckons it were all a plot between him and the queen's fella.'
'Prince Phillip ?'
'Is that the queen's fella ?'
'It is.'
''im then.' She dipped her fried bread into the yolk of her egg causing yellow juice to seep out across her plate.
'I've heard that story but I think it was all probably an accident.'
'I hate the lot of 'em anyway.' Clearly a young woman of sound judgement thought Lauren.
'I'm all for a republic.'
'Yer what ?'
'Never mind.' Maybe the discussion about the finer points of the constitution could wait for another day.

   Lauren drank from her tea and considered getting another. It was probably fair to let Beth finish her food before launching into the story.
'That were good.'
'Did you enjoy it ?' For some reason the sight of a smiling, temporarily contented Beth gave Lauren a small jolt of satisfaction. At least she'd given the girl a proper meal.
'Aye, it were alright. Now are you gonna tell me what this is all about or am I going to have had a wasted trip ?'
   Lauren looked at Beth's empty plate and the smear of brown sauce on the corner of her lips and thought its probably not been entirely wasted.
'It's about Robert. I've found some things out about him that I thought you should know.' Beth's posture stiffened.
'You're not going to tell me a load of crap to try and put me off him so you can

have a crack are you ?' She bristled.
'No, you have to try and trust me here Beth. I'm really not interested in Robert anymore. You'll understand why when I've told you what I'm about to tell you.'
'Go on then.'
'Last week when I was walking home Robert tried to attack me.' There was no point beating about the bush. She wasn't Mature Bessie.
'Yer what ?'
'I'd been drinking at the pub with some friends and Robert followed me home.'
'That were the other night when he went out. Said he was seeing you or summat. I didn't make owt of it like, I was knackered and didn't fancy a row so I left him to it.'
'Except he wasn't seeing me, not properly. I was meeting other people. He's been following me about, after work, when I go out, that kind of thing.'
'You're joking me aren't yer ?'
'I wish I was.'
'I can't believe it. You're just trying to fuck with me 'ead you. I know what you're like.' Her face had turned red and the her voice was becoming raised. The pensioner couple on the next table looked up from their breakfasts, casting a nosy glance in their direction.
'I'm not, I promise. Can we just keep it down.' Lauren really didn't need another scene.
'He attacked yer, you say ?' Beth huddled in, her voice lowered almost to the point of a whisper.
'Just as I was turning into my street he grabbed hold of me and pushed me down an alley. He was really threatening.'
'Did you tell police ?'
'I did, they've asked me to make a statement and whether or not I want to press charges.'
'What did you say ?'
'I told them I hadn't made up my mind. I wanted to see you first.'
'I'll keep him out yer way. I promise. The bastard shouldn't 'ave done that to you. You're his mate.'
'I was his mate.'
'Is that it ?'
'No, unfortunately it's not.'
'Can I 'ave a large Danish ?' Beth grinned sheepishly. 'If we're stopping like.'

   Lauren ordered them both more drinks and a two large Danish pastries.
'The thing is Beth.'
   Lauren was about to launch into the second difficult part of the Robert P.Gorman story when the café door was flung open. In stormed an incendiary faced Robert. He charged across to their table and made a grab for the pushchair. Noticing him just in time Beth instinctively threw herself across it. Robert dramatically halted in his tracks, and turned towards the seated Lauren.
'Please will you leave my fiancée alone Lauren.' He was shaking, his voice was raised and the eyes of everyone in the café had turned towards their table.

'Fiancée ?'
'Fuck off will you Rob. I'm talking to Lauren.' Beth looked at him, her arms stretched out across the tiny confused and concerned face of her little boy.
'Well I forbid it Bethany. I don't think you should be mixing with her.' He was close to tears again, his head twitching furiously.
'Robert please calm down will you.' Lauren got to her feet, trying her hardest not to provoke him any further. Beth didn't seem to have any such qualms.
'Who the fuck do you think you are Rob ? Get out of my face right now or there won't be any fucking wedding.' The middle-aged waitress in the blue pinny came across to their table.
'Could you take your arguments outside please folks. You're upsetting my other customers.'
'Look I'm really sorry about all this we were…' Lauren tried to explain.
'This bloke is hassling us, he won't leave us alone. Could you get rid of him.' Beth was much more direct.
'Beth please ?' Now the tears began to roll down Robert's face. Rejection. That's what really hurt.
'Just go home Rob.' She looked at him with undisguised disgust. What had he become ? The waitress tried to take Robert by the arm but he pulled it sharply out of the way.
'Get your fucking hands off me.'
'Sir, if you don't leave my premises I'm afraid I'll have to call the police.'
'I'm not going anywhere.'

   The thick-set man in blue overalls and reflective jacket who had been quietly watching the proceedings from his perch across the other side of the café now wandered across to their table.
'Is this gent giving you problems ladies ?' He asked in a gently controlled West Yorkshire accent.
'Aye, he is. He won't leave, will you Rob.' Beth taunted her blubbering boyfriend.
'Come on now mate. Time to go home and leave the ladies to their conversation.' He placed his hand on Robert's shoulder.
'Get your fucking hands off me.' He turned his contorted angry face to the man.
'Now let's not have any trouble shall we.'
'If you don't take your hands off me I'll push you through that window.' The workman didn't seem unduly threatened. He raised an eyebrow and smiled.
'Ooh like that now is it ?' He was twice Robert's size and unlikely to be pushed anywhere. Beth was grinning. Lauren didn't know where to look as every eye in the place fixed on their table. A group of five young lads in tracksuits and baseball caps were loitering outside, their faces pressed up against the window trying to make out the activity inside.
'Come on Robert, nobody wants any trouble. I'll take you home if you like.' Lauren reached for his arm.
'You just keep away you dirty fucking slut.' Robert was jabbing his finger at her, his face twisted and full of fury just as it had been the night of the attack.

   The workman took him firmly by the waist and attempted to move him towards

the door, Robert quickly swung his arms, picked up the empty glass that had contained Beth's Coke and slammed it down on the closely-cropped head of his attacker. The man let out a guttural scream, loosened his grip and put his hands to his bleeding head, the shattered glass spraying across the floor of the café.
'Now look what you made me do you dirty cheating bitch.' He wagged his finger at Lauren accusingly.
The rest of the staff had come out from the kitchen to see what was going on. A burly looking chef with greasy black hair wiped his hands on his apron , whilst a teenage waitress helped the concussed workman to another table. The middle-aged waitress who appeared to be running the place was using the phone on the wall behind the counter to contact the police.
'I can't believe you just did that you lunatic.' Lauren grabbed hold of him. This was more than she could stand. He had pushed her well beyond her limits. She rarely lost her temper, not properly, it was kept in reserve for very special degrees of annoyance. When it was unleashed it coursed through her like a force of nature. Robert was just about to experience its full force for himself.
'I thought you were fucking alright you, you took me in. I thought you were just a bit shy and lonely but you're an absolute fucking mentalist. How dare you do this to me Robert ? What the fuck do you think you're playing at ?'
   She was shaking him, anger pulsing through every pore. Beth stood open-mouthed as Christopher who until now had been concerned but bravely quiet, started to cry. Sensing the danger, Beth pushed the pushchair away from the table whilst the middle-aged waitress gestured for her to go through the doors into the kitchen and safety.
'And why don't you tell Beth about what happened at the library Robert ? Why don't you let her know why you got the sack ?'
'Who told you that ?' A look of blind panic crossed his face.
   Lauren seeing his discomfort seized the moment.
'You didn't want to be reminded of that little incident did you ? You're lucky that you're not being burnt out of your poxy flat by a lynch-mob on the hunt for paedos.'
   Robert's tears returned, this time in heavy uncontrollable sobs.
'It wasn't like that Lauren. It wasn't fucking like that. It was a misunderstanding for god's sake.' He held out his hands, imploring her to believe him.
   Lauren was too far gone to notice.
'Was attacking me a misunderstanding ? Was smashing a glass over a strangers head a fucking misunderstanding ?'
'Please Lauren, not here, please don't do this to me.' He was wobbling on his feet, his face completely ashen.
'You were the one who burst in here. You were the one who must have been watching us again like a fucking stalker. I didn't want any of this. It's you Robert. You bring it on yourself, you do this to yourself.'
   Suddenly his eyes looked skywards , his legs buckled and he fell to the floor. At just that moment a couple of police officers entered the café and scurried across to Robert's prone figure. Lauren stood above him, her whole body shaking, her heart

in her mouth, and beads of sweat glistening on her brow. Her anger was spent. It was all done. The policeman looked up at her.
'OK madam, we'll take over now.'

Lauren sat down on the chair and stared out of the window. A large crowd of goggle-eyed onlookers had amassed on the pavement and were staring in blind disbelief at what they'd just seen. One of the teenage waitresses brought her a glass of water. An ambulance crew quickly followed and helped the woozy and confused workman, his wound oozing red mess down his reflective jacket, off to get some treatment. As Robert slowly came around the female police officer sat down next to Lauren.
'Now, would you like to tell me what this has all been about ?'
Just where did she begin ?

Someone to drive her home

Francis picked her up from the police station, his face drawn, the bags under his eyes looking heavier by the day.
'It never ends at the minute does it.' He sighed.
'Don't give me hassle Francis.' Lauren buckled her seat-belt and leaned back in the passenger seat. The purple rosary beads that hung from his car mirror glistened in the street light.
'I'm not going to. I'm just feeling a bit out of my depth .You know I don't like controversy.'
'You're out of your depth ? How do you think I feel.' Her head was thumping mercilessly. It had been a very long afternoon. They pulled out of the car park of the Fulford Road station. Francis tapped the steering wheel at irregular intervals as he silently negotiated the inner ring-road and headed back towards home. His Scissor Sisters cassette played low on the car stereo providing an incongruous upbeat accompaniment.
'And where are Beth and the baby now.' He finally spoke, curiosity getting the better of him.
'They're at her mum's.'
'Did you meet her ?'
'I saw her briefly in the waiting room.' Lauren sat back in the passenger seat with her eyes closed. She'd seen more than enough of the world today. Her body was exhausted with rage.
'What was she like.'
'Like Beth but older.'
Francis nodded.
'And where is…'
'He's still being interviewed. Could be charged for the assault.'

'He needs locking up.'
Lauren didn't say anything.
'They know everything now.' As they pulled into their street, Lauren finally spoke.
'Everything ?'
'I told Beth and her mum everything I knew. Beth wants to get onto the council to get a new flat. Away from Robert. Her mum wants her to live at home with her. Possibly go to college.'
'But she doesn't want to ?' The car pulled up outside their house in the space it had vacated half an hour or so earlier.
'She's an independent little so-and-so.' Lauren unbuckled her belt as the car came to a halt.
'Is that why you get on ? ' Francis smiled at her, as he eased on the handbrake and flicked off his cassette.
'Aye, s'pose so,' she found just enough energy to smile back. Bless St. Francis. He always made the world right.
'You're even sounding like her now.'

The world moves on

Lauren suddenly had a panicked thought. Was her passport still in date ? She'd applied for one years ago prior to a proposed Interail tour of Europe. In the end the trip didn't happen and the passport wasn't needed. Where had she put it ? It had popped up unexpectedly countless times over the past ten years, now when she wanted it she couldn't find the damn thing. Finally she discovered it lurking at the bottom of her knicker draw. After getting over the shock of seeing her passport photo she saw the expiry date was three months away. It was still good to go. So that was her 22 year old self sealed under plastic film at the back of her never used passport. She looked sort of confident and content. Lauren tried to remember where she thought she'd be by now. She vaguely recollected having thoughts of being a writer, maybe living with someone. Definitely not married though. Did children play any part in her thoughts back then ? There had been conversations with Millie on the subject. Millie always knew where she wanted to be.
'Married to a wealthy bloke, a couple of kids, lady of leisure. That kind of thing.'
'That would just bore me stupid.'
'I think access to a credit card or two might ameliorate my boredom. Good looks and a six-pack would help as well.'
'Well I hope you eventually bump into him.'
'Me too.'
Now it seems as if she just had.

'It's going to be a massive wedding.' Millie's excitement was threatening to overflow at any point. 'In this lovely little clapper-board church in Karl's home town. His parents are really pulling out all the stops. And guess what ?' She spoke at double-speed, barely pausing for breath.

'What ?' Lauren was trying her hardest to be enthusiastic for her friend. It wasn't easy.
'His parents are going to pay for my family and friends to come over and stay. Just how cool is that ?'
'Sounds fantastic.' It was a generous offer, but still.
'They've got this lovely big place. You're going to love it. His older sister lives nearby, she's married to this real estate guy called Don, there place is nearly as big. The plan is for me, mum and dad and the bridesmaid to stay at hers. Which would be you of course…'
'Of course.' Lauren suddenly had a nightmare vision of herself in a bridesmaids dress in some Stepford style American town full of perfect wholesome apple pie women. It wasn't pleasant. Actually, the thought of mincing around in a big frock didn't do much for her full-stop. It would only be for one day. At least there would be little danger of the bride being upstaged she thought.
'Oh it's going to be amazing Lauren. I can't wait to see you and tell you all about it. Only a few days now.'
'Yeah, not long.' She was counting the days, but not in a good sense, more in an 'oh my god, I have to sit in a tin box several thousand feet in the air for seven hours with a load of smelly strangers,' kind of way.

Francis had been busy buying new clothes for his New York holiday. He came home ladened down with bags from Next and M&S. These were his staple shops. He was a man of simple tastes and knew what he liked.
'I've bought a couple of new jumpers, a new scarf and hat set, a nice pair of cords oh and these.' From a Schuh bag he pulled out a box. Opening it he showed a perfect white pair of Dunlop Green Flash trainers to Lauren.
'Oooh Green Flash, very nice.' Impressive. She wouldn't have minded a pair herself.
'Well, I've heard you going on about them and thought I'd get myself a pair. We used to wear these in PE back in my day.'
'Retro-chic Francis, very now.' Lauren grinned at him.
'Well, I didn't want to look like an old fuddy-duddy next to you youngsters in Noo Yorik.' He mimicked a New York accent and waved his open hands in a showbiz fashion. It seemed to be almost compulsory to end any conversation about the city at the moment with a stab at the lingo.   Lauren picked up the Rough Guide for the thousandth time. It would be good. It would definitely be good she kept telling herself. Seeing Millie as well. Her oldest, closest friend. Her partner in crime. Wouldn't that be fantastic ? Of course it would.

Wouldn't it ?

The future beckons

The 9.15 train pulled into Kings Cross Station. A purposeful crowd of hassled looking people stepped onto the platform and headed off to their places of work.

The train had filled up steadily as they moved further south, passing endless flat empty fields and anonymous commuter towns. She had found a comfortable berth by a window and kept her head buried in her newspaper, book and magazine as a means to fend off unnecessary conversation. As a rule, she hated public transport, but as a non-driver it was a painful necessity. There was always the possibility of being jammed into a window seat by a nutter with a runaway mouth and a personal hygiene problem. Even worse, once or twice she'd been chatted up on the train by eager faced young men with holdalls. Poor things, what did they know ?

   Lauren moved quickly amongst the herd without really knowing where she was going. The tube map confused her, but a finger placed on the line from Kings Cross to where she was ultimately heading began to make matters slightly clearer. A ticket was purchased from a blank confusing machine and soon she was underneath the station, standing on the platform with a massed rank of faceless humanity. Already she was feeling homesick for little York. A handful of serious looking commuters in expensive suits and long coats had jumped on the train at York with her. They must commute all the way to London from York every day. It was only two or so hours, it was probably do-able. Maybe that's what she could do ? Live with Francis then get the train every day. No, don't be ridiculous. The train fare alone would swallow up her salary and Francis would hit the roof. If she was going to make this leap into a new life there couldn't be any looking back.

   She jumped on the right tube train, managed to remember where to change and eventually came back above ground just streets away from the offices of Forward Arc. The tube journey had been grim. Packed in like sardines with determinedly glum faces from right across the planet. Other people might have been inspired at this point, Lauren just felt a little trapped.

    She had hoped to purchase something new to wear for the interview, but in the end she had gone dressed in a navy blue trouser suit that had been lurking at the back of her wardrobe for just such an occasion. Wearing it felt odd and the cut was showing its age. Accent had been fairly laid back on the dress code front, at least for the creative team. She had frequently rolled into work in a pair of jeans, and Barry never seemed to change out of his faded Red Dwarf t-shirt. She wondered what Barry was doing now ? Probably sat smoking a roll-up whilst poring over his drawing board in the attic study of his little Acomb house. Maybe in a while he'd knock-off make himself a cup of tea and then take his black Labrador for a run in West Bank Park. It would have been nice to have seen a friendly face amongst the throng of people. No matter, she was here for a purpose and couldn't allow herself to drift off into melancholy. Not today.

     The offices of Forward Arc were bright, colourful and furnished in stuff that looked as if it had come straight from the pages of an up to the minute design catalogue. An impossibly upbeat young man with shiny black shoes, no older than 25 led her through to the interview room where she was met by three senior staff. One guy, in his mid-forties was a senior executive, a skinny woman with a smokers smile who looked vaguely contemptuous of Lauren's appearance headed up human resources and another man, around about her age, good looking with dark brown eyes, olive skin and shoulder length curly hair was introduced as the head of the creative team. She was sure he had given her an admiring glance as she sat down which helped to bolster her confidence after the negative vibes she'd been picking up from the woman from HR.

In the end the interview went as well as could be expected. She managed to answer all the questions that were posed quite quickly and efficiently. Once proceedings got under way her nerves dissipated. The guy from the creative team discussed some of the ideas he'd seen in the samples of work she'd sent in with her application. Lauren even managed to share a joke which was received in the right spirit. Leaving the offices she felt pleased with her performance. It was quite a revelation. The first interview she'd been to in over a decade and it went swimmingly. She bought herself a copy of the Evening Standard and a Time Out for the journey back. She tried hard to imagine herself living in the capital, travelling on the tube, swanning around the offices of Forward Arc, actually advancing in her career for once. The thought was as equally exciting as it was terrifying. Her confidence in her ability to handle such a transition was growing daily. The interview had strengthened her confidence further. Even if this opportunity didn't ultimately land her way, then there would be others.

Then as the train pulled back into York, the winter sun failing as the floodlights came on underneath the city walls she felt a different kind of emotional pull. There sitting in the car park with his engine running, just as he promised was Francis. He waved at her gleefully, as Lauren ran across to jump in the passenger seat.
'So ?' He asked.
'So what?'
'So how did it go ? Are we going to lose you to London then. Did you get your head turned ?'
'It was OK actually. Yeah, it was OK.'
'There, I told you that would happen. You're too big for this little town Lauren.'
'We'll see shall we.'

I want to be a part of it

The alarm buzzed furiously. It was 2:30 Am but it wasn't a mistake. Their flight left Manchester at 7:45 and they had to be there in time to check-in. Francis was fussing around full of energy. He'd hardly slept, packed and unpacked his case, flossed his teeth, attempted a restyle of his thinning, receding hair and then collapsed on the sofa in the front room. He was wringing his hands and humming show tunes as a means of distraction. Lauren by way of contrast had to drag herself painfully from her comfortable bed. So this was it. She stood stirring her third mug of coffee in half an hour.
'You'll be needing the toilet every five minutes.'
'Hmmm.' Her eyelids could barely open. Lauren was not a morning person, particularly when that morning began before three.

'Now are you sure you've got all you need ?' Francis hadn't been convinced that the hasty packing that Lauren had undertaken had covered all possible meteorological bases. How could she be so blasé ? Being found without the right coat was a faux-pas too far for Francis to contemplate. Particularly somewhere as hip and stylish as New York.
'Hmmm.' She scratched her head.
'It's going to be cold out there.'
'It is.' Every word thumped home into her half-awake brain.
'I'm not getting any impression of urgency from you here. You're about to go to New York, you could try and be excited.'
'It's hard to be excited at this time of the morning. My bed is calling.' So it was. Her soft cotton sheet, her lovely big duvet. Man, it was good that bed. The mattress now fitted her shape perfectly. Bed was a lovely old friend. She was going to miss that bed.
'You can sleep on the plane.'
'Don't mention that.' Lauren winced.
'What ?'
'The plane. I don't want to think about it until I absolutely have to.'
'Fair enough. It's really nothing to worry about.' Francis flung a hand up dismissively.
'Says the man with a hip flask full of whisky and some sleeping pills.'
'I can assure you that after I've downed them I won't be worrying in the slightest.'
'I'm not surprised. Just stay awake until we get going won't you.'

   A taxi was due to pick them up at 3.25 to take them down to the railway station. Francis stood peering anxiously around the curtain in the front room, hopping from one foot to the other. Lauren thought he might be about to wet himself.
'Where is he ?' Francis examined his watch.
'It's not time yet. Give him chance.' Up until then Francis had been bearable. Now he was beginning to slip into mildly irritating. Bloody hell, the house was cold. She wrapped her arms around herself and once again thought longingly about the cosy refuge that she'd been so rudely dragged from at such an early hour. To go on a damn plane as well. It just wasn't right. Wait a minute, oldest, bestest friend, trip of a lifetime and all that. You had to suffer for your friends.
'Our train goes at ten to four we need to get there. Maybe I should I have booked at it for 3.15.'
'Well, we didn't. Just chill out, we've got loads of time.'
'I'm not so sure. Did I turn off all the switches ?'
'Yes, we turned off all the switches, pulled out the plugs, Sally from next door will be watering the plants and checking everything's ok.' I bet she will thought Lauren. She'll be rifling through my knicker drawer looking for anything incriminating, the nosy, good for nothing, think she's it little…
'Did I cancel the milk ?' Francis looked alarmed.
'Francis, we don't have a milkman.'
'We don't ?' He looked at her confused. Lauren shook her head. Then the phone

rang. They both froze.

'Who would call at this time of morning ?' Francis asked rhetorically.

'Could be Millie, seeing if we've left.' Lauren was thinking aloud. It continued to ring. It sounded cold and persistent in this bitter early hour.

'Would she do that ?' Francis wasn't convinced.

'Probably not. Shall we leave it.'

'I think we should.' But he didn't seem very sure.

'What if it's an emergency ? It could be a parent.'

'You're right, shall I get it ?'

Lauren nodded. Francis caught the phone on the last ring before it was due to click into the answering service.

'It's for you. A woman.' Francis handed her the phone.

'Is that Lauren Seymour ?' It was a voice she vaguely recognised but her brain couldn't register.

'It is ?'

'Oh, sorry to disturb you like this, I believe we've spoken before. It's Maggie Curran again at York District Hospital.'

'Yes we have. Is this an emergency ?'

'It's a bit of a case of déjà vu I'm afraid. It's your friend, Mr Gorman. We've got him at the hospital again.'

'Did he…'

'No nothing like that. I'm afraid there's been a bit of an unfortunate incident. He was brought here by the police. He's been attacked.'

'Where ? What happened ?'

'All we know at the present moment is that people broke into his home and beat him up. He's not conscious at the moment, he's in a very bad way. We've got you down as his next of kin. That's why we called. Is that right ?'

'He doesn't have any family.' Of course. There was only ever her. She was shackled to him because he had no other and her conscience wouldn't allow her to break free. Francis was looking at his watch, his face grave and concerned.

'Will you be coming down in the morning to see him ? The police may wish to speak to you as well.'

'I'm…'

But she couldn't say what she was doing. What was she doing ? Standing in the front room with a suitcase and an expectant housemate, about to fly half way across the world. It wasn't what she did was it ? Of course something would intervene. It always did.

'OK, well I'll leave it with you.' The voice sounded confused as to the relationship between the injured man and this woman on the other end of the phone. Maggie Curran wasn't the only one confused. 'I go off shift at 6, but if you want to get in touch with one of my colleagues they should be able to give you a bit more information. He's very poorly, but we think he'll be OK.'

'Right.'

'I do apologise for having to be the bearer of bad news again.'

Lauren tried to think of something appropriate to say but the words wouldn't

come. The conversation over she stood frozen to the spot, staring into space.
'It's him isn't it ?' Francis asked.
Lauren nodded blankly.
'He's in hospital.'
'Tried to top himself again did he ? Ashamed of all he's done.' Francis tapped his watch distractedly. He didn't need any of this.
'No, he got attacked. He got beaten up in his flat.'
'Probably no less than he deserves.'
'Francis !' Lauren could feel herself wanting to cry but she was determined to resist the impending tears. The sound of a car pulling into the street and gliding to a halt outside their house stopped them both in their tracks. Moments later a car horn sounded.
'That's it. We're off.' Francis picked up his case and headed towards the hall door. Lauren remained rooted to the spot. 'Come on Lauren. It's time. We're going to New York.' But she didn't move. She just stared at him not sure if she knew how to put one foot in front of the other anymore. Francis walked across and took her by the arm. 'Don't do this to me now Lauren, please let's just go.' His voice was far from it's usual assured self. It was panicked and desperate, 'we've got to go.' The car horn beeped for a second time.
'I can't go.' She slowly mouthed.
'Yes you can, come on.' He tried his hardest to reassure her. 'In a few hours time we'll be flying out to see your oldest and bestest friend in the world. Imagine that.'
'I can't leave him. It's my fault.'
'Please, we haven't got time to discuss this now, please let's just go. You can call the hospital from the airport. He'll pull through, he's a strong boy.'
'No. It's no good. I can't.' She shook her head. The taxi driver again beeped his horn impatiently.
'If we don't get out there in a minute he's going to be gone. Now this is your last chance. We're going to New York.'
'You go,' she gave him an anguished look, her face imploring him to leave, 'please.' Francis looked at her. She was completely immobile, her face was cold, her eyes distant and withdrawn.
'I can't believe you're choosing him over Millie and I ? What do I tell her when I get there. How will she feel ?'
'Please go Francis.'
   He gave her one last saddened look before picking up his case, dragging it and his heavy heart out of the front door. A few seconds later she heard the taxi door slam and the car pull away. Her opportunity had gone. Robert P.Gorman had intervened again.

The truth hurts

The WPC who had spoken to her in the café was waiting for her when she arrived at the hospital.
'Sorry to have meet again under such circumstances Ms Seymour.'
'That's OK.' But it was far from OK.
'I just needed to fill you in with what has been going on here. There was an attack on Mr Gorman at his flat last night. A couple of men in balaclavas broke down his door and beat him up. They left him unconscious and then overturned his flat. They also spray painted graffiti all over the walls of the property.' She spoke with the same cold matter-of-fact tone. This was just another day at the office for her. At the end of her shift she could go home and tell her partner all about the weird guy and his peculiar relationship with the stroppy tall woman. They'd both laugh, knock back another glass of wine before settling down for a cuddle on the sofa whilst watching the soaps.
'Graffiti ? What like ?'
'I think it suggested that Mr Gorman was a paedophile.'
'Oh.' She should have expected it. People could be unforgiving if they got wind of ugly rumours. What had she expected to happen when she spilled the beans on Robert's past ? Understanding and forgiveness ? It was never likely.
'We've already apprehended the men we believe to be responsible for it. One of the tenants saw them leave the block and jump into a red Ford Mondeo. He took down the number and we traced it to a Mr Mark Hardy of Acomb.'
'Hardy ?' That immediately rang an alarm bell. 'I know that surname.'
'Yes, we believe Mr Hardy to be the older brother of a Bethany Hardy who previously lived next door to Mr Gorman.'
'They had a relationship.'
'Yes, he was accompanied in the attack by Bethany Hardy's father.'
'I thought he was in prison.' It was hard to keep up.
'Released a couple of weeks ago. He could well be going back inside for this.'
'I don't know what to say.' She had secretly half-expected this. Nothing good could have come of trying to play this one by the book. It was always going to end with someone getting hurt. Maybe all of them.
'Needless to say we think Mr Gorman has made a number of enemies. He does appear to have something of a history.'
'I don't know much about it.'
'You are his next of kin ?'
'So I've been told. He's got no family at all.'
'I think your friend may well need a new start somewhere.' The WPC did her best to look sympathetic. It wasn't fooling anyone, least of all Lauren.
'He's not my friend.'
'He's not ? Oh, I presumed as you were here that…'
'He's just someone I know, that's all.'
'Well, we will obviously be talking to him about all this. There may be some assistance we can give him.'
'Of course.'
'Are you OK Ms Seymour ? Can I get you anything ?'

'I don't know.'
'Sorry ?'
'I don't know if I'm OK.' How did she begin to describe how she now felt ?
'Would you like me to get a doctor or a nurse or something ?'
'I just want to see him.'

   Robert was hooked up to a drip and a couple of monitors, his face was black and blue, he had massive cuts which had received stitches under his lips and eyes. His eyelids were shut and in the grey light of the hospital room he looked like a damaged corpse. It was an ugly and unexpected sight. She paused open-mouthed for a while trying to take in what it was that was stretched out before her.
   Lauren sat down on the chair next to the bed and stared at the far wall listening to the beep of the monitor. Seconds passed, the body slowly stirred, a hand tensed and untensed, eyelids flickered open.
'Thanks for coming.' A strained feeble voice finally spoke. 'You didn't have to.'
'No, I didn't. I don't know why I'm here.' She refused to make eye-contact and instead kept her attention firmly fixed on the far wall.
'I'm sorry about everything.'
'OK.' They both fell into silence. Now it was Lauren's turn to speak. Finally she looked him the eye. 'This can't go on Robert. You can't keep doing this to me.'
'I didn't want this Lauren. I wanted to let you go.'
'Really ? It doesn't feel like it. I feel like I'm shackled to you.'
'As I said, you didn't have to come.'
   That was the truth. Just how easy would it have been to have ignored the call and jump in the taxi with Francis ? She'd now be half-way across the Atlantic, miles from the demands of this sorry state of a man. Why was she here ? As of yet, she was unable to properly answer. But here she was whilst Francis sat next to an empty seat on the Manchester to New York plane.
'Have you heard from Beth ?'
'No, nothing. She doesn't want anything to do with me. I bet she asked them to do this.'
'Maybe.' It was possible. That girl was as hard as nails but was this really her style ?
'I don't know Robert. I shouldn't be involved in any of this.'
'But you are though.'
  Lauren didn't reply.
'What are you going to do ? I think you should think about a new start somewhere. Where nobody knows you.'
'Run away like a dirty nonce you mean.'
'No I didn't mean.' That wasn't what she'd said. 'Anyway, I don't know what to think. You've never told me what happened.'
'It's not something to be proud of.' He seemed exasperated, confused as to why anyone would want to quiz him now. Did he really think his current condition gave him immunity from his history ? There could be no hiding places.
'No. Did you do the things you are meant to have done ?' Lauren was not going to be restrained by his current feeble condition. There had been far too much treading

on eggshells and look where it had got them both.

'It was all a misunderstanding. I can't talk about it now.'

'You either tell me now or I leave here beginning to believe the graffiti they left in your flat.' Her voice was firm and to the point.

'Alright, alright,' he sighed, then took a deep breath. 'I'd never had a girlfriend. This young girl came onto me quite strongly. Sent me love letters, suggestive cards, told me that she thought the world of me. I didn't know what to think.'

'And ?'

'Then one week after our group the other kids had left and she hung around talking to me.'

'Then what ?'

'I tried to kiss her.'

'You did what ?' Did the idiocy of this man no know bounds ?

'I know I shouldn't have. It was stupid of me, but she was acting all provocative and leading me on.'

'Oh for fucks sake Robert.' She disgustedly jammed her chair away from him, the legs making a dull scrape on the floor. 'You do realise that's what all paedophiles say don't you ? That somehow the kid wanted it. That they were asking for it.'

'I know but I didn't do anything with her.' His voice was anguished and upset. 'She pulled away from me screaming, told the rest of the library staff what had happened and I got suspended.'

'And why did the case against you fail ?'

'I'd kept the notes and cards I'd received from her. The police confronted her with them and she broke down. It was all just messy.'

'None of this excuses the fact that you as a person left in the care of a child, because that's what she was Robert, attempted to take advantage of her.' The stupid, stupid, stupid, little man. Robert wasn't a dark continent. He was an open book with the words "fuck-up" written across the front in bold heavy type.

'I know and if I could turn back the clock.' He pleaded for an ounce of sympathy. It wasn't about to be forthcoming.

'You should have thought of that. And what about Beth ? Where does she fit in.'

'It was after you bought me my new clothes, she'd started taking more interest in me. I was flattered by it. Like I said, I'd never had a girlfriend.'

'Did you not think it could look suspicious with your history ?'

'Of course I did, I'm not completely clueless.'

'I'm not so sure.'

'Anyway, we never slept together.'

'What ?' Lauren had just presumed.

'Me and Beth. We never did anything. She wouldn't sleep with me and I didn't mind as the thought scared me shitless. She wanted us to be boyfriend and girlfriend but not sleep together. I agreed as it kept things simpler. I just liked her company.'

'You're joking ?' Just liked her company ? A man happily foregoing sex ? Robert was even weirder than she'd realised.

'No, you were my first.'

'Oh.' There went the bombshell.

'That's why I think I was so upset.' Could this begin to explain his behaviour ? Like hell it could.
'Doesn't excuse the fact that you stalked me for weeks. What the fuck were you thinking ?'
'I wasn't thinking anything that was just it. I think I fell in love with you.'
'Fuck off did you.' The 'L' word hadn't been completely unexpected, yet that did little to appease the offence it caused to her ears.
'Don't say that.' What had he expected ? A similar declaration from Lauren ?
'You didn't love me Robert, you were just obsessed. You wouldn't know the meaning of the word.'
'I did love you. I do love you. I liked Beth but I love you.'
'No you fucking don't .' She slammed the edge of the bed with her hand. 'You don't get it do you ? You have completely fucked up where I'm concerned. You stalked me, you threaten me, you call me every name under the sun and leave me lying in my own piss in a back alley. Then you humiliate me in public and glass a guy who tried to intervene. That's not love Robert. That's fucking obsession.'
'Please Lauren, none of this need have happened.'
'Oh what ?' Her patience had finally snapped 'It was all a misunderstanding was it ? Like with the girl in the library.'
'That's not fair.'
'Isn't it ? Well that's just tough. I missed a flight to New York to be here with you. I've probably fucked up my relationship with my two closest friends because of this.'
'So you must feel something for me. Otherwise you wouldn't be here.'
'Robert all I feel for you is pity. It's just doing enough to ameliorate my contempt.'
'Is there someone else ?'
'First lesson in one night stands Robert, because that's all it ever was, is that once it's done with you move on. You don't stalk your partner, you don't threaten them, you don't fuck with their head. I could have slept with countless blokes since I drunkenly, foolishly shagged you and it would be none of your business. A shag, is a shag, is a shag. It's a lark, then it's done. Not every time you jump into bed with someone means that wedding bells will soon be ringing.'
'Have you ?'
'As I said, that's none of your business.'
'Please say you feel something for me.'
'What, and lie to you ?'
'Did you never ?'
'Alright, for a brief moment I thought we could perhaps be friends. That we could get along, go to the cinema occasionally, have a drink together.'
'Only friends.'
'Only ever friends.' That was her story and she was sticking to it.
'Now what ?'
'Now, I want you to get the hell out of York and out of my life.' She pointed towards the door as if the badly bruised and broken Robert could have jumped up and left there and then. 'I want you to move on because believe it or not, I still think

you can put all this behind you.'

'You do ?' It was the first piece of encouragement she'd given him all morning. 'Just about.'

They sat in silence. Robert's eyes slowly closed and Lauren heard the sound of his heavy, drawn out breath. He was sleeping. She quietly rose to her feet and stepped away from the bandaged shape. He looked peaceful lying there, out of harms way. Walking to the door, she took one last look at him and wondered how all this had begun.

The silence from New York had been deafening. Lauren wondered whether she should attempt to make contact with Millie just yet. Maybe she should wait until Francis returned home. Would he still be speaking to her when he did arrive back ? Would he still want her living with him ? Lauren knew that this had been a major betrayal of their relationship. The understanding they shared had been ruptured. At the end of the day, she had been given a split-second choice between her two closest friends and Robert, and had chosen Robert. Only she could begin to answer why she had done that. Despite her guilt at the wasted ticket, which she intended to compensate Francis for upon his return, Lauren had an instinctive feeling that she'd made the right decision. Why that should be so though, she had as yet little or no idea. There had been a finality about this last encounter with Robert. She didn't suspect she'd be hearing from him again.

Time to move on

The last of the Wednesday morning stragglers had gone home. Students mainly, a few casualties from the weekly rock night at Ziggys winded their way back to their shared houses. One young woman was singing a word perfect verse of Motorcycle Emptiness by the Manic Street Preachers as she went. She weaved her solitary way through the dark empty streets, pressing her nose against the window of the fast food chicken takeaway on Pavement, before heading up the Shambles, and on towards her home. In her drunken haze these old streets could belong to her.

For a brief few hours York would be silent. There was hardly a car in sight anywhere in the centre of the city. One or two homeless individuals wandered looking for shelter against the February weather. A premature blackbird sang a lonely song from a tree along the banks of the river, as a dark figure sat at a table outside the King's Arms on the banks of the Ouse. The pub had featured in thousands of photos down the years. Its regular flooding a source of amazement for tourists, a fact of life for the landlord.

The last few days had been wet up in the Dales. The great Yorkshire rivers that began high in the hills were sending their dark peaty contents down into the heart of the ancient city. The water coursed, swirled and bubbled its way. It was within an inch or two of breaking its banks yet again. Another wet day would see the final push it needed to send it over the edge, seeping steadily into the neat front rooms of the folks who had paid for a river view.

The figure on the bank stood up and gazed at the water, seemingly lost deep in thought. If there had been anyone watching they would have seen it pause, then look up towards the sky at the clouds that were being blown across the almost full moon. It hesitated for a moment longer. Then it turned, walked away from the banks and began to climb the steep steps that led up to the road and the bridge above. It walked slowly, deliberately, running a distracted arm along the top of the bridge until it paused nearly half-way across.

Again it looked around, saw an empty taxi fly past and out of sight until once again it was completely alone. Then it placed both hands on the top of the faded stone bridge, levered itself up with its arms and sat down, dangling its legs over the side. Glancing down at the water flowing quickly beneath it, it seemed to wobble for a moment, until a left arm reached out and steadied itself. It fixed a tight grip, rose onto its knees then straightened up, slowly loosening the steady hand. There it stood balancing on the narrow stone surface of the bridge in the moonlight. It again glanced downwards at the reflection of the moon and the streetlight on the dark, swirling waters below. If it was waiting for a passing piece of humanity to spot it there then it would wait in vain. The street remained empty. Instead, the figure spread out its arms as wide and as straight as they would go, looked up towards the heavens and advanced its feet over the edge until gravity took hold. Down it dropped, its arms now raised high above its head, hands clasped together. If the figure could speak it would have spoken of how quickly all this had seemed to happen. The decisive clarity that had impelled it this far. The feeling of calm it felt before it hit the water and plummeted far below into the rushing brown torrent. It would of mentioned how the when the water began to fill its lungs, carrying the detritus of green rolling fields, the remnants of dry stone walls, and all those wind-blown invaders that made this place their home, a slow feeling of fulfilment had replaced those of fear. It would have said how its last moments were not tragic, but contented, the confusion of its life melting away in the gentle embrace of the icy waters. It maybe would have told how for once, it had felt little pain as the light that had shot through the murk of the enveloping water finally disappeared from its dying view.

So now what ?

Lauren recognised the print on the envelope. It was in the same style as the one she had received inviting her for an interview at Forward Arc. She picked it off the mat along with the menu from the dodgy looking kebab house that accompanied it. She took the letter through to the front room and sat down on the sofa examining the envelope. Over the past few days she had been sleeping in. With no job to go to and no housemate to accommodate there had been little preventing her from catching up on her precious sleep. She held the letter just before her eyes and hesitated. Deep breath Lauren :

'Here goes.'

Then quickly, urgently she ripped open the envelope, her hesitation now firmly behind her. Pulling out and unfolding the letter she saw the now familiar purple Forward Arc logo and began to read.
'Dear Ms Seymour.'
Good start thought Lauren. *Ms*. Very grown up career woman. Quickly, what does it say ?
'We are writing to offer you the position of Senior Copywriter here at Forward Arc.'
Lauren's hand dropped the letter. That couldn't be right. She curled her legs up under her and looked at the letter lying on the floor. No this wasn't in the script. After a minute or two, she reached down and picked it up. The job offer was still there. She hadn't misread it, and if she were dreaming surely Francis would have walked out of the kitchen wearing lederhosen and talking with the voice of Russell Brand by now. But he hadn't so this must be real.

Reading on it asked her to call the head of the creative team to discuss when she wanted to start work. Then she read the figure next to the starting salary.
'Fuck me !'
It was nearly twice what she had been earning at Accent. 'That can't be right.' The letter signed off with a cheery, *'we look forward to your acceptance and welcoming you to the successful team here at Forward Arc.'*

So now what ?

Picking up the threads

If everything was still as planned then Francis was due home tomorrow. Lauren had received no word from him or Millie since his departure. Part of her had hoped for an angry phone call from her best friend demanding to know what had happened. But it hadn't materialised. Instead there had been an almost week long silence. It was as if she had been written out of the script. This only served to exacerbate the tension. Still Lauren felt little regret for doing what she had done. It had not been part of her plans to get a phone call from the hospital moments before they were due to leave but it all had a kind of tidy logic. Her business with Robert was unfinished. It had needed to reach a conclusion, for her to finally come nearer to understanding him, to tying up this curious period of her life. She needed to hear Robert tell her exactly what had happened with the girl in the library. Her questions couldn't be left unanswered.

She was still unsure about her feelings towards him. There were far too many grey areas in his past for her to truly ever allow herself to stop distrusting the man.

Equally however, she had seen much in his character that suggested he was far from just a one-dimensional deviant oddball. Robert. P.Gorman had potential of that she was certain. But he needed professional help. It had perhaps been wrong of her to think that she could be the person to help him become a properly functioning member of the human race. She liked to think she might have assisted that process just a little. If he could get his head together, move somewhere new, maybe secure some gainful employment, meet some new people and begin to find his identity. Then perhaps the story could turn for Robert. Other people had done and experienced much worse than him and managed to turn their lives around. From the moment his parents died and he went to live with his over protective nan his life had taken a tragic trajectory. It was almost as if some cruel hand had plotted the whole thing from the beginning, and was now sitting back and watching the fragments of his broken life with ill-disguised satisfaction.

Lauren wasn't expecting the figure, huddled in an oversized parka coat who now stood on her doorstep. It was Beth, her familiar sallow complexion and knotted brow, her premature look of complete world weariness, lightened only by her undoubted beauty and leftover innocence. Her hands were wrapped tight around her middle, her hard eyes were wide and staring, she sniffed and looked at Lauren.
'Beth ?'
'He's dead.' It was clear she'd been crying.
'I'm sorry.'
'Robert's dead.'

They both sat at the small dining table at the far end of the living room.
'We got a call from the police this morning. Someone in a barge down by Bishopthorpe saw his body floating past. Police search boat picked him up a bit further down.' Beth was remarkably still and matter of fact about it all.
'How did they know to call you ?'
'He'd tied a plastic envelope to his coat with stuff in it about who he was and who to contact if he got found.'
'Poor Robert.'
'It's what he wanted.'
'Yes.'
Lauren too felt something. An inner-stillness, a tentative little light inside her that held back any grief or regret. That may yet come, but for now all she felt was calm. That, and a steady sense of connection with the girl sitting opposite.
Beth offered Lauren a cigarette.
'I thought you were trying to give up.'
'I was'
They sat in silence drawing on their cigarettes, Beth's hand had a slight tremor. 'It weren't me that wanted him done in y'know.'
'No ?'
'I'd told mam not tell anyone but she gabbed like. News got back to me brother. Some lad were having a go at him about his sister being with a paedo. He called me

dad, they got off their heads and went round to sort him out.'
'Do you think he was ?'

Beth perhaps knew Robert better than anyone. Lauren had presumed that the younger woman's influence on Robert was detrimental to his well-being, in actual fact it could have been the making of him. He would have learnt some valuable lessons about women and about life, the nature of love and perhaps heartbreak. He could have grown with her. Emotionally he was never a man of 33, but a stunted problematic adolescent. The fates had conspired to make him so.

'Nah. I don't think he were a paedo. He never tried owt on. Sometimes I wished he would.'
'He was very fond of you.'
'Aye, but he loved you.'
'I'm not sure it was love.'

Whatever Robert's misplaced and mixed-up feelings towards Lauren, she knew she could never grace them with the "L" word. That was what she had been secretly nurturing inside her towards Matt, what Robert felt could surely never be anything like that.

'It were summat.'
'Was there a note ?'
'Just a bit of paper that said summat about it being "time to move on"' Lauren remembered her final words to Robert as he lay in his hospital bed. 'P'raps it's time for all of us to move on now.' Beth looked at her seeking some kind of recognition. Lauren smiled at the younger woman and held her hand.
'I've been offered a job. In London.'
'Nice one.'
'What about you. How are you going to move on ?'
'I think I'm gonna go t'college.'
'Good for you Beth. You're a bright girl.' This was the best news Lauren had heard in weeks. It surpassed her own job offer by several degrees of brightness.
'Aye, so people tell me.'
'You should listen to them.'
'I want to be a psychologist.'
'I think you'd be a good one.'
'D'ye reckon ?'
'Yeah, you're good at getting inside peoples heads.'
'For better or worse.' Beth sighed.
'What about Robert, what do you think made him tick ?'

Beth leaned back in her chair, stubbed out the remains of her cigarette and folded her hands.
'He just wanted folk to like him.'
'And hardly anyone did.'
'No, that were the problem. Nobody gave him a chance. That were why he fell for that girl at the library I reckon. She showed him a bit of attention like and he lost his 'ead. It wasn't right, but it didn't make him a paedo.'

In reality they were unlikely to ever know what had really gone on that afternoon in the library three years earlier. The girl involved would know the truth, but Lauren had no intention of attempting to track her down. All these remains would go the same way as Robert. No more stones would be upturned. No secrets would be uncovered with their never ending knot of time-wound threads tying the past to the future. They all needed to step out from all that had gone before and start something new, free from the pieces of someone else's history. Robert's story was over. Now they could all begin a new chapter of their own.

Beth eventually fell asleep on the sofa in the front room. Lauren found her sleep reassuring. She covered her with a blanket, placed a kiss on her cheek and then telephoned her mother. Her broad York accent was broken with sobs. She thanked Lauren for looking out for her daughter and expressed her sadness at all that had happened.

Then Lauren contacted the police. Speaking to an officer of the law had been an all to familiar experience for her of late. She wanted it to end. There would have to be an inquest, then he could be laid to rest. The police were trying to locate any extended family. Apparently there was a second cousin in Australia who had never met him but who sent his condolences. Other than that they kept drawing blanks. Under the circumstances the body would have to be released to his friends. As things currently stood this was Beth, her mum and Lauren herself.

After Beth had awoke, Lauren cooked them both tinned ravioli on toast and they sat watching Neighbours together whilst they demolished it. Being alongside Beth made Lauren feel marginally more at ease in the world today. She was a special young woman and Lauren felt privileged that circumstance had thrown them together like this. They made an unlikely pair.

Lauren arranged for a taxi to take Beth back to her mum's house, but promised to be in touch the next day to discuss how they were going to say goodbye to Robert P.Gorman.

Lauren again found sleep difficult to come by that night. She had spent time fiddling around on Myspace, checking Ebay for second hand clothes and reading the online papers. She'd also gone through her box of mementos, found her photograph of Matt and kissed it goodnight. She had been here before of course, but Robert was no Matt. The sense of loss she felt now was not that she had experienced when she had learnt of the news of Matt's death. This was of a different tenor altogether. She had perhaps been guilty of mixing the two men up in her mind. Attempting to intervene in the life of a troubled Robert had become a means to attempt to make amends for not intervening anymore than she had in the life of a troubled Matt. His death had been largely unforeseen, in the case of Robert , the possibility that he might try to make good his earlier failed attempt couldn't be ruled out.

If she had intended on stopping that tragic deed ever coming to pass then she had failed. There was no way of hiding from that fact, but perhaps her real failure had been in presuming that she, and she alone, could be the one who would make a difference. It had been arrogant of her to ever think that she knew what was best for Robert P.Gorman. She rarely knew what was best for herself. Nobody did. We pretended enough. Applied a wonky narrative to our decisions. Told ourselves and others that it was all for the best, that A followed B, but in the end everything was chance and circumstance. She knew that now. Maybe she'd stop being so hard on herself.

It might have been that Robert's earlier attempt had succeeded. She might have read about his demise in the local paper and come to connect his name with the strange boy she knew as an undergraduate. Perhaps like so much that happened locally, it might just have passed her by. As things turned out it hadn't passed her by. Robert had been given a couple more months of life on the planet. Two months in which he got his wardrobe sorted, found his first girlfriend, saw his first film at the cinema and lost his virginity. At least he hadn't died with his cherry intact. Thinking of this, Lauren managed a weak smile and finally lay down in her bed. Francis was due home tomorrow and there was much to tell him, a lot to explain, and a whole heap of forgiveness to seek.

The princess diaries

'The bastard.' Millie was in floods of dramatic theatrical tears. 'The two-timing, fucking bollock twat !' She punched the sofa repeatedly with the back of her clenched fist, and stomped her ballet-pump covered foot on the carpet.
'Let it all out,' thought Lauren.
'Well I did tell you hon, as soon as I set eyes on the boy I could tell.' Francis was knocking back a large measure of left-over Christmas Baileys.
'Shagging his best mate ! Can you believe how that made me feel Lauren?' Her mascara had run down her face, making her look like an extra from a school production of the Rocky Horror Show.
'No I guess I probably can't.' Lauren couldn't honestly say she was sorry to hear this news.
'Gay. I should have guessed. Now he decides to tell me. After I've given up my life, moved country, promised to marry him. The fucking bastard.' She tugged at her hair and gave the sofa another kick.

Francis winced and turned away.
'She's been like this all the way home.' He whispered to Lauren. He had been the one who had first suggested that big Alpha-Male hetero love stud Karl might not be as red-blooded as he made out. 'Marriage of convenience, didn't want to tell his folks that he fantasised about sleeping with the male lead, rather than playing the male lead. In my experience it's always the men who like to pretend they're big macho manly blokes who are the biggest queens on the block.' He smiled wickedly at Lauren. 'Such a shame. Whereas your preening girlie men are invariably all women mad.' He necked the last of his Baileys. 'Mother nature is one mixed-up bitter old fucker.'
'They're a dark continent are men.' Lauren gave her best friend a hug.
'Why didn't I listen to you Lauren ? You said it was all too sudden.' Millie couldn't possibly look more self-pitying.

'Cos you thought you were in love babes, it's not a crime.'
'But what was I thinking ?' She grabbed her cheeks and pulled them down.
'You wanted to believe in the fairy tale. You've always been a princess.'
'And look where it got me ?'
'Not that I've done much better have I ?'
'At least you've not made a fool of yourself like me. What am I going to tell everyone ?'
'Don't worry about that now. We'll sort it out.'
'And you, how are you doing ?' She put a hand on Lauren's cheek, and then gently moved a wisp of her hair from her face. 'It must have all been fucking terrible for you. I'm sorry for not being very sympathetic.' She was going to cry again.
'We're getting by. It'll work out alright.'
'And the job ? I've not asked about the job.' Francis remembered.
'Yeah, Franny said you'd had an interview or something ?'
'I did, and they offered me it. I can start in a couple of weeks.'
'So that means…' His face dropped as he realised that his housemate of nearly a decade would soon be moving on.
'I could be moving to London.'
'Will be moving to London. You've got to go do it babes, it'd be so cool for you.'
Millie held onto Lauren for dear life. Lauren in turn relaxed into the familiar sweet warm scent of her bestest, oldest friend in the whole wide world and wondered what happened next.
'I'm frightened I might be falling for the fairy-tale though Mills. Do we do happily ever after you and me ?'

The river flows

Five figures gathered around the edge of the bleak ragged moorland overlooking the vast expanse of the Hole of Horcum. The bulk of Francis, his face beginning to show the relentless passage of the years stood before the other four, his back to the drop at the point where the moor ran into sky. Millie held onto Lauren's arm , whilst Beth and her mum huddled under Beth's parka coat. In her arms, Beth's mum held a contented chattering baby Christopher.
'Friends,' began Francis, ' in all honesty, none of us really knew Robert that well. He was a lonely young man who entered our lives in a remarkable and unsuspected fashion. He touched all of us in some way and now he has gone we are left wondering what all of this might have meant. None of us will ever know for sure. Perhaps there is little meaning in these random events. All I do know is that we have a duty to give the boy a better send off than any reception he ever received in life.' He had judged the mood just right, that tender, special man. 'Lauren, if you'd like to come forward and do the honours.'

Lauren had been holding a cheap cremation urn containing the last remains of Robert. P.Gorman. She walked to the edge of the moor, held up the urn and spoke :
'To Robert.'

'To Robert,' they all chorused in return.

   She turned, unscrewed the lid and threw the contents out and down into the Hole Of Horcum, shaking the urn until every last fragment of his scorched remains had gone. They swirled in the breeze, then floated slowly downwards like a dirty descending cloud. She watched them disappear slowly out of sight, then looked up at the blue arc of the sky, the fresh wind blown in from the North Sea refreshing her spirit.

   On the way home Francis had taken them all into a fish restaurant just off the city's outer -ring road, for sit down fish, chips and mushy peas, washed down by bottles of lager and cups of tea. Francis had proposed a toast;
'To those of us who never got the chance to shine, may the rest of us use our light wisely.'
   Lauren held his arm and whispered in his ear.
'Where do you get all this from ? You should consider becoming a priest.'
'Now it's funny you should mention that.' He tapped his nose and winked before returning to his giant plate of chips and beer battered haddock.

   After their food, Francis had parked the car into which they'd all squeezed, in the car park on Marygate. Together they'd walked slowly down by the banks of the river in the direction of the Ings, the giant flood meadows that kept the city dry from the overflowing waters of the swollen Ouse. The sun had been slowly sinking, bringing to a close a February day that had been ripe with the promise of spring. No one had been saying much. They just walked together, at times some of them linked arms or held hands, at others each was seemingly lost in their own individual thoughts. Millie had appeared relieved to be home. Francis contemplated losing his housemate, whilst Beth and her mum perhaps dared to think that life might be beginning to take a turn for the better. Millie had hogged Christopher's pushchair, and she seemed to be getting on splendidly with his mum and nan.
   'We won't have many more chances to do this Lauren Seymour.' Francis had grabbed Lauren by the arm and delayed her from the rest of the ambling party.
'I wouldn't be so sure.' Lauren held him tightly. They walked on a little before she spoke again. 'You know how you said you always wanted to be a priest when you were little.'
'Oh yes, it was all I ever dreamt of. They had such lovely outfits.'
'Well I used to fantasise about being a writer. A proper one, not a poxy copy hack.'
'There's nothing wrong with being a copywriter.'
'Maybe not, but I think I've got a book in me.'
'Well I do hope it's not lodged anywhere delicate.'
   She laughed and thumped his chest playfully with the palm of her hand.
   The river passed them by in the opposite direction, as timeless as the sun that now set beyond the Ings, casting a red shadow under Clifton Bridge. A pair of ducks quacked conspiratorially as the unlikely group turned around and made their way slowly back to the car in the failing late winter light. The giant clanging bell of Great Peter marked time as another hour got tugged along by the muddy water, out of the

ancient city and home to the sea.

Visit the Take Me Out website

www.takemeoutabook.moonfruit.com

Or the book's very own Myspace page

www.myspace.com/takemeoutabook

TAKE ME OUT

Is a

GARBLED NOISE PRODUCTION

www.garblednoise.moonfruit.com

ABOUT THE AUTHOR

Martyn Clayton is a writer and photographer, who like Lauren lives in York, enjoys a crisp sandwich, listening to his CD collection and tries his hardest not to bother anyone. He regularly reads Heat magazine and the NME. He'd like to see an end to the monarchy. When he grows up he'd like to have cheekbones but he doesn't know anyone called Robert.

Visit him at his obligatory Myspace page :

www.myspace.com/martynclayton